PENGUIN CLASSICS

THE HAUNTED DOLLS' HOUSE AND OTHER GHOST STORIES

MONTAGUE RHODES JAMES was born in 1862 at Goodnestone, in Kent, but spent most of his early years at Livermere Hall in Suffolk. He attended Temple Grove preparatory school and Eton before beginning a long association with King's College, Cambridge, first as a student (1882), then as a fellow (1887), dean (1889), tutor (1900), and provost (1905). He was also director of the Fitzwilliam Museum in Cambridge (1893–1908). His first volume of ghost stories, *Ghost-Stories of an Antiquary*, appeared in 1904, followed by three other volumes: *More Ghost Stories of an Antiquary* (1911), *A Thin Ghost* (1919), and *A Warning to the Curious* (1925). His *Collected Ghost Stories* appeared in 1931. In 1918 he became provost of Eton, remaining in that office for the rest of his life. Throughout his career James published many distinguished works of scholarship, especially on medieval manuscripts, biblical apocrypha, and church history; among his important publications were *The Wanderings and Homes of Manuscripts* (1919) and *The Apocryphal New Testament* (1924). His autobiography, *Eton and King's*, was issued in 1926. Among his many honors was the Order of Merit, bestowed upon him by King George V in 1930. James, who never married, died in 1936.

S. T. JOSHI is a widely published writer and editor. He has edited three Penguin Classics editions of H. P. Lovecraft's horror tales as well as Algernon Blackwood's *Ancient Sorceries and Other Strange Stories* (2002) and Lord Dunsany's *In the Land of Time and Other Fantasy Tales* (2004). Among his critical and biographical works are *The Weird Tale* (1990), *H. P. Lovecraft: A Life* (1996), and *The Modern Weird Tale* (2001). He has edited works by Ambrose Bierce, H. L. Mencken, and other writers. He lives with his wife in upstate New York.

M. R. JAMES

The Haunted Dolls' House
and
Other Ghost Stories

THE COMPLETE GHOST STORIES
OF M. R. JAMES,
VOLUME 2

Edited with an Introduction and Notes by
S. T. JOSHI

PENGUIN BOOKS

PENGUIN BOOKS

Published by the Penguin Group

Penguin Group (USA) Inc., 375 Hudson Street, New York, New York 10014, U.S.A.

Penguin Group (Canada), 90 Eglinton Avenue East, Suite 700, Toronto, Ontario, Canada M4P 2Y3
(a division of Pearson Penguin Canada Inc.)

Penguin Books Ltd, 80 Strand, London WC2R 0RL, England

Penguin Ireland, 25 St Stephen's Green, Dublin 2, Ireland (a division of Penguin Books Ltd)

Penguin Group (Australia), 250 Camberwell Road, Camberwell, Victoria 3124, Australia
(a division of Pearson Australia Group Pty Ltd)

Penguin Books India Pvt Ltd, 11 Community Centre, Panchsheel Park, New Delhi - 110 017, India

Penguin Group (NZ), cnr Airborne and Rosedale Roads, Albany, Auckland 1310, New Zealand
(a division of Pearson New Zealand Ltd)

Penguin Books (South Africa) (Pty) Ltd, 24 Sturdee Avenue, Rosebank, Johannesburg 2196, South Africa

Penguin Books Ltd, Registered Offices:
80 Strand, London WC2R 0RL, England

First published in Penguin Books 2006

5   7   9   10   8   6   4

Introduction copyright © S. T. Joshi, 2006
All rights reserved

The copyrighted stories in this collection are reprinted by arrangement with Nicholas Rhodes James.

LIBRARY OF CONGRESS CATALOGING IN PUBLICATION DATA
James, M. R. (Montague Rhodes), 1862–1936.
The complete ghost stories of M.R. James. Volume 2,
The haunted dolls' house and other ghost stories / M.R. James ; edited with an introduction
and notes by S.T. Joshi.
p. cm.—(Penguin classics)
Includes all stories from A thin ghost and others (1919)
and A warning to the curious and other ghost stories (1925), and other stories.
ISBN 0 14 30.3992 X
1. Ghost stories, English. I. Joshi, S. T., 1958– II. Title.
III. Title: Haunted dolls' house and other ghost stories. IV. Series.
PR6019.A565A6 2006
823'.912—dc22   2006046023

Printed in the United States of America
Set in Sabon

Contents

Introduction

It is generally agreed that the tales in M. R. James's final two collections of ghost stories, *A Thin Ghost and Others* (1919) and *A Warning to the Curious* (1925), to say nothing of the stories that he gathered only in his *Collected Ghost Stories* (1931) or did not collect at all, are generally inferior to those of his two landmark volumes, *Ghost-Stories of an Antiquary* (1904) and *More Ghost Stories of an Antiquary* (1911). And yet, for a writer as accomplished as James, even his lesser work—and this includes essays, fragments, and even letters—remains of compelling interest. In his final two decades of life, scholarship and administrative burdens remained paramount in his sphere of interests—it was, after all, at this time that he produced such monuments as his edition of *The Apocryphal New Testament* (1924) and his translation of the fairy-tales of Hans Christian Andersen from the Danish (1930)—but the writing of ghost stories (which James acknowledged was the only type of fiction he cared to write) was more than the production of an idle hour.

A Thin Ghost and Others appeared shortly after James became provost of Eton in 1918—an occasion on which he received congratulations from Thomas Hardy, A. E. Housman, the archbishop of Canterbury, and other notables. The war was over, much to James's relief; there is some evidence that he felt a certain guilt at pursuing arcane scholarship at King's College, Cambridge, while others were dying in the battlefields of Europe. Unlike the stories in his first two collections, which take for their settings a large segment of the European continent, from France and Germany to Sweden and Denmark, his later

tales stay pretty close to home. All are set in England, most of
them in out-of-the-way rustic sites where disproof of the supernatural phenomena on display is difficult. It is as if James himself, after spending much of his youth and early adulthood in
wide-ranging travels for scholarly and antiquarian purposes,
felt the need to reestablish his roots with the country of his
birth—especially with the rural countryside, where he mani-
festly felt far more at home than in the frenetic megalopolis of
London. The extraordinary felicity that James displayed in devising fictitious names for his settings is enviable: it requires
a careful consultation of a gazeteer of England to determine
that none of the sites mentioned in "A View from a Hill"—
Fulnaker Abbey, Oldbourne Church, Lambsfield, Wanstone,
Ackford, and Thorfield—have any existence except in James's
imagination.

But to say that the names of James's locales are fictitious is
one thing; it is a very different thing to say that they are purely
imaginary. His extensive travels, by foot and by bicycle,
throughout his native land had rendered every county familiar. It does not, perhaps, take much effort to determine that
Seaburgh, in "A Warning to the Curious," is a thin disguise for
Aldeburgh, in Suffolk, or that, in "The Uncommon Prayer-
book," the imaginary towns of Stanford St. Thomas and Stanford Magdalene are probably based upon Stanford on Teme
and Stanford Bridge, in Hereford and Worcester. What all this
suggests is that James was becoming increasingly disinclined to
mask the autobiographical details that form the core of genuine
experience at the foundation of many of his tales. This feature
may be exhibited most clearly in some of the tales he gathered
only in his *Collected Ghost Stories* or did not collect, or publish, at all. It is scarcely to be denied that James himself is the
narrator of "Wailing Well," a tale that sent shivers through the
Boy Scout troop to whom he read it in 1927; "The Fenstanton
Witch," although set in the eighteenth century, draws clearly
upon James's intimate familiarity with the history and topography of King's College, where he was successively a King's
scholar, fellow, dean, and provost.

James's later tales appear to display a fascination with the *technique* of the ghost story—specifically, with the attempt to render the supernatural plausible in light of the increasingly militant materialism and secularism (exhibited by such Cambridge thinkers as Lytton Strachey, John Maynard Keynes, and Bertrand Russell) that was dominating intellectual thought in his day. Naïve exhibitions of ghosts and vampires were clearly out of the question; extreme indirection now had to be employed. This focus on technique perhaps reaches its apex in "Two Doctors," which even so devoted a partisan as Michael Cox calls "one of Monty's least successful stories."[1] And yet, this story hardly deserves the bad press it has received, for it proves to be an extraordinarily clever supernatural detective story (James was devoted to mystery and detective tales, to the extent that in one of his articles on ghost stories he makes a casual and unexplained reference to Captain Hastings, the sidekick of Agatha Christie's Hercule Poirot) in which all the pieces of the puzzle are laid out for the reader clever enough to place them in their correct sequence and bestow upon them their correct significance.

Another device much used by James in his later tales to create verisimilitude, and to overcome the hard-headed skeptic's natural incredulity in the face of the supernatural, was narrative distancing. This device is carried perhaps to excess in such a tale as "The Residence at Whitminster," in which a first-person narrator, acting as a kind of editor, redacts the notes of a Dr. Ashton, letters by Mary Oldys (the niece of Henry Oldys, Dr. Ashton's successor at the collegiate church at Whitminster), the diary of a Mr. Spearman (Mary's fiancé), and other documents, all in the effort to present with the utmost indirectness, and with what politicians would later term plausible deniability, the supernatural phenomena on display.

It is possible that this obsession with technique was the result of James's exhaustive study of the history and theory of the ghostly tale, a work chiefly undertaken in the 1920s as a concomitant to his fascination with one of the leading Victorian practitoners of the weird tale, Joseph Sheridan Le Fanu (1814–1873). James testifies that he pored through entire runs of such periodicals as the *Dublin University Magazine* and *All the Year Round* in the hunt for previously unattributed works by Le Fanu; and although he erred in a few cases, his work did result in the addition of several tales to the Le Fanu corpus, as exemplified by James's landmark edition of Le Fanu's *Madam Crowl's Ghost and Other Tales of Mystery* (1923). It is very likely that this work led James to reformulate, or at any rate refine, his own nebulous views on what constitutes a ghost story and how it should best be told.

His first words on the matter occur in the brief preface to *More Ghost Stories of an Antiquary*.[2] Here, in a very short space, he manages to outline three principles of ghost story writing: 1) "the setting should be fairly familiar and the majority of the characters and their talk such as you may meet or hear any day"; 2) "the ghost should be malevolent or odious"; 3) "the technical terms of 'occultism' . . . tend to put the mere ghost story . . . upon a quasi-scientific plane, and to call into play faculties quite other than imaginative." In his later writings on the ghost story—such as his introduction to V. H. Collins's *Ghosts and Marvels* (1924), "Some Remarks on Ghost Stories" (1929), and "Ghosts—Treat Them Gently!" (1931)— James does not so much revise as lend further nuance to these principles.

And yet, there is a question as to how faithfully James himself adhered to his own dicta when writing ghost stories. The notion of "familiarity," especially as regards characterization and setting (both of time and of place), was for James a matter of some elasticity. Although he remarks that a setting as remote as the twelfth or thirteenth century is not likely to induce a reader to remark, "If I'm not careful, something of this kind may happen to me!," we quickly see that any number of James's tales are set, or at least begin, in the seventeenth, eighteenth, or early nineteenth century. James of course does not require absolute contemporaneity: he does remark in the introduction to *Ghosts and Marvels* that

For the ghost story a slight haze of distance is desirable. "Thirty years ago," "Not long before the war," are very proper openings. If a really remote date be chosen, there is more than one way of

bringing the reader in contact with it. The finding of documents
about it can be made plausible; or you may begin with your apparition and go back over the years to tell the cause of it; or . . .
you may set the scene directly in the desired epoch, which I think
is hardest to do with success.

It can readily be seen that James has adopted each of these op-
tions in his various tales. And yet, I believe that James's own
antiquarianism allowed him to believe that even the seventeenth
century was a period of relative recency that requires only the
citing of certain telling historical details to elicit the reader's
sense of vital reality. Whether the passing of another full century since the writing of James's earliest ghost stories—and,
perhaps more significantly, the collapse of historical learning even
on the part of many readers who claim to be well educated—
has rendered this conception a bit more dubious is something
for which James cannot be held responsible.

But James exemplified brilliantly in his own work his corresponding principles of "atmosphere and a nicely managed
crescendo." He goes on to state: "Let us, then, be introduced to
the actors in a placid way; let us see them going about their ordinary business, undisturbed by forebodings, pleased with their
surroundings, and into this calm environment let the ominous
thing put out its head, unobtrusively at first, and then more insistently, until it holds the stage." Here James may have been
combating the luridness that he censured in many of the Gothic
novels of the late eighteenth and early nineteenth centuries—a
luridness whose recrudescence he would also censure in some
of the pulp magazine fiction of the 1920s and 1930s. Curiously,
James's enunciation of this principle places him strikingly in ac-
cord with the dominant tendency of post–World War II horror
fiction, when such writers as Ray Bradbury, Shirley Jackson,
and Richard Matheson chose to emphasize the ordinariness of
their characters as they encounter the supernatural, in conscious contrast to what came to be regarded as the over-the-top
flamboyancy of H. P. Lovecraft and his disciples. It could well
be said that this principle has now been carried somewhat to
excess in the bestselling work of Stephen King, Peter Straub,

and Dean Koontz, who are so focused on the mundane lives of their mundane characters that the supernatural phenomenon—which, one would suppose, is the *raison d'être* of their work—is given short shrift.

As it is, James found himself increasingly critical of much of the supernatural literature of both his predecessors and his contemporaries. His disdain for Poe's masterwork, "Ligeia," is scarcely concealed by the remark: "Evidently in many people's judgments it ranks as a classic." In "Some Remarks on Ghost Stories" the drumbeat of negativity continues: after lavishing praise upon the Victorians, especially Le Fanu, James finds that Bram Stoker's *Dracula* "suffers by excess"; that his friend E. F. Benson "sins occasionally by stepping over the line of legitimate horridness"; that Ambrose Bierce is "sometimes unpardonable"; that the psychic detective stories of Algernon Blackwood and of K. and Hesketh Pearson err by overreliance on occultism; and so on and so forth. But James reserves his greatest condemnation for the material contained in the *Not at Night* anthologies assembled by Christine Campbell Thomson, most of which derived from the American pulp magazine *Weird Tales:* "These [stories] are merely nauseating, and it is very easy to be nauseating." In fact, James is probably largely on target here: present-day devotees of pulp fiction only make themselves ridiculous by defending its literary worth *in toto* instead of the tiny fraction of work (chiefly the tales of Lovecraft, Clark Ashton Smith, Robert E. Howard, Henry S. Whitehead, and a very few others) that can legitimately be said to rise above the general level of formulaic hackwork.

But James lets down his hair entirely in a private letter not meant for publication—one he wrote to Nicholas Davies on January 12, 1928, shortly after receiving W. Paul Cook's magazine *The Recluse* (1927), containing H. P. Lovecraft's historical treatise "Supernatural Horror in Literature," which featured several glowing pages on James himself.[3] Beginning by remarking that Lovecraft's "style is of the most offensive," James goes on to condemn Matthew Gregory Lewis's *The Monk* (it "is really not fit to be read"), Mary Shelley's *Frankenstein* (which "fails to impress me as it should"), Edward Bulwer-Lytton's

"The Haunted and the Haunters" (which is "boomed above its merits"), Bierce (who "to my thinking oversteps the mark"), Robert W. Chambers (whose supernatural novels "are horrid & nasty"), Arthur Machen (who "has a nasty after-taste: rather a foul mind I think, but clever as they make 'em"), and so on. In general, "the moderns are apt to be either woolly or too nasty for me."

James, certainly, is entitled to his opinions, but it is evident that his emphasis on reticence and indirection has betrayed him into wholesale condemnations of authors and works that have far more merit than he was willing to acknowledge. James remained devoted to the ghostly tales of such writers as H. Russell Wakefield, A. M. Burrage, Walter de la Mare, and their congeners; the one American he seems to have appreciated unreservedly is Mary E. Wilkins Freeman, author of *The Wind in the Rose-bush and Other Stories of the Supernatural* (1903), as richly evocative of the history and landscape of New Engand as James's own tales are of those of England. His distaste for any admixture of sexual imagery in the supernatural tale is what no doubt led him to condemn Arthur Machen, whose "The Great God Pan" evoked the outrage of many other critics as the outpouring of a "foul mind."

And yet, on this whole issue, James himself may not have followed his own counsel as strictly as he seemed to fancy. There is no denying a certain element of "horridness" in much of James's own work, however artfully and indirectly it is conveyed. From beginning to end of his career as a writer of ghost stories he could unleash such hideous displays as the following:

> On the left side of his chest there opened a black and gaping rent; and there fell upon Stephen's brain, rather than upon his ear, the impression of one of those hungry and desolate cries that he had heard resounding over the woods of Aswarby all that evening.
> —"Lost Hearts"

> [T]hey saw a round body covered with fire—the size of a man's head—appear very suddenly, then seem to collapse and fall back. This, five or six times; then a similar ball leapt into the air and

fell on the grass, where after a moment it lay still. The Bishop went as near as he dared to it, and saw—what but the remains of an enormous spider, veinous and scarred! —"The Ash-Tree"

I was conscious of a most horrible smell of mould, and of a cold kind of face pressed against my own, and moving slowly over it, and of several—I don't know how many—legs or arms or tentacles or something clinging to my body. I screamed out . . . like a beast, and fell away backward from the step on which I stood. —"The Treasure of Abbot Thomas"

But in the chalk pit it was that poor Uncle Henry's body was found, with a sack over the head, the throat horribly mangled. It was a peaked corner of the sack sticking out of the soil that attracted attention. I cannot bring myself to write in greater detail. —"The Story of a Disappearance and an Appearance"

You don't need to be told that he was dead. . . . His mouth was full of sand and stones, and his teeth and jaws were broken to bits. I only glanced once at his face. —"A Warning to the Curious"

Have scarecrows bare bony feet? Do their heads loll on to their shoulders? Have they iron collars and links of chain about their necks? Can they get up and move, if never so stiffly, across a floor, with wagging head and arms close at their sides? and shiver? —"Rats"

Of course, it is unjust to rip out these passages from their contexts; they are no doubt what James specified as the culmination of a "nicely managed crescendo." And even here, the reticence that James so valued comes into play: the simple sentences "I cannot bring myself to write in greater detail" and "I only glanced once at his face" evoke far more horror than any amount of blood-and-thunder grisliness ever could, and one can be assured that, had James lived another two or three generations, he would have emphatically bestowed his mark of approval on such masters of subtlety as Robert Aickman, Ramsey Campbell, T. E. D. Klein, and Thomas Ligotti rather than on their noisier contemporaries, Dennis Wheatley, Stephen King, John Saul, and Clive Barker. In horror fiction, less is almost always more, and even the most florid word-painting (or, in film, special-effects violence and grue) pales in comparison to what the sensitive imagination can envision when properly stimulated.

Aside from H. P. Lovecraft, no writer of supernatural fiction has achieved such celebrity on such a relatively small body of work as M. R. James. Even the least of his ghost stories exhibits a craftsmanship and attention to detail that must be the envy of more hasty and prolific scriveners, while the fertility of conception that allowed him to ring so many ingenious changes upon the one topos of the ghost or revenant can only elicit our admiration. James and his disciples have attracted a small cadre of devotees intent on preserving their work, if only by means of the small press, and, more valuably, on explicating its smallest particulars. But James's ghost stories are far more than the property of a coterie: by revealing to the full the possibilities of aesthetic achievement in the tale of supernatural horror, they become a contribution to the literature of the ages.

Suggestions for Further Reading

A. PRIMARY

James's ghost stories were issued in four slim volumes published in the United Kingdom by Edward Arnold: *Ghost-Stories of an Antiquary* (1904); *More Ghost Stories of an Antiquary* (1911); *A Thin Ghost and Others* (1919); and *A Warning to the Curious* (1925). Only the third volume appeared in the United States during James's lifetime (Longmans, Green, 1919). The complete contents of these volumes (aside from their prefaces) were included in *The Collected Ghost Stories of M. R. James* (Edward Arnold, 1931), a volume that has been frequently reprinted under various titles (e.g., *The Penguin Complete Ghost Stories of M. R. James* [Penguin, 1984]). This omnibus also includes five additional stories along with a new preface and the essay "Stories I Have Tried to Write." *The Five Jars* (Edward Arnold, 1922) is a children's fantasy; it was not published in the United States in James's lifetime. James also prepared a notable edition of the stories of Joseph Sheridan Le Fanu, *Madam Crowl's Ghost and Other Tales of Mystery* (George Bell & Sons, 1923). His autobiography, *Eton and King's*, was published by Williams & Norgate in 1926.

There are numerous selections of James's ghost stories, the most notable being *Casting the Runes and Other Ghost Stories*, edited by Michael Cox (Oxford University Press/World's Classics, 1987), with substantial introduction and notes. Curiously, the 2002 reprint removes Cox's introduction and notes and substitutes an introduction by Michael Chabon. Cox has written another weighty introduction to another collection, *The*

Ghost Stories of M. R. James (Oxford University Press, 1986).
Peter Haining's *M. R. James: The Book of the Supernatural*
(Foulsham, 1979; published in the United States as *M. R. James:
The Book of Ghost Stories* [Stein & Day, 1982]) contains a
wealth of obscure writings by James and other ancillary material. Rosemary Pardoe's compilation, *The Fenstanton Witch
and Others* (Haunted Library, 1999), is a valuable assemblage
of James's ghost-story fragments and other writings.

In a class by itself is *A Pleasing Terror: The Complete Supernatural Writings of M. R. James*, edited by Barbara and Christo-
pher Roden (Ash-Tree Press, 2001). It not only contains the
complete contents of all four collections of ghost stories, but also
all the uncollected tales (including some fragments), *The Five
Jars*, his various writings on the ghost story, and several interesting works of criticism. The works by James are annotated
(Michael Cox's annotations from *Casting the Runes* are included
for the stories in that volume), although the notes (not excluding
Cox's) are not written with quite the scholarly rigor that one
might expect; there are also a few errors and omissions. But on
the whole, it is an admirable compilation, and it is unfortunate
that it was limited to 1,000 copies and is now out of print.

It is surprising that little has been done with the abundance
of James's surviving letters. Gwendolen McBryde issued a
charming if expurgated volume of James's letters to her as *Letters to a Friend* (Edward Arnold, 1956), but little of his other
correspondence has seen print.

James's scholarly work divides broadly into several discrete
categories. One group is his descriptive catalogues of manuscripts. He cataloged the manuscripts of all the colleges of
Cambridge University, including Jesus (1895), Sidney Sussex
(1895), Peterhouse (1899), Trinity (1900–04; four volumes),
Emmanuel (1904), Christ's (1905), Clare (1905), Pembroke
(1905), Queen's (1905), Gonville and Caius (1907–08; two
volumes), Trinity Hall (1907), Corpus Christi (1909–13; seven
parts), Magdalene (1909), St. John's (1913), and St. Catherine's
(1925). Other catalogues include: *A Descriptive Catalogue of
the Manuscripts in the Library of Eton College* (1895); *A
Descriptive Catalogue of the Manuscripts in the Fitzwilliam*

Museum (1895); *A Descriptive Catalogue of Fifty Manuscripts from the Collection of Henry Yates Thompson* (1898); *The Manuscripts in the Library at Lambeth Palace, a revised edition with Claude Jenkins,* (1900, 1930–32, five parts); *The Manuscripts of Westminster Abbey* with J. A. Robinson (1908); *A Descriptive Catalogue of the Latin Manuscripts in the John Rylands Library at Manchester* (1921, two volumes); *Bibliotheca Pepysiana* (1923); *A Catalogue of the Medieval Manuscripts in the University Library, Aberdeen* (1932); *The Bohun Manuscripts* with E. G. Millar (1936).

Another group is his editions of and treatises on biblical apocrypha and apocalyptic works: *The Gospel According to Peter, and the Revelation of Peter: Two Lectures* with J. A. Robinson (1892); *Apocrypha Anecdota* (two series, 1893, 1897); *The Trinity College Apocalypse* (1909); *The Second Epistle General of Peter and the General Epistle of Jude* (1912); *Old Testament Legends* (1913); *The Lost Apocrypha of the Old Testament* (1920); *The Apocalypse in Latin and French* (1922); *The Apocryphal New Testament* (1924); *Latin Infancy Gospels* (1927); *The Apocalypse in Art* (1931); *The Dublin Apocalypse* (1932); *The New Testament* with Delia Lyttelton (1934–36; four volumes).

James also prepared editions and translations of works of medieval Latin and other languages: *The Life and Miracles of St. William of Norwich by Thyomas of Monmouth* with Augustus Jessopp (1896); Walter Map, *De Nugis Curialium* (edition, 1914; translation, 1923); *The Biblical Antiquities of Philo* (1917); Hans Christian Andersen, *Forty Stories,* translated from Danish (1930).

More general discussions of libraries, manuscripts, and associated matters include *The Ancient Libraries of Canterbury and Dover* (1903); *The Wanderings and Homes of Manuscripts* (1919); *Abbeys* (1925); *Suffolk and Norfolk* (1930).

James prolifically contributed scholarly articles and reviews to many journals, most notably to the *Classical Review, Eton College Chronicle, English Historical Review, Journal of Theological Studies,* and the *Proceedings of the Cambridge Antiquarian Society.*

The most comprehensive bibliography of James's work can

now be found in "A Bibliography of the Published Works of Montague Rhodes James" by Nicholas Rogers, in *The Legacy of M. R. James,* edited by Lynda Dennison (Shaun Tyas, 2001), pp. 239–67. It supersedes the bibliographies by A. F. Scholfield in S. G. Lubbock's memoir (1939) and in Richard William Pfaff's biography (1980), for which see below.

B. SECONDARY

Of the two biographies of James, Richard William Pfaff's *Montague Rhodes James* (Scolar Press, 1980) exhaustively and meticulously treats James's scholarly writings. Michael Cox's *M. R. James: An Informal Portrait* (Oxford University Press, 1983) is a good complement, providing details on James's personal life (with liberal quotations of unpublished letters) and valuable information on the ghost stories. S. G. Lubbock's *A Memoir of Montague Rhodes James* (Cambridge University Press, 1939) is an affecting tribute. *The Legacy of M. R. James,* edited by Lynda Dennison (Shaun Tyas, 2001), presents papers from the 1995 Cambridge Symposium on James and is exclusively devoted to James's scholarly work.

Critical analysis of James's ghost stories has not been produced in great abundance. H. P. Lovecraft's warmly appreciative pages on James in "Supernatural Horror in Literature," *Recluse,* (1927) were read by James himself and received with mixed impressions. Chapters on James in general studies of supernatural fiction, such as Peter Penzoldt's *The Supernatural in Fiction* (Peter Nevill, 1952), Julia Briggs's *Night Visitors: The Rise and Fall of the English Ghost Story* (Faber & Faber, 1977), Jack Sullivan's *Elegant Nightmares: The English Ghost Story from Le Fanu to Blackwood* (Ohio University Press, 1978), and Edward Wagenknecht's *Seven Masters of Supernatural Fiction* (Greenwood Press, 1991) are variously informative. My own chapter on James in *The Weird Tale* (University of Texas Press, 1990) now strikes me as a bit uncharitable. Austin Warren's "The Marvels of M. R. James, Antiquary" in *Connections* (University of Michigan Press, 1970) is more descriptive than analytical, but makes some good points regarding James's techniques of ghost story writing.

The occasional journal *Ghosts & Scholars*, edited by Rosemary Pardoe (thirty-three issues published between 1979 and 2001), although largely devoted to "stories in the tradition of M. R. James," includes a substantial number of interesting articles and notes on James, including annotations of stories not included in Cox's *Casting the Runes* (these annotations are now included in *A Pleasing Terror*). It has now been succeeded by the *Ghosts & Scholars M. R. James Newsletter* (2002f.) edited by Rosemary Pardoe. See also *Formidable Visitants*, edited by Roger Johnson (1999), a tribute to *Ghosts & Scholars* on its twentieth anniversary.

Many of the better articles on James's ghost stories, along with several original essays, appear in *Warnings to the Curious: A Sheaf of Criticism on M. R. James*, edited by Rosemary Pardoe and myself (Hippocampus Press, 2007).

General articles on James include:

Mary Butts, "The Art of Montagu [*sic*] James," *London Mercury* 29 (February 1934), 306–17 (a rather effusive essay that discusses James's economy of means and his "low" characters).

Brian Cowlishaw, " 'A Warning to the Curious': Victorian Science and the Awful Unconscious in M. R. James's Ghost Stories," *Victorian Newsletter*, No. 94 (Fall 1998), 36–42 (a provocative study of James's use of nineteenth-century science in his depiction of ghosts).

Penny Fielding, "Reading Rooms: M. R. James and the Library of Modernity," *Modern Fiction Studies* 46 (Fall 2000), 749–71 (an unhelpfully pedantic study of the sociological significance of the library in James's work).

Stephen Gaselee, "Montague Rhodes James: 1862–1936," *Proceedings of the British Academy* 22 (1936), 418–33 (a touching memoir by one who had known James for thirty-five years).

Linda J. Holland-Toll, "From Haunted Gardens to Lurking Wendigos: Liminal and Wild Places in M. R. James and Algernon Blackwood," *Studies in Weird Fiction* No. 25 (Summer 2001), 12–17 (a penetrating study of the "bad place" archetype in James and Blackwood).

Shane Leslie, "Montague Rhodes James," *Quarterly Review* 304 (January 1966), 45–56 (a warm but somewhat haphazard memoir, focusing on James's scholarly work).

Simon MacCulloch, "The Toad in the Study: M. R. James, H. P. Lovecraft and Forbidden Knowledge," *Ghosts & Scholars* No. 20 (1995), 38–43; No. 21 (1996), 37–42; No. 22 (1996), 40–46; No. 23 (1997), 54–60. Reprinted in *Studies in Weird Fiction* No. 20 (Winter 1997), 2–12; No. 21 (Summer 1997), 17–28 (a wide-ranging and closely argued discussion of the theme of "forbidden knowledge" in James and Lovecraft; perhaps the best single article on James).

Michael A. Mason, "On Not Letting Them Lie: Moral Significance in the Ghost Stories of M. R. James," *Studies in Short Fiction* 19 (1982), 253–60 (on the moral overtones of James's protagonists and ghosts).

Robert Michalski, "The Malice of Inanimate Objects: Exchange in M. R. James's Ghost Stories," *Extrapolation* 37 (Spring 1996), 46–62 (a strained and implausible sociological interpretation of James's tales).

Samuel D. Russell, "Irony and Horror: The Art of M. R. James," *Haunted* No. 2 (December 1964), 43–52; No. 3 (June 1968), 96–106 (reprinted in *PT* 609–30) (a sound general overview of James's ghost stories).

Norman Scarfe, "The Strangeness Present: M. R. James's Suffolk," *Country Life* No. 4655 (6 November 1986), 1416–19 (a discussion of the use of Suffolk topography in James's tales).

Jacqueline Simpson, " 'The Rules of Folklore' in the Ghost Stories of M. R. James," *Folklore* 108 (1997), 9–18 (an exhaustive study of the use of folklore in James's work).

Devendra P. Varma, "The Ghost Stories of M. R. James: Artistic Exponent of the Victorian Macabre," *Indian Journal of English Studies* NS 4 (1983), 73–81 (a sensitive essay on James's technique of writing ghost stories).

Ron Weighell, "Dark Devotions: M. R. James and the Magical Tradition," *Ghosts & Scholars* No. 6 (1984) 20–30 (profound study of James's use of magic and occultism).

Other articles on specific stories are cited in the notes.

A Note on the Text

The texts of the first fifteen stories in this book are taken from *The Collected Ghost Stories of M. R. James* (1931), which appear to represent James's final wishes for these tales. The texts of "The Experiment" and "The Malice of Inanimate Objects" are taken from *A Pleasing Terror* (2001); the text of "A Vignette" is taken from its first appearance in the *London Mercury* (November 1936). For the text of "The Fenstanton Witch," see the introductory note to that story. "Twelve Medieval Ghost-Stories" has been taken from its first appearance in *English Historical Review* (July 1922). In the appendix, the introduction to *Ghosts and Marvels* (1924) is taken from that volume; "Some Remarks on Ghost Stories" is taken from its first appearance in the London *Bookman* (December 1929); "Ghosts—Treat Them Gently!" is taken from *A Pleasing Terror;* the preface to *Collected Ghost Stories* and "Stories I Have Tried to Write" are taken from *Collected Ghost Stories* (1931).

I trust that my introduction and commentary testify sufficiently to my indebtedness to the work of some of the leading James scholars, including Richard William Pfaff, Michael Cox, Rosemary Pardoe, and several others. I am grateful to Keith B. Johnston, Stefan Dziemianowicz, and Simon Vivian of Eton College for assistance in the writing of the notes and for supplying some necessary source materials.

A Note on the Text

The Haunted Dolls' House
and
Other Ghost Stories

THE RESIDENCE
AT WHITMINSTER

Dr. Ashton—Thomas Ashton, Doctor of Divinity—sat in his study, habited in a dressing-gown, and with a silk cap on his shaven head—his wig being for the time taken off and placed on its block on a side table. He was a man of some fifty-five years, strongly made, of a sanguine complexion, an angry eye, and a long upper lip. Face and eye were lighted up at the moment when I picture him by the level ray of an afternoon sun that shone in upon him through a tall sash window, giving on the west. The room into which it shone was also tall, lined with bookcases, and, where the wall showed between them, panelled. On the table near the doctor's elbow was a green cloth, and upon it what he would have called a silver standish—a tray with inkstands—quill pens, a calf-bound book or two, some papers, a church-warden pipe and brass tobacco-box, a flask cased in plaited straw, and a liqueur glass. The year was 1730, the month December, the hour somewhat past three in the afternoon.

I have described in these lines pretty much all that a superficial observer would have noted when he looked into the room. What met Dr. Ashton's eye when he looked out of it, sitting in his leather armchair? Little more than the tops of the shrubs and fruit-trees of his garden could be seen from that point, but the red-brick wall of it was visible in almost all the length of its western side. In the middle of that was a gate—a double gate of rather elaborate iron scroll-work, which allowed something of a view beyond. Through it he could see that the ground sloped away almost at once to a bottom, along which a stream must run, and rose steeply from it on the other side, up to a field that was park-like in character, and thickly studded with oaks, now, of course, leafless. They did not stand so thick together but that some glimpse of sky and horizon could be seen between their stems. The sky was now golden and the horizon, a horizon of distant woods, it seemed, was purple.

But all that Dr. Ashton could find to say, after contemplating this prospect for many minutes, was: "Abominable!"

A listener would have been aware, immediately upon this, of the sound of footsteps coming somewhat hurriedly in the direction of the study: by the resonance he could have told that they were traversing a much larger room. Dr. Ashton turned round in his chair as the door opened, and looked expectant. The incomer was a lady—a stout lady in the dress of the time: though I have made some attempt at indicating the doctor's costume, I will not enterprise that of his wife—for it was Mrs. Ashton who now entered. She had an anxious, even a sorely distracted, look, and it was in a very disturbed voice that she almost whispered to Dr. Ashton, putting her head close to his, "He's in a very sad way, love, worse, I'm afraid." "Tt—tt, is he really?" and he leaned back and looked in her face. She nodded. Two solemn bells, high up, and not far away, rang out the half-hour at this moment. Mrs. Ashton started. "Oh, do you think you can give order that the minster clock be stopped chiming to-night? 'Tis just over his chamber, and will keep him from sleeping, and to sleep is the only chance for him, that's certain." "Why, to be sure, if there were need, real need, it could be done, but not upon any light occasion. This Frank, now, do you assure me that his recovery stands upon it?" said Dr. Ashton: his voice was loud and rather hard. "I do verily believe it," said his wife. "Then, if it must be, bid Molly run across to Simpkins and say on my authority that he is to stop the clock chimes at sunset: and—yes—she is after that to say to my lord Saul that I wish to see him presently in this room." Mrs. Ashton hurried off.

Before any other visitor enters, it will be well to explain the situation.

Dr. Ashton was the holder, among other preferments, of a prebend in the rich collegiate church of Whitminster, one of the foundations which, though not a cathedral, survived Dissolution

and Reformation,[1] and retained its constitution and endow-
ments for a hundred years after the time of which I write. The
great church, the residences of the dean and the two prebendaries, the choir and its appurtenances, were all intact and in
working order. A dean who flourished soon after 1500 had
been a great builder, and had erected a spacious quadrangle of
red brick adjoining the church for the residence of the officials.
Some of these persons were no longer required: their offices
had dwindled down to mere titles, borne by clergy or lawyers
in the town and neighbourhood; and so the houses that had
been meant to accommodate eight or ten people were now shared
among three—the dean and the two prebendaries. Dr. Ashton's
included what had been the common parlour and the dining-hall
of the whole body. It occupied a whole side of the court, and at
one end had a private door into the minster. The other end, as we
have seen, looked out over the country.

So much for the house. As for the inmates, Dr. Ashton was a
wealthy man and childless, and he had adopted, or rather undertaken to bring up, the orphan son of his wife's sister. Frank
Sydall was the lad's name: he had been a good many months in
the house. Then one day came a letter from an Irish peer, the
Earl of Kildonan[2] (who had known Dr. Ashton at college), putting it to the doctor whether he would consider taking into his
family the Viscount Saul, the Earl's heir, and acting in some
sort as his tutor. Lord Kildonan was shortly to take up a post in
the Lisbon Embassy, and the boy was unfit to make the voyage:
"not that he is sickly," the Earl wrote, "though you'll find him
whimsical, or of late I've thought him so, and to confirm this,
'twas only to-day his old nurse came expressly to tell me he was
possess'd: but let that pass; I'll warrant you can find a spell to
make all straight. Your arm was stout enough in old days, and I
give you plenary authority to use it as you see fit. The truth is,
he has here no boys of his age or quality to consort with, and is
given to moping about in our raths[3] and graveyards: and he
brings home romances that fright my servants out of their wits.
So there are you and your lady forewarned." It was perhaps
with half an eye open to the possibility of an Irish bishopric (at
which another sentence in the Earl's letter seemed to hint) that

Dr. Ashton accepted the charge of my Lord Viscount Saul and of the 200 guineas a year that were to come with him.

So he came, one night in September. When he got out of the chaise that brought him, he went first and spoke to the postboy and gave him some money, and patted the neck of his horse. Whether he made some movement that scared it or not, there was very nearly a nasty accident, for the beast started violently, and the postilion being unready was thrown and lost his fee, as he found afterwards, and the chaise lost some paint on the gateposts, and the wheel went over the man's foot who was taking out the baggage. When Lord Saul came up the steps into the light of the lamp in the porch to be greeted by Dr. Ashton, he was seen to be a thin youth of, say, sixteen years old, with straight black hair and the pale colouring that is common to such a figure. He took the accident and commotion calmly enough, and expressed a proper anxiety for the people who had been, or might have been, hurt: his voice was smooth and pleasant, and without any trace, curiously, of an Irish brogue.

Frank Sydall was a younger boy, perhaps of eleven or twelve, but Lord Saul did not for that reject his company. Frank was able to teach him various games he had not known in Ireland, and he was apt at learning them; apt, too, at his books, though he had had little or no regular teaching at home. It was not long before he was making a shift to puzzle out the inscriptions on the tombs in the minster, and he would often put a question to the doctor about the old books in the library that required some thought to answer. It is to be supposed that he made himself very agreeable to the servants, for within ten days of his coming they were almost falling over each other in their efforts to oblige him. At the same time, Mrs. Ashton was rather put to it to find new maidservants; for there were several changes, and some of the families in the town from which she had been accustomed to draw seemed to have no one available. She was forced to go farther afield than was usual.

These generalities I gather from the doctor's notes in his diary and from letters. They are generalities, and we should like, in view of what has to be told, something sharper and more detailed. We get it in entries which begin late in the year, and, I think, were posted up all together after the final incident: but they cover so few days in all that there is no need to doubt that the writer could remember the course of things accurately.

On a Friday morning it was that a fox, or perhaps a cat, made away with Mrs. Ashton's most prized black cockerel, a bird without a single white feather on its body. Her husband had told her often enough that it would make a suitable sacrifice to Æsculapius;[4] that had discomfited her much, and now she would hardly be consoled. The boys looked everywhere for traces of it: Lord Saul brought in a few feathers, which seemed to have been partially burnt on the garden rubbish-heap. It was on the same day that Dr. Ashton, looking out of an upper window, saw the two boys playing in the corner of the garden at a game he did not understand. Frank was looking earnestly at something in the palm of his hand. Saul stood behind him and seemed to be listening. After some minutes he very gently laid his hand on Frank's head, and almost instantly thereupon, Frank suddenly dropped whatever it was that he was holding, clapped his hands to his eyes, and sank down on the grass. Saul, whose face expressed great anger, hastily picked the object up, of which it could only be seen that it was glittering, put it in his pocket, and turned away, leaving Frank huddled up on the grass. Dr. Ashton rapped on the window to attract their attention, and Saul looked up as if in alarm, and then springing to Frank, pulled him up by the arm and led him away. When they came in to dinner, Saul explained that they had been acting a part of the tragedy of Radamistus, in which the heroine reads the future fate of her father's kingdom by means of a glass ball held in her hand, and is overcome by the terrible events she has seen.[5] During this explanation Frank said nothing, only looked rather bewilderedly at Saul. He must, Mrs. Ashton thought, have contracted a chill from the wet of the grass, for that evening he was certainly feverish and disordered; and the disorder was of the mind as well as the body, for he seemed to have something he wished to say to Mrs. Ashton, only a press of household affairs prevented her from paying attention to him; and when she went, according to her habit, to see that the light in the boys' chamber had been taken away, and to bid them

good night, he seemed to be sleeping, though his face was unnaturally flushed, to her thinking: Lord Saul, however, was pale
and quiet, and smiling in his slumber.

Next morning it happened that Dr. Ashton was occupied in
church and other business, and unable to take the boys' lessons.
He therefore set them tasks to be written and brought to him.
Three times, if not oftener, Frank knocked at the study door, and
each time the doctor chanced to be engaged with some visitor,
and sent the boy off rather roughly, which he later regretted.
Two clergymen were at dinner this day, and both remarked—
being fathers of families—that the lad seemed sickening for a
fever, in which they were too near the truth, and it had been
better if he had been put to bed forthwith: for a couple of hours
later in the afternoon he came running into the house, crying
out in a way that was really terrifying, and rushing to Mrs. Ashton, clung about her, begging her to protect him, and saying,
"Keep them off! keep them off!" without intermission. And it
was now evident that some sickness had taken strong hold of
him. He was therefore got to bed in another chamber from that
in which he commonly lay, and the physician brought to him:
who pronounced the disorder to be grave and affecting the lad's
brain, and prognosticated a fatal end to it if strict quiet were
not observed, and those sedative remedies used which he should
prescribe.

We are now come by another way to the point we had reached
before. The minster clock has been stopped from striking, and
Lord Saul is on the threshold of the study.

"What account can you give of this poor lad's state?" was
Dr. Ashton's first question. "Why, sir, little more than you know
already, I fancy. I must blame myself, though, for giving him a
fright yesterday when we were acting that silly play you saw. I
fear I made him take it more to heart than I meant." "How
so?" "Well, by telling him foolish tales I had picked up in Ireland of what we call the second sight." "*Second* sight! What
kind of sight might that be?" "Why, you know our ignorant
people pretend that some are able to foresee what is to come—
sometimes in a glass, or in the air, maybe, and at Kildonan we
had an old woman that pretended to such a power. And I dare

say I coloured the matter more highly than I should: but I never dreamed Frank would take it so near as he did." "You were wrong, my lord, very wrong, in meddling with such superstitious matters at all, and you should have considered whose house you were in, and how little becoming such actions are to my character and person or to your own: but pray how came it that you, acting, as you say, a play, should fall upon anything that could so alarm Frank?" "That is what I can hardly tell, sir: he passed all in a moment from rant about battles and lovers and Cleodora and Antigenes[6] to something I could not follow at all, and then dropped down as you saw." "Yes: was that at the moment when you laid your hand on the top of his head?" Lord Saul gave a quick look at his questioner—quick and spiteful—and for the first time seemed unready with an answer. "About that time it may have been," he said. "I have tried to recollect myself, but I am not sure. There was, at any rate, no significance in what I did then." "Ah!" said Dr. Ashton, "well, my lord, I should do wrong were I not to tell you that this fright of my poor nephew may have very ill consequences to him. The doctor speaks very despondingly of his state." Lord Saul pressed his hands together and looked earnestly upon Dr. Ashton. "I am willing to believe you had no bad intention, as assuredly you could have no reason to bear the poor boy malice: but I cannot wholly free you from blame in the affair." As he spoke, the hurrying steps were heard again, and Mrs. Ashton came quickly into the room, carrying a candle, for the evening had by this time closed in. She was greatly agitated. "O come!" she cried, "come directly. I'm sure he is going." "Going? Frank? Is it possible? Already?" With some such incoherent words the doctor caught up a book of prayers from the table and ran out after his wife. Lord Saul stopped for a moment where he was. Molly, the maid, saw him bend over and put both hands to his face. If it were the last words she had to speak, she said afterwards, he was striving to keep back a fit of laughing. Then he went out softly, following the others.

Mrs. Ashton was sadly right in her forecast. I have no inclination to imagine the last scene in detail. What Dr. Ashton records is, or may be taken to be, important to the story. They asked Frank if he would like to see his companion, Lord Saul, once again. The boy was quite collected, it appears, in these moments. "No," he said, "I do not want to see him; but you should tell him I am afraid he will be very cold." "What do you mean, my dear?" said Mrs. Ashton. "Only that," said Frank; "but say to him besides that I am free of them now, but he should take care. And I am sorry about your black cockerel, Aunt Ashton; but he said we must use it so, if we were to see all that could be seen."

Not many minutes after, he was gone. Both the Ashtons were grieved, she naturally most; but the doctor, though not an emotional man, felt the pathos of the early death: and, besides, there was the growing suspicion that all had not been told him by Saul, and that there was something here which was out of his beaten track. When he left the chamber of death, it was to walk across the quadrangle of the residence to the sexton's house. A passing bell, the greatest of the minster bells, must be rung, a grave must be dug in the minster yard, and there was now no need to silence the chiming of the minster clock. As he came slowly back in the dark, he thought he must see Lord Saul again. That matter of the black cockerel—trifling as it might seem—would have to be cleared up. It might be merely a fancy of the sick boy, but if not, was there not a witch-trial he had read, in which some grim little rite of sacrifice had played a part? Yes, he must see Saul.

I rather guess these thoughts of his than find written authority for them. That there was another interview is certain: certain also that Saul would (or, as he said, could) throw no light on Frank's words: though the message, or some part of it, appeared to affect him horribly. But there is no record of the talk in detail. It is only said that Saul sat all that evening in the study, and when he bid good night, which he did most reluctantly, asked for the doctor's prayers.

The month of January was near its end when Lord Kildonan, in the Embassy at Lisbon, received a letter that for once gravely disturbed that vain man and neglectful father. Saul was dead. The scene at Frank's burial had been very distressing. The day was awful in blackness and wind: the bearers, staggering blindly along under the flapping black pall, found it a hard job, when they emerged from the porch of the minster, to make their way to the grave. Mrs. Ashton was in her room—women did not then go to their kinsfolk's funerals—but Saul was there, draped in the mourning cloak of the time, and his face was white and fixed as that of one dead, except when, as was noticed three or four times, he suddenly turned his head to the left and looked over his shoulder. It was then alive with a terrible expression of listening fear. No one saw him go away: and no one could find him that evening. All night the gale buffeted the high windows of the church, and howled over the upland and roared through the woodland. It was useless to search in the open: no voice of shouting or cry for help could possibly be heard. All that Dr. Ashton could do was to warn the people about the college, and the town constables, and to sit up, on the alert for any news, and this he did. News came early next morning, brought by the sexton, whose business it was to open the church for early prayers at seven, and who sent the maid rushing upstairs with wild eyes and flying hair to summon her master. The two men dashed across to the south door of the minster, there to find Lord Saul clinging desperately to the great ring of the door, his head sunk between his shoulders, his stockings in rags, his shoes gone, his legs torn and bloody.

This was what had to be told to Lord Kildonan, and this really ends the first part of the story. The tomb of Frank Sydall and of the Lord Viscount Saul, only child and heir to William Earl of Kildonan, is one: a stone altar tomb in Whitminster churchyard.

Dr. Ashton lived on for over thirty years in his prebendal house, I do not know how quietly, but without visible disturbance. His successor preferred a house he already owned in the town, and left that of the senior prebendary vacant. Between them these two men saw the eighteenth century out and the nineteenth in; for Mr. Hindes, the successor of Ashton, became prebendary at nine-and-twenty and died at nine-and-eighty. So that it was not till 1823 or 1824 that anyone succeeded to the post who intended to make the house his home. The man who did so was Dr. Henry Oldys, whose name may be known to

some of my readers as that of the author of a row of volumes
labelled *Oldys's Works,* which occupy a place that must be honoured, since it is so rarely touched, upon the shelves of many a
substantial library.

Dr. Oldys, his niece, and his servants took some months to
transfer furniture and books from his Dorsetshire parsonage
to the quadrangle of Whitminster, and to get everything into
place. But eventually the work was done, and the house (which,
though untenanted, had always been kept sound and weather-
tight) woke up, and like Monte Cristo's mansion at Auteuil,
lived, sang, and bloomed once more.[7] On a certain morning in
June it looked especially fair, as Dr. Oldys strolled in his garden
before breakfast and gazed over the red roof at the minster
tower with its four gold vanes, backed by a very blue sky, and
very white little clouds.

"Mary," he said, as he seated himself at the breakfast-table
and laid down something hard and shiny on the cloth, "here's a
find which the boy made just now. You'll be sharper than I if
you can guess what it's meant for." It was a round and perfectly
smooth tablet—as much as an inch thick—of what seemed
clear glass. "It is rather attractive, at all events," said Mary: she
was a fair woman, with light hair and large eyes, rather a devotee of literature. "Yes," said her uncle, "I thought you'd be
pleased with it. I presume it came from the house: it turned up
in the rubbish-heap in the corner." "I'm not sure that I do like
it, after all," said Mary, some minutes later. "Why in the world
not, my dear?" "I don't know, I'm sure. Perhaps it's only
fancy." "Yes, only fancy and romance, of course. What's that
book, now—the name of that book, I mean, that you had your
head in all yesterday?" "*The Talisman,*[8] Uncle. Oh, if this
should turn out to be a talisman, how enchanting it would be!"
"Yes, *The Talisman*: ah, well, you're welcome to it, whatever it
is: I must be off about my business. Is all well in the house?
Does it suit you? Any complaints from the servants' hall?"
"No, indeed, nothing could be more charming. The only
soupçon of a complaint besides the lock of the linen closet,
which I told you of, is that Mrs. Maple says she cannot get rid
of the sawflies[9] out of that room you pass through at the other

end of the hall. By the way, are you sure you like your bed-room? It is a long way off from anyone else, you know." "Like it? To be sure I do; the farther off from you, my dear, the better. There, don't think it necessary to beat me: accept my apologies. But what are sawflies? Will they eat my coats? If not, they may have the room to themselves for what I care. We are not likely to be using it." "No, of course not. Well, what she calls sawflies are those reddish things like a daddy-long-legs,[10] but smaller,* and there are a great many of them perching about that room, certainly. I don't like them, but I don't fancy they are mischie-vous." "There seem to be several things you don't like this fine morning," said her uncle, as he closed the door. Miss Oldys re-mained in her chair looking at the tablet, which she was holding in the palm of her hand. The smile that had been on her face faded slowly from it and gave place to an expression of curios-ity and almost strained attention. Her reverie was broken by the entrance of Mrs. Maple, and her invariable opening, "Oh, Miss, could I speak to you a minute?"

A letter from Miss Oldys to a friend in Lichfield, begun a day or two before, is the next source for this story. It is not de-void of traces of the influence of that leader of female thought in her day, Miss Anna Seward, known to some as the Swan of Lichfield.[11]

"My sweetest Emily will be rejoiced to hear that we are at length—my beloved uncle and myself—settled in the house that now calls us master—nay, master and mistress—as in past ages it has called so many others. Here we taste a mingling of mod-ern elegance and hoary antiquity, such as has never ere now graced life for either of us. The town, small as it is, affords us some reflection, pale indeed, but veritable, of the sweets of po-lite intercourse: the adjacent country numbers amid the occu-pants of its scattered mansions some whose polish is annually refreshed by contact with metropolitan splendour, and others whose robust and homely geniality is, at times, and by way of contrast, not less cheering and acceptable. Tired of the parlours

---

*Apparently the ichneumon fly (*Ophion obscurum*), and not the true sawfly, is meant.

and drawing-rooms of our friends, we have ready to hand a
refuge from the clash of wits or the small talk of the day amid
the solemn beauties of our venerable minster, whose silver
chimes daily 'knoll us to prayer,'[12] and in the shady walks of
whose tranquil graveyard we muse with softened heart, and
ever and anon with moistened eye, upon the memorials of the
young, the beautiful, the aged, the wise, and the good."

Here there is an abrupt break both in the writing and the style.

"But my dearest Emily, I can no longer write with the care
which you deserve, and in which we both take pleasure. What I
have to tell you is wholly foreign to what has gone before. This
morning my uncle brought in to breakfast an object which had
been found in the garden; it was a glass or crystal tablet of this
shape (a little sketch is given), which he handed to me, and
which, after he left the room, remained on the table by me. I
gazed at it, I know not why, for some minutes, till called away
by the day's duties; and you will smile incredulously when I say
that I seemed to myself to begin to descry reflected in it objects
and scenes which were not in the room where I was. You will
not, however, think it strange that after such an experience I
took the first opportunity to seclude myself in my room with
what I now half believed to be a talisman of mickle might.[13] I
was not disappointed. I assure you, Emily, by that memory
which is dearest to both of us, that what I went through this afternoon transcends the limits of what I had before deemed
credible. In brief, what I saw, seated in my bedroom, in the
broad daylight of summer, and looking into the crystal depth of
that small round tablet, was this. First, a prospect, strange to
me, of an enclosure of rough and hillocky grass, with a grey
stone ruin in the midst, and a wall of rough stones about it. In
this stood an old, and very ugly, woman in a red cloak and
ragged skirt, talking to a boy dressed in the fashion of maybe a
hundred years ago. She put something which glittered into his
hand, and he something into hers, which I saw to be money, for
a single coin fell from her trembling hand into the grass. The
scene passed: I should have remarked, by the way, that on the
rough walls of the enclosure I could distinguish bones, and even
a skull, lying in a disorderly fashion. Next, I was looking upon

two boys; one the figure of the former vision, the other younger. They were in a plot of garden, walled round, and this garden, in spite of the difference in arrangement, and the small size of the trees, I could clearly recognize as being that upon which I now look from my window. The boys were engaged in some curious play, it seemed. Something was smouldering on the ground. The elder placed his hands upon it, and then raised them in what I took to be an attitude of prayer: and I saw, and started at seeing, that on them were deep stains of blood. The sky above was overcast. The same boy now turned his face towards the wall of the garden, and beckoned with both his raised hands, and as he did so I was conscious that some moving objects were becoming visible over the top of the wall—whether heads or other parts of some animal or human forms I could not tell. Upon the instant the elder boy turned sharply, seized the arm of the younger (who all this time had been poring over what lay on the ground), and both hurried off. I then saw blood upon the grass, a little pile of bricks, and what I thought were black feathers scattered about. That scene closed, and the next was so dark that perhaps the full meaning of it escaped me. But what I seemed to see was a form, at first crouching low among trees or bushes that were being threshed by a violent wind, then running very swiftly, and constantly turning a pale face to look behind him, as if he feared a pursuer: and, indeed, pursuers were following hard after him. Their shapes were but dimly seen, their number—three or four, perhaps—only guessed. I suppose they were on the whole more like dogs than anything else, but dogs such as we have seen they assuredly were not. Could I have closed my eyes to this horror, I would have done so at once, but I was helpless. The last I saw was the victim darting beneath an arch and clutching at some object to which he clung: and those that were pursuing him overtook him, and I seemed to hear the echo of a cry of despair. It may be that I became unconscious: certainly I had the sensation of awaking to the light of day after an interval of darkness. Such, in literal truth, Emily, was my vision—I can call it by no other name—of this afternoon. Tell me, have I not been the unwilling witness of some episode of a tragedy connected with this very house?"

The letter is continued next day. "The tale of yesterday was not completed when I laid down my pen. I said nothing of my experiences to my uncle—you know, yourself, how little his robust common sense would be prepared to allow of them, and how in his eyes the specific remedy would be a black draught[14] or a glass of port. After a silent evening, then—silent, not sullen—I retired to rest. Judge of my terror, when, not yet in bed, I heard what I can only describe as a distant bellow, and knew it for my uncle's voice, though never in my hearing so exerted before. His sleeping-room is at the farther extremity of this large house, and to gain access to it one must traverse an antique hall some eighty feet long, a lofty panelled chamber, and two unoccupied bedrooms. In the second of these—a room almost devoid of furniture—I found him, in the dark, his candle lying smashed on the floor. As I ran in, bearing a light, he clasped me in arms that trembled for the first time since I have known him, thanked God, and hurried me out of the room. He would say nothing of what had alarmed him. 'To-morrow, to-morrow,' was all I could get from him. A bed was hastily improvised for him in the room next to my own. I doubt if his night was more restful than mine. I could only get to sleep in the small hours, when daylight was already strong, and then my dreams were of the grimmest—particularly one which stamped itself on my brain, and which I must set down on the chance of dispersing the impression it has made. It was that I came up to my room with a heavy foreboding of evil oppressing me, and went with a hesitation and reluctance I could not explain to my chest of drawers. I opened the top drawer, in which was nothing but ribbons and handkerchiefs, and then the second, where was as little to alarm, and then, O heavens, the third and last: and there was a mass of linen neatly folded: upon which, as I looked with a curiosity that began to be tinged with horror, I perceived a movement in it, and a pink hand was thrust out of the folds and began to grope feebly in the air. I could bear it no more, and rushed from the room, clapping the door after me, and strove with all my force to lock it. But the key would not turn in the wards, and from within the room came a sound of rustling and bumping, drawing nearer and nearer to the door.

Why I did not flee down the stairs I know not. I continued grasping the handle, and mercifully, as the door was plucked from my hand with an irresistible force, I awoke. You may not think this very alarming, but I assure you it was so to me.

"At breakfast to-day my uncle was very uncommunicative, and I think ashamed of the fright he had given us; but afterwards he inquired of me whether Mr. Spearman was still in town, adding that he thought that was a young man who had some sense left in his head. I think you know, my dear Emily, that I am not inclined to disagree with him there, and also that I was not unlikely to be able to answer his question. To Mr. Spearman he accordingly went, and I have not seen him since. I must send this strange budget of news to you now, or it may have to wait over more than one post."

The reader will not be far out if he guesses that Miss Mary and Mr. Spearman made a match of it not very long after this month of June. Mr. Spearman was a young spark, who had a good property in the neighbourhood of Whitminster, and not unfrequently about this time spent a few days at the "King's Head," ostensibly on business. But he must have had some leisure, for his diary is copious, especially for the days of which I am telling the story. It is probable to me that he wrote this episode as fully as he could at the bidding of Miss Mary.

"Uncle Oldys (how I hope I may have the right to call him so before long!) called this morning. After throwing out a good many short remarks on indifferent topics, he said, 'I wish, Spearman, you'd listen to an odd story and keep a close tongue about it just for a bit, till I get more light on it.' 'To be sure,' said I, 'you may count on me.' 'I don't know what to make of it,' he said. 'You know my bedroom. It is well away from everyone else's, and I pass through the great hall and two or three other rooms to get to it.' 'Is it at the end next the minster, then?' I asked. 'Yes, it is: well, now, yesterday morning my Mary told me that the room next before it was infested with some sort of fly that the housekeeper couldn't get rid of. That may be the explanation, or it may not. What do you think?' 'Why,' said I, 'you've not yet told me what has to be explained.' 'True enough, I don't believe I have; but by the by, what are these

sawflies? What's the size of them?' I began to wonder if he was
touched in the head. 'What I call a sawfly,' I said very patiently,
'is a red animal, like a daddy-long-legs, but not so big, perhaps
an inch long, perhaps less. It is very hard in the body, and to
me'—I was going to say 'particularly offensive,' but he broke
in, 'Come, come; an inch or less. That won't do.' 'I can only tell
you,' I said, 'what I know. Would it not be better if you told me
from first to last what it is that has puzzled you, and then I may
be able to give you some kind of an opinion.' He gazed at me
meditatively. 'Perhaps it would,' he said. 'I told Mary only to-
day that I thought you had some vestiges of sense in your head.'
(I bowed my acknowledgments.) 'The thing is, I've an odd kind
of shyness about talking of it. Nothing of the sort has happened
to me before. Well, about eleven o'clock last night, or after, I
took my candle and set out for my room. I had a book in my
other hand—I always read something for a few minutes before
I drop off to sleep. A dangerous habit: I don't recommend it:
but *I* know how to manage my light and my bed curtains. Now
then, first, as I stepped out of my study into the great hall that's
next to it, and shut the door, my candle went out. I supposed
I had clapped the door behind me too quick, and made a
draught, and I was annoyed, for I'd no tinder-box nearer than
my bedroom. But I knew my way well enough, and went on.
The next thing was that my book was struck out of my hand in
the dark: if I said twitched out of my hand it would better express the sensation. It fell on the floor. I picked it up, and went
on, more annoyed than before, and a little startled. But as you
know, that hall has many windows without curtains, and in
summer nights like these it's easy to see not only where the furniture is, but whether there's anyone or anything moving: and
there was no one—nothing of the kind. So on I went through
the hall and through the audit chamber next to it, which also
has big windows, and then into the bedrooms which lead to my
own, where the curtains were drawn, and I had to go slower
because of steps here and there. It was in the second of those
rooms that I nearly got my *quietus*.[15] The moment I opened the
door of it I felt there was something wrong. I thought twice, I
confess, whether I shouldn't turn back and find another way

there is to my room rather than go through that one. Then I was ashamed of myself, and thought what people call better of it, though I don't know about "better" in this case. If I was to describe my experience exactly, I should say this: there was a dry, light, rustling sound all over the room as I went in, and then (you remember it was perfectly dark) something seemed to rush at me, and there was—I don't know how to put it—a sensation of long thin arms, or legs, or feelers, all about my face, and neck, and body. Very little strength in them, there seemed to be, but, Spearman, I don't think I was ever more horrified or disgusted in all my life, that I remember: and it does take something to put me out. I roared out as loud as I could, and flung away my candle at random, and, knowing I was near the window, I tore at the curtain and somehow let in enough light to be able to see something waving which I knew was an insect's leg, by the shape of it: but, Lord, what a size! Why, the beast must have been as tall as I am. And now you tell me sawflies are an inch long or less. What do you make of it, Spearman?'

" 'For goodness' sake finish your story first,' I said. 'I never heard anything like it.' 'Oh,' said he, 'there's no more to tell. Mary ran in with a light, and there was nothing there. I didn't tell her what was the matter. I changed my room for last night, and I expect for good.' 'Have you searched this odd room of yours?' I said. 'What do you keep in it?' 'We don't use it,' he answered. 'There's an old press there, and some little other furniture.' 'And in the press?' said I. 'I don't know; I never saw it opened, but I do know that it's locked.' 'Well, I should have it looked into, and, if you had time, I own to having some curiosity to see the place myself.' 'I didn't exactly like to ask you, but that's rather what I hoped you'd say. Name your time and I'll take you there.' 'No time like the present,' I said at once, for I saw he would never settle down to anything while this affair was in suspense. He got up with great alacrity, and looked at me, I am tempted to think, with marked approval. 'Come along,' was all he said, however; and was pretty silent all the way to his house. My Mary (as he calls her in public, and I in private) was summoned, and we proceeded to the room. The Doctor had gone so far as to tell her that he had had something

of a fright there last night, of what nature he had not yet di-
vulged; but now he pointed out and described, very briefly, the
incidents of his progress. When we were near the important
spot, he pulled up, and allowed me to pass on. 'There's the
room,' he said. 'Go in, Spearman, and tell us what you find.'
Whatever I might have felt at midnight, noonday I was sure
would keep back anything sinister, and I flung the door open
with an air and stepped in. It was a well-lighted room, with its
large window on the right, though not, I thought, a very airy
one. The principal piece of furniture was the gaunt old press of
dark wood. There was, too, a four-post bedstead, a mere skele-
ton which could hide nothing, and there was a chest of drawers.
On the window-sill and the floor near it were the dead bodies of
many hundred sawflies, and one torpid one which I had some
satisfaction in killing. I tried the door of the press, but could
not open it: the drawers, too, were locked. Somewhere, I was
conscious, there was a faint rustling sound, but I could not lo-
cate it, and when I made my report to those outside, I said nothing of it. But, I said, clearly the next thing was to see what was
in those locked receptacles. Uncle Oldys turned to Mary. 'Mrs.
Maple,' he said, and Mary ran off—no one, I am sure, steps like
her—and soon came back at a soberer pace, with an elderly lady
of discreet aspect.

   " 'Have you the keys of these things, Mrs. Maple?' said Uncle
Oldys. His simple words let loose a torrent (not violent, but copious) of speech: had she been a shade or two higher in the social scale, Mrs. Maple might have stood as the model for Miss
Bates.[16]

   " 'Oh, Doctor, and Miss, and you too, sir,' she said, acknowl-
edging my presence with a bend, 'them keys! who was that
again that come when first we took over things in this house—a
gentleman in business it was, and I gave him his luncheon in the
small parlour on account of us not having everything as we
should like to see it in the large one—chicken, and apple-pie,
and a glass of madeira—dear, dear, you'll say I'm running on,
Miss Mary; but I only mention it to bring back my recollection;
and there it comes—Gardner, just the same as it did last week
with the artichokes and the text of the sermon. Now that Mr.

Gardner, every key I got from him were labelled to itself, and each and every one was a key of some door or another in this house, and sometimes two; and when I say door, my meaning is door of a room, not like such a press as this is. Yes, Miss Mary, I know full well, and I'm just making it clear to your uncle and you too, sir. But now there *was* a box which this same gentleman he give over into my charge, and thinking no harm after he was gone I took the liberty, knowing it was your uncle's property, to rattle it: and unless I'm most surprisingly deceived, in that box there was keys, but what keys, that, Doctor, is known Elsewhere, for open the box, no that I would not do.'

"I wondered that Uncle Oldys remained as quiet as he did under this address. Mary, I knew, was amused by it, and he probably had been taught by experience that it was useless to break in upon it. At any rate he did not, but merely said at the end, 'Have you that box handy, Mrs. Maple? If so, you might bring it here.' Mrs. Maple pointed her finger at him, either in accusation or in gloomy triumph. 'There,' she said, 'was I to choose out the very words out of your mouth, Doctor, them would be the ones. And if I've took it to my own rebuke one half a dozen times, it's been nearer fifty. Laid awake I have in my bed, sat down in my chair I have, the same you and Miss Mary gave me the day I was twenty year in your service, and no person could desire a better—yes, Miss Mary, but it *is* the truth, and well we know who it is would have it different if he could. "All very well," says I to myself, "but pray, when the Doctor calls you to account for that box, what are you going to say?" No, Doctor, if you was some masters I've heard of and I was some servants I could name, I should have an easy task before me, but things being, humanly speaking, what they are, the one course open to me is just to say to you that without Miss Mary comes to my room and helps me to my recollection, which her wits *may* manage what's slipped beyond mine, no such box as that, small though it be, will cross your eyes this many a day to come.'

" 'Why, dear Mrs. Maple, why didn't you tell me before that you wanted me to help you to find it?' said my Mary. 'No, never mind telling me why it was: let us come at once and look for it.'

They hastened off together. I could hear Mrs. Maple beginning an explanation which, I doubt not, lasted into the farthest recesses of the housekeeper's department. Uncle Oldys and I were left alone. 'A valuable servant,' he said, nodding towards the door. 'Nothing goes wrong under her: the speeches are seldom over three minutes.' 'How will Miss Oldys manage to make her remember about the box?' I asked.

" 'Mary? Oh, she'll make her sit down and ask her about her aunt's last illness, or who gave her the china dog on the mantelpiece—something quite off the point. Then, as Maple says, one thing brings up another, and the right one will come round sooner than you could suppose. There! I believe I hear them coming back already.'

"It was indeed so, and Mrs. Maple was hurrying on ahead of Mary with the box in her outstretched hand, and a beaming face. 'What was it,' she cried as she drew near, 'what was it as I said, before ever I come out of Dorsetshire to this place? Not that I'm a Dorset woman myself, nor had need to be. "Safe bind, safe find," and there it was in the place where I'd put it— what?—two months back, I dare say.' She handed it to Uncle Oldys, and he and I examined it with some interest, so that I ceased to pay attention to Mrs. Ann Maple for the moment, though I know that she went on to expound exactly where the box had been, and in what way Mary had helped to refresh her memory on the subject.

"It was an oldish box, tied with pink tape and sealed, and on the lid was pasted a label inscribed in old ink, 'The Senior Prebendary's House, Whitminster.' On being opened it was found to contain two keys of moderate size, and a paper, on which, in the same hand as the label, was 'Keys of the Press and Box of Drawers standing in the disused Chamber.' Also this: 'The Effects in this Press and Box are held by me, and to be held by my successors in the Residence, in trust for the noble Family of Kildonan, if claim be made by any survivor of it. I having made all the Enquiry possible to myself am of the opinion that that noble House is wholly extinct: the last Earl having been, as is notorious, cast away at sea, and his only Child and Heire deceas'd in my House (the Papers as to which melancholy

Casualty were by me repos'd in the same Press in this year of our Lord 1753, 21 March). I am further of opinion that unless grave discomfort arise, such persons, not being of the Family of Kildonan, as shall become possess'd of these keys, will be well advised to leave matters as they are: which opinion I do not express without weighty and sufficient reason; and am Happy to have my Judgment confirm'd by the other Members of this College and Church who are conversant with the Events referr'd to in this Paper. Tho. Ashton, *S.T.P., Præb. senr*. Will. Blake, *S.T.P., Decanus*. Hen. Goodman, *S.T.B., Præb. junr*.'[17]

" 'Ah!' said Uncle Oldys, 'grave discomfort! So he thought there might be something. I suspect it was that young man,' he went on, pointing with the key to the line about the 'only Child and Heire.' 'Eh, Mary? The viscounty of Kildonan was Saul.' 'How *do* you know that, Uncle?' said Mary. 'Oh, why not? it's all in Debrett[18]—two little fat books. But I meant the tomb by the lime walk. He's there. What's the story, I wonder? Do you know it, Mrs. Maple? and, by the way, look at your sawflies by the window there.'

"Mrs. Maple, thus confronted with two subjects at once, was a little put to it to do justice to both. It was no doubt rash in Uncle Oldys to give her the opportunity. I could only guess that he had some slight hesitation about using the key he held in his hand.

" 'Oh them flies, how bad they was, Doctor and Miss, this three or four days: and you, too, sir, you wouldn't guess, none of you! And how they come, too! First we took the room in hand, the shutters was up, and had been, I dare say, years upon years, and not a fly to be seen. Then we got the shutter bars down with a deal of trouble and left it so for the day, and next day I sent Susan in with the broom to sweep about, and not two minutes hadn't passed when out she come into the hall like a blind thing, and we had regular to beat them off her. Why, her cap and her hair, you couldn't see the colour of it, I do assure you, and all clustering round her eyes, too. Fortunate enough she's not a girl with fancies, else if it had been me, why only the tickling of the nasty things would have drove me out of my wits. And now there they lay like so many dead things. Well, they was lively enough on the Monday, and now here's Thursday, is it, or no, Friday. Only to come near the door and you'd hear them pattering up against it, and once you opened it, dash at you, they would, as if they'd eat you. I couldn't help thinking to myself, "If you was bats, where should we be this night?" Nor you can't cresh 'em, not like a usual kind of a fly. Well, there's something to be thankful for, if we could but learn by it. And then this tomb, too,' she said, hastening on to her second point to elude any chance of interruption, 'of them two poor young lads. I say poor, and yet when I recollect myself, I was at tea with Mrs. Simpkins, the sexton's wife, before you come, Doctor and Miss Mary, and that's a family has been in the place, what? I dare say a hundred years in that very house, and could put their hand on any tomb or yet grave in all the yard and give you name and age. And his account of that young man, Mr. Simpkins's I mean to say—*well!*" She compressed her lips and nodded several times. 'Tell us, Mrs. Maple,' said Mary. 'Go on,' said Uncle Oldys. 'What about him?' said I. 'Never was such a thing seen in this place, not since Queen Mary's times and the Pope and all,' said Mrs. Maple. 'Why, do you know he lived in this very house, him and them that was with him, and for all I can tell in this identical room' (she shifted her feet uneasily on the floor). 'Who was with him? Do you mean the people of the house?' said Uncle Oldys suspiciously. 'Not to call people, Doctor, dear no,' was the answer; 'more what he brought with him from Ireland, I believe it was. No, the people in the house was the last to hear anything of his goings-on. But in the town not a family but knew how he stopped out at night: and them that was with him, why, they were such as would strip the skin from the child in its grave; and a withered heart makes an ugly thin ghost, says Mr. Simpkins. But they turned on him at the last, he says, and there's the mark still to be seen on the minster door where they run him down. And that's no more than the truth, for I got him to show it to myself, and that's what he said. A lord he was, with a Bible name of a wicked king, whatever his godfathers could have been thinking of.' 'Saul was the name,' said Uncle Oldys. 'To be sure it was Saul, Doctor, and thank you; and now isn't it King Saul that we read of raising up the dead ghost that was slumbering in its tomb till he disturbed it,[19] and isn't that a strange thing, this young lord to have such a name, and Mr. Simpkins's grandfather to see him out of his window of a dark night going about from one grave to another in the yard with a candle, and them that was with him following through the grass at his heels: and one night him to come right up to old Mr. Simpkins's window that gives on the yard and press his face up against it to find out if there was anyone in the room that could see him: and only just time there was for old Mr. Simpkins to drop down like, quiet, just under the window and hold his breath, and not stir till he heard him stepping away again, and this rustling-like in the grass after him as he went, and then when he looked out of his window in the morning there was treadings in the grass and a dead man's bone. Oh, he was a cruel child for certain, but he had to pay in the end, and after.' 'After?' said Uncle Oldys, with a frown. 'Oh yes, Doctor, night after night in old Mr. Simpkins's time, and his son, that's our Mr. Simpkins's father, yes, and our own Mr. Simpkins too. Up against that same window, particular when they've had a fire of a chilly evening, with his face right on the panes, and his hands fluttering out, and his mouth open and shut, open and shut, for a minute or more, and then gone off in the dark yard. But open the window at such times, no, that they dare not do, though they could find it in their heart to pity the poor thing, that pinched up with the cold, and seemingly fading away to a nothink as the years passed on. Well, indeed, I believe it is no more than the truth what our Mr. Simpkins says on his own grandfather's word, "A withered heart makes an ugly thin ghost."' 'I dare say,' said Uncle Oldys suddenly: so suddenly that Mrs. Maple stopped short. 'Thank you. Come away, all of you.' 'Why, *Uncle*,' said Mary, 'are you not going to open the press after all?' Uncle Oldys blushed, actually blushed. 'My dear,' he said, 'you are at liberty to call me a coward, or applaud me as a prudent man, whichever you please. But I am neither going to open that press nor that chest of drawers myself, nor am I going to hand over the keys to you or to any other person. Mrs. Maple, will you kindly see about getting a man or two to move those pieces of furniture into the garret?' 'And

when they do it, Mrs. Maple,' said Mary, who seemed to me—
I did not then know why—more relieved than disappointed by
her uncle's decision, 'I have something that I want put with the
rest; only quite a small packet.'

"We left that curious room not unwillingly, I think. Uncle
Oldys's orders were carried out that same day. And so," con-
cludes Mr. Spearman, "Whitminster has a Bluebeard's chamber, and, I am rather inclined to suspect, a Jack-in-the-box,
awaiting some future occupant of the residence of the senior
prebendary."

THE DIARY OF
MR. POYNTER

The sale-room of an old and famous firm of book auctioneers in London is, of course, a great meeting-place for collectors, librarians, and dealers: not only when an auction is in progress, but perhaps even more notably when books that are coming on for sale are upon view. It was in such a sale-room that the remarkable series of events began which were detailed to me not many months ago by the person whom they principally affected—namely, Mr. James Denton, M.A., F.S.A., etc., etc., sometime of Trinity Hall, now, or lately, of Rendcomb Manor in the county of Warwick.[1]

He, on a certain spring day in a recent year, was in London for a few days upon business connected principally with the furnishing of the house which he had just finished building at Rendcomb. It may be a disappointment to you to learn that Rendcomb Manor was new; that I cannot help. There had, no doubt, been an old house; but it was not remarkable for beauty or interest. Even had it been, neither beauty nor interest would have enabled it to resist the disastrous fire which about a couple of years before the date of my story had razed it to the ground. I am glad to say that all that was most valuable in it had been saved, and that it was fully insured. So that it was with a comparatively light heart that Mr. Denton was able to face the task of building a new and considerably more convenient dwelling for himself and his aunt who constituted his whole *ménage*.

Being in London, with time on his hands, and not far from the sale-room at which I have obscurely hinted, Mr. Denton thought that he would spend an hour there upon the chance of finding, among that portion of the famous Thomas collection

of MSS., which he knew to be then on view, something bearing
upon the history or topography of his part of Warwickshire.

He turned in accordingly, purchased a catalogue and as-
cended to the sale-room, where, as usual, the books were disposed in cases and some laid out upon the long tables. At the
shelves, or sitting about at the tables, were figures, many of
whom were familiar to him. He exchanged nods and greetings
with several, and then settled down to examine his catalogue
and note likely items. He had made good progress through
about two hundred of the five hundred lots—every now and
then rising to take a volume from the shelf and give it a cursory
glance—when a hand was laid on his shoulder, and he looked
up. His interrupter was one of those intelligent men with a
pointed beard and a flannel shirt, of whom the last quarter of
the nineteenth century was, it seems to me, very prolific.

It is no part of my plan to repeat the whole conversation
which ensued between the two. I must content myself with stat-
ing that it largely referred to common acquaintances, e.g., to
the nephew of Mr. Denton's friend who had recently married
and settled in Chelsea, to the sister-in-law of Mr. Denton's
friend who had been seriously indisposed, but was now better,
and to a piece of china which Mr. Denton's friend had purchased some months before at a price much below its true
value. From which you will rightly infer that the conversation
was rather in the nature of a monologue. In due time, however,
the friend bethought himself that Mr. Denton was there for a
purpose, and said he, "What are you looking out for in particular? I don't think there's much in this lot." "Why, I thought
there might be some Warwickshire collections, but I don't see
anything under Warwick in the catalogue." "No, apparently
not," said the friend. "All the same, I believe I noticed something like a Warwickshire diary. What was the name again?
Drayton? Potter? Painter—either a P or a D, I feel sure." He
turned over the leaves quickly. "Yes, here it is. Poynter. Lot 486.
That might interest you. There are the books, I think: out on
the table. Someone has been looking at them. Well, I must be
getting on. Good-bye—you'll look us up, won't you? Couldn't
you come this afternoon? we've got a little music about four.

Well, then, when you're next in town." He went off. Mr. Denton looked at his watch and found to his confusion that he
could spare no more than a moment before retrieving his luggage and going for the train. The moment was just enough to
show him that there were four largish volumes of the diary—
that it concerned the years about 1710, and that there seemed
to be a good many insertions in it of various kinds. It seemed
quite worth while to leave a commission of five and twenty
pounds for it, and this he was able to do, for his usual agent entered the room as he was on the point of leaving it.

That evening he rejoined his aunt at their temporary abode,
which was a small dower-house² not many hundred yards from
the Manor. On the following morning the two resumed a discussion that had now lasted for some weeks as to the equipment
of the new house. Mr. Denton laid before his relative a statement of the results of his visit to town—particulars of carpets,
of chairs, of wardrobes, and of bedroom china. "Yes, dear,"
said his aunt, "but I don't see any chintzes here. Did you go
to ——?" Mr. Denton stamped on the floor (where else, indeed,
could he have stamped?). "Oh dear, oh dear," he said, "the one
thing I missed. I *am* sorry. The fact is I was on my way there
and I happened to be passing Robins's." His aunt threw up her
hands. "Robins's! Then the next thing will be another parcel of
horrible old books at some outrageous price. I do think, James,
when I am taking all this trouble for you, you might contrive to
remember the one or two things which I specially begged you
to see after. It's not as if I was asking it for myself. I don't know
whether you think I get any pleasure out of it, but if so I can assure you it's very much the reverse. The thought and worry and
trouble I have over it you have no idea of, and *you* have simply
to go to the shops and order the things." Mr. Denton inter-
posed a moan of penitence. "Oh, aunt——" "Yes, that's all very
well, dear, and I don't want to speak sharply, but you *must* know
how very annoying it is: particularly as it delays the whole of
our business for I can't tell how long: here is Wednesday—the
Simpsons come to-morrow, and you can't leave them. Then on
Saturday we have friends, as you know, coming for tennis. Yes,
indeed, you spoke of asking them yourself, but, of course, I had

to write the notes, and it is ridiculous, James, to look like that. We must occasionally be civil to our neighbours: you wouldn't like to have it said we were perfect bears. What was I saying? Well, anyhow it comes to this, that it must be Thursday in next week at least, before you can go to town again, and until we have decided upon the chintzes it is impossible to settle upon one single other thing."

Mr. Denton ventured to suggest that as the paint and wall-papers had been dealt with, this was too severe a view: but this his aunt was not prepared to admit at the moment. Nor, indeed, was there any proposition he could have advanced which she would have found herself able to accept. However, as the day went on, she receded a little from this position: examined with lessening disfavour the samples and price lists submitted by her nephew, and even in some cases gave a qualified approval to his choice.

As for him, he was naturally somewhat dashed by the consciousness of duty unfulfilled, but more so by the prospect of a lawn-tennis party, which, though an inevitable evil in August, he had thought there was no occasion to fear in May. But he was to some extent cheered by the arrival on the Friday morning of an intimation that he had secured at the price of £12 10s. the four volumes of Poynter's manuscript diary, and still more by the arrival on the next morning of the diary itself.

The necessity of taking Mr. and Mrs. Simpson for a drive in the car on Saturday morning and of attending to his neighbours and guests that afternoon prevented him from doing more than open the parcel until the party had retired to bed on the Saturday night. It was then that he made certain of the fact, which he had before only suspected, that he had indeed acquired the diary of Mr. William Poynter, Squire of Acrington[3] (about four miles from his own parish)—that same Poynter who was for a time a member of the circle of Oxford antiquaries, the centre of which was Thomas Hearne,[4] and with whom Hearne seems ultimately to have quarrelled—a not uncommon episode in the career of that excellent man. As is the case with Hearne's own collections, the diary of Poynter contained a good many notes from printed books, descriptions of coins and other antiquities that had been brought to his notice, and drafts of letters on these subjects, besides the chronicle of everyday events. The description in the sale-catalogue had given Mr. Denton no idea of the amount of interest which seemed to lie in the book, and he sat up reading in the first of the four volumes until a reprehensibly late hour.

On the Sunday morning, after church, his aunt came into the study and was diverted from what she had been going to say to him by the sight of the four brown leather quartos on the table. "What are these?" she said suspiciously. "New, aren't they? Oh! are these the things that made you forget my chintzes? I thought so. Disgusting. What did you give for them, I should like to know? Over Ten Pounds? James, it is really sinful. Well, if you have money to throw away on this kind of thing, there *can* be no reason why you should not subscribe—and subscribe handsomely—to my anti-Vivisection League.[5] There is not, indeed, James, and I shall be very seriously annoyed if—. Who did you say wrote them? Old Mr. Poynter, of Acrington? Well, of course, there is some interest in getting together old papers about this neighbourhood. But Ten Pounds!" She picked up one of the volumes—not that which her nephew had been reading—and opened it at random, dashing it to the floor the next instant with a cry of disgust as an earwig fell from between the pages. Mr. Denton picked it up with a smothered expletive and said, "Poor book! I think you're rather hard on Mr. Poynter." "Was I, my dear? I beg his pardon, but you know I cannot abide those horrid creatures. Let me see if I've done any mischief." "No, I think all's well: but look here what you've opened him on." "Dear me, yes, to be sure! How very interesting. Do unpin it, James, and let me look at it."

It was a piece of patterned stuff about the size of the quarto page, to which it was fastened by an old-fashioned pin. James detached it and handed it to his aunt, carefully replacing the pin in the paper.

Now, I do not know exactly what the fabric was; but it had a design printed upon it, which completely fascinated Miss Denton. She went into raptures over it, held it against the wall, made James do the same, that she might retire to contemplate it

from a distance: then pored over it at close quarters, and ended
her examination by expressing in the warmest terms her appre-
ciation of the taste of the ancient Mr. Poynter who had had
the happy idea of preserving this sample in his diary. "It is a
most charming pattern," she said, "and remarkable too. Look,
James, how delightfully the lines ripple. It reminds one of hair,
very much, doesn't it? And then these knots of ribbon at intervals. They give just the relief of colour that is wanted. I
wonder—" "I was going to say," said James with deference, "I
wonder if it would cost much to have it copied for our curtains." "Copied? how could you have it copied, James?" "Well,
I don't know the details, but I suppose that is a printed pattern,
and that you could have a block cut from it in wood or metal."
"Now, really, that is a capital idea, James. I am almost inclined
to be glad that you were so—that you forgot the chintzes on
Wednesday. At any rate, I'll promise to forgive and forget if you
get this *lovely* old thing copied. No one will have anything in
the least like it, and mind, James, we won't allow it to be sold.
Now I *must* go, and I've totally forgotten what it was I came in
to say: never mind, it'll keep."

After his aunt had gone James Denton devoted a few minutes to examining the pattern more closely than he had yet
had a chance of doing. He was puzzled to think why it should
have struck Miss Denton so forcibly. It seemed to him not specially remarkable or pretty. No doubt it was suitable enough
for a curtain pattern: it ran in vertical bands, and there was
some indication that these were intended to converge at the
top. She was right, too, in thinking that these main bands re-
sembled rippling—almost curling—tresses of hair. Well, the
main thing was to find out by means of trade directories, or
otherwise, what firm would undertake the reproduction of an
old pattern of this kind. Not to delay the reader over this portion of the story, a list of likely names was made out, and Mr.
Denton fixed a day for calling on them, or some of them, with
his sample.

The first two visits which he paid were unsuccessful: but
there is luck in odd numbers. The firm in Bermondsey[6] which
was third on his list was accustomed to handling this line. The

evidence they were able to produce justified their being entrusted with the job. "Our Mr. Cattell" took a fervent personal interest in it. "It's 'eartrending, isn't it, sir," he said, "to picture the quantity of reelly lovely medeevial stuff of this kind that lays wellnigh unnoticed in many of our residential country 'ouses: much of it in peril, I take it, of being cast aside as so much rubbish. What is it Shakespeare says—unconsidered trifles.[7] Ah, I often say he 'as a word for us all, sir. I say Shakespeare, but I'm well aware all don't 'old with me there—I 'ad something of an upset the other day when a gentleman came in—a titled man, too, he was, and I think he told me he'd wrote on the topic, and I 'appened to cite out something about 'Ercules and the painted cloth.[8] Dear me, you never see such a pother. But as to this, what you've kindly confided to us, it's a piece of work we shall take a reel enthusiasm in achieving it out to the very best of our ability. What man 'as done, as I was observing only a few weeks back to another esteemed client, man can do, and in three to four weeks' time, all being well, we shall 'ope to lay before you evidence to that effect, sir. Take the address, Mr. 'Iggins, if you please."

Such was the general drift of Mr. Cattell's observations on the occasion of his first interview with Mr. Denton. About a month later, being advised that some samples were ready for his inspection, Mr. Denton met him again, and had, it seems, reason to be satisfied with the faithfulness of the reproduction of the design. It had been finished off at the top in accordance with the indication I mentioned, so that the vertical bands joined. But something still needed to be done in the way of matching the colour of the original. Mr. Cattell had suggestions of a technical kind to offer, with which I need not trouble you. He had also views as to the general desirability of the pattern which were vaguely adverse. "You say you don't wish this to be supplied excepting to personal friends equipped with a authorization from yourself, sir. It shall be done. I quite understand your wish to keep it exclusive: lends a catchit, does it not, to the suite? What's every man's, it's been said, is no man's."

"Do you think it would be popular if it were generally obtainable?" asked Mr. Denton.

"I 'ardly think it, sir," said Cattell, pensively clasping his beard. "I 'ardly think it. Not popular: it wasn't popular with the man that cut the block, was it, Mr. 'Iggins?"

"Did he find it a difficult job?"

"He'd no call to do so, sir; but the fact is that the artistic temperament—and our men are artists, sir, every one of them—true artists as much as many that the world styles by that term—it's apt to take some strange 'ardly accountable likes or dislikes, and here was an example. The twice or thrice that I went to inspect his progress: language I could understand, for that's 'abitual to him, but reel distaste for what I should call a dainty enough thing, I did not, nor am I now able to fathom. It seemed," said Mr. Cattell, looking narrowly upon Mr. Denton, "as if the man scented something almost Hevil in the design."

"Indeed? did he tell you so? I can't say I see anything sinister in it myself."

"Neether can I, sir. In fact I said as much. 'Come, Gatwick,' I said, 'what's to do here? What's the reason of your prejudice—for I can call it no more than that?' But, no! no explanation was forthcoming. And I was merely reduced, as I am now, to a shrug of the shoulders, and a *cui bono*. However, here it is," and with that the technical side of the question came to the front again.

The matching of the colours for the background, the hem, and the knots of ribbon was by far the longest part of the business, and necessitated many sendings to and fro of the original pattern and of new samples. During part of August and September, too, the Dentons were away from the Manor. So that it was not until October was well in that a sufficient quantity of the stuff had been manufactured to furnish curtains for the three or four bedrooms which were to be fitted up with it.

On the feast of Simon and Jude[9] the aunt and nephew returned from a short visit to find all completed, and their satisfaction at the general effect was great. The new curtains, in particular, agreed to admiration with their surroundings. When Mr. Denton was dressing for dinner, and took stock of his room, in which there was a large amount of the chintz dis-

THE DIARY OF MR. POYNTER

played, he congratulated himself over and over again on the luck which had first made him forget his aunt's commission and had then put into his hands this extremely effective means of remedying his mistake. The pattern was, as he said at dinner, so restful and yet so far from being dull. And Miss Denton—who, by the way, had none of the stuff in her own room—was much disposed to agree with him.

At breakfast next morning he was induced to qualify his satisfaction to some extent—but very slightly. "There is one thing I rather regret," he said, "that we allowed them to join up the vertical bands of the pattern at the top. I think it would have been better to leave that alone."

"Oh?" said his aunt interrogatively.

"Yes: as I was reading in bed last night they kept catching my eye rather. That is, I found myself looking across at them every now and then. There was an effect as if someone kept peeping out between the curtains in one place or another, where there was no edge, and I think that was due to the joining up of the bands at the top. The only other thing that troubled me was the wind."

"Why, I thought it was a perfectly still night."

"Perhaps it was only on my side of the house, but there was enough to sway my curtains and rustle them more than I wanted."

That night a bachelor friend of James Denton's came to stay, and was lodged in a room on the same floor as his host, but at the end of a long passage, half-way down which was a red baize door, put there to cut off the draught and intercept noise.

. The party of three had separated. Miss Denton a good first, the two men at about eleven. James Denton, not yet inclined for bed, sat him down in an arm-chair and read for a time. Then he dozed, and then he woke, and bethought himself that his brown spaniel, which ordinarily slept in his room, had not come upstairs with him. Then he thought he was mistaken: for happening to move his hand which hung down over the arm of the chair within a few inches of the floor, he felt on the back of it just the slightest touch of a surface of hair, and stretching it out in that direction he stroked and patted a rounded something. But the feel of it, and still more the fact that instead of a responsive movement, absolute stillness greeted his touch, made him look over the arm. What he had been touching rose to meet him. It was in the attitude of one that had crept along the floor on its belly, and it was, so far as could be recollected, a human figure. But of the face which was now rising to within a few inches of his own no feature was discernible, only hair. Shapeless as it was, there was about it so horrible an air of menace that as he bounded from his chair and rushed from the room he heard himself moaning with fear: and doubtless he did right to fly. As he dashed into the baize door that cut the passage in two, and—forgetting that it opened towards him—beat against it with all the force in him, he felt a soft ineffectual tearing at his back which, all the same, seemed to be growing in power, as if the hand, or whatever worse than a hand was there, were becoming more material as the pursuer's rage was more concentrated. Then he remembered the trick of the door—he got it open—he shut it behind him—he gained his friend's room, and that is all we need know.

It seems curious that, during all the time that had elapsed since the purchase of Poynter's diary, James Denton should not have sought an explanation of the presence of the pattern that had been pinned into it. Well, he had read the diary through without finding it mentioned, and had concluded that there was nothing to be said. But, on leaving Rendcomb Manor (he did not know whether for good), as he naturally insisted upon doing on the day after experiencing the horror I have tried to put into words, he took the diary with him. And at his seaside lodgings he examined more narrowly the portion whence the pattern had been taken. What he remembered having suspected about it turned out to be correct. Two or three leaves were pasted together, but written upon, as was patent when they were held up to the light. They yielded easily to steaming, for the paste had lost much of its strength and they contained something relevant to the pattern.

The entry was made in 1707.

"Old Mr. Casbury, of Acrington, told me this day much of

young Sir Everard Charlett, whom he remember'd Commoner of University College,[10] and thought was of the same Family as Dr. Arthur Charlett, now master of ye Coll. This Charlett was a personable young gent., but a loose atheistical companion, and a great Lifter, as they then call'd the hard drinkers, and for what I know do so now. He was noted, and subject to severall censures at different times for his extravagancies: and if the full history of his debaucheries had bin known, no doubt would have been expell'd ye Coll., supposing that no interest had been imploy'd on his behalf, of which Mr. Casbury had some suspicion. He was a very beautiful person, and constantly wore his own Hair, which was very abundant, from which, and his loose way of living, the cant name for him was Absalom,[11] and he was accustom'd to say that indeed he believ'd he had shortened old David's days, meaning his father, Sir Job Charlett, an old worthy cavalier.[12]

"Note that Mr. Casbury said that he remembers not the year of Sir Everard Charlett's death, but it was 1692 or 3. He died suddenly in October. [Several lines describing his unpleasant habits and reputed delinquencies are omitted.] Having seen him in such topping spirits the night before, Mr. Casbury was amaz'd when he learn'd the death. He was found in the town ditch, the hair as was said pluck'd clean off his head. Most bells in Oxford rung out for him, being a nobleman, and he was buried next night in St. Peter's in the East. But two years after, being to be moved to his country estate by his successor, it was said the coffin, breaking by mischance, proved quite full of Hair: which sounds fabulous, but yet I believe precedents are upon record, as in Dr. Plot's *History of Staffordshire*.[13]

"His chambers being afterwards stripp'd, Mr. Casbury came by part of the hangings of it, which 'twas said this Charlett had design'd expressly for a memoriall of his Hair, giving the Fellow that drew it a lock to work by, and the piece which I have fasten'd in here was parcel of the same, which Mr. Casbury gave to me. He said he believ'd there was a subtlety in the drawing, but had never discover'd it himself, nor much liked to pore upon it."

———

The money spent upon the curtains might as well have been
thrown into the fire, as they were. Mr. Cattell's comment upon
what he heard of the story took the form of a quotation from
Shakespeare. You may guess it without difficulty. It began with
the words "There are more things."[14]

AN EPISODE OF
CATHEDRAL HISTORY

There was once a learned gentleman who was deputed to examine and report upon the archives of the Cathedral of Southminster.[1] The examination of these records demanded a very considerable expenditure of time: hence it became advisable for him to engage lodgings in the city: for though the Cathedral body were profuse in their offers of hospitality, Mr. Lake felt that he would prefer to be master of his day. This was recognized as reasonable. The Dean eventually wrote advising Mr. Lake, if he were not already suited, to communicate with Mr. Worby, the principal Verger, who occupied a house convenient to the church and was prepared to take in a quiet lodger for three or four weeks. Such an arrangement was precisely what Mr. Lake desired. Terms were easily agreed upon, and early in December, like another Mr. Datchery[2] (as he remarked to himself), the investigator found himself in the occupation of a very comfortable room in an ancient and "cathedraly" house.

One so familiar with the customs of Cathedral churches, and treated with such obvious consideration by the Dean and Chapter[3] of this Cathedral in particular, could not fail to command the respect of the Head Verger. Mr. Worby even acquiesced in certain modifications of statements he had been accustomed to offer for years to parties of visitors. Mr. Lake, on his part, found the Verger a very cheery companion, and took advantage of any occasion that presented itself for enjoying his conversation when the day's work was over.

One evening, about nine o'clock, Mr. Worby knocked at his lodger's door. "I've occasion," he said, "to go across to the Cathedral, Mr. Lake, and I think I made you a promise when I did so next I would give you the opportunity to see what it looks like at night time. It's quite fine and dry outside, if you care to come."

"To be sure I will; very much obliged to you, Mr. Worby, for thinking of it, but let me get my coat."

"Here it is, sir, and I've another lantern here that you'll find advisable for the steps, as there's no moon."

"Anyone might think we were Jasper and Durdles, over again, mightn't they?" said Lake, as they crossed the close, for he had ascertained that the Verger had read *Edwin Drood*.[4]

"Well, so they might," said Mr. Worby, with a short laugh, "though I don't know whether we ought to take it as a compliment. Odd ways, I often think, they had at that Cathedral, don't it seem so to you, sir? Full choral matins at seven o'clock in the morning all the year round. Wouldn't suit our boys' voices nowadays, and I think there's one or two of the men would be applying for a rise if the Chapter was to bring it in— particular the alltoes."

They were now at the south-west door. As Mr. Worby was unlocking it, Lake said, "Did you ever find anybody locked in here by accident?"

"Twice I did. One was a drunk sailor; however he got in I don't know. I s'pose he went to sleep in the service, but by the time I got to him he was praying fit to bring the roof in. Lor'! what a noise that man did make! said it was the first time he'd been inside a church for ten years, and blest if ever he'd try it again. The other was an old sheep: them boys it was, up to their games. That was the last time they tried it on, though. There, sir, now you see what we look like; our late Dean used now and again to bring parties in, but he preferred a moonlight night, and there was a piece of verse he'd coat to 'em, relating to a Scotch cathedral, I understand; but I don't know; I almost think the effect's better when it's all dark-like. Seems to add to the size and heighth. Now if you won't mind stopping somewhere in the nave while I go up into the choir where my business lays, you'll see what I mean."

Accordingly Lake waited, leaning against a pillar, and watched the light wavering along the length of the church, and up the steps into the choir, until it was intercepted by some screen or other furniture, which only allowed the reflection to be seen on the piers and roof. Not many minutes had passed before Worby reappeared at the door of the choir and by waving his lantern signalled to Lake to rejoin him.

"I suppose it *is* Worby, and not a substitute," thought Lake to himself, as he walked up the nave. There was, in fact, nothing untoward. Worby showed him the papers which he had come to fetch out of the Dean's stall, and asked him what he thought of the spectacle: Lake agreed that it was well worth seeing. "I suppose," he said, as they walked towards the altar-steps together, "that you're too much used to going about here at night to feel nervous—but you must get a start every now and then, don't you, when a book falls down or a door swings to?"

"No, Mr. Lake, I can't say I think much about noises, not nowadays: I'm much more afraid of finding an escape of gas or a burst in the stove pipes than anything else. Still there have been times, years ago. Did you notice that plain altar-tomb there—fifteenth century we say it is, I don't know if you agree to that? Well, if you didn't look at it, just come back and give it a glance, if you'd be so good." It was on the north side of the choir, and rather awkwardly placed: only about three feet from the enclosing stone screen. Quite plain, as the Verger had said, but for some ordinary stone panelling. A metal cross of some size on the northern side (that next to the screen) was the solitary feature of any interest.

Lake agreed that it was not earlier than the Perpendicular period:[5] "but," he said, "unless it's the tomb of some remarkable person, you'll forgive me for saying that I don't think it's particularly noteworthy."

"Well, I can't say as it is the tomb of anybody noted in 'istory," said Worby, who had a dry smile on his face, "for we don't own any record whatsoever of who it was put up to. For all that, if you've half an hour to spare, sir, when we get back to the house, Mr. Lake, I could tell you a tale about that tomb. I won't begin on it now; it strikes cold here, and we don't want to be dawdling about all night."

"Of course I should like to hear it immensely."

"Very well, sir, you shall. Now if I might put a question to
you," he went on, as they passed down the choir aisle, "in our
little local guide—and not only there, but in the little book on
our Cathedral in the series⁶—you'll find it stated that this portion of the building was erected previous to the twelfth century.
Now of course I should be glad enough to take that view, but—
mind the step, sir—but, I put it to you—does the lay of the
stone 'ere in this portion of the wall (which he tapped with his
key), does it to your eye carry the flavour of what you might
call Saxon masonry? No, I thought not; no more it does to me:
now, if you'll believe me, I've said as much to those men—one's
the librarian of our Free Libry here, and the other came down
from London on purpose—fifty times, if I have once, but I
might just as well have talked to that bit of stonework. But
there it is, I suppose every one's got their opinions."

The discussion of this peculiar trait of human nature occupied
Mr. Worby almost up to the moment when he and Lake re-
entered the former's house. The condition of the fire in Lake's
sitting-room led to a suggestion from Mr. Worby that they
should finish the evening in his own parlour. We find them accordingly settled there some short time afterwards.

Mr. Worby made his story a long one, and I will not undertake to tell it wholly in his own words, or in his own order. Lake
committed the substance of it to paper immediately after hearing it, together with some few passages of the narrative which
had fixed themselves *verbatim* in his mind; I shall probably find
it expedient to condense Lake's record to some extent.

Mr. Worby was born, it appeared, about the year 1828. His
father before him had been connected with the Cathedral, and
likewise his grandfather. One or both had been choristers, and
in later life both had done work as mason and carpenter respectively about the fabric. Worby himself, though possessed, as he
frankly acknowledged, of an indifferent voice, had been drafted
into the choir at about ten years of age.

It was in 1840 that the wave of the Gothic revival smote the
Cathedral of Southminster. "There was a lot of lovely stuff went
then, sir," said Worby, with a sigh. "My father couldn't hardly
believe it when he got his orders to clear out the choir. There was

a new dean just come in—Dean Burscough it was—and my father had been 'prenticed to a good firm of joiners in the city, and knew what good work was when he saw it. Crool it was, he used to say: all that beautiful wainscot oak, as good as the day it was put up, and garlands-like of foliage and fruit, and lovely old gilding work on the coats of arms and the organ pipes. All went to the timber yard—every bit except some little pieces worked up in the Lady Chapel, and 'ere in this overmantel. Well—I may be mistook, but I say our choir never looked as well since. Still there was a lot found out about the history of the church, and no doubt but what it did stand in need of repair. There was very few winters passed but what we'd lose a pinnicle." Mr. Lake expressed his concurrence with Worby's views of restoration, but owns to a fear about this point lest the story proper should never be reached. Possibly this was perceptible in his manner.

Worby hastened to reassure him, "Not but what I could carry on about that topic for hours at a time, and do do when I see my opportunity. But Dean Burscough he was very set on the Gothic period, and nothing would serve him but everything must be made agreeable to that. And one morning after service he appointed for my father to meet him in the choir, and he came back after he'd taken off his robes in the vestry, and he'd got a roll of paper with him, and the verger that was then brought in a table, and they begun spreading it out on the table with prayer books to keep it down, and my father helped 'em, and he saw it was a picture of the inside of a choir in a Cathedral; and the Dean—he was a quick-spoken gentleman—he says, 'Well, Worby, what do you think of that?' 'Why,' says my father, 'I don't think I 'ave the pleasure of knowing that view. Would that be Hereford Cathedral,[7] Mr. Dean?' 'No, Worby,' says the Dean, 'that's Southminster Cathedral as we hope to see it before many years.' 'In-deed, sir,' says my father, and that was all he did say—leastways to the Dean—but he used to tell me he felt reelly faint in himself when he looked round our choir as I can remember it, all comfortable and furnished-like, and then see this nasty little dry picter, as he called it, drawn out by some London architect. Well, there I am again. But you'll see what I mean if you look at this old view."

Worby reached down a framed print from the wall. "Well, the long and the short of it was that the Dean he handed over to my father a copy of an order of the Chapter that he was to clear out every bit of the choir—make a clean sweep—ready for the new work that was being designed up in town, and he was to put it in hand as soon as ever he could get the breakers together. Now then, sir, if you look at that view, you'll see where the pulpit used to stand: that's what I want you to notice, if you please." It was, indeed, easily seen; an unusually large structure of timber with a domed sounding-board, standing at the east end of the stalls on the north side of the choir, facing the bishop's throne. Worby proceeded to explain that during the alterations, services were held in the nave, the members of the choir being thereby disappointed of an anticipated holiday, and the organist in particular incurring the suspicion of having wilfully damaged the mechanism of the temporary organ that was hired at considerable expense from London.

The work of demolition began with the choir screen and organ loft, and proceeded gradually eastwards, disclosing, as Worby said, many interesting features of older work. While this was going on, the members of the Chapter were, naturally, in and about the choir a great deal, and it soon became apparent to the elder Worby—who could not help overhearing some of their talk—that, on the part of the senior Canons especially, there must have been a good deal of disagreement before the policy now being carried out had been adopted. Some were of opinion that they should catch their deaths of cold in the return-stalls, unprotected by a screen from the draughts in the nave: others objected to being exposed to the view of persons in the choir aisles, especially, they said, during the sermons, when they found it helpful to listen in a posture which was liable to misconstruction. The strongest opposition, however, came from the oldest of the body, who up to the last moment objected to the removal of the pulpit. "You ought not to touch it, Mr. Dean," he said with great emphasis one morning, when the two were standing before it: "you don't know what mischief you may do." "Mischief? it's not a work of any particular merit, Canon." "Don't call me Canon," said the old man with great asperity, "that is, for thirty years I've been known as Dr. Ayloff, and I shall be obliged, Mr. Dean, if you would kindly humour me in that matter. And as to the pulpit (which I've preached from for thirty years, though I don't insist on that), all I'll say is, I *know* you're doing wrong in moving it." "But what sense could there be, my dear Doctor, in leaving it where it is, when we're fitting up the rest of the choir in a totally different *style?* What reason could be given—apart from the look of the thing?" "Reason! reason!" said old Dr. Ayloff; "if you young men—if I may say so without any disrespect, Mr. Dean—if you'd only listen to reason a little, and not be always asking for it, we should get on better. But there, I've said my say." The old gentleman hobbled off, and as it proved, never entered the Cathedral again. The season—it was a hot summer—turned sickly on a sudden. Dr. Ayloff was one of the first to go, with some affection[8] of the muscles of the thorax, which took him painfully at night. And at many services the number of choirmen and boys was very thin.

Meanwhile the pulpit had been done away with. In fact, the sounding-board (part of which still exists as a table in a summerhouse in the palace garden) was taken down within an hour or two of Dr. Ayloff's protest. The removal of the base—not effected without considerable trouble—disclosed to view, greatly to the exultation of the restoring party, an altar-tomb—the tomb, of course, to which Worby had attracted Lake's attention that same evening. Much fruitless research was expended in attempts to identify the occupant; from that day to this he has never had a name put to him. The structure had been most carefully boxed in under the pulpit-base, so that such slight ornament as it possessed was not defaced; only on the north side of it there was what looked like an injury; a gap between two of the slabs composing the side. It might be two or three inches across. Palmer, the mason, was directed to fill it up in a week's time, when he came to do some other small jobs near that part of the choir.

The season was undoubtedly a very trying one. Whether the church was built on a site that had once been a marsh, as was suggested, or for whatever reason, the residents in its immediate neighbourhood had, many of them, but little enjoyment of the exquisite sunny days and the calm nights of August and September. To several of the older people—Dr. Ayloff, among others, as we have seen—the summer proved downright fatal, but even among the younger, few escaped either a sojourn in bed for a matter of weeks, or at the least, a brooding sense of oppression, accompanied by hateful nightmares. Gradually there formulated itself a suspicion—which grew into a conviction—that the alterations in the Cathedral had something to say in the matter. The widow of a former old verger, a pensioner of the Chapter of Southminster, was visited by dreams, which she retailed to her friends, of a shape that slipped out of the little door of the south transept as the dark fell in, and flitted—taking a fresh direction every night—about the Close, disappearing for a while in house after house, and finally emerging again when the night sky was paling. She could see nothing of it, she said, but that it was a moving form: only she had an impression that when it returned to the church, as it seemed to do in the end of the dream, it turned its head: and then, she could not tell why, but she thought it had red eyes. Worby remembered hearing the old lady tell this dream at a tea-party in the house of the chapter clerk. Its recurrence might, perhaps, he said, be taken as a symptom of approaching illness; at any rate before the end of September the old lady was in her grave.

The interest excited by the restoration of this great church was not confined to its own county. One day that summer an F.S.A.,[9] of some celebrity, visited the place. His business was to write an account of the discoveries that had been made, for the Society of Antiquaries, and his wife, who accompanied him, was to make a series of illustrative drawings for his report. In the morning she employed herself in making a general sketch of the choir; in the afternoon she devoted herself to details. She first drew the newly-exposed altar-tomb, and when that was finished, she called her husband's attention to a beautiful piece of diaper-ornament[10] on the screen just behind it, which had, like the tomb itself, been completely concealed by the pulpit. Of course, he said, an illustration of that must be made; so she seated herself on the tomb and began a careful drawing which occupied her till dusk.

Her husband had by this time finished his work of measuring and description, and they agreed that it was time to be getting back to their hotel. "You may as well brush my skirt, Frank," said the lady, "it must have got covered with dust, I'm sure." He obeyed dutifully; but, after a moment, he said, "I don't know whether you value this dress particularly, my dear, but I'm inclined to think it's seen its best days. There's a great bit of it gone." "Gone? Where?" said she. "I don't know where it's gone, but it's off at the bottom edge behind here." She pulled it hastily into sight, and was horrified to find a jagged tear extending some way into the substance of the stuff; very much, she said, as if a dog had rent it away. The dress was, in any case, hopelessly spoilt, to her great vexation, and though they looked everywhere, the missing piece could not be found. There were many ways, they concluded, in which the injury might have come about, for the choir was full of old bits of woodwork with nails sticking out of them. Finally, they could only suppose that one of these had caused the mischief, and that the workmen, who had been about all day, had carried off the particular piece with the fragment of dress still attached to it.

It was about this time, Worby thought, that his little dog began to wear an anxious expression when the hour for it to be put into the shed in the back yard approached. (For his mother had ordained that it must not sleep in the house.) One evening, he said, when he was just going to pick it up and carry it out, it looked at him "like a Christian, and waved its 'and, I was going to say—well, you know 'ow they do carry on sometimes, and the end of it was I put it under my coat, and 'uddled it upstairs— and I'm afraid I as good as deceived my poor mother on the subject. After that the dog acted very artful with 'iding itself under the bed for half an hour or more before bed-time came, and we worked it so as my mother never found out what we'd done." Of course Worby was glad of its company anyhow, but more particularly when the nuisance that is still remembered in Southminster as "the crying" set in.

"Night after night," said Worby, "that dog seemed to know it was coming; he'd creep out, he would, and snuggle into the bed and cuddle right up to me shivering, and when the crying

come he'd be like a wild thing, shoving his head under my arm,
and I was fully near as bad. Six or seven times we'd hear it, not
more, and when he'd dror out his 'ed again I'd know it was over
for that night. What was it like, sir? Well, I never heard but one
thing that seemed to hit it off. I happened to be playing about in
the Close, and there was two of the Canons met and said 'Good
morning' one to another. 'Sleep well last night?' says one—it
was Mr. Henslow that one, and Mr. Lyall was the other.[11]
'Can't say I did,' says Mr. Lyall, 'rather too much of Isaiah
xxxiv. 14 for me.' 'xxxiv. 14,' says Mr. Henslow, 'what's that?'
'You call yourself a Bible reader!' says Mr. Lyall. (Mr. Henslow,
you must know, he was one of what used to be termed Simeon's
lot—pretty much what we should call the Evangelical party.)[12]
'You go and look it up.' I wanted to know what he was getting
at myself, and so off I ran home and got out my own Bible, and
there it was: 'the satyr shall cry to his fellow.' Well, I thought, is
that what we've been listening to these past nights? and I tell
you it made me look over my shoulder a time or two. Of course
I'd asked my father and mother about what it could be before
that, but they both said it was most likely cats: but they spoke
very short, and I could see they was troubled. My word! that
was a noise—'ungry-like, as if it was calling after someone that
wouldn't come. If ever you felt you wanted company, it would
be when you was waiting for it to begin again. I believe two or
three nights there was men put on to watch in different parts of
the Close: but they all used to get together in one corner, the
nearest they could to the High Street, and nothing came of it.

"Well, the next thing was this. Me and another of the boys—
he's in business in the city now as a grocer, like his father before
him—we'd gone up in the choir after morning service was over,
and we heard old Palmer the mason bellowing to some of his
men. So we went up nearer, because we knew he was a rusty old
chap and there might be some fun going. It appears Palmer' d
told this man to stop up the chink in that old tomb. Well, there
was this man keeping on saying he'd done it the best he could,
and there was Palmer carrying on like all possessed about it.
'Call that making a job of it?' he says. 'If you had your rights
you'd get the sack for this. What do you suppose I pay you your

wages for? What do you suppose I'm going to say to the Dean and Chapter when they come round, as come they may do any time, and see where you've been bungling about covering the 'ole place with mess and plaster and Lord knows what?' 'Well, master, I done the best I could,' says the man; 'I don't know no more than what you do 'ow it come to fall out this way. I tamped it right in the 'ole,' he says, 'and now it's fell out,' he says, 'I never see.'

"'Fell out?' says old Palmer, 'why it's nowhere near the place. Blowed out, you mean'; and he picked up a bit of plaster, and so did I, that was laying up against the screen, three or four feet off, and not dry yet; and old Palmer he looked at it curious-like, and then he turned round on me and he says, 'Now then, you boys, have you been up to some of your games here?' 'No,' I says, 'I haven't, Mr. Palmer; there's none of us been about here till just this minute'; and while I was talking the other boy, Evans, he got looking in through the chink, and I heard him draw in his breath, and he came away sharp and up to us, and says he, 'I believe there's something in there. I saw something shiny.' 'What! I dare say!' says old Palmer; 'well, I ain't got time to stop about there. You, William, you go off and get some more stuff and make a job of it this time; if not, there'll be trouble in my yard,' he says.

"So the man he went off, and Palmer too, and us boys stopped behind, and I says to Evans, 'Did you really see anything in there?' 'Yes,' he says, 'I did indeed.' So then I says, 'Let's shove something in and stir it up.' And we tried several of the bits of wood that was laying about, but they were all too big. Then Evans he had a sheet of music he'd brought with him, an anthem or a service, I forget which it was now, and he rolled it up small and shoved it in the chink; two or three times he did it, and nothing happened. 'Give it me, boy,' I said, and I had a try. No, nothing happened. Then, I don't know why I thought of it, I'm sure, but I stooped down just opposite the chink and put my two fingers in my mouth and whistled—you know the way— and at that I seemed to think I heard something stirring, and I says to Evans, 'Come away,' I says; 'I don't like this.' 'Oh, rot,' he says, 'give me that roll,' and he took it and shoved it in. And

I don't think ever I see anyone go so pale as he did. 'I say, Worby,' he says, 'it's caught, or else someone's got hold of it.' 'Pull it out or leave it,' I says. 'Come and let's get off.' So he gave a good pull, and it came away. Leastways most of it did, but the end was gone. Torn off it was, and Evans looked at it for a second and then he gave a sort of a croak and let it drop, and we both made off out of there as quick as ever we could. When we got outside Evans says to me, 'Did you see the end of that paper?' 'No,' I says, 'only it was torn.' 'Yes, it was,' he says, 'but it was wet too, and black!' Well, partly because of the fright we had, and partly because that music was wanted in a day or two, and we knew there'd be a set-out[13] about it with the organist, we didn't say nothing to anyone else, and I suppose the workmen they swept up the bit that was left along with the rest of the rubbish. But Evans, if you were to ask him this very day about it, he'd stick to it he saw that paper wet and black at the end where it was torn."

After that the boys gave the choir a wide berth, so that Worby was not sure what was the result of the mason's renewed mending of the tomb. Only he made out from fragments of conversation dropped by the workmen passing through the choir that some difficulty had been met with, and that the governor—Mr. Palmer to wit—had tried his own hand at the job. A little later, he happened to see Mr. Palmer himself knocking at the door of the Deanery and being admitted by the butler. A day or so after that, he gathered from a remark his father let fall at breakfast that something a little out of the common was to be done in the Cathedral after morning service on the morrow. "And I'd just as soon it was to-day," his father added; "I don't see the use of running risks." " 'Father,' I says, 'what are you going to do in the Cathedral to-morrow?' And he turned on me as savage as I ever see him—he was a wonderful good-tempered man as a general thing, my poor father was. 'My lad,' he says, 'I'll trouble you not to go picking up your elders' and betters' talk: it's not manners and it's not straight. What I'm going to do or not going to do in the Cathedral to-morrow is none of your business: and if I catch sight of you hanging about the place to-morrow after your work's done, I'll send you home with a flea in your ear. Now you mind that.' Of course I said I was very sorry and that, and equally of course I went off and laid my plans with Evans. We knew there was a stair up in the corner of the transept which you can get up to the triforium, and in them days the door to it was pretty well always open, and even if it wasn't we knew the key usually laid under a bit of matting hard by. So we made up our minds we'd be putting away music and that, next morning while the rest of the boys was clearing off, and then slip up the stairs and watch from the triforium if there was any signs of work going on.

"Well, that same night I dropped off asleep as sound as a boy does, and all of a sudden the dog woke me up, coming into the bed, and thought I, now we're going to get it sharp, for he seemed more frightened than usual. After about five minutes sure enough came this cry. I can't give you no idea what it was like; and so near too—nearer than I'd heard it yet—and a funny thing, Mr. Lake, you know what a place this Close is for an echo, and particular if you stand this side of it. Well, this crying never made no sign of an echo at all. But, as I said, it was dreadful near this night; and on the top of the start I got with hearing it, I got another fright; for I heard something rustling outside in the passage. Now to be sure I thought I was done; but I noticed the dog seemed to perk up a bit, and next there was someone whispered outside the door, and I very near laughed out loud, for I knew it was my father and mother that had got out of bed with the noise. 'Whatever is it?' says my mother. 'Hush! I don't know,' says my father, excited-like, 'don't disturb the boy. I hope he didn't hear nothing.'

"So, me knowing they were just outside, it made me bolder, and I slipped out of bed across to my little window—giving on the Close—but the dog he bored right down to the bottom of the bed—and I looked out. First go off I couldn't see anything. Then right down in the shadow under a buttress I made out what I shall always say was two spots of red—a dull red it was—nothing like a lamp or a fire, but just so as you could pick 'em out of the black shadow. I hadn't but just sighted 'em when it seemed we wasn't the only people that had been disturbed, because I see a window in a house on the left-hand side become lighted up, and the light moving. I just turned my head to make sure of it, and then looked back into the shadow for those two red things, and they were gone, and for all I peered about and stared, there was not a sign more of them. Then come my last fright that night—something come against my bare leg—but that was all right: that was my little dog had come out of bed, and prancing about making a great to-do, only holding his tongue, and me seeing he was quite in spirits again, I took him back to bed and we slept the night out!

"Next morning I made out to tell my mother I'd had the dog in my room, and I was surprised, after all she'd said about it before, how quiet she took it. 'Did you?' she says. 'Well, by good rights you ought to go without your breakfast for doing such a thing behind my back: but I don't know as there's any great harm done, only another time you ask my permission, do you hear?' A bit after that I said something to my father about having heard the cats again. '*Cats?*' he says; and he looked over at my poor mother, and she coughed and he says, 'Oh! ah! yes, cats. I believe I heard 'em myself.'

"That was a funny morning altogether: nothing seemed to go right. The organist he stopped in bed, and the minor Canon he forgot it was the 19th day and waited for the *Venite*;[14] and after a bit the deputy he set off playing the chant for evensong, which was a minor; and then the Decani[15] boys were laughing so much they couldn't sing, and when it came to the anthem the solo boy he got took with the giggles, and made out his nose was bleeding, and shoved the book at me what hadn't practised the verse and wasn't much of a singer if I had known it. Well, things was rougher, you see, fifty years ago, and I got a nip from the counter-tenor behind me that I remembered.

"So we got through somehow, and neither the men nor the boys weren't by way of waiting to see whether the Canon in residence—Mr. Henslow it was—would come to the vestries and fine 'em, but I don't believe he did: for one thing I fancy he'd read the wrong lesson for the first time in his life, and knew it. Anyhow, Evans and me didn't find no difficulty in slipping up the stairs as I told you, and when we got up we laid ourselves down flat on our stomachs where we could just stretch our heads out over the old tomb, and we hadn't but just done so when we heard the verger that was then, first shutting the iron porch-gates and locking the south-west door, and then the transept door, so we knew there was something up, and they meant to keep the public out for a bit.

. "Next thing was, the Dean and the Canon come in by their door on the north, and then I see my father, and old Palmer, and a couple of their best men, and Palmer stood a talking for a bit with the Dean in the middle of the choir. He had a coil of rope and the men had crows.[16] All of 'em looked a bit nervous. So there they stood talking, and at last I heard the Dean say, 'Well, I've no time to waste, Palmer. If you think this'll satisfy South-minster people, I'll permit it to be done; but I must say this, that never in the whole course of my life have I heard such arrant nonsense from a practical man as I have from you. Don't you agree with me, Henslow?' As far as I could hear Mr. Henslow said something like 'Oh well! we're told, aren't we, Mr. Dean, not to judge others?'[17] And the Dean he gave a kind of sniff, and walked straight up to the tomb, and took his stand behind it with his back to the screen, and the others they come edging up rather gingerly. Henslow, he stopped on the south side and scratched on his chin, he did. Then the Dean spoke up: 'Palmer,' he says, 'which can you do easiest, get the slab off the top, or shift one of the side slabs?'

"Old Palmer and his men they pottered about a bit looking round the edge of the top slab and sounding the sides on the south and east and west and everywhere but the north. Henslow said something about it being better to have a try at the south side, because there was more light and more room to move about in. Then my father, who'd been watching of them, went round to the north side, and knelt down and felt of the slab by the chink, and he got up and dusted his knees and says to the Dean: 'Beg pardon, Mr. Dean, but I think if Mr. Palmer'll try this here slab he'll find it'll come out easy enough. Seems to me one of the men could prise it out with his crow by means of this chink.' 'Ah! thank you, Worby,' says the Dean;

'that's a good suggestion. Palmer, let one of your men do that, will you?'

"So the man come round, and put his bar in and bore on it, and just that minute when they were all bending over, and we boys got our heads well over the edge of the triforium, there come a most fearful crash down at the west end of the choir, as if a whole stack of big timber had fallen down a flight of stairs. Well, you can't expect me to tell you everything that happened all in a minute. Of course there was a terrible commotion. I heard the slab fall out, and the crowbar on the floor, and I heard the Dean say, 'Good God!'

"When I looked down again I saw the Dean tumbled over on the floor, the men was making off down the choir, Henslow was just going to help the Dean up, Palmer was going to stop the men (as he said afterwards) and my father was sitting on the altar step with his face in his hands. The Dean he was very cross. 'I wish to goodness you'd look where you're coming to, Henslow,' he says. 'Why you should all take to your heels when a stick of wood tumbles down I cannot imagine'; and all Henslow could do, explaining he was right away on the other side of the tomb, would not satisfy him.

"Then Palmer came back and reported there was nothing to account for this noise and nothing seemingly fallen down, and when the Dean finished feeling of himself they gathered round—except my father, he sat where he was—and someone lighted up a bit of candle and they looked into the tomb. 'Nothing there,' says the Dean, 'what did I tell you? Stay! here's something. What's this? a bit of music paper, and a piece of torn stuff—part of a dress it looks like. Both quite modern—no interest whatever. Another time perhaps you'll take the advice of an educated man'—or something like that, and off he went, limping a bit, and out through the north door, only as he went he called back angry to Palmer for leaving the door standing open. Palmer called out 'Very sorry, sir,' but he shrugged his shoulders, and Henslow says, 'I fancy Mr. Dean's mistaken. I closed the door behind me, but he's a little upset.' Then Palmer says, 'Why, where's Worby?' and they saw him sitting on the step and went up to him. He was recovering himself, it seemed, and wiping his forehead, and Palmer helped him up on to his legs, as I was glad to see.

"They were too far off for me to hear what they said, but my father pointed to the north door in the aisle, and Palmer and Henslow both of them looked very surprised and scared. After a bit, my father and Henslow went out of the church, and the others made what haste they could to put the slab back and plaster it in. And about as the clock struck twelve the Cathedral was opened again and us boys made the best of our way home.

"I was in a great taking to know what it was had given my poor father such a turn, and when I got in and found him sitting in his chair taking a glass of spirits, and my mother standing looking anxious at him, I couldn't keep from bursting out and making confession where I'd been. But he didn't seem to take on, not in the way of losing his temper. 'You was there, was you? Well, did you see it?' 'I see everything, father,' I said, 'except when the noise came.' 'Did you see what it was knocked the Dean over?' he says, 'that what come out of the monument? You didn't? Well, that's a mercy.' 'Why, what was it, father?' I said. 'Come, you must have seen it,' he says. '*Didn't* you see? A thing like a man, all over hair, and two great eyes to it?'

"Well, that was all I could get out of him that time, and later on he seemed as if he was ashamed of being so frightened, and he used to put me off when I asked him about it. But years after, when I was got to be a grown man, we had more talk now and again on the matter, and he always said the same thing. 'Black it was,' he'd say, 'and a mass of hair, and two legs, and the light caught on its eyes.'

"Well, that's the tale of that tomb, Mr. Lake; it's one we don't tell to our visitors, and I should be obliged to you not to make any use of it till I'm out of the way. I doubt Mr. Evans'll feel the same as I do, if you ask him."

This proved to be the case. But over twenty years have passed by, and the grass is growing over both Worby and Evans; so Mr. Lake felt no difficulty about communicating his notes—taken

in 1890—to me. He accompanied them with a sketch of the
tomb and a copy of the short inscription on the metal cross
which was affixed at the expense of Dr. Lyall to the centre of
the northern side. It was from the Vulgate of Isaiah xxxiv., and
consisted merely of the three words—

IBI CUBAVIT LAMIA.[18]

THE STORY OF A DISAPPEARANCE AND AN APPEARANCE

The letters which I now publish were sent to me recently by a person who knows me to be interested in ghost stories. There is no doubt about their authenticity. The paper on which they are written, the ink, and the whole external aspect put their date beyond the reach of question.

The only point which they do not make clear is the identity of the writer. He signs with initials only, and as none of the envelopes of the letters are preserved, the surname of his correspondent—obviously a married brother—is as obscure as his own. No further preliminary explanation is needed, I think. Luckily the first letter supplies all that could be expected.

LETTER I

GREAT CIIRISHALL,[1] *Dec.* 22, 1837.

MY DEAR ROBERT,—It is with great regret for the enjoyment I am losing, and for a reason which you will deplore equally with myself, that I write to inform you that I am unable to join your circle for this Christmas: but you will agree with me that it is unavoidable when I say that I have within these few hours received a letter from Mrs. Hunt at B——, to the effect that our Uncle Henry has suddenly and mysteriously disappeared, and begging me to go down there immediately and join the search that is being made for him. Little as I, or you either, I think, have ever seen of Uncle, I naturally feel that this is not a request that can be regarded lightly, and accordingly I propose to go to B—— by this afternoon's mail, reaching it late in the evening. I

shall not go to the Rectory, but put up at the King's Head, and
to which you may address letters. I enclose a small draft, which
you will please make use of for the benefit of the young people.
I shall write you daily (supposing me to be detained more than
a single day) what goes on, and you may be sure, should the
business be cleared up in time to permit of my coming to the
Manor after all, I shall present myself. I have but a few minutes
at disposal. With cordial greetings to you all, and many regrets,
believe me, your affectionate Bro.,

                                              W. R.

LETTER II

KING'S HEAD, *Dec.* 23, '37.

MY DEAR ROBERT,—In the first place, there is as yet no news
of Uncle H., and I think you may finally dismiss any idea—I
won't say hope—that I might after all "turn up" for Xmas.
However, my thoughts will be with you, and you have my best
wishes for a really festive day. Mind that none of my nephews or
nieces expend any fraction of their guineas on presents for me.

Since I got here I have been blaming myself for taking this affair of Uncle H. too easily. From what people here say, I gather
that there is very little hope that he can still be alive; but
whether it is accident or design that carried him off I cannot
judge. The facts are these. On Friday the 19th, he went as usual
shortly before five o'clock to read evening prayers at the Church;
and when they were over the clerk brought him a message, in
response to which he set off to pay a visit to a sick person at an
outlying cottage the better part of two miles away. He paid the
visit, and started on his return journey at about half-past six.
This is the last that is known of him. The people here are very
much grieved at his loss; he had been here many years, as you
know, and though, as you also know, he was not the most genial of men, and had more than a little of the *martinet* in his
composition, he seems to have been active in good works, and
unsparing of trouble to himself.

Poor Mrs. Hunt, who has been his housekeeper ever since she

left Woodley,[2] is quite overcome: it seems like the end of the world to her. I am glad that I did not entertain the idea of taking quarters at the Rectory; and I have declined several kindly offers of hospitality from people in the place, preferring as I do to be independent, and finding myself very comfortable here.

You will, of course, wish to know what has been done in the way of inquiry and search. First, nothing was to be expected from investigation at the Rectory; and to be brief, nothing has transpired. I asked Mrs. Hunt—as others had done before—whether there was either any unfavourable symptom in her master such as might portend a sudden stroke, or attack of illness, or whether he had ever had reason to apprehend any such thing: but both she, and also his medical man, were clear that this was not the case. He was quite in his usual health. In the second place, naturally, ponds and streams have been dragged, and fields in the neighbourhood which he is known to have visited last, have been searched—without result. I have myself talked to the parish clerk and—more important—have been to the house where he paid his visit.

There can be no question of any foul play on these people's part. The one man in the house is ill in bed and very weak: the wife and the children of course could do nothing themselves, nor is there the shadow of a probability that they or any of them should have agreed to decoy poor Uncle H. out in order that he might be attacked on the way back. They had told what they knew to several other inquirers already, but the woman repeated it to me. The Rector was looking just as usual: he wasn't very long with the sick man—"He ain't," she said, "like some what has a gift in prayer; but there, if we was all that way, 'owever would the chapel people get their living?" He left some money when he went away, and one of the children saw him cross the stile into the next field. He was dressed as he always was: wore his bands—I gather he is nearly the last man remaining who does so—at any rate in this district.

You see I am putting down everything. The fact is that I have nothing else to do, having brought no business papers with me; and, moreover, it serves to clear my own mind, and may suggest points which have been overlooked. So I shall continue to write all that passes, even to conversations if need be—you may read or not as you please, but pray keep the letters. I have another reason for writing so fully, but it is not a very tangible one.

You may ask if I have myself made any search in the fields near the cottage. Something—a good deal—has been done by others, as I mentioned; but I hope to go over the ground to-morrow. Bow Street[3] has now been informed, and will send down by to-night's coach, but I do not think they will make much of the job. There is no snow, which might have helped us. The fields are all grass. Of course I was on the *qui vive*[4] for any indication to-day both going and returning; but there was a thick mist on the way back, and I was not in trim for wandering about unknown pastures, especially on an evening when bushes looked like men, and a cow lowing in the distance might have been the last trump. I assure you, if Uncle Henry had stepped out from among the trees in a little copse which borders the path at one place, carrying his head under his arm, I should have been very little more uncomfortable than I was. To tell you the truth, I was rather expecting something of the kind. But I must drop my pen for the moment: Mr. Lucas, the curate, is announced.

Later. Mr. Lucas has been, and gone, and there is not much beyond the decencies of ordinary sentiment to be got from him. I can see that he has given up any idea that the Rector can be alive, and that, so far as he can be, he is truly sorry. I can also discern that even in a more emotional person than Mr. Lucas, Uncle Henry was not likely to inspire strong attachment.

Besides Mr. Lucas, I have had another visitor in the shape of my Boniface[5]—mine host of the "King's Head"—who came to see whether I had everything I wished, and who really requires the pen of a Boz[6] to do him justice. He was very solemn and weighty at first. "Well, sir," he said, "I suppose we must bow our 'ead beneath the blow, as my poor wife had used to say. So far as I can gather there's been neither hide nor yet hair of our late respected incumbent scented out as yet; not that he was what the Scripture terms a hairy man[7] in any sense of the word."

I said—as well as I could—that I supposed not, but could not help adding that I had heard he was sometimes a little difficult to deal with. Mr. Bowman looked at me sharply for a moment, and then passed in a flash from solemn sympathy to impassioned declamation. "When I think," he said, "of the language that man see fit to employ to me in this here parlour over no more a matter than a cask of beer—such a thing as I told him might happen any day of the week to a man with a family— though as it turned out he was quite under a mistake, and that I knew at the time, only I was that shocked to hear him I couldn't lay my tongue to the right expression."

He stopped abruptly and eyed me with some embarrassment. I only said, "Dear me, I'm sorry to hear you had any little differences: I suppose my uncle will be a good deal missed in the parish?" Mr. Bowman drew a long breath. "Ah, yes!" he said; "your uncle! You'll understand me when I say that for the moment it had slipped my remembrance that he was a relative; and natural enough, I must say, as it should, for as to you bearing any resemblance to—to him, the notion of any such a thing is clean ridiculous. All the same, 'ad I 'ave bore it in my mind, you'll be among the first to feel, I'm sure, as I should have abstained my lips, or rather I should *not* have abstained my lips with no such reflections."

I assured him that I quite understood, and was going to have asked him some further questions, but he was called away to see after some business. By the way, you need not take it into your head that he has anything to fear from the inquiry into poor Uncle Henry's disappearance—though, no doubt, in the watches of the night it will occur to him that *I* think he has, and I may expect explanations to-morrow.

I must close this letter: it has to go by the late coach.

LETTER III

Dec. 25, '37.

MY DEAR ROBERT,—This is a curious letter to be writing on Christmas Day, and yet after all there is nothing much in it. Or there may be—you shall be the judge. At least, nothing decisive. The Bow Street men practically say that they have no clue. The length of time and the weather conditions have made all tracks so faint as to be quite useless: nothing that belonged to the dead man—I'm afraid no other word will do—has been picked up.

As I expected, Mr. Bowman was uneasy in his mind this morning; quite early I heard him holding forth in a very distinct voice—purposely so, I thought—to the Bow Street officers in the bar, as to the loss that the town had sustained in their Rector, and as to the necessity of leaving no stone unturned (he was very great on this phrase) in order to come at the truth. I suspect him of being an orator of repute at convivial meetings.

When I was at breakfast he came to wait on me, and took an opportunity when handing a muffin to say in a low tone, "I 'ope, sir, you reconize as my feelings towards your relative is not actuated by any taint of what you may call melignity—you can leave the room, Elizar, I will see the gentleman 'as all he requires with my own hands—I ask your pardon, sir, but you must be well aware a man is not always master of himself: and when that man has been 'urt in his mind by the application of expressions which I will go so far as to say 'ad not ought to have been made use of (his voice was rising all this time and his face growing redder); no, sir; and 'ere, if you will permit of it, I should like to explain to you in a very few words the exact state of the bone of contention. This cask—I might more truly call it a firkin—of beer—"

I felt it was time to interpose, and said that I did not see that it would help us very much to go into that matter in detail. Mr. Bowman acquiesced, and resumed more calmly:

"Well, sir, I bow to your ruling, and as you say, be that here or be it there, it don't contribute a great deal, perhaps, to the present question. All I wish you to understand is that I am as prepared as you are yourself to lend every hand to the business we have afore us, and—as I took the opportunity to say as much to the Orficers not three-quarters of an hour ago—to leave no stone unturned as may throw even a spark of light on this painful matter."

In fact, Mr. Bowman did accompany us on our exploration, but though I am sure his genuine wish was to be helpful, I am afraid he did not contribute to the serious side of it. He appeared to be under the impression that we were likely to meet either Uncle Henry or the person responsible for his disappearance, walking about the fields, and did a great deal of shading his eyes with his hand and calling our attention, by pointing with his stick, to distant cattle and labourers. He held several long conversations with old women whom we met, and was very strict and severe in his manner, but on each occasion returned to our party saying, "Well, I find she don't seem to 'ave no connexion with this sad affair. I think you may take it from me, sir, as there's little or no light to be looked for from that quarter; not without she's keeping somethink back intentional."

We gained no appreciable result, as I told you at starting; the Bow Street men have left the town, whether for London or not I am not sure.

This evening I had company in the shape of a bagman,[8] a smartish fellow. He knew what was going forward, but though he has been on the roads for some days about here, he had nothing to tell of suspicious characters—tramps, wandering sailors or gipsies. He was very full of a capital Punch and Judy Show he had seen this same day at W——, and asked if it had been here yet, and advised me by no means to miss it if it does come. The best Punch and the best Toby dog, he said, he had ever come across. Toby dogs, you know, are the last new thing in the shows. I have only seen one myself, but before long all the men will have them.

Now why, you will want to know, do I trouble to write all this to you? I am obliged to do it, because it has something to do with another absurd trifle (as you will inevitably say), which in my present state of rather unquiet fancy—nothing more, perhaps—I have to put down. It is a dream, sir, which I am going to record, and I must say it is one of the oddest I have had. Is there anything in it beyond what the bagman's talk and Uncle Henry's disappearance could have suggested? You, I repeat, shall judge: I am not in a sufficiently cool and judicial frame to do so.

It began with what I can only describe as a pulling aside of curtains: and I found myself seated in a place—I don't know whether indoors or out. There were people—only a few—on either side of me, but I did not recognize them, or indeed think much about them. They never spoke, but, so far as I remember, were all grave and pale-faced and looked fixedly before them. Facing me there was a Punch and Judy Show, perhaps rather larger than the ordinary ones, painted with black figures on a reddish-yellow ground. Behind it and on each side was only darkness, but in front there was a sufficiency of light. I was "strung up" to a high degree of expectation and looked every moment to hear the pan-pipes and the Roo-too-too-it.[9] Instead of that there came suddenly an enormous—I can use no other word—an enormous single toll of a bell, I don't know from how far off—somewhere behind. The little curtain flew up and the drama began.

I believe someone once tried to re-write Punch as a serious tragedy; but whoever he may have been, this performance would have suited him exactly. There was something Satanic about the hero. He varied his methods of attack: for some of his victims he lay in wait, and to see his horrible face—it was yellowish white, I may remark—peering round the wings made me think of the Vampyre in Fuseli's foul sketch.[10] To others he was polite and carneying—particularly to the unfortunate alien who can only say *Shallabalah*—though what Punch said I never could catch. But with all of them I came to dread the moment of death. The crack of the stick on their skulls, which in the ordinary way delights me, had here a crushing sound as if the bone was giving way, and the victims quivered and kicked as they lay. The baby—it sounds more ridiculous as I go on—the baby, I am sure, was alive. Punch wrung its neck, and if the choke or squeak which it gave were not real, I know nothing of reality.

The stage got perceptibly darker as each crime was consummated, and at last there was one murder which was done quite in the dark, so that I could see nothing of the victim, and took some time to effect. It was accompanied by hard breathing and horrid muffled sounds, and after it Punch came and sat on the footboard and fanned himself and looked at his shoes, which were bloody, and hung his head on one side, and sniggered in so deadly a fashion that I saw some of those beside me cover their faces, and I would gladly have done the same. But in the meantime the scene behind Punch was clearing, and showed, not the usual house front, but something more ambitious—a grove of trees and the gentle slope of a hill, with a very natural—in fact, I should say a real—moon shining on it. Over this there rose slowly an object which I soon perceived to be a human figure with something peculiar about the head—what, I was unable at first to see. It did not stand on its feet, but began creeping or dragging itself across the middle distance towards Punch, who still sat back to it; and by this time, I may remark (though it did not occur to me at the moment) that all pretence of this being a puppet show had vanished. Punch was still Punch, it is true, but, like the others, was in some sense a live creature, and both moved themselves at their own will.

When I next glanced at him he was sitting in malignant reflection; but in another instant something seemed to attract his attention, and he first sat up sharply and then turned round, and evidently caught sight of the person that was approaching him and was in fact now very near. Then, indeed, did he show unmistakable signs of terror: catching up his stick, he rushed towards the wood, only just eluding the arm of his pursuer, which was suddenly flung out to intercept him. It was with a revulsion which I cannot easily express that I now saw more or less clearly what this pursuer was like. He was a sturdy figure clad in black, and, as I thought, wearing bands: his head was covered with a whitish bag.

The chase which now began lasted I do not know how long, now among the trees, now along the slope of the field, sometimes both figures disappearing wholly for a few seconds, and only some uncertain sounds letting one know that they were still afoot. At length there came a moment when Punch, evidently exhausted, staggered in from the left and threw himself down among the trees. His pursuer was not long after him, and came looking uncertainly from side to side. Then, catching sight of the figure on the ground, he too threw himself down—his back was turned to the audience—with a swift motion twitched the covering from his head, and thrust his face into that of Punch. Everything on the instant grew dark.

There was one long, loud, shuddering scream, and I awoke to find myself looking straight into the face of—what in all the world do you think? but—a large owl, which was seated on my window-sill immediately opposite my bed-foot, holding up its wings like two shrouded arms. I caught the fierce glance of its yellow eyes, and then it was gone. I heard the single enormous bell again—very likely, as you are saying to yourself, the church clock; but I do not think so—and then I was broad awake.

All this, I may say, happened within the last half-hour. There was no probability of my getting to sleep again, so I got up, put on clothes enough to keep me warm, and am writing this rigmarole in the first hours of Christmas Day. Have I left out anything? Yes; there was no Toby dog, and the names over the front of the Punch and Judy booth were Kidman and Gallop, which were certainly not what the bagman told me to look out for.

By this time, I feel a little more as if I could sleep, so this shall be sealed and wafered.

LETTER IV

Dec. 26, '37.

MY DEAR ROBERT,—All is over. The body has been found. I do not make excuses for not having sent off my news by last night's mail, for the simple reason that I was incapable of putting pen to paper. The events that attended the discovery bewildered me so completely that I needed what I could get of a night's rest to enable me to face the situation at all. Now I can give you my journal of the day, certainly the strangest Christmas Day that ever I spent or am likely to spend.

The first incident was not very serious. Mr. Bowman had, I think, been keeping Christmas Eve, and was a little inclined to be captious: at least, he was not on foot very early, and to judge from what I could hear, neither men or maids could do anything to please him. The latter were certainly reduced to tears; nor am I sure that Mr. Bowman succeeded in preserving a manly composure. At any rate, when I came downstairs, it was in a broken voice that he wished me the compliments of the season, and a little later on, when he paid his visit of ceremony at breakfast, he was far from cheerful: even Byronic, I might almost say, in his outlook on life.[11]

"I don't know," he said, "if you think with me, sir; but every Christmas as comes round the world seems a hollerer thing to me. Why, take an example now from what lays under my own eye. There's my servant Eliza—been with me now for going on fifteen years. I thought I could have placed my confidence in Elizar, and yet this very morning—Christmas morning too, of all the blessed days in the year—with the bells a ringing and—and—all like that—I say, this very morning, had it not have been for Providence watching over us all, that girl would have put—indeed I may go so far to say, 'ad put the cheese on your breakfast-table—" He saw I was about to speak, and waved his hand at me. "It's all very well for you to say, 'Yes, Mr. Bowman, but you took away the cheese and locked it up in the cupboard,' which I did, and have the key here, or if not the actual key, one very much about the same size. That's true enough, sir, but what do you think is the effect of that action on me? Why, it's no exaggeration for me to say that the ground is cut from under my feet. And yet when I said as much to Eliza, not nasty, mind you, but just firm-like, what was my return? 'Oh,' she says: 'well,' she says, 'there wasn't no bones broke, I suppose.' Well, sir, it 'urt me, that's all I can say: it 'urt me, and I don't like to think of it now."

There was an ominous pause here, in which I ventured to say something like, "Yes, very trying," and then asked at what hour the church service was to be. "Eleven o'clock," Mr. Bowman said with a heavy sigh. "Ah, you won't have no such discourse from poor Mr. Lucas as what you would have done from our late Rector. Him and me may have had our little differences, and did do, more's the pity."

I could see that a powerful effort was needed to keep him off the vexed question of the cask of beer, but he made it. "But I will say this, that a better preacher, nor yet one to stand faster by his rights, or what he considered to be his rights—however, that's not the question now—I for one, never set under. Some might say, 'Was he a eloquent man?' and to that my answer

would be: 'Well, there you've a better right per'aps to speak of
your own uncle than what I have.' Others might ask, 'Did he
keep a hold of his congregation?' and there again I should reply, 'That depends.' But as I say—yes, Eliza, my girl, I'm
coming—eleven o'clock, sir, and you inquire for the King's
Head pew." I believe Eliza had been very near the door, and
shall consider it in my vail.[12]

The next episode was church: I felt Mr. Lucas had a difficult
task in doing justice to Christmas sentiments, and also to the
feeling of disquiet and regret which, whatever Mr. Bowman
might say, was clearly prevalent. I do not think he rose to the
occasion. I was uncomfortable. The organ wolved[13]—you know
what I mean: the wind died—twice in the Christmas Hymn,
and the tenor bell, I suppose owing to some negligence on the
part of the ringers, kept sounding faintly about once in a
minute during the sermon. The clerk sent up a man to see to it,
but he seemed unable to do much. I was glad when it was over.
There was an odd incident, too, before the service. I went in
rather early, and came upon two men carrying the parish bier
back to its place under the tower. From what I overheard them
saying, it appeared that it had been put out by mistake, by
someone who was not there. I also saw the clerk busy folding
up a moth-eaten velvet pall—not a sight for Christmas Day.

I dined soon after this, and then, feeling disinclined to go out,
took my seat by the fire in the parlour, with the last number of
Pickwick,[14] which I had been saving up for some days. I
thought I could be sure of keeping awake over this, but I turned
out as bad as our friend Smith. I suppose it was half-past two
when I was roused by a piercing whistle and laughing and talking voices outside in the market-place. It was a Punch and
Judy—I had no doubt the one that my bagman had seen at
W——. I was half delighted, half not—the latter because my
unpleasant dream came back to me so vividly; but, anyhow, I
determined to see it through, and I sent Eliza out with a crown-
piece to the performers and a request that they would face my
window if they could manage it.

· The show was a very smart new one; the names of the propri-
etors, I need hardly tell you, were Italian, Foresta and Calpigi.

The Toby dog was there, as I had been led to expect. All B——
turned out, but did not obstruct my view, for I was at the large
first-floor window and not ten yards away.

The play began on the stroke of a quarter to three by the
church clock. Certainly it was very good; and I was soon relieved to find that the disgust my dream had given me for
Punch's onslaughts on his ill-starred visitors was only transient.
I laughed at the demise of the Turncock, the Foreigner, the Beadle, and even the baby. The only drawback was the Toby dog's
developing a tendency to howl in the wrong place. Something
had occurred, I suppose, to upset him, and something considerable: for, I forget exactly at what point, he gave a most lamen-
table cry, leapt off the footboard, and shot away across the
market-place and down a side street. There was a stage-wait,
but only a brief one. I suppose the men decided that it was no
good going after him, and that he was likely to turn up again at
night.

We went on. Punch dealt faithfully with Judy, and in fact
with all comers; and then came the moment when the gallows
was erected, and the great scene with Mr. Ketch was to be en-
acted. It was now that something happened of which I can certainly not yet see the import fully. You have witnessed an
execution, and know what the criminal's head looks like with the
cap on. If you are like me, you never wish to think of it again,
and I do not willingly remind you of it. It was just such a head
as that, that I, from my somewhat higher post, saw in the inside
of the show-box; but at first the audience did not see it. I expected it to emerge into their view, but instead of that there
slowly rose for a few seconds an uncovered face, with an expression of terror upon it, of which I have never imagined the
like. It seemed as if the man, whoever he was, was being
forcibly lifted, with his arms somehow pinioned or held back,
towards the little gibbet on the stage. I could just see the night-
capped head behind him. Then there was a cry and a crash. The
whole show-box fell over backwards; kicking legs were seen
among the ruins, and then two figures—as some said; I can only
answer for one—were visible running at top speed across the
square and disappearing in a lane which leads to the fields.

Of course everybody gave chase. I followed; but the pace was killing, and very few were in, literally, at the death. It happened in a chalk pit: the man went over the edge quite blindly and broke his neck. They searched everywhere for the other, until it occurred to me to ask whether he had ever left the market-place. At first everyone was sure that he had; but when we came to look, he was there, under the showbox, dead too.

But in the chalk pit it was that poor Uncle Henry's body was found, with a sack over the head, the throat horribly mangled. It was a peaked corner of the sack sticking out of the soil that attracted attention. I cannot bring myself to write in greater detail.

I forgot to say the men's real names were Kidman and Gallop. I feel sure I have heard them, but no one here seems to know anything about them.

I am coming to you as soon as I can after the funeral. I must tell you when we meet what I think of it all.

TWO DOCTORS

It is a very common thing, in my experience, to find papers shut up in old books; but one of the rarest things to come across any such that are at all interesting. Still it does happen, and one should never destroy them unlooked at. Now it was a practice of mine before the war occasionally to buy old ledgers of which the paper was good, and which possessed a good many blank leaves, and to extract these and use them for my own notes and writings. One such I purchased for a small sum in 1911. It was tightly clasped, and its boards were warped by having for years been obliged to embrace a number of extraneous sheets. Three-quarters of this inserted matter had lost all vestige of importance for any living human being: one bundle had not. That it belonged to a lawyer is certain, for it is endorsed: *The strangest case I have yet met,* and bears initials, and an address in Gray's Inn.[1] It is only materials for a case, and consists of statements by possible witnesses. The man who would have been the defendant or prisoner seems never to have appeared. The *dossier* is not complete, but, such as it is, it furnishes a riddle in which the supernatural appears to play a part. You must see what you can make of it.

The following is the setting and the tale as I elicit it.

The scene is Islington[2] in 1718, and the time the month of June: a countrified place, therefore, and a pleasant season. Dr. Abell was walking in his garden one afternoon waiting for his horse to be brought round that he might set out on his visits for the day. To him entered his confidential servant, Luke Jennett, who had been with him twenty years.

"I said I wished to speak to him, and what I had to say might take some quarter of an hour. He accordingly bade me go into his study, which was a room opening on the terrace path where he was walking, and came in himself and sat down. I told him that, much against my will, I must look out for another place. He inquired what was my reason, in consideration I had been so long with him. I said if he would excuse me he would do me a great kindness, because (this appears to have been common form even in 1718) I was one that always liked to have everything pleasant about me. As well as I can remember, he said that was his case likewise, but he would wish to know why I should change my mind after so many years, and, says he, 'you know there can be no talk of a remembrance of you in my will if you leave my service now.' I said I had made my reckoning of that.

" 'Then,' says he, 'you must have some complaint to make, and if I could I would willingly set it right.' And at that I told him, not seeing how I could keep it back, the matter of my former affidavit and of the bedstaff in the dispensing-room, and said that a house where such things happened was no place for me. At which he, looking very black upon me, said no more, but called me fool, and said he would pay what was owing me in the morning; and so, his horse being waiting, went out. So for that night I lodged with my sister's husband near Battle Bridge[3] and came early next morning to my late master, who then made a great matter that I had not lain in his house and stopped a crown out of my wages owing.

"After that I took service here and there, not for long at a time, and saw no more of him till I came to be Dr. Quinn's man at Dodds Hall in Islington."

There is one very obscure part in this statement—namely, the reference to the former affidavit and the matter of the bedstaff. The former affidavit is not in the bundle of papers. It is to be feared that it was taken out to be read because of its special oddity, and not put back. Of what nature the story was may be guessed later, but as yet no clue has been put into our hands.

The Rector of Islington, Jonathan Pratt, is the next to step forward. He furnishes particulars of the standing and reputation of Dr. Abell and Dr. Quinn, both of whom lived and practised in his parish.

"It is not to be supposed," he says, "that a physician should be a regular attendant at morning and evening prayers, or at the Wednesday lectures, but within the measure of their ability I would say that both these persons fulfilled their obligations as loyal members of the Church of England. At the same time (as you desire my private mind) I must say, in the language of the schools, *distinguo*.[4] Dr. A. was to me a source of perplexity, Dr. Q. to my eye a plain, honest believer, not inquiring over closely into points of belief, but squaring his practice to what lights he had. The other interested himself in questions to which Providence, as I hold, designs no answer to be given us in this state: he would ask me, for example, what place I believed those beings now to hold in the scheme of creation which by some are thought neither to have stood fast when the rebel angels fell, nor to have joined with them to the full pitch of their transgression.

"As was suitable, my first answer to him was a question, What warrant he had for supposing any such beings to exist? for that there was none in Scripture I took it he was aware. It appeared—for as I am on the subject, the whole tale may be given—that he grounded himself on such passages as that of the satyr which Jerome tells us conversed with Antony;[5] but thought too that some parts of Scripture might be cited in support. 'And besides,' said he, 'you know 'tis the universal belief among those that spend their days and nights abroad, and I would add that if your calling took you so continuously as it does me about the country lanes by night, you might not be so surprised as I see you to be by my suggestion.' 'You are then of John Milton's mind,' I said, 'and hold that

> Millions of spiritual creatures walk the earth
> Unseen, both when we wake and when we sleep.'[6]

"'I do not know,' he said, 'why Milton should take upon himself to say "unseen"; though to be sure he was blind when he wrote that. But for the rest, why, yes, I think he was in the right.' 'Well,' I said, 'though not so often as you, I am not seldom called abroad pretty late; but I have no mind of meeting a satyr in our Islington lanes in all the years I have been here; and if you have had the better luck, I am sure the Royal Society[7] would be glad to know of it.'

"I am reminded of these trifling expressions because Dr. A. took them so ill, stamping out of the room in a huff with some such word as that these high and dry parsons had no eyes but for a prayer-book or a pint of wine.

"But this was not the only time that our conversation took a remarkable turn. There was an evening when he came in, at first seeming gay and in good spirits, but afterwards as he sat and smoked by the fire falling into a musing way; out of which to rouse him I said pleasantly that I supposed he had had no meetings of late with his odd friends. A question which did effectually arouse him, for he looked most wildly, and as if scared, upon me, and said, 'You were never there? I did not see you. Who brought you?' And then in a more collected tone, 'What was this about a meeting? I believe I must have been in a doze.' To which I answered that I was thinking of fauns and centaurs in the dark lane, and not of a witches' Sabbath; but it seemed he took it differently.

" 'Well,' said he, 'I can plead guilty to neither; but I find you very much more of a sceptic than becomes your cloth. If you care to know about the dark lane you might do worse than ask my housekeeper that lived at the other end of it when she was a child.' 'Yes,' said I, 'and the old women in the almshouse and the children in the kennel. If I were you, I would send to your brother Quinn for a bolus[8] to clear your brain.' 'Damn Quinn,' says he; 'talk no more of him: he has embezzled four of my best patients this month; I believe it is that cursed man of his, Jennett, that used to be with me, his tongue is never still; it should be nailed to the pillory if he had his deserts.' This, I may say, was the only time of his showing me that he had any grudge against either Dr. Quinn or Jennett, and as was my business, I did my best to persuade him he was mistaken in them. Yet it could not be denied that some respectable families in the parish had given him the cold shoulder, and for no reason that they were willing to allege. The end was that he said he had not done so ill at Islington but that he could afford to live at ease elsewhere when he chose, and anyhow he bore Dr. Quinn no malice. I think I now remember what observation of mine drew him into the train of thought which he next pursued. It was, I believe, my mentioning some juggling tricks which my brother in the East Indies had seen at the court of the Rajah of Mysore. 'A convenient thing enough,' said Dr. Abell to me, 'if by some arrangement a man could get the power of communicating motion and energy to inanimate objects.' 'As if the axe should move itself against him that lifts it; something of that kind?' 'Well, I don't know that that was in my mind so much; but if you could summon such a volume from your shelf or even order it to open at the right page.'

"He was sitting by the fire—it was a cold evening—and stretched out his hand that way, and just then the fire-irons, or at least the poker, fell over towards him with a great clatter, and I did not hear what else he said. But I told him that I could not easily conceive of an arrangement, as he called it, of such a kind that would not include as one of its conditions a heavier payment than any Christian would care to make; to which he assented. 'But,' he said, 'I have no doubt these bargains can be made very tempting, very persuasive. Still, you would not favour them, eh, Doctor? No, I suppose not.'

"This is as much as I know of Dr. Abell's mind, and the feeling between these men. Dr. Quinn, as I said, was a plain, honest creature, and a man to whom I would have gone—indeed I have before now gone to him—for advice on matters of business. He was, however, every now and again, and particularly of late, not exempt from troublesome fancies. There was certainly a time when he was so much harassed by his dreams that he could not keep them to himself, but would tell them to his acquaintances and among them to me. I was at supper at his house, and he was not inclined to let me leave him at my usual time. 'If you go,' he said, 'there will be nothing for it but I must go to bed and dream of the chrysalis.' 'You might be worse off,' said I. 'I do not think it,' he said, and he shook himself like a man who is displeased with the complexion of his thoughts. 'I only meant,' said I, 'that a chrysalis is an innocent thing.' 'This one is not,' he said, 'and I do not care to think of it.'

"However, sooner than lose my company he was fain to tell

me (for I pressed him) that this was a dream which had come to him several times of late, and even more than once in a night. It was to this effect, that he seemed to himself to wake under an extreme compulsion to rise and go out of doors. So he would dress himself and go down to his garden door. By the door there stood a spade which he must take, and go out into the garden, and at a particular place in the shrubbery, somewhat clear, and upon which the moon shone (for there was always in his dream a full moon), he would feel himself forced to dig. And after some time the spade would uncover something light-coloured, which he would perceive to be a stuff, linen or woollen, and this he must clear with his hands. It was always the same: of the size of a man and shaped like the chrysalis of a moth, with the folds showing a promise of an opening at one end.

"He could not describe how gladly he would have left all at this stage and run to the house, but he must not escape so easily. So with many groans, and knowing only too well what to expect, he parted these folds of stuff, or, as it sometimes seemed to be, membrane, and disclosed a head covered with a smooth pink skin, which breaking as the creature stirred, showed him his own face in a state of death. The telling of this so much disturbed him that I was forced out of mere compassion to sit with him the greater part of the night and talk with him upon indifferent subjects. He said that upon every recurrence of this dream he woke and found himself, as it were, fighting for his breath."

Another extract from Luke Jennett's long continuous statement comes in at this point.

"I never told tales of my master, Dr. Abell, to anybody in the neighbourhood. When I was in another service I remember to have spoken to my fellow-servants about the matter of the bed-staff, but I am sure I never said either I or he were the persons concerned, and it met with so little credit that I was affronted and thought best to keep it to myself. And when I came back to Islington and found Dr. Abell still there, who I was told had left the parish, I was clear that it behoved me to use great discretion, for indeed I was afraid of the man, and it is certain I was no party to spreading any ill report of him. My master,

Dr. Quinn, was a very just, honest man, and no maker of mischief. I am sure he never stirred a finger nor said a word by way of inducement to a soul to make them leave going to Dr. Abell and come to him; nay, he would hardly be persuaded to attend them that came, until he was convinced that if he did not they would send into the town for a physician rather than do as they had hitherto done.

"I believe it may be proved that Dr. Abell came into my master's house more than once. We had a new chambermaid out of Hertfordshire, and she asked me who was the gentleman that was looking after the master, that is Dr. Quinn, when he was out, and seemed so disappointed that he was out. She said whoever he was he knew the way of the house well, running at once into the study and then into the dispensing-room, and last into the bedchamber. I made her tell me what he was like, and what she said was suitable enough to Dr. Abell; but besides she told me she saw the same man at church, and someone told her that was the Doctor.

"It was just after this that my master began to have his bad nights, and complained to me and other persons, and in particular what discomfort he suffered from his pillow and bedclothes. He said he must buy some to suit him, and should do his own marketing. And accordingly brought home a parcel which he said was of the right quality, but where he bought it we had then no knowledge, only they were marked in thread with a coronet and a bird. The women said they were of a sort not commonly met with and very fine, and my master said they were the comfortablest he ever used, and he slept now both soft and deep. Also the feather pillows were the best sorted and his head would sink into them as if they were a cloud: which I have myself remarked several times when I came to wake him of a morning, his face being almost hid by the pillow closing over it.

"I had never any communication with Dr. Abell after I came back to Islington, but one day when he passed me in the street and asked me whether I was not looking for another service, to which I answered I was very well suited where I was, but he said I was a tickleminded[9] fellow and he doubted not he should soon hear I was on the world again, which indeed proved true."

Dr. Pratt is next taken up where he left off.

"On the 16th I was called up out of my bed soon after it was light—that is about five—with a message that Dr. Quinn was dead or dying. Making my way to his house I found there was no doubt which was the truth. All the persons in the house except the one that let me in were already in his chamber and standing about his bed, but none touching him. He was stretched in the midst of the bed, on his back, without any disorder, and indeed had the appearance of one ready laid out for burial. His hands, I think, were even crossed on his breast. The only thing not usual was that nothing was to be seen of his face, the two ends of the pillow or bolster appearing to be closed quite over it. These I immediately pulled apart, at the same time rebuking those present, and especially the man, for not at once coming to the assistance of his master. He, however, only looked at me and shook his head, having evidently no more hope than myself that there was anything but a corpse before us.

"Indeed it was plain to anyone possessed of the least experience that he was not only dead, but had died of suffocation. Nor could it be conceived that his death was accidentally caused by the mere folding of the pillow over his face. How should he not, feeling the oppression, have lifted his hands to put it away? whereas not a fold of the sheet which was closely gathered about him, as I now observed, was disordered. The next thing was to procure a physician. I had bethought me of this on leaving my house, and sent on the messenger who had come to me to Dr. Abell; but I now heard that he was away from home, and the nearest surgeon was got, who, however, could tell no more, at least without opening the body, than we already knew.

"As to any person entering the room with evil purpose (which was the next point to be cleared), it was visible that the bolts of the door were burst from their stanchions, and the stanchions broken away from the door-post by main force; and there was a sufficient body of witness, the smith among them, to testify that this had been done but a few minutes before I came. The chamber being, moreover, at the top of the house, the window was neither easy of access nor did it show any sign

of an exit made that way, either by marks upon the sill or foot-
prints below upon soft mould."

The surgeon's evidence forms of course part of the report of
the inquest, but since it has nothing but remarks upon the
healthy state of the larger organs and the coagulation of blood
in various parts of the body, it need not be reproduced. The verdict was "Death by the visitation of God."

Annexed to the other papers is one which I was at first inclined to suppose had made its way among them by mistake.
Upon further consideration I think I can divine a reason for its
presence.

It relates to the rifling of a mausoleum in Middlesex which
stood in a park (now broken up), the property of a noble family which I will not name. The outrage was not that of an ordinary resurrection man. The object, it seemed likely, was theft.
The account is blunt and terrible. I shall not quote it. A dealer
in the North of London suffered heavy penalties as a receiver of
stolen goods in connexion with the affair.

THE HAUNTED DOLLS' HOUSE

"I suppose you get stuff of that kind through your hands pretty often?" said Mr. Dillet, as he pointed with his stick to an object which shall be described when the time comes: and when he said it, he lied in his throat, and knew that he lied. Not once in twenty years—perhaps not once in a lifetime—could Mr. Chittenden, skilled as he was in ferreting out the forgotten treasures of half a dozen counties, expect to handle such a specimen. It was collectors' palaver, and Mr. Chittenden recognized it as such.

"Stuff of that kind, Mr. Dillet! It's a museum piece, that is."

"Well, I suppose there are museums that'll take anything."

"I've seen one, not as good as that, years back," said Mr. Chittenden thoughtfully. "But that's not likely to come into the market: and I'm told they 'ave some fine ones of the period over the water. No: I'm only telling you the truth, Mr. Dillet, when I say that if you was to place an unlimited order with me for the very best that could be got—and you know I 'ave facilities for getting to know of such things, and a reputation to maintain—well, all I can say is, I should lead you straight up to that one and say, 'I can't do no better for you than that, sir.' "

"Hear, hear!" said Mr. Dillet, applauding ironically with the end of his stick on the floor of the shop. "How much are you sticking the innocent American buyer for it, eh?"

"Oh, I shan't be over hard on the buyer, American or otherwise. You see, it stands this way, Mr. Dillet—if I knew just a bit more about the pedigree—"

"Or just a bit less," Mr. Dillet put in.

"Ha, ha! you will have your joke, sir. No, but as I was saying, if I knew just a little more than what I do about the piece—though anyone can see for themselves it's a genuine thing, every last corner of it, and there's not been one of my men allowed to so much as touch it since it came into the shop—there'd be another figure in the price I'm asking."

"And what's that: five and twenty?"

"Multiply that by three and you've got it, sir. Seventy-five's my price."

"And fifty's mine," said Mr. Dillet.

The point of agreement was, of course, somewhere between the two, it does not matter exactly where—I think sixty guineas. But half an hour later the object was being packed, and within an hour Mr. Dillet had called for it in his car and driven away. Mr. Chittenden, holding the cheque in his hand, saw him off from the door with smiles, and returned, still smiling, into the parlour where his wife was making the tea. He stopped at the door.

"It's gone," he said.

"Thank God for that!" said Mrs. Chittenden, putting down the teapot. "Mr. Dillet, was it?"

"Yes, it was."

"Well, I'd sooner it was him than another."

"Oh, I don't know; he ain't a bad feller, my dear."

"Maybe not, but in my opinion he'd be none the worse for a bit of a shake up."

"Well, if that's your opinion, it's my opinion he's put himself into the way of getting one. Anyhow, *we* shan't have no more of it, and that's something to be thankful for."

And so Mr. and Mrs. Chittenden sat down to tea.

And what of Mr. Dillet and of his new acquisition? What it was, the title of this story will have told you. What it was like, I shall have to indicate as well as I can.

There was only just room enough for it in the car, and Mr. Dillet had to sit with the driver: he had also to go slow, for though the rooms of the Dolls' House had all been stuffed carefully with soft cotton-wool, jolting was to be avoided, in view of the immense number of small objects which thronged them; and the ten-mile drive was an anxious time for him, in spite of all the precautions he insisted upon. At last his front door was reached, and Collins, the butler, came out.

"Look here, Collins, you must help me with this thing—it's a delicate job. We must get it out upright, see? It's full of little things that mustn't be displaced more than we can help. Let's see, where shall we have it? (After a pause for consideration.) Really, I think I shall have to put it in my own room, to begin with at any rate. On the big table—that's it."

It was conveyed—with much talking—to Mr. Dillet's spacious room on the first floor, looking out on the drive. The sheeting was unwound from it, and the front thrown open, and for the next hour or two Mr. Dillet was fully occupied in extracting the padding and setting in order the contents of the rooms.

When this thoroughly congenial task was finished, I must say that it would have been difficult to find a more perfect and attractive specimen of a Dolls' House in Strawberry Hill Gothic[1] than that which now stood on Mr. Dillet's large kneehole table, lighted up by the evening sun which came slanting through three tall sash-windows.

It was quite six feet long, including the Chapel or Oratory which flanked the front on the left as you faced it, and the stable on the right. The main block of the house was, as I have said, in the Gothic manner: that is to say, the windows had pointed arches and were surmounted by what are called ogival hoods, with crockets[2] and finials such as we see on the canopies of tombs built into church walls. At the angles were absurd turrets covered with arched panels. The Chapel had pinnacles and buttresses, and a bell in the turret and coloured glass in the windows. When the front of the house was open you saw four large rooms, bedroom, dining-room, drawing-room and kitchen, each with its appropriate furniture in a very complete state.

The stable on the right was in two storeys, with its proper complement of horses, coaches and grooms, and with its clock and Gothic cupola for the clock bell.

Pages, of course, might be written on the outfit of the mansion—how many frying-pans, how many gilt chairs, what pictures, carpets, chandeliers, four-posters, table linen, glass, crockery and plate it possessed; but all this must be left to the imagination. I will only say that the base or plinth on which the house stood (for it was fitted with one of some depth which allowed of a flight of steps to the front door and a terrace, partly balustraded) contained a shallow drawer or drawers in which were neatly stored sets of embroidered curtains, changes of raiment for the inmates, and, in short, all the materials for an infinite series of variations and refittings of the most absorbing and delightful kind.

"Quintessence of Horace Walpole, that's what it is: he must have had something to do with the making of it." Such was Mr. Dillet's murmured reflection as he knelt before it in a reverent ecstasy. "Simply wonderful! this is my day and no mistake. Five hundred pound coming in this morning for that cabinet which I never cared about, and now this tumbling into my hands for a tenth, at the very most, of what it would fetch in town. Well, well! It almost makes one afraid something'll happen to counter it. Let's have a look at the population, anyhow."

Accordingly, he set them before him in a row. Again, here is an opportunity, which some would snatch at, of making an inventory of costume: I am incapable of it.

There were a gentleman and lady, in blue satin and brocade respectively. There were two children, a boy and a girl. There was a cook, a nurse, a footman, and there were the stable servants, two postilions, a coachman, two grooms.

"Anyone else? Yes, possibly."

The curtains of the four-poster in the bedroom were closely drawn round all four sides of it, and he put his finger in between them and felt in the bed. He drew the finger back hastily, for it almost seemed to him as if something had—not stirred, perhaps, but yielded—in an odd live way as he pressed it. Then he put back the curtains, which ran on rods in the proper manner, and extracted from the bed a white-haired old gentleman in a long linen night-dress and cap, and laid him down by the rest. The tale was complete.

Dinner-time was now near, so Mr. Dillet spent but five minutes in putting the lady and children into the drawing-room, the gentleman into the dining-room, the servants into the kitchen and stables, and the old man back into his bed. He retired into his dressing-room next door, and we see and hear no more of him until something like eleven o'clock at night.

His whim was to sleep surrounded by some of the gems of his collection. The big room in which we have seen him contained his bed: bath, wardrobe, and all the appliances of dressing were in a commodious room adjoining: but his four-poster, which itself was a valued treasure, stood in the large room where he sometimes wrote, and often sat, and even received visitors. Tonight he repaired to it in a highly complacent frame of mind.

There was no striking clock within earshot—none on the staircase, none in the stable, none in the distant church tower. Yet it is indubitable that Mr. Dillet was startled out of a very pleasant slumber by a bell tolling One.

He was so much startled that he did not merely lie breathless with wide-open eyes, but actually sat up in his bed.

He never asked himself, till the morning hours, how it was that, though there was no light at all in the room, the Dolls' House on the kneehole table stood out with complete clearness. But it was so. The effect was that of a bright harvest moon shining full on the front of a big white stone mansion—a quarter of a mile away it might be, and yet every detail was photographically sharp. There were trees about it, too—trees rising behind the chapel and the house. He seemed to be conscious of the scent of a cool still September night. He thought he could hear an occasional stamp and clink from the stables, as of horses stirring. And with another shock he realized that, above the house, he was looking, not at the wall of his room with its pictures, but into the profound blue of a night sky.

There were lights, more than one, in the windows, and he quickly saw that this was no four-roomed house with a movable front, but one of many rooms, and staircases—a real house, but seen as if through the wrong end of a telescope. "You mean to show me something," he muttered to himself, and he gazed earnestly on the lighted windows. They would in real life have been shuttered or curtained, no doubt, he thought; but, as it was, there was nothing to intercept his view of what was being transacted inside the rooms.

Two rooms were lighted—one on the ground floor to the

right of the door, one upstairs, on the left—the first brightly enough, the other rather dimly. The lower room was the dining-room: a table was laid, but the meal was over, and only wine and glasses were left on the table. The man of the blue satin and the woman of the brocade were alone in the room, and they were talking very earnestly, seated close together at the table, their elbows on it: every now and again stopping to listen, as it seemed. Once *he* rose, came to the window and opened it and put his head out and his hand to his ear. There was a lighted ta-per in a silver candlestick on a sideboard. When the man left the window he seemed to leave the room also; and the lady, taper in hand, remained standing and listening. The expression on her face was that of one striving her utmost to keep down a fear that threatened to master her—and succeeding. It was a hateful face, too; broad, flat and sly. Now the man came back and she took some small thing from him and hurried out of the room. He, too, disappeared, but only for a moment or two. The front door slowly opened and he stepped out and stood on the top of the *perron*,³ looking this way and that; then turned towards the upper window that was lighted, and shook his fist.

It was time to look at that upper window. Through it was seen a four-post bed: a nurse or other servant in an arm-chair, evi-dently sound asleep; in the bed an old man lying: awake, and, one would say, anxious, from the way in which he shifted about and moved his fingers, beating tunes on the coverlet. Beyond the bed a door opened. Light was seen on the ceiling, and the lady came in: she set down her candle on a table, came to the fireside and roused the nurse. In her hand she had an old-fashioned wine bottle, ready uncorked. The nurse took it, poured some of the contents into a little silver saucepan, added some spice and sugar from casters on the table, and set it to warm on the fire. Mean-while the old man in the bed beckoned feebly to the lady, who came to him, smiling, took his wrist as if to feel his pulse, and bit her lip as if in consternation. He looked at her anxiously, and then pointed to the window, and spoke. She nodded, and did as the man below had done; opened the casement and listened— perhaps rather ostentatiously: then drew in her head and shook it, looking at the old man, who seemed to sigh.

By this time the posset⁴ on the fire was steaming, and the nurse poured it into a small two-handled silver bowl and brought it to the bedside. The old man seemed disinclined for it and was waving it away, but the lady and the nurse together bent over him and evidently pressed it upon him. He must have yielded, for they supported him into a sitting position, and put it to his lips. He drank most of it, in several draughts, and they laid him down. The lady left the room, smiling good-night to him, and took the bowl, the bottle and the silver saucepan with her. The nurse returned to the chair, and there was an interval of complete quiet.

Suddenly the old man started up in his bed—and he must have uttered some cry, for the nurse started out of her chair and made but one step of it to the bedside. He was a sad and terrible sight—flushed in the face, almost to blackness, the eyes glaring whitely, both hands clutching at his heart, foam at his lips.

For a moment the nurse left him, ran to the door, flung it wide open, and, one supposes, screamed aloud for help, then darted back to the bed and seemed to try feverishly to soothe him—to lay him down—anything. But as the lady, her husband, and several servants, rushed into the room with horrified faces, the old man collapsed under the nurse's hands and lay back, and the features, contorted with agony and rage, relaxed slowly into calm.

A few moments later, lights showed out to the left of the house, and a coach with flambeaux drove up to the door. A white-wigged man in black got nimbly out and ran up the steps, carrying a small leather trunk-shaped box. He was met in the doorway by the man and his wife, she with her handker-chief clutched between her hands, he with a tragic face, but retaining his self-control. They led the new-comer into the dining-room, where he set his box of papers on the table, and, turning to them, listened with a face of consternation at what they had to tell. He nodded his head again and again, threw out his hands slightly, declined, it seemed, offers of refreshment and lodging for the night, and within a few minutes came slowly down the steps, entering the coach and driving off the way he had come. As the man in blue watched him from the top of the steps, a smile not pleasant to see stole slowly over his fat white face. Darkness fell over the whole scene as the lights of the coach disappeared.

But Mr. Dillet remained sitting up in the bed: he had rightly guessed that there would be a sequel. The house front glimmered out again before long. But now there was a difference. The lights were in other windows, one at the top of the house, the other illuminating the range of coloured windows of the chapel. How he saw through these is not quite obvious, but he did. The interior was as carefully furnished as the rest of the establishment, with its minute red cushions on the desks, its Gothic stall-canopies, and its western gallery and pinnacled organ with gold pipes. On the centre of the black and white pavement was a bier: four tall candles burned at the corners. On the bier was a coffin covered with a pall of black velvet.

As he looked the folds of the pall stirred. It seemed to rise at one end: it slid downwards: it fell away, exposing the black coffin with its silver handles and name-plate. One of the tall candlesticks swayed and toppled over. Ask no more, but turn, as Mr. Dillet hastily did, and look in at the lighted window at the top of the house, where a boy and girl lay in two truckle-beds,⁵ and a four-poster for the nurse rose above them. The nurse was not visible for the moment; but the father and mother were there, dressed now in mourning, but with very little sign of mourning in their demeanour. Indeed, they were laughing and talking with a good deal of animation, sometimes to each other, and sometimes throwing a remark to one or other of the children, and again laughing at the answers. Then the father was seen to go on tiptoe out of the room, taking with him as he went a white garment that hung on a peg near the door. He shut the door after him. A minute or two later it was slowly opened again, and a muffled head poked round it. A bent form of sinister shape stepped across to the truckle-beds, and suddenly stopped, threw up its arms and revealed, of course, the father, laughing. The children were in agonies of terror, the boy with the bedclothes over his head, the girl throwing herself out of bed into her mother's arms. Attempts at consolation followed— the parents took the children on their laps, patted them, picked up the white gown and showed there was no harm in it, and so forth; and at last putting the children back into bed, left the room with encouraging waves of the hand. As they left it, the nurse came in, and soon the light died down.

Still Mr. Dillet watched immovable.

A new sort of light—not of lamp or candle—a pale ugly light, began to dawn around the door-case at the back of the room. The door was opening again. The seer does not like to dwell upon what he saw entering the room: he says it might be described as a frog—the size of a man—but it had scanty white hair about its head. It was busy about the truckle-beds, but not for long. The sound of cries—faint, as if coming out of a vast distance—but, even so, infinitely appalling, reached the ear.

There were signs of a hideous commotion all over the house: lights moved along and up, and doors opened and shut, and running figures passed within the windows. The clock in the stable turret tolled one, and darkness fell again.

It was only dispelled once more, to show the house front. At the bottom of the steps dark figures were drawn up in two lines, holding flaming torches. More dark figures came down the steps, bearing, first one, then another small coffin. And the lines of torch-bearers with the coffins between them moved silently onward to the left.

The hours of night passed on—never so slowly, Mr. Dillet thought. Gradually he sank down from sitting to lying in his bed—but he did not close an eye: and early next morning he sent for the doctor.

The doctor found him in a disquieting state of nerves, and recommended sea-air. To a quiet place on the East Coast he accordingly repaired by easy stages in his car.

One of the first people he met on the sea front was Mr. Chittenden, who, it appeared, had likewise been advised to take his wife away for a bit of a change.

Mr. Chittenden looked somewhat askance upon him when they met: and not without cause.

"Well, I don't wonder at you being a bit upset, Mr. Dillet. What? yes, well, I might say 'orrible upset, to be sure, seeing what me and my poor wife went through ourselves. But I put it to you, Mr. Dillet, one of two things: was I going to scrap a lovely piece like that on the one 'and, or was I going to tell customers: 'I'm selling you a regular picture-palace-dramar in reel life of the olden time, billed to perform regular at one o'clock A.M.'? Why, what would you 'ave said yourself? And next thing you know, two Justices of the Peace[6] in the back parlour, and pore Mr. and Mrs. Chittenden off in a spring cart to the County Asylum and everyone in the street saying, 'Ah, I thought it 'ud come to that. Look at the way the man drank!'—and me next door, or next door but one, to a total abstainer, as you know. Well, there was my position. What? Me 'ave it back in the shop? Well, what do *you* think? No, but I'll tell you what I will do. You shall have your money back, bar the ten pound I paid for it, and you make what you can."

Later in the day, in what is offensively called the "smoke-room" of the hotel, a murmured conversation between the two went on for some time.

"How much do you really know about that thing, and where it came from?"

"Honest, Mr. Dillet, I don't know the 'ouse. Of course, it came out of the lumber room of a country 'ouse—that anyone could guess. But I'll go as far as say this, that I believe it's not a hundred miles from this place. Which direction and how far I've no notion. I'm only judging by guess-work. The man as I actually paid the cheque to ain't one of my regular men, and I've lost sight of him; but I 'ave the idea that this part of the country was his beat, and that's every word I can tell you. But now, Mr. Dillet, there's one thing that rather physicks[7] me. That old chap,—I suppose you saw him drive up to the door— I thought so: now, would he have been the medical man, do you take it? My wife would have it so, but I stuck to it that was the lawyer, because he had papers with him, and one he took out was folded up."

"I agree," said Mr. Dillet. "Thinking it over, I came to the conclusion that was the old man's will, ready to be signed."

"Just what I thought," said Mr. Chittenden, "and I took it that will would have cut out the young people, eh? Well, well! It's been a lesson to me, I know that. I shan't buy no more dolls' houses, nor waste no more money on the pictures—and as to this business of poisonin' grandpa, well, if I know myself, I never 'ad much of a turn for that. Live and let live: that's bin my motto throughout life, and I ain't found it a bad one."

Filled with these elevated sentiments, Mr. Chittenden retired to his lodgings. Mr. Dillet next day repaired to the local Institute, where he hoped to find some clue to the riddle that absorbed him. He gazed in despair at a long file of the Canterbury and York Society's publications of the Parish Registers of the district.[8] No print resembling the house of his nightmare was among those that hung on the staircase and in the passages. Disconsolate, he found himself at last in a derelict room, staring at a dusty model of a church in a dusty glass case: *Model of St. Stephen's Church, Coxham.*[9] *Presented by J. Merewether, Esq., of Ilbridge House, 1877. The work of his ancestor James Merewether, d. 1786.* There was something in the fashion of it that reminded him dimly of his horror. He retraced his steps to a wall map he had noticed, and made out that Ilbridge House was in Coxham Parish. Coxham was, as it happened, one of the parishes of which he had retained the name when he glanced over the file of printed registers, and it was not long before he found in them the record of the burial of Roger Milford, aged 76, on the 11th of September, 1757, and of Roger and Elizabeth Merewether, aged 9 and 7, on the 19th of the same month. It seemed worth while to follow up this clue, frail as it was; and in the afternoon he drove out to Coxham. The east end of the north aisle of the church is a Milford chapel, and on its north wall are tablets to the same persons; Roger, the elder, it seems, was distinguished by all the qualities which adorn "the Father, the Magistrate, and the Man": the memorial was erected by his attached daughter Elizabeth, "who did not long survive the loss of a parent ever solicitous for her welfare, and of two amiable children." The last sentence was plainly an addition to the original inscription.

A yet later slab told of James Merewether, husband of Elizabeth, "who in the dawn of life practised, not without success, those arts which, had he continued their exercise, might in the opinion of the most competent judges have earned for him the name of the British Vitruvius:[10] but who, overwhelmed by the visitation which deprived him of an affectionate partner and a blooming offspring, passed his Prime and Age in a secluded yet elegant Retirement: his grateful Nephew and Heir indulges a pious sorrow by this too brief recital of his excellences."

The children were more simply commemorated. Both died on the night of the 12th of September.

Mr. Dillet felt sure that in Ilbridge House he had found the scene of his drama. In some old sketch-book, possibly in some old print, he may yet find convincing evidence that he is right. But the Ilbridge House of to-day is not that which he sought; it is an Elizabethan erection of the forties, in red brick with stone quoins and dressings. A quarter of a mile from it, in a low part of the park, backed by ancient, stag-horned, ivy-strangled trees and thick undergrowth, are marks of a terraced platform overgrown with rough grass. A few stone balusters lie here and there, and a heap or two, covered with nettles and ivy, of wrought stones with badly-carved crockets. This, someone told Mr. Dillet, was the site of an older house.

As he drove out of the village, the hall clock struck four, and Mr. Dillet started up and clapped his hands to his ears. It was not the first time he had heard that bell.

Awaiting an offer from the other side of the Atlantic, the dolls' house still reposes, carefully sheeted, in a loft over Mr. Dillet's stables, whither Collins conveyed it on the day when Mr. Dillet started for the sea coast.

———

[It will be said, perhaps, and not unjustly, that this is no more than a variation on a former story of mine called *The Mezzotint*. I can only hope that there is enough of variation in the setting to make the repetition of the *motif* tolerable.]

THE UNCOMMON
PRAYER-BOOK

I

Mr. Davidson was spending the first week in January alone in a
country town. A combination of circumstances had driven him
to that drastic course: his nearest relations were enjoying winter
sports abroad, and the friends who had been kindly anxious to
replace them had an infectious complaint in the house. Doubtless he might have found someone else to take pity on him.
"But," he reflected, "most of them have made up their parties,
and, after all, it is only for three or four days at most that I have
to fend for myself, and it will be just as well if I can get a move
on with my introduction to the Leventhorp Papers. I might use
the time by going down as near as I can to Gaulsford and making acquaintance with the neighbourhood. I ought to see the remains of Leventhorp House,[1] and the tombs in the church."

The first day after his arrival at the Swan Hotel at Longbridge[2]
was so stormy that he got no farther than the tobacconist's. The
next, comparatively bright, he used for his visit to Gaulsford,
which interested him more than a little, but had no ulterior consequences. The third, which was really a pearl of a day for early
January, was too fine to be spent indoors. He gathered from the
landlord that a favourite practice of visitors in the summer was to
take a morning train to a couple of stations westward, and walk
back down the valley of the Tent, through Stanford St. Thomas
and Stanford Magdalene, both of which were accounted highly
picturesque villages. He closed with this plan, and we now find
him seated in a third-class carriage at 9.45 A.M., on his way to
Kingsbourne Junction, and studying the map of the district.[3]

One old man was his only fellow-traveller, a piping old man, who seemed inclined for conversation. So Mr. Davidson, after going through the necessary versicles and responses about the weather, inquired whether he was going far.

"No, sir, not far, not this morning, sir," said the old man. "I ain't only goin' so far as what they call Kingsbourne Junction. There isn't but two stations betwixt here and there. Yes, they calls it Kingsbourne Junction."

"I'm going there, too," said Mr. Davidson.

"Oh, indeed, sir; do you know that part?"

"No, I'm only going for the sake of taking a walk back to Longbridge, and seeing a bit of the country."

"Oh, indeed, sir! Well, 'tis a beautiful day for a gentleman as enjoys a bit of a walk."

"Yes, to be sure. Have you got far to go when you get to Kingsbourne?"

"No, sir, I ain't got far to go, once I get to Kingsbourne Junction. I'm agoin' to see my daughter, sir. She live at Brockstone.⁴ That's about two mile across the fields from what they call Kingsbourne Junction, that is. You've got that marked down on your map, I expect, sir."

"I expect I have. Let me see, Brockstone, did you say? Here's Kingsbourne, yes; and which way is Brockstone—toward the Stanfords? Ah, I see it: Brockstone Court, in a park. I don't see the village, though."

"No, sir, you wouldn't see no village of Brockstone. There ain't only the Court and the Chapel at Brockstone."

"Chapel? Oh, yes, that's marked here, too. The Chapel; close by the Court, it seems to be. Does it belong to the Court?"

"Yes, sir, that's close up to the Court, only a step. Yes, that belong to the Court. My daughter, you see, sir, she's the keeper's wife now, and she live at the Court and look after things now the family's away."

"No one living there now, then?"

"No, sir, not for a number of years. The old gentleman, he lived there when I was a lad; and the lady, she lived on after him to very near upon ninety years of age. And then she died, and them that have it now, they've got this other place, in

Warwickshire I believe it is, and they don't do nothin' about lettin' the Court out; but Colonel Wildman, he have the shooting, and young Mr. Clark, he's the agent, he come over once in so many weeks to see to things, and my daughter's husband, he's the keeper."

"And who uses the Chapel? just the people round about, I suppose."

"Oh, no, no one don't use the Chapel. Why, there ain't no one to go. All the people about, they go to Stanford St. Thomas Church; but my son-in-law, he go to Kingsbourne Church now, because the gentleman at Stanford, he have this Gregory singin',⁵ and my son-in-law, he don't like that; he say he can hear the old donkey brayin' any day of the week, and he like something a little cheerful on the Sunday." The old man drew his hand across his mouth and laughed. "That's what my son-in-law say; he say he can hear the old donkey," etc., *da capo*.

Mr. Davidson also laughed as honestly as he could, thinking meanwhile that Brockstone Court and Chapel would probably be worth including in his walk; for the map showed that from Brockstone he could strike the Tent Valley quite as easily as by following the main Kingsbourne-Longbridge road. So, when the mirth excited by the remembrance of the son-in-law's *bon mot* had died down, he returned to the charge, and ascertained that both the Court and the Chapel were of the class known as "old-fashioned places," and that the old man would be very willing to take him thither, and his daughter would be happy to show him whatever she could.

"But that ain't a lot, sir, not as if the family was livin' there; all the lookin'-glasses is covered up, and the paintin's, and the curtains and carpets folded away; not but what I dare say she could show you a pair just to look at, because she go over them to see as the morth shouldn't get into 'em."

"I shan't mind about that, thank you; if she can show me the inside of the Chapel, that's what I'd like best to see."

"Oh, she can show you that right enough, sir. She have the key of the door, you see, and most weeks she go in and dust about. That's a nice Chapel, that is. My son-in-law, he say he'll be bound they didn't have none of this Gregory singin' there.

Dear! I can't help but smile when I think of him sayin' that about th' old donkey. 'I can hear him bray,' he say, 'any day of the week'; and so he can, sir; that's true, anyway."

The walk across the fields from Kingsbourne to Brockstone was very pleasant. It lay for the most part on the top of the country, and commanded wide views over a succession of ridges, plough and pasture, or covered with dark-blue woods—all ending, more or less abruptly, on the right, in headlands that overlooked the wide valley of a great western river. The last field they crossed was bounded by a close copse, and no sooner were they in it than the path turned downward very sharply, and it became evident that Brockstone was neatly fitted into a sudden and very narrow valley. It was not long before they had glimpses of groups of smokeless stone chimneys, and stone-tiled roofs, close beneath their feet; and, not many minutes after that, they were wiping their shoes at the back-door of Brockstone Court; while the keeper's dogs barked very loudly in unseen places, and Mrs. Porter, in quick succession, screamed at them to be quiet, greeted her father, and begged both her visitors to step in.

II

It was not to be expected that Mr. Davidson should escape being taken through the principal rooms of the Court, in spite of the fact that the house was entirely out of commission. Pictures, carpets, curtains, furniture, were all covered up or put away, as old Mr. Avery had said; and the admiration which our friend was very ready to bestow had to be lavished on the proportions of the rooms, and on the one painted ceiling, upon which an artist who had fled from London in the plague-year[6] had depicted the Triumph of Loyalty and Defeat of Sedition. In this Mr. Davidson could show an unfeigned interest. The portraits of Cromwell, Ireton, Bradshaw, Peters,[7] and the rest, writhing in carefully-devised torments, were evidently the part of the design to which most pains had been devoted.

"That were the old Lady Sadleir[8] had that paintin' done, same as the one what put up the Chapel. They say she were the first that went up to London to dance on Oliver Cromwell's grave." So said Mr. Avery, and continued musingly, "Well, I suppose she got some satisfaction to her mind, but I don't know as I should want to pay the fare to London and back just for that; and my son-in-law, he say the same; he say he don't know as he should have cared to pay all that money only for that. I was tellin' the gentleman as we come along in the train, Mary, what your 'Arry says about this Gregory singin' down at Stanford here. We 'ad a bit of a laugh over that, sir, didn't us?"

"Yes, to be sure we did; ha! ha!" Once again Mr. Davidson strove to do justice to the pleasantry of the keeper. "But," he said, "if Mrs. Porter can show me the Chapel, I think it should be now, for the days aren't long, and I want to get back to Longbridge before it falls quite dark."

Even if Brockstone Court has not been illustrated in *Rural Life*[9] (and I think it has not), I do not propose to point out its excellences here; but of the Chapel a word must be said. It stands about a hundred yards from the house, and has its own little graveyard and trees about it. It is a stone building about seventy feet long, and in the Gothic style, as that style was understood in the middle of the seventeenth century. On the whole it resembles some of the Oxford college chapels as much as anything, save that it has a distinct chancel, like a parish church, and a fanciful domed bell-turret at the south-west angle.

When the west door was thrown open, Mr. Davidson could not repress an exclamation of pleased surprise at the completeness and richness of the interior. Screen-work, pulpit, seating, and glass—all were of the same period; and as he advanced into the nave and sighted the organ-case with its gold embossed pipes in the western gallery, his cup of satisfaction was filled. The glass in the nave windows was chiefly armorial; and in the chancel were figure-subjects, of the kind that may be seen at Abbey Dore, of Lord Scudamore's work.[10]

But this is not an archæological review.

While Mr. Davidson was still busy examining the remains of the organ (attributed to one of the Dallams,[11] I believe), old Mr. Avery had stumped up into the chancel and was lifting the dust-cloths from the blue-velvet cushions of the stall-desks. Evidently it was here that the family sat.

Mr. Davidson heard him say in a rather hushed tone of surprise, "Why, Mary, here's all the books open agin!"

The reply was in a voice that sounded peevish rather than surprised. "Tt-tt-tt, well, there, I never!"

Mrs. Porter went over to where her father was standing, and they continued talking in a lower key. Mr. Davidson saw plainly that something not quite in the common run was under discussion; so he came down the gallery stairs and joined them. There was no sign of disorder in the chancel any more than in the rest of the Chapel, which was beautifully clean; but the eight folio Prayer-Books on the cushions of the stall-desks were indubitably open.

Mrs. Porter was inclined to be fretful over it. "Whoever can it be as does it?" she said: "for there's no key but mine, nor yet door but the one we come in by, and the winders is barred, every one of 'em; I don't like it, father, that I don't."

"What is it, Mrs. Porter? Anything wrong?" said Mr. Davidson.

"No, sir, nothing reely wrong, only these books. Every time, pretty near, that I come in to do up the place, I shuts 'em and spreads the cloths over 'em to keep off the dust, ever since Mr. Clark spoke about it, when I first come; and yet there they are again, and always the same page—and as I says, whoever it can be as does it with the door and winders shut; and as I says, it makes anyone feel queer comin' in here alone, as I 'ave to do, not as I'm given that way myself, not to be frightened easy, I mean to say; and there's not a rat in the place—not as no rat wouldn't trouble to do a thing like that, do you think, sir?"

"Hardly, I should say; but it sounds very queer. Are they always open at the same place, did you say?"

"Always the same place, sir, one of the psalms it is, and I didn't particular notice it the first time or two, till I see a little red line of printing, and it's always caught my eye since."

Mr. Davidson walked along the stalls and looked at the open books. Sure enough, they all stood at the same page: Psalm cix., and at the head of it, just between the number and the *Deus laudem*, was a rubric, "For the 25th day of April." Without pretending to minute knowledge of the history of the Book of Common Prayer, he knew enough to be sure that this was a very odd and wholly unauthorized addition to its text; and though he remembered that April 25 is St. Mark's Day, he could not imagine what appropriateness this very savage psalm[12] could have to that festival. With slight misgivings he ventured to turn over the leaves to examine the title-page, and knowing the need for particular accuracy in these matters, he devoted some ten minutes to making a line-for-line transcript of it. The date was 1653; the printer called himself Anthony Cadman. He turned to the list of proper psalms for certain days; yes, added to it was that same inexplicable entry: *For the 25th day of April: the 109th Psalm.* An expert would no doubt have thought of many other points to inquire into, but this antiquary, as I have said, was no expert. He took stock, however, of the binding—a handsome one of tooled blue leather, bearing the arms that figured in several of the nave windows in various combinations.

"How often," he said at last to Mrs. Porter, "have you found these books lying open like this?"

"Reely I couldn't say, sir, but it's a great many times now. Do you recollect, father, me telling you about it the first time I noticed it?"

"That I do, my dear; you was in a rare taking, and I don't so much wonder at it; that was five year ago I was paying you a visit at Michaelmas time, and you come in at tea-time, and says you, 'Father, there's the books laying open under the cloths agin'; and I didn't know what my daughter was speakin' about, you see, sir, and I says, 'Books?' just like that, I says; and then it all came out. But as Harry says,—that's my son-in-law, sir,— 'whoever it can be,' he says, 'as does it, because there ain't only the one door, and we keeps the key locked up,' he says, 'and the winders is barred, every one on 'em. Well,' he says, 'I lay once I could catch 'em at it, they wouldn't do it a second time,' he says. And no more they wouldn't, I don't believe, sir. Well, that was five year ago, and it's been happenin' constant ever since by your account, my dear. Young Mr. Clark, he don't seem to think much to it; but then he don't live here, you see, and 'tisn't his business to come and clean up here of a dark afternoon, is it?"

"I suppose you never notice anything else odd when you are at work here, Mrs. Porter?" said Mr. Davidson.

"No, sir, I do not," said Mrs. Porter, "and it's a funny thing to me I don't, with the feeling I have as there's someone settin' here—no, it's the other side, just within the screen—and lookin' at me all the time I'm dustin' in the gallery and pews. But I never yet see nothin' worse than myself, as the sayin' goes, and I kindly hope I never may."

III

In the conversation that followed (there was not much of it), nothing was added to the statement of the case. Having parted on good terms with Mr. Avery and his daughter, Mr. Davidson addressed himself to his eight-mile walk. The little valley of Brockstone soon led him down into the broader one of the Tent, and on to Stanford St. Thomas, where he found refreshment.

We need not accompany him all the way to Longbridge. But as he was changing his socks before dinner, he suddenly paused and said half-aloud, "By Jove, that is a rum thing!" It had not occurred to him before how strange it was that any edition of the Prayer-Book should have been issued in 1653, seven years before the Restoration, five years before Cromwell's death, and when the use of the book, let alone the printing of it, was penal.[13] He must have been a bold man who put his name and a date on that title-page. Only, Mr. Davidson reflected, it probably was not his name at all, for the ways of printers in difficult times were devious.

As he was in the front hall of the Swan that evening, making some investigations about trains, a small motor stopped in front of the door, and out of it came a small man in a fur coat, who stood on the steps and gave directions in a rather yapping foreign accent to his chauffeur. When he came into the hotel, he was seen to be black-haired and pale-faced, with a little pointed beard, and gold pince-nez; altogether, very neatly turned out.

He went to his room, and Mr. Davidson saw no more of him till dinner-time. As they were the only two dining that night, it was not difficult for the new-comer to find an excuse for falling into talk; he was evidently wishing to make out what brought Mr. Davidson into that neighbourhood at that season.

"Can you tell me how far it is from here to Arlingworth?"[14] was one of his early questions; and it was one which threw some light on his own plans; for Mr. Davidson recollected having seen at the station an advertisement of a sale at Arlingworth Hall, comprising old furniture, pictures, and books. This, then, was a London dealer.

"No," he said, "I've never been there. I believe it lies out by Kingsbourne—it can't be less than twelve miles. I see there's a sale there shortly."

The other looked at him inquisitively, and he laughed. "No," he said, as if answering a question, "you needn't be afraid of my competing; I'm leaving this place to-morrow."

This cleared the air, and the dealer, whose name was Homberger, admitted that he was interested in books, and thought there might be in these old country-house libraries something to repay a journey. "For," said he, "we English have always this marvellous talent for accumulating rarities in the most unexpected places, ain't it?"

And in the course of the evening he was most interesting on the subject of finds made by himself and others. "I shall take the occasion after this sale to look round the district a bit; perhaps you could inform me of some likely spots, Mr. Davidson?"

But Mr. Davidson, though he had seen some very tempting locked-up book-cases at Brockstone Court, kept his counsel. He did not really like Mr. Homberger.

Next day, as he sat in the train, a little ray of light came to illuminate one of yesterday's puzzles. He happened to take out an almanac-diary that he had bought for the new year, and it occurred to him to look at the remarkable events for April 25. There it was: "St. Mark. Oliver Cromwell born, 1599."

That, coupled with the painted ceiling, seemed to explain a good deal. The figure of old Lady Sadleir became more substantial to his imagination, as of one in whom love for Church and King had gradually given place to intense hate of the power that had silenced the one and slaughtered the other. What curious evil service was that which she and a few like her had been wont to celebrate year by year in that remote valley? and how in the world had she managed to elude authority? And again, did not this persistent opening of the books agree oddly with the other traits of her portrait known to him? It would be interesting for anyone who chanced to be near Brockstone on the twenty-fifth of April to look in at the Chapel and see if anything exceptional happened. When he came to think of it, there seemed to be no reason why he should not be that person himself; he, and if possible, some congenial friend. He resolved that so it should be.

Knowing that he knew really nothing about the printing of Prayer-Books, he realized that he must make it his business to get the best light on the matter without divulging his reasons. I may say at once that his search was entirely fruitless. One writer of the early part of the nineteenth century, a writer of rather windy and rhapsodical chat about books, professed to have heard of a special anti-Cromwellian issue of the Prayer-Book in the very midst of the Commonwealth period. But he did not claim to have seen a copy, and no one had believed him. Looking into this matter, Mr. Davidson found that the statement was based on letters from a correspondent who had lived near Longbridge; so he was inclined to think that the Brockstone Prayer-Books were at the bottom of it, and had excited a momentary interest.

Months went on, and St. Mark's Day came near. Nothing interfered with Mr. Davidson's plans of visiting Brockstone, or with those of the friend whom he had persuaded to go with him, and to whom alone he had confided the puzzle. The same 9.45 train which had taken him in January took them now to Kingsbourne; the same field-path led them to Brockstone. But to-day they stopped more than once to pick a cowslip; the distant woods and ploughed uplands were of another colour, and in the copse there was, as Mrs. Porter said, "a regular charm of birds; why you couldn't hardly collect your mind sometimes with it."

She recognized Mr. Davidson at once, and was very ready to do the honours of the Chapel. The new visitor, Mr. Witham, was as much struck by the completeness of it as Mr. Davidson had been. "There can't be such another in England," he said.

"Books open again, Mrs. Porter?" said Davidson, as they walked up to the chancel.

"Dear, yes, I expect so, sir," said Mrs. Porter, as she drew off the cloths. "Well, there!" she exclaimed the next moment, "if they ain't shut! That's the first time ever I've found 'em so. But it's not for want of care on my part, I do assure you, gentlemen, if they wasn't, for I felt the cloths the last thing before I shut up last week, when the gentleman had done photografting the heast winder, and every one was shut, and where there was ribbons left, I tied 'em. Now I think of it, I don't remember ever to 'ave done that before, and per'aps, whoever it is, it just made the difference to 'em. Well, it only shows, don't it? if at first you don't succeed, try, try, try again."

Meanwhile the two men had been examining the books, and now Davidson spoke.

"I'm sorry to say I'm afraid there's something wrong here, Mrs. Porter. These are not the same books."

It would make too long a business to detail all Mrs. Porter's outcries, and the questionings that followed. The upshot was this. Early in January the gentleman had come to see over the Chapel, and thought a great deal of it, and said he must come back in the spring weather and take some photografts. And only a week ago he had drove up in his motoring car, and a very 'eavy box with the slides in it, and she had locked him in because he said something about a long explosion, and she was afraid of some damage happening; and he says, no, not explosion, but it appeared the lantern what they take the slides with worked very slow; and so he was in there the best part of an hour and she come and let him out, and he drove off with his box and all and gave her his visiting-card, and oh, dear, dear, to think of such a thing! he must have changed the books and took the old ones away with him in his box.

"What sort of man was he?"

"Oh, dear, he was a small-made gentleman, if you can call

him so after the way he've behaved, with black hair, that is if it was hair, and gold eye-glasses, if they was gold; reely, one don't know what to believe. Sometimes I doubt he weren't a reel Englishman at all, and yet he seemed to know the language, and had the name on his visiting-card like anybody else might."

"Just so; might we see the card? Yes; T. W. Henderson, and an address somewhere near Bristol. Well, Mrs. Porter, it's quite plain this Mr. Henderson, as he calls himself, has walked off with your eight Prayer-Books and put eight others about the same size in place of them. Now listen to me. I suppose you must tell your husband about this, but neither you nor he must say one word about it to anyone else. If you'll give me the address of the agent,—Mr. Clark, isn't it?—I will write to him and tell him exactly what has happened, and that it really is no fault of yours. But, you understand, we must keep it very quiet; and why? Because this man who has stolen the books will of course try to sell them one at a time—for I may tell you they are worth a good deal of money—and the only way we can bring it home to him is by keeping a sharp look out and saying nothing."

By dint of repeating the same advice in various forms, they succeeded in impressing Mrs. Porter with the real need for silence, and were forced to make a concession only in the case of Mr. Avery, who was expected on a visit shortly. "But you may be safe with father, sir," said Mrs. Porter. "Father ain't a talkin' man."

It was not quite Mr. Davidson's experience of him; still, there were no neighbours at Brockstone, and even Mr. Avery must be aware that gossip with anybody on such a subject would be likely to end in the Porters having to look out for another situation.

A last question was whether Mr. Henderson, so-called, had anyone with him.

"No, sir, not when he come he hadn't; he was working his own motoring car himself, and what luggage he had, let me see: there was his lantern and this box of slides inside the carriage, which I helped him into the Chapel and out of it myself with it, if only I'd knowed! And as he drove away under the big yew tree by the monument, I see the long white bundle laying on the

top of the coach, what I didn't notice when he drove up. But he
set in front, sir, and only the boxes inside behind him. And do
you reely think, sir, as his name weren't Henderson at all? Oh,
dear me, what a dreadful thing! Why, fancy what trouble it
might bring to a innocent person that might never have set foot
in the place but for that!"

They left Mrs. Porter in tears. On the way home there was
much discussion as to the best means of keeping watch upon
possible sales. What Henderson-Homberger (for there could be
no real doubt of the identity) had done was, obviously, to bring
down the requisite number of folio Prayer-Books—disused copies
from college chapels and the like, bought ostensibly for the sake
of the bindings, which were superficially like enough to the old
ones—and to substitute them at his leisure for the genuine articles. A week had now passed without any public notice being
taken of the theft. He would take a little time himself to find
out about the rarity of the books, and would ultimately, no
doubt, "place" them cautiously. Between them, Davidson and
Witham were in a position to know a good deal of what was
passing in the book-world, and they could map out the ground
pretty completely. A weak point with them at the moment was
that neither of them knew under what other name or names
Henderson-Homberger carried on business. But there are ways
of solving these problems.

And yet all this planning proved unnecessary.

IV

We are transported to a London office on this same 25th of
April. We find there, within closed doors, late in the day, two
police inspectors, a commissionaire, and a youthful clerk. The
two latter, both rather pale and agitated in appearance, are sitting on chairs and being questioned.

"How long do you say you've been in this Mr. Poschwitz's
employment? Six months? And what was his business? Attended sales in various parts and brought home parcels of
books. Did he keep a shop anywhere? No? Disposed of 'em

here and there, and sometimes to private collectors. Right. Now then, when did he go out last? Rather better than a week ago? Tell you where he was going? No? Said he was going to start next day from his private residence, and shouldn't be at the office—that's here, eh?—before two days; you was to attend as usual. Where is his private residence? Oh, that's the address, Norwood[15] way; I see. Any family? Not in this country? Now, then, what account do you give of what's happened since he came back? Came back on the Tuesday, did he? and this is the Saturday. Bring any books? One package; where is it? In the safe? You got the key? No, to be sure, it's open, of course. How did he seem when he got back—cheerful? Well, but how do you mean—curious? Thought he might be in for an illness: he said that, did he? Odd smell got in his nose, couldn't get rid of it; told you to let him know who wanted to see him before you let 'em in? That wasn't usual with him? Much the same all Wednesday, Thursday, Friday. Out a good deal; said he was going to the British Museum. Often went there to make inquiries in the way of his business. Walked up and down a lot in the office when he was in. Anyone call in on those days? Mostly when he was out. Anyone find him in? Oh, Mr. Collinson? Who's Mr. Collinson? An old customer; know his address? All right, give it us afterwards. Well, now, what about this morning? You left Mr. Poschwitz's here at twelve and went home. Anybody see you? Commissionaire, you did? Remained at home till summoned here. Very well.

"Now, commissionaire; we have your name—Watkins, eh? Very well, make your statement; don't go too quick, so as we can get it down."

"I was on duty 'ere later than usual, Mr. Potwitch 'aving asked me to remain on, and ordered his lunching to be sent in, which came as ordered. I was in the lobby from eleven-thirty on, and see Mr. Bligh [the clerk] leave at about twelve. After that no one come in at all except Mr. Potwitch's lunching come at one o'clock and the man left in five minutes' time. Towards the afternoon I became tired of waitin' and I come upstairs to this first floor. The outer door what lead to the orfice stood open, and I come up to the plate-glass door here. Mr. Potwitch he was standing behind the table smoking a cigar, and he laid it down on the mantelpiece and felt in his trouser pockets and took out a key and went across to the safe. And I knocked on the glass, thinkin' to see if he wanted me to come and take away his tray; but he didn't take no notice, bein' engaged with the safe door. Then he got it open and stooped down and seemed to be lifting up a package off of the floor of the safe. And then, sir, I see what looked to be like a great roll of old shabby white flannel, about four to five feet high, fall for'ards out of the inside of the safe right against Mr. Potwitch's shoulder as he was stooping over; and Mr. Potwitch, he raised himself up as it were, resting his hands on the package, and gave a exclamation. And I can't hardly expect you should take what I says, but as true as I stand here I see this roll had a kind of a face in the upper end of it, sir.[16] You can't be more surprised than what I was, I can assure you, and I've seen a lot in me time. Yes, I can describe it if you wish it, sir; it was very much the same as this wall here in colour [the wall had an earth-coloured distemper] and it had a bit of a band tied round underneath. And the eyes, well they was dry-like, and much as if there was two big spiders' bodies in the holes. Hair? no, I don't know as there was much hair to be seen; the flannel-stuff was over the top of the 'ead. I'm very sure it warn't what it should have been. No, I only see it in a flash, but I took it in like a photograft—wish I hadn't. Yes, sir, it fell right over on to Mr. Potwitch's shoulder, and this face hid in his neck,—yes, sir, about where the injury was,—more like a ferret going for a rabbit than anythink else; and he rolled over, and of course I tried to get in at the door; but as you know, sir, it were locked on the inside, and all I could do, I rung up everyone, and the surgeon come, and the police and you gentlemen, and you know as much as what I do. If you won't be requirin' me any more to-day I'd be glad to be getting off home; it's shook me up more than I thought for."

"Well," said one of the inspectors, when they were left alone; and "Well?" said the other inspector; and, after a pause, "What's the surgeon's report again? You've got it there. Yes. Effect on the blood like the worst kind of snake-bite; death almost instantaneous. I'm glad of that, for his sake; he was a nasty sight. No case for detaining this man Watkins, anyway; we know all about him. And what about this safe, now? We'd better go over it again; and, by the way, we haven't opened that package he was busy with when he died."

"Well, handle it careful," said the other; "there might be this snake in it, for what you know. Get a light into the corners of the place, too. Well, there's room for a shortish person to stand up in; but what about ventilation?"

"Perhaps," said the other slowly, as he explored the safe with an electric torch, "perhaps they didn't require much of that. My word! it strikes warm coming out of that place! like a vault, it is. But here, what's this bank-like of dust all spread out into the room? That must have come there since the door was opened; it would sweep it all away if you moved it—see? Now what do you make of that?"

"Make of it? About as much as I make of anything else in this case. One of London's mysteries this is going to be, by what I can see. And I don't believe a photographer's box full of large-size old-fashioned Prayer-Books is going to take us much further. For that's just what your package is."

It was a natural but hasty utterance. The preceding narrative shows that there was, in fact, plenty of material for constructing a case; and when once Messrs. Davidson and Witham had brought their end to Scotland Yard, the join-up was soon made, and the circle completed.

To the relief of Mrs. Porter, the owners of Brockstone decided not to replace the books in the Chapel; they repose, I believe, in a safe-deposit in town. The police have their own methods of keeping certain matters out of the newspapers; otherwise, it can hardly be supposed that Watkins's evidence about Mr. Poschwitz's death could have failed to furnish a good many head-lines of a startling character to the press.

A NEIGHBOUR'S
LANDMARK

Those who spend the greater part of their time in reading or writing books are, of course, apt to take rather particular notice of accumulations of books when they come across them. They will not pass a stall, a shop, or even a bedroom-shelf without reading some title, and if they find themselves in an unfamiliar library, no host need trouble himself further about their entertainment. The putting of dispersed sets of volumes together, or the turning right way up of those which the dusting housemaid has left in an apoplectic condition, appeals to them as one of the lesser Works of Mercy.[1] Happy in these employments, and in occasionally opening an eighteenth-century octavo, to see "what it is all about," and to conclude after five minutes that it deserves the seclusion it now enjoys, I had reached the middle of a wet August afternoon at Betton Court—

"You begin in a deeply Victorian manner," I said; "is this to continue?"

"Remember, if you please," said my friend, looking at me over his spectacles, "that I am a Victorian by birth and education, and that the Victorian tree may not unreasonably be expected to bear Victorian fruit. Further, remember that an immense quantity of clever and thoughtful Rubbish is now being written about the Victorian age. Now," he went on, laying his papers on his knee, "that article, 'The Stricken Years,' in *The Times* Literary Supplement[2] the other day,—able? of course it is able; but, oh! my soul and body, do just hand it over here, will you? it's on the table by you."

"I thought you were to read me something you had written," I said, without moving, "but, of course—"

"Yes, I know," he said. "Very well, then, I'll do that first. But I *should* like to show you afterwards what I mean. However—" And he lifted the sheets of paper and adjusted his spectacles.

—at Betton Court, where, generations back, two country-house libraries had been fused together, and no descendant of either stock had ever faced the task of picking them over or getting rid of duplicates. Now I am not setting out to tell of rarities I may have discovered, of Shakespeare quartos bound up in volumes of political tracts, or anything of that kind, but of an experience which befell me in the course of my search—an experience which I cannot either explain away or fit into the scheme of my ordinary life.

It was, I said, a wet August afternoon, rather windy, rather warm. Outside the window great trees were stirring and weeping. Between them were stretches of green and yellow country (for the Court stands high on a hill-side), and blue hills far off, veiled with rain. Up above was a very restless and hopeless movement of low clouds travelling north-west. I had suspended my work—if you call it work—for some minutes to stand at the window and look at these things, and at the greenhouse roof on the right with the water sliding off it, and the Church tower that rose behind that. It was all in favour of my going steadily on; no likelihood of a clearing up for hours to come. I, therefore, returned to the shelves, lifted out a set of eight or nine volumes, lettered "Tracts," and conveyed them to the table for closer examination.

They were for the most part of the reign of Anne. There was a good deal of *The Late Peace, The Late War, The Conduct of the Allies*:[3] there were also *Letters to a Convocation Man*; *Sermons preached at St. Michael's, Queenhithe*; *Enquiries into a late Charge of the Rt. Rev. the Lord Bishop of Winchester* (or more probably Winton) *to his Clergy*:[4] things all very lively once, and indeed still keeping so much of their old sting that I was tempted to betake myself into an arm-chair in the window, and give them more time than I had intended. Besides, I was somewhat tired by the day. The Church clock struck four, and it really was four, for in 1889 there was no saving of daylight. So I settled myself. And first I glanced over some of the War pamphlets, and pleased myself by trying to pick out Swift by his style from among the undistinguished.[5] But the War pamphlets needed more knowledge of the geography of the Low Countries than I had. I turned to the Church, and read several pages of what the Dean of Canterbury said to the Society for Promoting Christian Knowledge on the occasion of their anniversary meeting in 1711.[6] When I turned over to a Letter from a Beneficed Clergyman in the Country to the Bishop of C . . . . r, I was becoming languid, and I gazed for some moments at the following sentence without surprise:

"This Abuse (for I think myself justified in calling it by that name) is one which I am persuaded Your Lordship would (if 'twere known to you) exert your utmost efforts to do away. But I am also persuaded that you know no more of its existence than (in the words of the Country Song)

'That which walks in Betton Wood
Knows why it walks or why it cries.' "[7]

Then indeed I did sit up in my chair, and run my finger along the lines to make sure that I had read them right. There was no mistake. Nothing more was to be gathered from the rest of the pamphlet. The next paragraph definitely changed the subject: "But I have said enough upon this *Topick*" were its opening words. So discreet, too, was the namelessness of the Beneficed Clergyman that he refrained even from initials, and had his letter printed in London.

The riddle was of a kind that might faintly interest anyone: to me, who have dabbled a good deal in works of folk-lore, it was really exciting. I was set upon solving it—on finding out, I mean, what story lay behind it; and, at least, I felt myself lucky in one point, that, whereas I might have come on the paragraph in some College Library far away, here I was at Betton, on the very scene of action.

The Church clock struck five, and a single stroke on a gong followed. This, I knew, meant tea. I heaved myself out of the deep chair, and obeyed the summons.

My host and I were alone at the Court. He came in soon, wet

from a round of landlord's errands, and with pieces of local news which had to be passed on before I could make an opportunity of asking whether there was a particular place in the parish that was still known as Betton Wood.

"Betton Wood," he said, "was a short mile away, just on the crest of Betton Hill, and my father stubbed up the last bit of it when it paid better to grow corn than scrub oaks. Why do you want to know about Betton Wood?"

"Because," I said, "in an old pamphlet I was reading just now, there are two lines of a country song which mention it, and they sound as if there was a story belonging to them. Someone says that someone else knows no more of whatever it may be—

'Than that which walks in Betton Wood
Knows why it walks or why it cries.'"

"Goodness," said Philipson, "I wonder whether that was why . . . I must ask old Mitchell." He muttered something else to himself, and took some more tea, thoughtfully.

"Whether that was why—?" I said.

"Yes, I was going to say, whether that was why my father had the Wood stubbed up. I said just now it was to get more ploughland, but I don't really know if it was. I don't believe he ever broke it up: it's rough pasture at this moment. But there's one old chap at least who'd remember something of it—old Mitchell." He looked at his watch. "Blest if I don't go down there and ask him. I don't think I'll take you," he went on; "he's not so likely to tell anything he thinks is odd if there's a stranger by."

"Well, mind you remember every single thing he does tell. As for me, if it clears up, I shall go out, and if it doesn't, I shall go on with the books."

It did clear up, sufficiently at least to make me think it worth while to walk up the nearest hill and look over the country. I did not know the lie of the land; it was the first visit I had paid to Philipson, and this was the first day of it. So I went down the garden and through the wet shrubberies with a very open mind, and offered no resistance to the indistinct impulse—was it, however, so very indistinct?—which kept urging me to bear to the left whenever there was a forking of the path. The result was that after ten minutes or more of dark going between dripping rows of box and laurel and privet, I was confronted by a stone arch in the Gothic style set in the stone wall which encircled the whole demesne. The door was fastened by a spring-lock, and I took the precaution of leaving this on the jar as I passed out into the road. That road I crossed, and entered a narrow lane between hedges which led upward; and that lane I pursued at a leisurely pace for as much as half a mile, and went on to the field to which it led. I was now on a good point of vantage for taking in the situation of the Court, the village, and the environment; and I leant upon a gate and gazed westward and downward.

I think we must all know the landscapes—are they by Birket Foster,[8] or somewhat earlier?—which, in the form of wood-cuts, decorate the volumes of poetry that lay on the drawing-room tables of our fathers and grandfathers—volumes in "Art Cloth, embossed bindings"; that strikes me as being the right phrase. I confess myself an admirer of them, and especially of those which show the peasant leaning over a gate in a hedge and surveying, at the bottom of a downward slope, the village church spire—embosomed amid venerable trees, and a fertile plain intersected by hedgerows, and bounded by distant hills, behind which the orb of day is sinking (or it may be rising) amid level clouds illumined by his dying (or nascent) ray. The expressions employed here are those which seem appropriate to the pictures I have in mind; and were there opportunity, I would try to work in the Vale, the Grove, the Cot, and the Flood. Anyhow, they are beautiful to me, these landscapes, and it was just such a one that I was now surveying. It might have come straight out of "Gems of Sacred Song, selected by a Lady" and given as a birthday present to Eleanor Philipson in 1852 by her attached friend Millicent Graves. All at once I turned as if I had been stung. There thrilled into my right ear and pierced my head a note of incredible sharpness, like the shriek of a bat, only ten times intensified—the kind of thing that makes one wonder if something has not given way in one's brain. I held my breath, and covered my ear, and shivered. Something in the circulation: another minute or two, I thought, and I return home. But I must fix the view a little more firmly in my mind. Only, when I turned to it again, the taste was gone out of it. The sun was down behind the hill, and the light was off the fields, and when the clock bell in the Church tower struck seven, I thought no longer of kind mellow evening hours of rest, and scents of flowers and woods on evening air; and of how someone on a farm a mile or two off would be saying "How clear Betton bell sounds to-night after the rain!"; but instead images came to me of dusty beams and creeping spiders and savage owls up in the tower, and forgotten graves and their ugly contents below, and of flying Time and all it had taken out of my life. And just then into my left ear—close as if lips had been put within an inch of my head, the frightful scream came thrilling again.

There was no mistake possible now. It *was* from outside. "With no language but a cry"[9] was the thought that flashed into my mind. Hideous it was beyond anything I had heard or have heard since, but I could read no emotion in it, and doubted if I could read any intelligence. All its effect was to take away every vestige, every possibility, of enjoyment, and make this no place to stay in one moment more. Of course there was nothing to be seen: but I was convinced that, if I waited, the thing would pass me again on its aimless, endless beat, and I could not bear the notion of a third repetition. I hurried back to the lane and down the hill. But when I came to the arch in the wall I stopped. Could I be sure of my way among those dank alleys, which would be danker and darker now! No, I confessed to myself that I was afraid: so jarred were all my nerves with the cry on the hill that I really felt I could not afford to be startled even by a little bird in a bush, or a rabbit. I followed the road which followed the wall, and I was not sorry when I came to the gate and the lodge, and descried Philipson coming up towards it from the direction of the village.

"And where have you been?" said he.

"I took that lane that goes up the hill opposite the stone arch in the wall."

"Oh! did you? Then you've been very near where Betton Wood used to be: at least, if you followed it up to the top, and out into the field."

And if the reader will believe it, that was the first time that I put two and two together. Did I at once tell Philipson what had happened to me? I did not. I have not had other experiences of the kind which are called super-natural, or -normal, or -physical, but, though I knew very well I must speak of this one before long, I was not at all anxious to do so; and I think I have read that this is a common case.

So all I said was: "Did you see the old man you meant to?"

"Old Mitchell? Yes, I did; and got something of a story out of him. I'll keep it till after dinner. It really is rather odd."

So when we were settled after dinner he began to report, faithfully, as he said, the dialogue that had taken place. Mitchell, not far off eighty years old, was in his elbow-chair. The married daughter with whom he lived was in and out preparing for tea.

After the usual salutations: "Mitchell, I want you to tell me something about the Wood."

"What Wood's that, Master Reginald?"

"Betton Wood. Do you remember it?"

Mitchell slowly raised his hand and pointed an accusing forefinger. "It were your father done away with Betton Wood, Master Reginald, I can tell you that much."

"Well, I know it was, Mitchell. You needn't look at me as if it were my fault."

"Your fault? No, I says it were your father done it, before your time."

"Yes, and I dare say if the truth was known, it was your father that advised him to do it, and I want to know why."

Mitchell seemed a little amused. "Well," he said, "my father were woodman to your father and your grandfather before him, and if he didn't know what belonged to his business, he'd oughter done. And if he did give advice that way, I suppose he might have had his reasons, mightn't he now?"

"Of course he might, and I want you to tell me what they were."

"Well now, Master Reginald, whatever makes you think as I

know what his reasons might 'a been I don't know how many year ago?"

"Well, to be sure, it is a long time, and you might easily have forgotten, if ever you knew. I suppose the only thing is for me to go and ask old Ellis what he can recollect about it."

That had the effect I hoped for.

"Old Ellis!" he growled. "First time ever I hear anyone say old Ellis were any use for any purpose. I should 'a thought you know'd better than that yourself, Master Reginald. What do you suppose old Ellis can tell you better'n what I can about Betton Wood, and what call have he got to be put afore me, I should like to know. His father warn't woodman on the place: he were ploughman—that's what he was, and so anyone could tell you what he knows; anyone could tell you that, I says."

"Just so, Mitchell, but if you know all about Betton Wood and won't tell me, why, I must do the next best I can, and try and get it out of somebody else; and old Ellis has been on the place very nearly as long as you have."

"That he ain't, not by eighteen months! Who says I wouldn't tell you nothing about the Wood? I ain't no objection; only it's a funny kind of a tale, and 'taint right to my thinkin' it should be all about the parish. You, Lizzie, do you keep in your kitchen a bit. Me and Master Reginald wants to have a word or two private. But one thing I'd like to know, Master Reginald, what come to put you upon asking about it to-day?"

"Oh! well, I happened to hear of an old saying about something that walks in Betton Wood. And I wondered if that had anything to do with its being cleared away: that's all."

"Well, you was in the right, Master Reginald, however you come to hear of it, and I believe I can tell you the rights of it better than anyone in this parish, let alone old Ellis. You see it came about this way: that the shortest road to Allen's Farm laid through the Wood, and when we was little my poor mother she used to go so many times in the week to the farm to fetch a quart of milk, because Mr. Allen what had the farm then under your father, he was a good man, and anyone that had a young family to bring up, he was willing to allow 'em so much in the week. But never you mind about that now. And my poor mother

she never liked to go through the Wood, because there was a lot
of talk in the place, and sayings like what you spoke about just
now. But every now and again, when she happened to be late
with her work, she'd have to take the short road through the
Wood, and as sure as ever she did, she'd come home in a rare
state. I remember her and my father talking about it, and he'd
say, 'Well, but it can't do you no harm, Emma,' and she'd say,
'Oh! but you haven't an idear of it, George. Why, it went right
through my head,' she says, 'and I came over all bewildered-
like, and as if I didn't know where I was. You see, George,' she
says, 'it ain't as if you was about there in the dusk. You always
goes there in the daytime, now don't you?' and he says: 'Why,
to be sure I do; do you take me for a fool?' And so they'd go on.
And time passed by, and I think it wore her out, because, you
understand, it warn't no use to go for the milk not till the afternoon, and she wouldn't never send none of us children instead,
for fear we should get a fright. Nor she wouldn't tell us about it
herself. 'No,' she says, 'it's bad enough for me. I don't want no
one else to go through it, nor yet hear talk about it.' But one
time I recollect she says, 'Well, first it's a rustling-like all along
in the bushes, coming very quick, either towards me or after me
according to the time, and then there comes this scream as appears to pierce right through from the one ear to the other, and
the later I am coming through, the more like I am to hear it
twice over; but thanks be, I never yet heard it the three times.'
And then I asked her, and I says: 'Why, that seems like someone
walking to and fro all the time, don't it?' and she says, 'Yes, it
do, and whatever it is she wants, I can't think': and I says, 'Is it
a woman, mother?' and she says, 'Yes, I've heard it is a woman.'

"Anyway, the end of it was my father he spoke to your father,
and told him the Wood was a bad wood. 'There's never a bit of
game in it, and there's never a bird's nest there,' he says, 'and it
ain't no manner of use to you.' And after a lot of talk, your father he come and see my mother about it, and he see she warn't
one of these silly women as gets nervish about nothink at all,
and he made up his mind there was somethink in it, and after
that he asked about in the neighbourhood, and I believe he
made out somethink, and wrote it down in a paper what very

like you've got up at the Court, Master Reginald. And then he gave the order, and the Wood was stubbed up. They done all the work in the daytime, I recollect, and was never there after three o'clock."

"Didn't they find anything to explain it, Mitchell? No bones or anything of that kind?"

"Nothink at all, Master Reginald, only the mark of a hedge and ditch along the middle, much about where the quickset hedge run now; and with all the work they done, if there had been anyone put away there, they was bound to find 'em. But I don't know whether it done much good, after all. People here don't seem to like the place no better than they did afore."

"That's about what I got out of Mitchell," said Philipson, "and as far as any explanation goes, it leaves us very much where we were. I must see if I can't find that paper."

"Why didn't your father ever tell you about the business?" I said.

"He died before I went to school, you know, and I imagine he didn't want to frighten us children by any such story. I can remember being shaken and slapped by my nurse for running up that lane towards the Wood when we were coming back rather late one winter afternoon: but in the daytime no one interfered with our going into the Wood if we wanted to—only we never did want."

"Hm!" I said, and then, "Do you think you'll be able to find that paper that your father wrote?"

"Yes," he said, "I do. I expect it's no farther away than that cupboard behind you. There's a bundle or two of things specially put aside, most of which I've looked through at various times, and I know there's one envelope labelled Betton Wood: but as there was no Betton Wood any more, I never thought it would be worth while to open it, and I never have. We'll do it now, though."

"Before you do," I said (I was still reluctant, but I thought this was perhaps the moment for my disclosure), "I'd better tell you I think Mitchell was right when he doubted if clearing away the Wood had put things straight." And I gave the account you have heard already: I need not say Philipson was interested.

"Still there?" he said. "It's amazing. Look here, will you come out there with me now, and see what happens?"

"I will do no such thing," I said, "and if you knew the feeling, you'd be glad to walk ten miles in the opposite direction. Don't talk of it. Open your envelope, and let's hear what your father made out."

He did so, and read me the three or four pages of jottings which it contained. At the top was written a motto from Scott's *Glenfinlas,* which seemed to me well-chosen:

"Where walks, they say, the shrieking ghost."[10]

Then there were notes of his talk with Mitchell's mother, from which I extract only this much. "I asked her if she never thought she saw anything to account for the sounds she heard. She told me, no more than once, on the darkest evening she ever came through the Wood; and then she seemed forced to look behind her as the rustling came in the bushes, and she thought she saw something all in tatters with the two arms held out in front of it coming on very fast, and at that she ran for the stile, and tore her gown all to flinders getting over it."

Then he had gone to two other people whom he found very shy of talking. They seemed to think, among other things, that it reflected discredit on the parish. However, one, Mrs. Emma Frost, was prevailed upon to repeat what her mother had told her. "They say it was a lady of title that married twice over, and her first husband went by the name of Brown, or it might have been Bryan ("Yes, there were Bryans at the Court before it came into our family," Philipson put in), and she removed her neighbour's landmark: leastways she took in a fair piece of the best pasture in Betton parish what belonged by rights to two children as hadn't no one to speak for them, and they say years after she went from bad to worse, and made out false papers to gain thousands of pounds up in London, and at last they was proved in law to be false, and she would have been tried and put to death very like, only she escaped away for the time. But no one can't avoid the curse that's laid on them that removes the landmark, and so we take it she can't leave Betton before someone take and put it right again."

At the end of the paper there was a note to this effect. "I regret that I cannot find any clue to previous owners of the fields adjoining the Wood. I do not hesitate to say that if I could discover their representatives, I should do my best to indemnify them for the wrong done to them in years now long past: for it is undeniable that the Wood is very curiously disturbed in the manner described by the people of the place. In my present ignorance alike of the extent of the land wrongly appropriated, and of the rightful owners, I am reduced to keeping a separate note of the profits derived from this part of the estate, and my custom has been to apply the sum that would represent the annual yield of about five acres to the common benefit of the parish and to charitable uses: and I hope that those who succeed me may see fit to continue this practice."

So much for the elder Mr. Philipson's paper. To those who, like myself, are readers of the State Trials[11] it will have gone far to illuminate the situation. They will remember how between the years 1678 and 1684 the Lady Ivy, formerly Theodosia Bryan, was alternately Plaintiff and Defendant in a series of trials in which she was trying to establish a claim against the Dean and Chapter of St. Paul's for a considerable and very valuable tract of land in Shadwell:[12] how in the last of those trials, presided over by L.C.J. Jeffreys,[13] it was proved up to the hilt that the deeds upon which she based her claim were forgeries executed under her orders: and how, after an information for perjury and forgery was issued against her, she disappeared completely—so completely, indeed, that no expert has ever been able to tell me what became of her.

Does not the story I have told suggest that she may still be heard of on the scene of one of her earlier and more successful exploits?

"That," said my friend, as he folded up his papers, "is a very faithful record of my one extraordinary experience. And now—"

But I had so many questions to ask him, as for instance, whether his friend had found the proper owner of the land, whether he had done anything about the hedge, whether the sounds were ever heard now, what was the exact title and date of his pamphlet, etc., etc., that bed-time came and passed, without his having an opportunity to revert to the Literary Supplement of *The Times*.

———

[Thanks to the researches of Sir John Fox, in his book on *The Lady Ivie's Trial* (Oxford, 1929), we now know that my heroine died in her bed in 1695, having—heaven knows how—been acquitted of the forgery, for which she had undoubtedly been responsible.]

A VIEW FROM A HILL

How pleasant it can be, alone in a first-class railway carriage, on the first day of a holiday that is to be fairly long, to dawdle through a bit of English country that is unfamiliar, stopping at every station. You have a map open on your knee, and you pick out the villages that lie to right and left by their church towers. You marvel at the complete stillness that attends your stoppage at the stations, broken only by a footstep crunching the gravel. Yet perhaps that is best experienced after sundown, and the traveller I have in mind was making his leisurely progress on a sunny afternoon in the latter half of June.

He was in the depths of the country. I need not particularize further than to say that if you divided the map of England into four quarters, he would have been found in the south-western of them.

He was a man of academic pursuits, and his term was just over. He was on his way to meet a new friend, older than himself. The two of them had met first on an official inquiry in town, had found that they had many tastes and habits in common, liked each other, and the result was an invitation from Squire Richards[1] to Mr. Fanshawe which was now taking effect.

The journey ended about five o'clock. Fanshawe was told by a cheerful country porter that the car from the Hall had been up to the station and left a message that something had to be fetched from half a mile farther on, and would the gentleman please to wait a few minutes till it came back? "But I see," continued the porter, "as you've got your bysticle, and very like you'd find it pleasanter to ride up to the 'All yourself. Straight up the road 'ere, and then first turn to the left—it ain't above two mile—and I'll see as your things is put in the car for you. You'll excuse me mentioning it, only I thought it were a nice evening for a ride. Yes, sir, very seasonable weather for the hay-makers: let me see, I have your bike ticket. Thank you, sir; much obliged: you can't miss your road, etc., etc."

The two miles to the Hall were just what was needed, after the day in the train, to dispel somnolence and impart a wish for tea. The Hall, when sighted, also promised just what was needed in the way of a quiet resting-place after days of sitting on committees and college-meetings. It was neither excitingly old nor depressingly new. Plastered walls, sash-windows, old trees, smooth lawns, were the features which Fanshawe noticed as he came up the drive. Squire Richards, a burly man of sixty odd, was awaiting him in the porch with evident pleasure.

"Tea first," he said, "or would you like a longer drink? No? All right, tea's ready in the garden. Come along, they'll put your machine away. I always have tea under the lime-tree by the stream on a day like this."

Nor could you ask for a better place. Midsummer afternoon, shade and scent of a vast lime-tree, cool, swirling water within five yards. It was long before either of them suggested a move. But about six, Mr. Richards sat up, knocked out his pipe, and said: "Look here, it's cool enough now to think of a stroll, if you're inclined? All right: then what I suggest is that we walk up the park and get on to the hill-side, where we can look over the country. We'll have a map, and I'll show you where things are; and you can go off on your machine, or we can take the car, ac-cording as you want exercise or not. If you're ready, we can start now and be back well before eight, taking it very easy."

"I'm ready. I should like my stick, though, and have you got any field-glasses? I lent mine to a man a week ago, and he's gone off Lord knows where and taken them with him."

Mr. Richards pondered. "Yes," he said, "I have, but they're not things I use myself, and I don't know whether the ones I have will suit you. They're old-fashioned, and about twice as heavy as they make 'em now. You're welcome to have them, but *I* won't carry them. By the way, what do you want to drink af-ter dinner?"

Protestations that anything would do were overruled, and a satisfactory settlement was reached on the way to the front hall, where Mr. Fanshawe found his stick, and Mr. Richards, after thoughtful pinching of his lower lip, resorted to a drawer in the hall-table, extracted a key, crossed to a cupboard in the panelling, opened it, took a box from the shelf, and put it on the table. "The glasses are in there," he said, "and there's some dodge of opening it, but I've forgotten what it is. You try." Mr. Fanshawe accordingly tried. There was no keyhole, and the box was solid, heavy and smooth: it seemed obvious that some part of it would have to be pressed before anything could happen. "The corners," said he to himself, "are the likely places; and infernally sharp corners they are too," he added, as he put his thumb in his mouth after exerting force on a lower corner.

"What's the matter?" said the Squire.

"Why, your disgusting Borgia box² has scratched me, drat it," said Fanshawe. The Squire chuckled unfeelingly. "Well, you've got it open, anyway," he said.

"So I have! Well, I don't begrudge a drop of blood in a good cause, and here are the glasses. They *are* pretty heavy, as you said, but I think I'm equal to carrying them."

"Ready?" said the Squire. "Come on then; we go out by the garden."

So they did, and passed out into the park, which sloped decidedly upwards to the hill which, as Fanshawe had seen from the train, dominated the country. It was a spur of a larger range that lay behind. On the way, the Squire, who was great on earthworks, pointed out various spots where he detected or imagined traces of war-ditches and the like. "And here," he said, stopping on a more or less level plot with a ring of large trees, "is Baxter's Roman villa." "Baxter?" said Mr. Fanshawe.

"I forgot; you don't know about him. He was the old chap I got those glasses from. I believe he made them. He was an old watch-maker down in the village, a great antiquary. My father gave him leave to grub about where he liked; and when he made a find he used to lend him a man or two to help him with the digging. He got a surprising lot of things together, and when he died—I dare say it's ten or fifteen years ago—I bought the

whole lot and gave them to the town museum. We'll run in one
of these days, and look over them. The glasses came to me with
the rest, but of course I kept them. If you look at them, you'll
see they're more or less amateur work—the body of them; naturally the lenses weren't his making."

"Yes, I see they are just the sort of thing that a clever work-
man in a different line of business might turn out. But I don't
see why he made them so heavy. And did Baxter actually find a
Roman villa here?"

"Yes, there's a pavement turfed over, where we're standing: it
was too rough and plain to be worth taking up, but of course
there are drawings of it: and the small things and pottery that
turned up were quite good of their kind. An ingenious chap, old
Baxter: he seemed to have a quite out-of-the-way instinct for
these things. He was invaluable to our archæologists. He used
to shut up his shop for days at a time, and wander off over the
district, marking down places, where he scented anything, on
the ordnance map; and he kept a book with fuller notes of the
places. Since his death, a good many of them have been sampled, and there's always been something to justify him."

"What a good man!" said Mr. Fanshawe.

"Good?" said the Squire, pulling up brusquely.

"I meant useful to have about the place," said Mr. Fanshawe.
"But was he a villain?"

"I don't know about that either," said the Squire; "but all I
can say is, if he was good, he wasn't lucky. And he wasn't liked:
I didn't like him," he added, after a moment.

"Oh?" said Fanshawe interrogatively.

"No, I didn't; but that's enough about Baxter: besides, this is
the stiffest bit, and I don't want to talk and walk as well."

Indeed it was hot, climbing a slippery grass slope that evening. "I told you I should take you the short way," panted the
Squire, "and I wish I hadn't. However, a bath won't do us any
harm when we get back. Here we are, and there's the seat."

A small clump of old Scotch firs crowned the top of the hill;
and, at the edge of it, commanding the cream of the view, was a
wide and solid seat, on which the two disposed themselves, and
wiped their brows, and regained breath.

"Now, then," said the Squire, as soon as he was in a condition to talk connectedly, "this is where your glasses come in.
But you'd better take a general look round first. My word! I've
never seen the view look better."

Writing as I am now with a winter wind flapping against
dark windows and a rushing, tumbling sea within a hundred
yards, I find it hard to summon up the feelings and words
which will put my reader in possession of the June evening
and the lovely English landscape of which the Squire was
speaking.

Across a broad level plain they looked upon ranges of great
hills, whose uplands—some green, some furred with woods—
caught the light of a sun, westering but not yet low. And all the
plain was fertile, though the river which traversed it was nowhere
seen. There were copses, green wheat, hedges and pasture-land:
the little compact white moving cloud marked the evening train.
Then the eye picked out red farms and grey houses, and nearer
home scattered cottages, and then the Hall, nestled under the hill.
The smoke of chimneys was very blue and straight. There was a
smell of hay in the air: there were wild roses on bushes hard by.
It was the acme of summer.

After some minutes of silent contemplation, the Squire began
to point out the leading features, the hills and valleys, and told
where the towns and villages lay. "Now," he said, "with the
glasses you'll be able to pick out Fulnaker Abbey. Take a line
across that big green field, then over the wood beyond it, then
over the farm on the knoll."

"Yes, yes," said Fanshawe. "I've got it. What a fine tower!"

"You must have got the wrong direction," said the Squire;
"there's not much of a tower about there that I remember, unless it's Oldbourne Church that you've got hold of. And if you
call that a fine tower, you're easily pleased."

"Well, I do call it a fine tower," said Fanshawe, the glasses
still at his eyes, "whether it's Oldbourne or any other. And it
must belong to a largish church; it looks to me like a central
tower—four big pinnacles at the corners, and four smaller ones
between. I must certainly go over there. How far is it?"

"Oldbourne's about nine miles, or less," said the Squire. "It's a long time since I've been there, but I don't remember thinking much of it. Now I'll show you another thing."

Fanshawe had lowered the glasses, and was still gazing in the Oldbourne direction. "No," he said, "I can't make out anything with the naked eye. What was it you were going to show me?"

"A good deal more to the left—it oughtn't to be difficult to find. Do you see a rather sudden knob of a hill with a thick wood on top of it? It's in a dead line with that single tree on the top of the big ridge."

"I do," said Fanshawe, "and I believe I could tell you without much difficulty what it's called."

"Could you now?" said the Squire. "Say on."

"Why, Gallows Hill," was the answer.

"How did you guess that?"

"Well, if you don't want it guessed, you shouldn't put up a dummy gibbet and a man hanging on it."

"What's that?" said the Squire abruptly. "There's nothing on that hill but wood."

"On the contrary," said Fanshawe, "there's a largish expanse of grass on the top and your dummy gibbet in the middle; and I thought there was something on it when I looked first. But I see there's nothing—or is there? I can't be sure."

"Nonsense, nonsense, Fanshawe, there's no such thing as a dummy gibbet, or any other sort, on that hill. And it's thick wood—a fairly young plantation. I was in it myself not a year ago. Hand me the glasses, though I don't suppose I can see anything." After a pause: "No, I thought not: they won't show a thing."

Meanwhile Fanshawe was scanning the hill—it might be only two or three miles away. "Well, it's very odd," he said, "it does look exactly like a wood without the glass." He took it again. "That *is* one of the oddest effects. The gibbet is perfectly plain, and the grass field, and there even seem to be people on it, and carts, or *a* cart, with men in it. And yet when I take the glass away, there's nothing. It must be something in the way this afternoon light falls: I shall come up earlier in the day when the sun's full on it."

"Did you say you saw people and a cart on that hill?" said the

Squire incredulously. "What should they be doing there at this time of day, even if the trees have been felled? Do talk sense—look again."

"Well, I certainly thought I saw them. Yes, I should say there were a few, just clearing off. And now—by Jove, it does look like something hanging on the gibbet. But these glasses are so beastly heavy I can't hold them steady for long. Anyhow, you can take it from me there's no wood. And if you'll show me the road on the map, I'll go there to-morrow."

The Squire remained brooding for some little time. At last he rose and said, "Well, I suppose that will be the best way to settle it. And now we'd better be getting back. Bath and dinner is my idea." And on the way back he was not very communicative.

They returned through the garden, and went into the front hall to leave sticks, etc., in their due place. And here they found the aged butler Patten evidently in a state of some anxiety. "Beg pardon, Master Henry," he began at once, "but someone's been up to mischief here, I'm much afraid." He pointed to the open box which had contained the glasses.

"Nothing worse than that, Patten?" said the Squire. "Mayn't I take out my own glasses and lend them to a friend? Bought with my own money, you recollect? At old Baxter's sale, eh?"

Patten bowed, unconvinced. "Oh, very well, Master Henry, as long as you know who it was. Only I thought proper to name it, for I didn't think that box'd been off its shelf since you first put it there; and, if you'll excuse me, after what happened. . . ." The voice was lowered, and the rest was not audible to Fanshawe. The Squire replied with a few words and a gruff laugh, and called on Fanshawe to come and be shown his room. And I do not think that anything else happened that night which bears on my story.

Except, perhaps, the sensation which invaded Fanshawe in the small hours that something had been let out which ought not to have been let out. It came into his dreams. He was walking in a garden which he seemed half to know, and stopped in front of a rockery made of old wrought stones, pieces of window tracery from a church, and even bits of figures. One of these moved his curiosity: it seemed to be a sculptured capital with scenes carved on it. He felt he must pull it out, and worked away, and, with an ease that surprised him, moved the stones that obscured it aside, and pulled out the block. As he did so, a tin label fell down by his feet with a little clatter. He picked it up and read on it: "On no account move this stone. Yours sincerely, J. Patten." As often happens in dreams, he felt that this injunction was of extreme importance; and with an anxiety that amounted to anguish he looked to see if the stone had really been shifted. Indeed it had; in fact, he could not see it anywhere. The removal had disclosed the mouth of a burrow, and he bent down to look into it. Something stirred in the blackness, and then, to his intense horror, a hand emerged—a clean right hand in a neat cuff and coat-sleeve, just in the attitude of a hand that means to shake yours. He wondered whether it would not be rude to let it alone. But, as he looked at it, it began to grow hairy and dirty and thin, and also to change its pose and stretch out as if to take hold of his leg. At that he dropped all thought of politeness, decided to run, screamed and woke himself up.

This was the dream he remembered; but it seemed to him (as, again, it often does) that there had been others of the same import before, but not so insistent. He lay awake for some little time, fixing the details of the last dream in his mind, and wondering in particular what the figures had been which he had seen or half seen on the carved capital. Something quite incongruous, he felt sure; but that was the most he could recall.

Whether because of the dream, or because it was the first day of his holiday, he did not get up very early; nor did he at once plunge into the exploration of the country. He spent a morning, half lazy, half instructive, in looking over the volumes of the County Archæological Society's transactions, in which were many contributions from Mr. Baxter on finds of flint implements, Roman sites, ruins of monastic establishments—in fact, most departments of archæology. They were written in an odd, pompous, only half-educated style. If the man had had more early schooling, thought Fanshawe, he would have been a very distinguished antiquary; or he might have been (he thus qualified his opinion a little later), but for a certain love of opposition and controversy, and, yes, a patronizing tone as of one possessing superior knowledge, which left an unpleasant taste. He might have been a very respectable artist. There was an imaginary restoration and elevation of a priory church which was very well conceived. A fine pinnacled central tower was a conspicuous feature of this; it reminded Fanshawe of that which he had seen from the hill, and which the Squire had told him must be Oldbourne. But it was not Oldbourne; it was Fulnaker Priory. "Oh, well," he said to himself, "I suppose Oldbourne Church may have been built by Fulnaker monks, and Baxter has copied Oldbourne tower. Anything about it in the letter-press? Ah, I see it was published after his death—found among his papers."

After lunch the Squire asked Fanshawe what he meant to do.

"Well," said Fanshawe, "I think I shall go out on my bike about four as far as Oldbourne and back by Gallows Hill. That ought to be a round of about fifteen miles, oughtn't it?"

"About that," said the Squire, "and you'll pass Lambsfield and Wanstone, both of which are worth looking at. There's a little glass at Lambsfield and the stone at Wanstone."

"Good," said Fanshawe, "I'll get tea somewhere, and may I take the glasses? I'll strap them on my bike, on the carrier."

"Of course, if you like," said the Squire. "I really ought to have some better ones. If I go into the town to-day, I'll see if I can pick up some."

"Why should you trouble to do that if you can't use them yourself?" said Fanshawe.

"Oh, I don't know; one ought to have a decent pair; and—well, old Patten doesn't think those are fit to use."

"Is he a judge?"

"He's got some tale: I don't know: something about old Baxter. I've promised to let him tell me about it. It seems very much on his mind since last night."

"Why that? Did he have a nightmare like me?"

"He had something: he was looking an old man this morning, and he said he hadn't closed an eye."

"Well, let him save up his tale till I come back."

"Very well, I will if I can. Look here, are you going to be

late? If you get a puncture eight miles off and have to walk
home, what then? I don't trust these bicycles: I shall tell them to
give us cold things to eat."

"I shan't mind that, whether I'm late or early. But I've got
things to mend punctures with. And now I'm off."

It was just as well that the Squire had made that arrangement
about a cold supper, Fanshawe thought, and not for the first
time, as he wheeled his bicycle up the drive about nine o'clock.
So also the Squire thought and said, several times, as he met
him in the hall, rather pleased at the confirmation of his want of
faith in bicycles than sympathetic with his hot, weary, thirsty,
and indeed haggard, friend. In fact, the kindest thing he found
to say was: "You'll want a long drink to-night? Cider-cup do?
All right. Hear that, Patten? Cider-cup, iced, lots of it." Then to
Fanshawe, "Don't be all night over your bath."

By half-past nine they were at dinner, and Fanshawe was re-
porting progress, if progress it might be called.

"I got to Lambsfield very smoothly, and saw the glass. It is very
interesting stuff, but there's a lot of lettering I couldn't read."

"Not with glasses?" said the Squire.

"Those glasses of yours are no manner of use inside a
church—or inside anywhere, I suppose, for that matter. But the
only places I took 'em into were churches."

"H'm! Well, go on," said the Squire.

"However, I took some sort of a photograph of the window,
and I dare say an enlargement would show what I want. Then
Wanstone; I should think that stone was a very out-of-the-way
thing, only I don't know about that class of antiquities. Has
anybody opened the mound it stands on?"

"Baxter wanted to, but the farmer wouldn't let him."

"Oh, well, I should think it would be worth doing. Anyhow,
the next thing was Fulnaker and Oldbourne. You know, it's
very odd about that tower I saw from the hill. Oldbourne
Church is nothing like it, and of course there's nothing over
thirty feet high at Fulnaker, though you can see it had a central
tower. I didn't tell you, did I? that Baxter's fancy drawing of
Fulnaker shows a tower exactly like the one I saw."

"So you thought, I dare say," put in the Squire.

"No, it wasn't a case of thinking. The picture actually *reminded* me of what I'd seen, and I made sure it was Oldbourne, well before I looked at the title."

"Well, Baxter had a very fair idea of architecture. I dare say what's left made it easy for him to draw the right sort of tower."

"That may be it, of course, but I'm doubtful if even a professional could have got it so exactly right. There's absolutely nothing left at Fulnaker but the bases of the piers which supported it. However, that isn't the oddest thing."

"What about Gallows Hill?" said the Squire. "Here, Patten, listen to this. I told you what Mr. Fanshawe said he saw from the hill."

"Yes, Master Henry, you did; and I can't say I was so much surprised, considering."

"All right, all right. You keep that till afterwards. We want to hear what Mr. Fanshawe saw to-day. Go on, Fanshawe. You turned to come back by Ackford and Thorfield, I suppose?"

"Yes, and I looked into both the churches. Then I got to the turning which goes to the top of Gallows Hill; I saw that if I wheeled my machine over the field at the top of the hill I could join the home road on this side. It was about half-past six when I got to the top of the hill, and there was a gate on my right, where it ought to be, leading into the belt of plantation."

"You hear that, Patten? A belt, he says."

"So I thought it was—a belt. But it wasn't. You were quite right, and I was hopelessly wrong. I *cannot* understand it. The whole top is planted quite thick. Well, I went on into this wood, wheeling and dragging my bike, expecting every minute to come to a clearing, and then my misfortunes began. Thorns, I suppose; first I realized that the front tyre was slack, then the back. I couldn't stop to do more than try to find the punctures and mark them; but even that was hopeless. So I ploughed on, and the farther I went, the less I liked the place."

"Not much poaching in that cover, eh, Patten?" said the Squire.

"No, indeed, Master Henry: there's very few cares to go—"

"No, I know: never mind that now. Go on, Fanshawe."

"I don't blame anybody for not caring to go there. I know I had all the fancies one least likes: steps crackling over twigs behind me, indistinct people stepping behind trees in front of me, yes, and even a hand laid on my shoulder. I pulled up very sharp at that and looked round, but there really was no branch or bush that could have done it. Then, when I was just about at the middle of the plot, I was convinced that there was someone looking down on me from above—and not with any pleasant intent. I stopped again, or at least slackened my pace, to look up. And as I did, down I came, and barked my shins abominably on, what do you think? a block of stone with a big square hole in the top of it. And within a few paces there were two others just like it. The three were set in a triangle. Now, do you make out what they were put there for?"

"I think I can," said the Squire, who was now very grave and absorbed in the story. "Sit down, Patten."

It was time, for the old man was supporting himself by one hand, and leaning heavily on it. He dropped into a chair, and said in a very tremulous voice, "You didn't go between them stones, did you, sir?"

"I did *not*," said Fanshawe, emphatically. "I dare say I was an ass, but as soon as it dawned on me where I was, I just shouldered my machine and did my best to run. It seemed to me as if I was in an unholy evil sort of graveyard, and I was most profoundly thankful that it was one of the longest days and still sunlight. Well, I had a horrid run, even if it was only a few hundred yards. Everything caught on everything: handles and spokes and carrier and pedals—caught in them viciously, or I fancied so. I fell over at least five times. At last I saw the hedge, and I couldn't trouble to hunt for the gate."

"There *is* no gate on my side," the Squire interpolated.

"Just as well I didn't waste time, then. I dropped the machine over somehow and went into the road pretty near head-first; some branch or something got my ankle at the last moment. Anyhow, there I was out of the wood, and seldom more thankful or more generally sore. Then came the job of mending my punctures. I had a good outfit and I'm not at all bad at the business;

but this was an absolutely hopeless case. It was seven when I got out of the wood, and I spent fifty minutes over one tyre. As fast as I found a hole and put on a patch, and blew it up, it went flat again. So I made up my mind to walk. That hill isn't three miles away, is it?"

"Not more across country, but nearer six by road."

"I thought it must be. I thought I couldn't have taken well over the hour over less than five miles, even leading a bike. Well, there's my story: where's yours and Patten's?"

"Mine? I've no story," said the Squire. "But you weren't very far out when you thought you were in a graveyard. There must be a good few of them up there, Patten, don't you think? They left 'em there when they fell to bits, I fancy."

Patten nodded, too much interested to speak. "Don't," said Fanshawe.

"Now then, Patten," said the Squire, "you've heard what sort of a time Mr. Fanshawe's been having. What do you make of it? Anything to do with Mr. Baxter? Fill yourself a glass of port, and tell us."

"Ah, that done me good, Master Henry," said Patten, after absorbing what was before him. "If you really wish to know what were in my thoughts, my answer would be clear in the affirmative. Yes," he went on, warming to his work, "I should say as Mr. Fanshawe's experience of to-day were very largely doo to the person you named. And I think, Master Henry, as I have some title to speak, in view of me 'aving been many years on speaking terms with him, and swore in to be jury on the Coroner's inquest near this time ten years ago, you being then, if you carry your mind back, Master Henry, travelling abroad, and no one 'ere to represent the family."

"Inquest?" said Fanshawe. "An inquest on Mr. Baxter, was there?"

"Yes, sir, on—on that very person. The facts as led up to that occurrence was these. The deceased was, as you may have gathered, a very peculiar individual in 'is 'abits—in my idear, at least, but all must speak as they find. He lived very much to himself, without neither chick nor child, as the saying is. And how he passed away his time was what very few could orfer a guess at."

"He lived unknown, and few could know when Baxter ceased to be,"[3] said the Squire to his pipe.

"I beg pardon, Master Henry, I was just coming to that. But when I say how he passed away his time—to be sure we know 'ow intent he was in rummaging and ransacking out all the 'istry of the neighbourhood and the number of things he'd managed to collect together—well, it was spoke of for miles round as Baxter's Museum, and many a time when he might be in the mood, and I might have an hour to spare, have he showed me his pieces of pots and what not, going back by his account to the times of the ancient Romans. However, you know more about that than what I do, Master Henry: only what I was a-going to say was this, as know what he might and interesting as he might be in his talk, there was something about the man— well, for one thing, no one ever remember to see him in church nor yet chapel at service-time. And that made talk. Our rector he never come in the house but once. 'Never ask me what the man said'; that was all anybody could ever get out of *him*. Then how did he spend his nights, particularly about this season of the year? Time and again the labouring men'd meet him coming back as they went out to their work, and he'd pass 'em by without a word, looking, they says, like someone straight out of the asylum. They see the whites of his eyes all round. He'd have a fish-basket with him, that they noticed, and he always come the same road. And the talk got to be that he'd made himself some business, and that not the best kind—well, not so far from where you was at seven o'clock this evening, sir.

"Well, now, after such a night as that, Mr. Baxter he'd shut up the shop, and the old lady that did for him had orders not to come in; and knowing what she did about his language, she took care to obey them orders. But one day it so happened, about three o'clock in the afternoon, the house being shut up as I said, there come a most fearful to-do inside, and smoke out of the windows, and Baxter crying out seemingly in an agony. So the man as lived next door he run round to the back premises and burst the door in, and several others come too. Well, he tell me he never in all his life smelt such a fearful—well, odour, as what there was in that kitchen-place. It seem as if Baxter had

been boiling something in a pot and overset it on his leg. There
he laid on the floor, trying to keep back the cries, but it was
more than he could manage, and when he seen the people come
in—oh, he was in a nice condition: if his tongue warn't blis-
tered worse than his leg it warn't his fault. Well, they picked
him up, and got him into a chair, and run for the medical man,
and one of 'em was going to pick up the pot, and Baxter, he
screams out to let it alone. So he did, but he couldn't see as
there was anything in the pot but a few old brown bones. Then
they says 'Dr. Lawrence'll be here in a minute, Mr. Baxter; he'll
soon put you to rights.' And then he was off again. He must be
got up to his room, he couldn't have the doctor come in there
and see all that mess—they must throw a cloth over it—
anything—the tablecloth out of the parlour; well, so they did.
But that must have been poisonous stuff in that pot, for it was
pretty near on two months afore Baxter were about agin. Beg
pardon, Master Henry, was you going to say something?"

"Yes, I was," said the Squire. "I wonder you haven't told me
all this before. However, I was going to say I remember old
Lawrence telling me he'd attended Baxter. He was a queer card,
he said. Lawrence was up in the bedroom one day, and picked
up a little mask covered with black velvet, and put it on in fun
and went to look at himself in the glass. He hadn't time for a
proper look, for old Baxter shouted out to him from the bed:
'Put it down, you fool! Do you want to look through a dead
man's eyes?' and it startled him so that he did put it down, and
then he asked Baxter what he meant. And Baxter insisted on
him handing it over, and said the man he bought it from was
dead, or some such nonsense. But Lawrence felt it as he handed
it over, and he declared he was sure it was made out of the front
of a skull. He bought a distilling apparatus at Baxter's sale, he
told me, but he could never use it: it seemed to taint everything,
however much he cleaned it. But go on, Patten."

"Yes, Master Henry, I'm nearly done now, and time, too, for
I don't know what they'll think about me in the servants' 'all.
Well, this business of the scalding was some few years before
Mr. Baxter was took, and he got about again, and went on just
as he'd used. And one of the last jobs he done was finishing up

them actual glasses what you took out last night. You see he'd
made the body of them some long time, and got the pieces of
glass for them, but there was somethink wanted to finish 'em,
whatever it was, I don't know, but I picked up the frame one
day, and I says: 'Mr. Baxter, why don't you make a job of this?'
And he says, 'Ah, when I've done that, you'll hear news, you
will: there's going to be no such pair of glasses as mine when
they're filled and sealed,' and there he stopped, and I says:
'Why, Mr. Baxter, you talk as if they was wine bottles: filled
and sealed—why, where's the necessity for that?' 'Did I say
filled and sealed?' he says. 'O, well, I was suiting my conversation to my company.' Well, then come round this time of year,
and one fine evening, I was passing his shop on my way home,
and he was standing on the step, very pleased with hisself, and
he says: 'All right and tight now: my best bit of work's finished,
and I'll be out with 'em to-morrow.' 'What, finished them
glasses?' I says, 'might I have a look at them?' 'No, no,' he says,
'I've put 'em to bed for to-night, and when I do show 'em you,
you'll have to pay for peepin', so I tell you.' And that, gentlemen, were the last words I heard that man say.

   "That were the 17th of June, and just a week after, there was
a funny thing happened, and it was doo to that as we brought in
'unsound mind' at the inquest, for barring that, no one as knew
Baxter in business could anyways have laid that against him.
But George Williams, as lived in the next house, and do now, he
was woke up that same night with a stumbling and tumbling
about in Mr. Baxter's premises, and he got out o' bed, and went
to the front window on the street to see if there was any rough
customers about. And it being a very light night, he could make
sure as there was not. Then he stood and listened, and he hear
Mr. Baxter coming down his front stair one step after another
very slow, and he got the idear as it was like someone bein'
pushed or pulled down and holdin' on to everythin' he could.
Next thing he hear the street door come open, and out come
Mr. Baxter into the street in his day-clothes, 'at and all, with his
arms straight down by his sides, and talking to hisself, and
shakin' his head from one side to the other, and walking in that
peculiar way that he appeared to be going as it were against his

own will. George Williams put up the window, and hear him say: 'O mercy, gentlemen!' and then he shut up sudden as if, he said, someone clapped his hand over his mouth, and Mr. Baxter threw his head back, and his hat fell off. And Williams see his face looking something pitiful, so as he couldn't keep from calling out to him: 'Why, Mr. Baxter, ain't you well?' and he was goin' to offer to fetch Dr. Lawrence to him, only he heard the answer: ' 'Tis best you mind your own business. Put in your head.' But whether it were Mr. Baxter said it so hoarse-like and faint, he never could be sure. Still there weren't no one but him in the street, and yet Williams was that upset by the way he spoke that he shrank back from the window and went and sat on the bed. And he heard Mr. Baxter's step go on and up the road, and after a minute or more he couldn't help but look out once more and he see him going along the same curious way as before. And one thing he recollected was that Mr. Baxter never stopped to pick up his 'at when it fell off, and yet there it was on his head. Well, Master Henry, that was the last anybody see of Mr. Baxter, leastways for a week or more. There was a lot of people said he was called off on business, or made off because he'd got into some scrape, but he was well known for miles round, and none of the railway-people nor the public-house people hadn't seen him; and then ponds was looked into and nothink found; and at last one evening Fakes the keeper come down from over the hill to the village, and he says he seen the Gallows Hill planting black with birds, and that were a funny thing, because he never see no sign of a creature there in his time. So they looked at each other a bit, and first one says: 'I'm game to go up,' and another says: 'So am I, if you are,' and half a dozen of 'em set out in the evening time, and took Dr. Lawrence with them, and you know, Master Henry, there he was between them three stones with his neck broke."

Useless to imagine the talk which this story set going. It is not remembered. But before Patten left them, he said to Fanshawe: "Excuse me, sir, but did I understand as you took out them glasses with you to-day? I thought you did; and might I ask, did you make use of them at all?"

"Yes. Only to look at something in a church."

"Oh, indeed, you took 'em into the church, did you, sir?"

"Yes, I did; it was Lambsfield church. By the way, I left them strapped on to my bicycle, I'm afraid, in the stable-yard."

"No matter for that, sir. I can bring them in the first thing to-morrow, and perhaps you'll be so good as to look at 'em then."

Accordingly, before breakfast, after a tranquil and well-earned sleep, Fanshawe took the glasses into the garden and directed them to a distant hill. He lowered them instantly, and looked at top and bottom, worked the screws, tried them again and yet again, shrugged his shoulders and replaced them on the hall-table.

"Patten," he said, "they're absolutely useless. I can't see a thing: it's as if someone had stuck a black wafer over the lens."

"Spoilt my glasses, have you?" said the Squire. "Thank you: the only ones I've got."

"You try them yourself," said Fanshawe, "I've done nothing to them."

So after breakfast the Squire took them out to the terrace and stood on the steps. After a few ineffectual attempts, "Lord, how heavy they are!" he said impatiently, and in the same instant dropped them on to the stones, and the lens splintered and the barrel cracked: a little pool of liquid formed on the stone slab. It was inky black, and the odour that rose from it is not to be described.

"Filled and sealed, eh?" said the Squire. "If I could bring myself to touch it, I dare say we should find the seal. So that's what came of his boiling and distilling, is it? Old Ghoul!"

"What in the world do you mean?"

"Don't you see, my good man? Remember what he said to the doctor about looking through dead men's eyes? Well, this was another way of it. But they didn't like having their bones boiled, I take it, and the end of it was they carried him off whither he would not. Well, I'll get a spade, and we'll bury this thing decently."

As they smoothed the turf over it, the Squire, handing the spade to Patten, who had been a reverential spectator, remarked to Fanshawe: "It's almost a pity you took that thing into the church: you might have seen more than you did. Baxter had them for a week, I make out, but I don't see that he did much in the time."

"I'm not sure," said Fanshawe, "there is that picture of Ful-naker Priory Church."

A WARNING TO
THE CURIOUS

The place on the east coast which the reader is asked to consider is Seaburgh. It is not very different now from what I remember it to have been when I was a child. Marshes intersected
by dykes to the south, recalling the early chapters of *Great Ex-*
pectations;[1] flat fields to the north, merging into heath; heath,
fir woods, and, above all, gorse, inland. A long sea-front and a
street: behind that a spacious church of flint, with a broad,
solid western tower and a peal of six bells. How well I remember their sound on a hot Sunday in August, as our party went
slowly up the white, dusty slope of road towards them, for the
church stands at the top of a short, steep incline. They rang
with a flat clacking sort of sound on those hot days, but when
the air was softer they were mellower too. The railway ran
down to its little terminus farther along the same road. There
was a gay white windmill just before you came to the station,
and another down near the shingle[2] at the south end of the
town, and yet others on higher ground to the north. There were
cottages of bright red brick with slate roofs . . . but why do I
encumber you with these commonplace details? The fact is that
they come crowding to the point of the pencil when it begins to
write of Seaburgh. I should like to be sure that I had allowed
the right ones to get on to the paper. But I forgot. I have not
quite done with the word-painting business yet.

Walk away from the sea and the town, pass the station, and
turn up the road on the right. It is a sandy road, parallel with
the railway, and if you follow it, it climbs to somewhat higher
ground. On your left (you are now going northward) is heath,
on your right (the side towards the sea) is a belt of old firs,

wind-beaten, thick at the top, with the slope that old seaside trees have; seen on the skyline from the train they would tell you in an instant, if you did not know it, that you were approaching a windy coast. Well, at the top of my little hill, a line of these firs strikes out and runs towards the sea, for there is a ridge that goes that way; and the ridge ends in a rather well-defined mound commanding the level fields of rough grass, and a little knot of fir trees crowns it. And here you may sit on a hot spring day, very well content to look at blue sea, white windmills, red cottages, bright green grass, church tower, and distant martello tower[3] on the south.

As I have said, I began to know Seaburgh as a child; but a gap of a good many years separates my early knowledge from that which is more recent. Still it keeps its place in my affections, and any tales of it that I pick up have an interest for me. One such tale is this: it came to me in a place very remote from Seaburgh, and quite accidentally, from a man whom I had been able to oblige—enough in his opinion to justify his making me his confidant to this extent.

I know all that country more or less (he said). I used to go to Seaburgh pretty regularly for golf in the spring. I generally put up at the "Bear," with a friend—Henry Long it was, you knew him perhaps—("Slightly," I said) and we used to take a sitting-room and be very happy there. Since he died I haven't cared to go there. And I don't know that I should anyhow after the particular thing that happened on our last visit.

It was in April, 19—, we were there, and by some chance we were almost the only people in the hotel. So the ordinary public rooms were practically empty, and we were the more surprised when, after dinner, our sitting-room door opened, and a young man put his head in. We were aware of this young man. He was rather a rabbity anæmic subject—light hair and light eyes—but not unpleasing. So when he said: "I beg your pardon, is this a private room?" we did not growl and say: "Yes, it is," but Long said, or I did—no matter which: "Please come in." "Oh, may I?" he said, and seemed relieved. Of course it was obvious that he wanted company; and as he was a reasonable kind of person—not the sort to bestow his whole family history on you—we urged him to make himself at home. "I dare say you find the other rooms rather bleak," I said. Yes, he did: but it was really too good of us, and so on. That being got over, he made some pretence of reading a book. Long was playing Patience, I was writing. It became plain to me after a few minutes that this visitor of ours was in rather a state of fidgets or nerves, which communicated itself to me, and so I put away my writing and turned to at engaging him in talk.

After some remarks, which I forget, he became rather confidential. "You'll think it very odd of me" (this was the sort of way he began), "but the fact is I've had something of a shock." Well, I recommended a drink of some cheering kind, and we had it. The waiter coming in made an interruption (and I thought our young man seemed very jumpy when the door opened), but after a while he got back to his woes again. There was nobody he knew in the place, and he did happen to know who we both were (it turned out there was some common acquaintance in town), and really he did want a word of advice, if we didn't mind. Of course we both said: "By all means," or "Not at all," and Long put away his cards. And we settled down to hear what his difficulty was.

"It began," he said, "more than a week ago, when I bicycled over to Froston,⁴ only about five or six miles, to see the church; I'm very much interested in architecture, and it's got one of those pretty porches with niches and shields. I took a photograph of it, and then an old man who was tidying up in the churchyard came and asked if I'd care to look into the church. I said yes, and he produced a key and let me in. There wasn't much inside, but I told him it was a nice little church, and he kept it very clean, 'but,' I said, 'the porch is the best part of it.' We were just outside the porch then, and he said, 'Ah, yes, that is a nice porch; and do you know, sir, what's the meanin' of that coat of arms there?'

"It was the one with the three crowns, and though I'm not much of a herald, I was able to say yes, I thought it was the old arms of the kingdom of East Anglia.⁵

" 'That's right, sir,' he said, 'and do you know the meanin' of them three crowns that's on it?'

"I said I'd no doubt it was known, but I couldn't recollect to have heard it myself.

" 'Well, then,' he said, 'for all you're a scholard, I can tell you something you don't know. Them's the three 'oly crowns what was buried in the ground near by the coast to keep the Germans from landing—ah, I can see you don't believe that. But I tell you, if it hadn't have been for one of them 'oly crowns bein' there still, them Germans would a landed here time and again, they would. Landed with their ships, and killed man, woman and child in their beds. Now then, that's the truth what I'm telling you, that is; and if you don't believe me, you ast the rector. There he comes: you ast him, I says.'

"I looked round, and there was the rector, a nice-looking old man, coming up the path; and before I could begin assuring my old man, who was getting quite excited, that I didn't disbelieve him, the rector struck in, and said: 'What's all this about, John? Good day to you, sir. Have you been looking at our little church?'

"So then there was a little talk which allowed the old man to calm down, and then the rector asked him again what was the matter.

" 'Oh,' he said, 'it warn't nothink, only I was telling this gentleman he'd ought to ast you about them 'oly crowns.'

" 'Ah, yes, to be sure,' said the rector, 'that's a very curious matter, isn't it? But I don't know whether the gentleman is interested in our old stories, eh?'

" 'Oh, he'll be interested fast enough,' says the old man, 'he'll put his confidence in what you tells him, sir; why, you known William Ager yourself, father and son too.'

"Then I put in a word to say how much I should like to hear all about it, and before many minutes I was walking up the village street with the rector, who had one or two words to say to parishioners, and then to the rectory, where he took me into his study. He had made out, on the way, that I really was capable of taking an intelligent interest in a piece of folk-lore, and not quite the ordinary tripper. So he was very willing to talk, and it is rather surprising to me that the particular legend he told me has not made its way into print before. His account of it was this: 'There has always been a belief in these parts in the three holy crowns. The old people say they were buried in different places near the coast to keep off the Danes or the French or the Germans. And they say that one of the three was dug up a long time ago, and another has disappeared by the encroaching of the sea, and one's still left doing its work, keeping off invaders. Well, now, if you have read the ordinary guides and histories of this county, you will remember perhaps that in 1687 a crown, which was said to be the crown of Redwald, King of the East Angles, was dug up at Rendlesham, and alas! alas! melted down before it was even properly described or drawn.[6] Well, Rendlesham isn't on the coast, but it isn't so very far inland, and it's on a very important line of access. And I believe that is the crown which the people mean when they say that one has been dug up. Then on the south you don't want me to tell you where there was a Saxon royal palace which is now under the sea, eh?[7] Well, there was the second crown, I take it. And up beyond these two, they say, lies the third.'

" 'Do they say where it is?' of course I asked.

"He said, 'Yes, indeed, they do, but they don't tell,' and his manner did not encourage me to put the obvious question. Instead of that I waited a moment, and said: 'What did the old man mean when he said you knew William Ager, as if that had something to do with the crowns?'

" 'To be sure,' he said, 'now that's another curious story. These Agers—it's a very old name in these parts, but I can't find that they were ever people of quality or big owners—these Agers say, or said, that their branch of the family were the guardians of the last crown. A certain old Nathaniel Ager was the first one I knew—I was born and brought up quite near here—and he, I believe, camped out at the place during the whole of the war of 1870. William, his son, did the same, I know, during the South African War.[8] And young William, *his* son, who has only died fairly recently, took lodgings at the cottage nearest the spot, and I've no doubt hastened his end, for he was a consumptive, by exposure and night watching. And he was the last of that branch. It was a dreadful grief to him to think that he was the last, but he could do nothing, the only relations at all near to him were in the colonies. I wrote letters for him to them imploring them to come over on business very important to the family, but there has been no answer. So the last of the holy crowns, if it's there, has no guardian now.'

"That was what the rector told me, and you can fancy how interesting I found it. The only thing I could think of when I left him was how to hit upon the spot where the crown was supposed to be. I wish I'd left it alone.

"But there was a sort of fate in it, for as I bicycled back past the churchyard wall my eye caught a fairly new gravestone, and on it was the name of William Ager. Of course I got off and read it. It said 'of this parish, died at Seaburgh, 19—, aged 28.' There it was, you see. A little judicious questioning in the right place, and I should at least find the cottage nearest the spot. Only I didn't quite know what was the right place to begin my questioning at. Again there was fate: it took me to the curiosity-shop down that way—you know—and I turned over some old books, and, if you please, one was a prayer-book of 1740 odd, in a rather handsome binding—I'll just go and get it, it's in my room."

He left us in a state of some surprise, but we had hardly time to exchange any remarks when he was back, panting, and handed us the book opened at the fly-leaf, on which was, in a straggly hand:

"Nathaniel Ager is my name and England is my nation,
Seaburgh is my dwelling-place and Christ is my Salvation,
When I am dead and in my Grave, and all my bones are rotton,
I hope the Lord will think on me when I am quite forgotton."

This poem was dated 1754, and there were many more entries of Agers, Nathaniel, Frederick, William, and so on, ending with William, 19—.

"You see," he said, "anybody would call it the greatest bit of luck. I did, but I don't now. Of course I asked the shopman about William Ager, and of course he happened to remember that he lodged in a cottage in the North Field and died there.

This was just chalking the road for me. I knew which the cottage must be: there is only one sizable one about there. The next thing was to scrape some sort of acquaintance with the people, and I took a walk that way at once. A dog did the business for me: he made at me so fiercely that they had to run out and beat him off, and then naturally begged my pardon, and we got into talk. I had only to bring up Ager's name, and pretend I knew, or thought I knew something of him, and then the woman said how sad it was him dying so young, and she was sure it came of him spending the night out of doors in the cold weather. Then I had to say: 'Did he go out on the sea at night?' and she said: 'Oh, no, it was on the hillock yonder with the trees on it.' And there I was.

"I know something about digging in these barrows: I've opened many of them in the down country. But that was with owner's leave, and in broad daylight and with men to help. I had to prospect very carefully here before I put a spade in: I couldn't trench across the mound, and with those old firs growing there I knew there would be awkward tree roots. Still the soil was very light and sandy and easy, and there was a rabbit hole or so that might be developed into a sort of tunnel. The going out and coming back at odd hours to the hotel was going to be the awkward part. When I made up my mind about the way to excavate I told the people that I was called away for a night, and I spent it out there. I made my tunnel: I won't bore you with the details of how I supported it and filled it in when I'd done, but the main thing is that I got the crown."

Naturally we both broke out into exclamations of surprise and interest. I for one had long known about the finding of the crown at Rendlesham and had often lamented its fate. No one has ever seen an Anglo-Saxon crown—at least no one had. But our man gazed at us with a rueful eye. "Yes," he said, "and the worst of it is I don't know how to put it back."

"Put it back?" we cried out. "Why, my dear sir, you've made one of the most exciting finds ever heard of in this country. Of course it ought to go to the Jewel House at the Tower.[9] What's your difficulty? If you're thinking about the owner of the land, and treasure-trove, and all that, we can certainly help you through. Nobody's going to make a fuss about technicalities in a case of this kind."

Probably more was said, but all he did was to put his face in his hands, and mutter: "I don't know how to put it back."

At last Long said: "You'll forgive me, I hope, if I seem impertinent, but are you *quite* sure you've got it?" I was wanting to ask much the same question myself, for of course the story did seem a lunatic's dream when one thought over it. But I hadn't quite dared to say what might hurt the poor young man's feelings. However, he took it quite calmly—really, with the calm of despair, you might say. He sat up and said: "Oh, yes, there's no doubt of that: I have it here, in my room, locked up in my bag. You can come and look at it if you like: I won't offer to bring it here."

We were not likely to let the chance slip. We went with him; his room was only a few doors off. The boots[10] was just collecting shoes in the passage: or so we thought: afterwards we were not sure. Our visitor—his name was Paxton—was in a worse state of shivers than before, and went hurriedly into the room, and beckoned us after him, turned on the light, and shut the door carefully. Then he unlocked his kit-bag, and produced a bundle of clean pocket-handkerchiefs in which something was wrapped, laid it on the bed, and undid it. I can now say I *have* seen an actual Anglo-Saxon crown. It was of silver—as the Rendlesham one is always said to have been—it was set with some gems, mostly antique intaglios and cameos, and was of rather plain, almost rough workmanship. In fact, it was like those you see on the coins and in the manuscripts. I found no reason to think it was later than the ninth century. I was intensely interested, of course, and I wanted to turn it over in my hands, but Paxton prevented me. "Don't *you* touch it," he said, "I'll do that." And with a sigh that was, I declare to you, dreadful to hear, he took it up and turned it about so that we could see every part of it. "Seen enough?" he said at last, and we nodded. He wrapped it up and locked it in his bag, and stood looking at us dumbly. "Come back to our room," Long said, "and tell us what the trouble is." He thanked us, and said: "Will you go first and see if—if the coast is clear?" That wasn't very intelligible, for our proceedings hadn't been, after all, very suspicious, and the hotel, as I said, was practically empty. However, we were beginning to have inklings of—we didn't know what, and anyhow nerves are infectious. So we did go, first peering out as we opened the door, and fancying (I found we both had the fancy) that a shadow, or more than a shadow—but it made no sound—passed from before us to one side as we came out into the passage. "It's all right," we whispered to Paxton—whispering seemed the proper tone—and we went, with him between us, back to our sitting-room. I was preparing, when we got there, to be ecstatic about the unique interest of what we had seen, but when I looked at Paxton I saw that would be terribly out of place, and I left it to him to begin.

"What *is* to be done?" was his opening. Long thought it right (as he explained to me afterwards) to be obtuse, and said: "Why not find out who the owner of the land is, and inform—" "Oh, no, no!" Paxton broke in impatiently, "I beg your pardon: you've been very kind, but don't you see it's *got* to go back, and I daren't be there at night, and daytime's impossible. Perhaps, though, you don't see: well, then, the truth is that I've never been alone since I touched it." I was beginning some fairly stupid comment, but Long caught my eye, and I stopped. Long said: "I think I do see, perhaps: but wouldn't it be—a relief—to tell us a little more clearly what the situation is?"

Then it all came out: Paxton looked over his shoulder and beckoned to us to come nearer to him, and began speaking in a low voice: we listened most intently, of course, and compared notes afterwards, and I wrote down our version, so I am confident I have what he told us almost word for word. He said: "It began when I was first prospecting, and put me off again and again. There was always somebody—a man—standing by one of the firs. This was in daylight, you know. He was never in front of me. I always saw him with the tail of my eye on the left or the right, and he was never there when I looked straight for him. I would lie down for quite a long time and take careful observations, and make sure there was no one, and then when I got up and began prospecting again, there he was. And he began to give me hints, besides; for wherever I put that prayer-book—short of locking it up, which I did at last—when I came back to my room it was always out on my table open at the fly-leaf where the names are, and one of my razors across it to keep it open. I'm sure he just can't open my bag, or something more would have happened. You see, he's light and weak, but all the same I daren't face him. Well, then, when I was making the tunnel, of course it was worse, and if I hadn't been so keen I should have dropped the whole thing and run. It was like someone scraping at my back all the time: I thought for a long time it was only soil dropping on me, but as I got nearer the—the crown, it was unmistakable. And when I actually laid it bare and got my fingers into the ring of it and pulled it out, there came a sort of cry behind me—oh, I can't tell you how desolate it was! And horribly threatening too. It spoilt all my pleasure in my find—cut it off that moment. And if I hadn't been the wretched fool I am, I should have put the thing back and left it. But I didn't. The rest of the time was just awful. I had hours to get through before I could decently come back to the hotel. First I spent time filling up my tunnel and covering my tracks, and all the while he was there trying to thwart me. Sometimes, you know, you see him, and sometimes you don't, just as he pleases, I think: he's there, but he has some power over your eyes. Well, I wasn't off the spot very long before sunrise, and then I had to get to the junction for Seaburgh, and take a train back. And though it was daylight fairly soon, I don't know if that made it much better. There were always hedges, or gorse-bushes, or park fences along the road—some sort of cover, I mean—and I was never easy for a second. And then when I began to meet people going to work, they always looked behind me very strangely: it might have been that they were surprised at seeing anyone so early; but I didn't think it was only that, and I don't now: they didn't look exactly at *me*. And the porter at the train was like that too. And the guard held open the door after I'd got into the carriage—just as he would if there was somebody else coming, you know. Oh, you may be very sure it isn't my fancy," he said with a dull sort of laugh. Then he went on: "And even if I do get it put back, he won't forgive me: I can tell that. And I was so happy a fortnight ago." He dropped into a chair, and I believe he began to cry.

We didn't know what to say, but we felt we must come to the rescue somehow, and so—it really seemed the only thing—we said if he was so set on putting the crown back in its place, we would help him. And I must say that after what we had heard it did seem the right thing. If these horrid consequences had come on this poor man, might there not really be something in the original idea of the crown having some curious power bound up with it, to guard the coast? At least, that was my feeling, and I think it was Long's too. Our offer was very welcome to Paxton, anyhow. When could we do it? It was nearing half-past ten. Could we contrive to make a late walk plausible to the hotel people that very night? We looked out of the window: there was a brilliant full moon—the Paschal moon.[11] Long undertook to tackle the boots and propitiate him. He was to say that we should not be much over the hour, and if we did find it so pleasant that we stopped out a bit longer we would see that he didn't lose by sitting up. Well, we were pretty regular customers of the hotel, and did not give much trouble, and were considered by the servants to be not under the mark in the way of tips; and so the boots *was* propitiated, and let us out on to the sea-front, and remained, as we heard later, looking after us. Paxton had a large coat over his arm, under which was the wrapped-up crown.

So we were off on this strange errand before we had time to think how very much out of the way it was. I have told this part quite shortly on purpose, for it really does represent the haste with which we settled our plan and took action. "The shortest way is up the hill and through the churchyard," Paxton said, as we stood a moment before the hotel looking up and down the front. There was nobody about—nobody at all. Seaburgh out of the season is an early, quiet place. "We can't go along the dyke by the cottage, because of the dog," Paxton also said, when I pointed to what I thought a shorter way along the front and across two fields. The reason he gave was good enough. We went up the road to the church, and turned in at the churchyard gate. I confess to having thought that there might be some lying there who might be conscious of our business: but if it was so, they were also conscious that one who was on their side, so to say, had us under surveillance, and we saw no sign of them. But under observation we felt we were, as I have never felt it at another time. Specially was it so when we passed out of the churchyard into a narrow path with close high hedges, through which we hurried as Christian did through that Valley;[12] and so got out into open fields. Then along hedges, though I would sooner have been in the open, where I could see if anyone was visible behind me; over a gate or two, and then a swerve to the left, taking us up on to the ridge which ended in that mound.

As we neared it, Henry Long felt, and I felt too, that there were what I can only call dim presences waiting for us, as well as a far more actual one attending us. Of Paxton's agitation all this time I can give you no adequate picture: he breathed like a hunted beast, and we could not either of us look at his face. How he would manage when we got to the very place we had not troubled to think: he had seemed so sure that that would not be difficult. Nor was it. I never saw anything like the dash with which he flung himself at a particular spot in the side of the mound, and tore at it, so that in a very few minutes the greater part of his body was out of sight. We stood holding the coat and that bundle of handkerchiefs, and looking, very fearfully, I must admit, about us. There was nothing to be seen: a line of dark firs behind us made one skyline, more trees and the church tower half a mile off on the right, cottages and a windmill on the horizon on the left, calm sea dead in front, faint barking of a dog at a cottage on a gleaming dyke between us and it: full moon making that path we know across the sea: the eternal whisper of the Scotch firs just above us, and of the sea in front. Yet, in all this quiet, an acute, an acrid consciousness of a restrained hostility very near us, like a dog on a leash that might be let go at any moment.

Paxton pulled himself out of the hole, and stretched a hand back to us. "Give it to me," he whispered, "unwrapped." We pulled off the handkerchiefs, and he took the crown. The moonlight just fell on it as he snatched it. We had not ourselves touched that bit of metal, and I have thought since that it was just as well. In another moment Paxton was out of the hole again and busy shovelling back the soil with hands that were already bleeding. He would have none of our help, though. It was much the longest part of the job to get the place to look undisturbed: yet—I don't know how—he made a wonderful success of it. At last he was satisfied, and we turned back.

We were a couple of hundred yards from the hill when Long suddenly said to him: "I say, you've left your coat there. That won't do. See?" And I certainly did see it—the long dark overcoat lying where the tunnel had been. Paxton had not stopped, however: he only shook his head, and held up the coat on his arm. And when we joined him, he said, without any excitement, but as if nothing mattered any more: "That wasn't my coat." And, indeed, when we looked back again, that dark thing was not to be seen.

Well, we got out on to the road, and came rapidly back that way. It was well before twelve when we got in, trying to put a good face on it, and saying—Long and I—what a lovely night it was for a walk. The boots was on the look-out for us, and we made remarks like that for his edification as we entered the hotel. He gave another look up and down the sea-front before he locked the front door, and said: "You didn't meet many people about, I s'pose, sir?" "No, indeed, not a soul," I said; at which I remember Paxton looked oddly at me. "Only I thought I see someone turn up the station road after you gentlemen," said the boots. "Still, you was three together, and I don't suppose he meant mischief." I didn't know what to say; Long merely said "Good night," and we went off upstairs, promising to turn out all lights, and to go to bed in a few minutes.

Back in our room, we did our very best to make Paxton take a cheerful view. "There's the crown safe back," we said; "very likely you'd have done better not to touch it" (and he heavily assented to that), "but no real harm has been done, and we shall never give this away to anyone who would be so mad as to go near it. Besides, don't you feel better yourself? I don't mind confessing," I said, "that on the way there I was very much inclined to take your view about—well, about being followed;

but going back, it wasn't at all the same thing, was it?" No, it wouldn't do: "*You've* nothing to trouble yourselves about," he said, "but I'm not forgiven. I've got to pay for that miserable sacrilege still. I know what you are going to say. The Church might help. Yes, but it's the body that has to suffer. It's true I'm not feeling that he's waiting outside for me just now. But—" Then he stopped. Then he turned to thanking us, and we put him off as soon as we could. And naturally we pressed him to use our sitting-room next day, and said we should be glad to go out with him. Or did he play golf, perhaps? Yes, he did, but he didn't think he should care about that to-morrow. Well, we recommended him to get up late and sit in our room in the morning while we were playing, and we would have a walk later in the day. He was very submissive and *piano* about it all: ready to do just what we thought best, but clearly quite certain in his own mind that what was coming could not be averted or palliated. You'll wonder why we didn't insist on accompanying him to his home and seeing him safe into the care of brothers or someone. The fact was he had nobody. He had had a flat in town, but lately he had made up his mind to settle for a time in Sweden, and he had dismantled his flat and shipped off his belongings, and was whiling away a fortnight or three weeks before he made a start. Anyhow, we didn't see what we could do better than sleep on it—or not sleep very much, as was my case—and see what we felt like to-morrow morning.

We felt very different, Long and I, on as beautiful an April morning as you could desire; and Paxton also looked very different when we saw him at breakfast. "The first approach to a decent night I seem ever to have had," was what he said. But he was going to do as we had settled: stay in probably all the morning, and come out with us later. We went to the links; we met some other men and played with them in the morning, and had lunch there rather early, so as not to be late back. All the same, the snares of death overtook him.

Whether it could have been prevented, I don't know. I think he would have been got at somehow, do what we might. Anyhow, this is what happened.

We went straight up to our room. Paxton was there, reading

quite peaceably. "Ready to come out shortly?" said Long, "say in half an hour's time?" "Certainly," he said: and I said we would change first, and perhaps have baths, and call for him in half an hour. I had my bath first, and went and lay down on my bed, and slept for about ten minutes. We came out of our rooms at the same time, and went together to the sitting-room. Paxton wasn't there—only his book. Nor was he in his room, nor in the downstair rooms. We shouted for him. A servant came out and said: "Why, I thought you gentlemen was gone out already, and so did the other gentleman. He heard you a-calling from the path there, and run out in a hurry, and I looked out of the coffee-room window, but I didn't see you. 'Owever, he run off down the beach that way."

Without a word we ran that way too—it was the opposite direction to that of last night's expedition. It wasn't quite four o'clock, and the day was fair, though not so fair as it had been, so there was really no reason, you'd say, for anxiety: with people about, surely a man couldn't come to much harm.

But something in our look as we ran out must have struck the servant, for she came out on the steps, and pointed, and said, "Yes, that's the way he went." We ran on as far as the top of the shingle bank, and there pulled up. There was a choice of ways: past the houses on the sea-front, or along the sand at the bottom of the beach, which, the tide being now out, was fairly broad. Or of course we might keep along the shingle between these two tracks and have some view of both of them; only that was heavy going. We chose the sand, for that was the loneliest, and someone *might* come to harm there without being seen from the public path.

Long said he saw Paxton some distance ahead, running and waving his stick, as if he wanted to signal to people who were on ahead of him. I couldn't be sure: one of these sea-mists was coming up very quickly from the south. There was someone, that's all I could say. And there were tracks on the sand as of someone running who wore shoes; and there were other tracks made before those—for the shoes sometimes trod in them and interfered with them—of someone not in shoes. Oh, of course, it's only my word you've got to take for all this: Long's dead, we'd no time or means to make sketches or take casts, and the next tide washed everything away. All we could do was to notice these marks as we hurried on. But there they were over and over again, and we had no doubt whatever that what we saw was the track of a bare foot, and one that showed more bones than flesh.

The notion of Paxton running after—after anything like this, and supposing it to be the friends he was looking for, was very dreadful to us. You can guess what we fancied: how the thing he was following might stop suddenly and turn round on him, and what sort of face it would show, half-seen at first in the mist—which all the while was getting thicker and thicker. And as I ran on wondering how the poor wretch could have been lured into mistaking that other thing for us, I remembered his saying, "He has some power over your eyes." And then I wondered what the end would be, for I had no hope now that the end could be averted, and—well, there is no need to tell all the dismal and horrid thoughts that flitted through my head as we ran on into the mist. It was uncanny, too, that the sun should still be bright in the sky and we could see nothing. We could only tell that we were now past the houses and had reached that gap there is between them and the old martello tower. When you are past the tower, you know, there is nothing but shingle for a long way—not a house, not a human creature, just that spit of land, or rather shingle, with the river on your right and the sea on your left.

But just before that, just by the martello tower, you remember there is the old battery, close to the sea. I believe there are only a few blocks of concrete left now: the rest has all been washed away, but at this time there was a lot more, though the place was a ruin. Well, when we got there, we clambered to the top as quick as we could to take breath and look over the shingle in front if by chance the mist would let us see anything. But a moment's rest we must have. We had run a mile at least. Nothing whatever was visible ahead of us, and we were just turning by common consent to get down and run hopelessly on, when we heard what I can only call a laugh: and if you can understand what I mean by a breathless, a lungless laugh, you

have it: but I don't suppose you can. It came from below, and
swerved away into the mist. That was enough. We bent over the
wall. Paxton was there at the bottom.

You don't need to be told that he was dead. His tracks
showed that he had run along the side of the battery, had
turned sharp round the corner of it, and, small doubt of it,
must have dashed straight into the open arms of someone who
was waiting there. His mouth was full of sand and stones, and
his teeth and jaws were broken to bits. I only glanced once at
his face.

At the same moment, just as we were scrambling down from
the battery to get to the body, we heard a shout, and saw a man
running down the bank of the martello tower. He was the care-
taker stationed there, and his keen old eyes had managed to descry through the mist that something was wrong. He had seen
Paxton fall, and had seen us a moment after, running up—
fortunate this, for otherwise we could hardly have escaped suspicion of being concerned in the dreadful business. Had he, we
asked, caught sight of anybody attacking our friend? He could
not be sure.

We sent him off for help, and stayed by the dead man till they
came with the stretcher. It was then that we traced out how he
had come, on the narrow fringe of sand under the battery wall.
The rest was shingle, and it was hopelessly impossible to tell
whither the other had gone.

What were we to say at the inquest? It was a duty, we felt,
not to give up, there and then, the secret of the crown, to be
published in every paper. I don't know how much you would
have told: but what we did agree upon was this: to say that we
had only made acquaintance with Paxton the day before, and
that he had told us he was under some apprehension of danger
at the hands of a man called William Ager. Also that we had
seen some other tracks besides Paxton's when we followed him
along the beach. But of course by that time everything was gone
from the sands.

No one had any knowledge, fortunately, of any William Ager
living in the district. The evidence of the man at the martello
tower freed us from all suspicion. All that could be done was to

return a verdict of wilful murder by some person or persons unknown.

Paxton was so totally without connections that all the inquiries that were subsequently made ended in a No Thoroughfare. And I have never been at Seaburgh, or even near it, since.

AN EVENING'S
ENTERTAINMENT

Nothing is more common form in old-fashioned books than the description of the winter fireside, where the aged grandam narrates to the circle of children that hangs on her lips story after story of ghosts and fairies, and inspires her audience with a pleasing terror. But we are never allowed to know what the stories were. We hear, indeed, of sheeted spectres with saucer eyes, and—still more intriguing—of "Rawhead and Bloody Bones" (an expression which the Oxford Dictionary traces back to 1550),[1] but the context of these striking images eludes us.

Here, then, is a problem which has long obsessed me; but I see no means of solving it finally. The aged grandams are gone, and the collectors of folklore began their work in England too late to save most of the actual stories which the grandams told. Yet such things do not easily die quite out, and imagination, working on scattered hints, may be able to devise a picture of an evening's entertainment, such an one as Mrs. Marcet's *Evening Conversations*, Mr. Joyce's *Dialogues on Chemistry*, and somebody else's *Philosophy in Sport made Science in Earnest*,[2] aimed at extinguishing by substituting for Error and Superstition the light of Utility and Truth; in some such terms as these:

Charles: I think, papa, that I now understand the properties of the lever, which you so kindly explained to me on Saturday; but I have been very much puzzled since then in thinking about the pendulum, and have wondered why it is that, when you stop it, the clock does not go on any more.

Papa: (You young sinner, have you been meddling with the clock in the hall? Come here to me! *No, this must be a gloss that has somehow crept into the text.*) Well, my boy, though I do not wholly approve of your conducting without my supervision experiments which may possibly impair the usefulness of a valuable scientific instrument, I will do my best to explain the principles of the pendulum to you. Fetch me a piece of stout whipcord from the drawer in my study, and ask cook to be so good as to lend you one of the weights which she uses in her kitchen.

And so we are off.

How different the scene in a household to which the beams of Science have not yet penetrated! The Squire, exhausted by a long day after the partridges, and replete with food and drink, is snoring on one side of the fireplace. His old mother sits opposite to him knitting, and the children (Charles and Fanny, not Harry and Lucy: they would never have stood it) are gathered about her knee.

Grandmother: Now, my dears, you must be very good and quiet, or you'll wake your father, and you know what'll happen then.

Charles: Yes, I know: he'll be woundy[3] cross-tempered and send us off to bed.

Grandmother (stops knitting and speaks with severity): What's that? Fie upon you, Charles! that's not a way to speak. Now I *was* going to have told you a story, but if you use suchlike words, I shan't. (*Suppressed outcry:* "Oh, granny!") Hush! hush! Now I believe you *have* woke your father!

Squire (thickly): Look here, mother, if you can't keep them brats quiet—

Grandmother: Yes, John, yes! it's too bad. I've been telling them if it happens again, off to bed they shall go.

Squire relapses.

Grandmother: There, now, you see, children, what did I tell you? you *must* be good and sit still. And I'll tell you what: tomorrow you shall go a-blackberrying, and if you bring home a nice basketful, I'll make you some jam.

Charles: Oh yes, granny, do! and I know where the best blackberries are: I saw 'em to-day.

Grandmother: And where's that, Charles?

Charles: Why, in the little lane that goes up past Collins's cottage.

Grandmother (laying down her knitting): Charles! whatever you do, don't you dare to pick one single blackberry in that lane. Don't you *know*—but there, how should you—what was I thinking of? Well, anyway, you mind what I say——

Charles and Fanny: But why, granny? Why shouldn't we pick 'em there?

Grandmother: Hush! hush! Very well then, I'll tell you all about it, only you mustn't interrupt. Now let me see. When I was quite a little girl that lane had a bad name, though it seems people don't remember about it now. And one day—dear me, just as it might be to-night—I told my poor mother when I came home to my supper—a summer evening it was—I told her where I'd been for my walk, and how I'd come back down that lane, and I asked her how it was that there were currant and gooseberry bushes growing in a little patch at the top of the lane. And oh, dear me, such a taking as she was in! She shook me and she slapped me, and says she, "You naughty, naughty child, haven't I forbid you twenty times over to set foot in that lane? and here you go dawdling down it at night-time," and so forth, and when she'd finished I was almost too much taken aback to say anything: but I did make her believe that was the first I'd ever heard of it; and that was no more than the truth. And then, to be sure, she was sorry she'd been so short with me, and to make up she told me the whole story after my supper. And since then I've often heard the same from the old people in the place, and had my own reasons besides for thinking there was something in it.

Now, up at the far end of that lane—let me see, is it on the right- or the left-hand side as you go up?—the left-hand side— you'll find a little patch of bushes and rough ground in the field, and something like a broken old hedge round about, and you'll notice there's some old gooseberry and currant bushes growing among it—or there used to be, for it's years now since I've been up that way. Well, that means there was a cottage stood there, of course; and in that cottage, before I was born or thought of, there lived a man named Davis. I've heard that he wasn't born in the parish, and it's true there's nobody of that name been living about here since I've known the place. But however that may be, this Mr. Davis lived very much to himself and very seldom went to the public-house, and he didn't work for any of the farmers, having as it seemed enough money of his own to get along. But he'd go to the town on market-days and take up his letters at the post-house where the mails called. And one day he came back from market, and brought a young man with him; and this young man and he lived together for some long time, and went about together, and whether he just did the work of the house for Mr. Davis, or whether Mr. Davis was his teacher in some way, nobody seemed to know. I've heard he was a pale, ugly young fellow and hadn't much to say for himself. Well, now, what did those two men do with themselves? Of course I can't tell you half the foolish things that the people got into their heads, and we know, don't we, that you mustn't speak evil when you aren't sure it's true, even when people are dead and gone. But as I said, those two were always about together, late and early, up on the downland and below in the woods: and there was one walk in particular that they'd take regularly once a month, to the place where you've seen that old figure cut out in the hill-side;[4] and it was noticed that in the summertime when they took that walk, they'd camp out all night, either there or somewhere near by. I remember once my father—that's your great-grandfather—told me he had spoken to Mr. Davis about it (for it's his land he lived on) and asked him why he was so fond of going there, but he only said: "Oh, it's a wonderful old place, sir, and I've always been fond of the old-fashioned things, and when him (that was his man he meant) and me are together there, it seems to bring back the old times so plain." And my father said, "Well," he said, "it may suit *you,* but *I* shouldn't like a lonely place like that in the middle of the night." And Mr. Davis smiled, and the young man, who'd been listening, said, "Oh, we don't want for company at such times," and my father said he couldn't help thinking Mr. Davis made some kind of sign, and the young man went on quick, as if to mend his words, and said, "That's to say, Mr. Davis and me's company enough for each other, ain't we, master? and then there's a beautiful air there of a summer night, and you can see all the country round under the moon, and it looks so different, seemingly, to what it do in the daytime. Why, all them barrows on the down—"

And then Mr. Davis cut in, seeming to be out of temper with the lad, and said, "Ah yes, they're old-fashioned places, ain't they, sir? Now, what would you think was the purpose of them?" And my father said (now, dear me, it seems funny, doesn't it, that I should recollect all this: but it took my fancy at the time, and though it's dull perhaps for you, I can't help finishing it out now), well, he said, "Why, I've heard, Mr. Davis, that they're all graves, and I know, when I've had occasion to plough up one, there's always been some old bones and pots turned up. But whose graves they are, I don't know: people say the ancient Romans were all about this country at one time, but whether they buried their people like that I can't tell." And Mr. Davis shook his head, thinking, and said, "Ah, to be sure: well they look to me to be older-like than the ancient Romans, and dressed different—that's to say, according to the pictures the Romans was in armour, and you didn't never find no armour, did you, sir, by what you said?" And my father was rather surprised and said, "I don't know that I mentioned anything about armour, but it's true I don't remember to have found any. But you talk as if you'd seen 'em, Mr. Davis," and they both of them laughed, Mr. Davis and the young man, and Mr. Davis said, "Seen 'em, sir? that would be a difficult matter after all these years. Not but what I should like well enough to know more about them old times and people, and what they worshipped and all." And my father said, "Worshipped? Well, I dare say they worshipped the old man on the hill." "Ah, indeed!" Mr. Davis said, "well, I shouldn't wonder," and my father went on and told them what he'd heard and read about the heathens and their sacrifices: what you'll learn some day for yourself, Charles, when you go to school and begin your Latin. And they seemed to be very much interested, both of them; but my father said he couldn't help thinking the most of what he was saying was no news to them. That was the only time he ever had much talk with Mr. Davis, and it stuck in his mind, particularly, he said, the young man's word about *not wanting for company*: because in those days there was a lot of talk in the villages round about—why, but for my father interfering, the people here would have ducked an old lady for a witch.

Charles: What does that mean, granny, ducked an old lady for a witch? Are there witches here now?

Grandmother: No, no, dear! why, what ever made me stray off like that? No, no, that's quite another affair. What I was going to say was that the people in other places round about believed that some sort of meetings went on at night-time on that hill where the man is, and that those who went there were up to no good. But don't you interrupt me now, for it's getting late. Well, I suppose it was a matter of three years that Mr. Davis and this young man went on living together: and then all of a sudden, a dreadful thing happened. I don't know if I ought to tell you. (*Outcries of* "Oh yes! yes, granny, you must," etc.). Well, then, you must promise not to get frightened and go screaming out in the middle of the night. ("No, no, we won't, of course not!") One morning very early towards the turn of the year, I think it was in September, one of the woodmen had to go up to his work at the top of the long covert just as it was getting light; and just where there were some few big oaks in a sort of clearing deep in the wood he saw at a distance a white thing that looked like a man through the mist, and he was in two minds about going on, but go on he did, and made out as he came near that it *was* a man, and more than that, it was Mr. Davis's young man: dressed in a sort of white gown he was, and hanging by his neck to the limb of the biggest oak, quite, quite dead: and near his feet there lay on the ground a hatchet all in a gore of blood. Well, what a terrible sight that was for anyone to come upon in that lonely place! This poor man was nearly out of his wits: he dropped everything he was carrying and ran as hard as ever he could straight down to the Parsonage, and woke them up and told what he'd seen. And old Mr. White, who was the parson then, sent him off to get two or three of the best men, the blacksmith and the church-wardens and what not, while he dressed himself, and all of them went up to this dreadful place with a horse to lay the poor body on and take it to the house. When they got there, everything was just as the woodman had said: but it was a terrible shock to them all to see how

the corpse was dressed, specially to old Mr. White, for it seemed
to him to be like a mockery of the church surplice that was on
it, only, he told my father, not the same in the fashion of it. And
when they came to take down the body from the oak tree they
found there was a chain of some metal round the neck and a little ornament like a wheel hanging to it on the front, and it was
very old looking, they said. Now in the meantime they had sent
off a boy to run to Mr. Davis's house and see whether he was at
home; for of course they couldn't but have their suspicions.
And Mr. White said they must send too to the constable of the
next parish, and get a message to another magistrate (he was a
magistrate himself), and so there was running hither and
thither. But my father as it happened was away from home that
night, otherwise they would have fetched him first. So then they
laid the body across the horse, and they say it was all they could
manage to keep the beast from bolting away from the time they
were in sight of the tree, for it seemed to be mad with fright.
However, they managed to bind the eyes and lead it down
through the wood and back into the village street; and there,
just by the big tree where the stocks are, they found a lot of the
women gathered together, and this boy whom they'd sent to
Mr. Davis's house lying in the middle, as white as paper, and
not a word could they get out of him, good or bad. So they saw
there was something worse yet to come, and they made the best
of their way up the lane to Mr. Davis's house. And when they
got near that, the horse they were leading seemed to go mad
again with fear, and reared up and screamed, and struck out
with its forefeet and the man that was leading it was as near as
possible being killed, and the dead body fell off its back. So Mr.
White bid them get the horse away as quick as might be, and
they carried the body straight into the living-room, for the door
stood open. And then they saw what it was that had given the
poor boy such a fright, and they guessed why the horse went
mad, for you know horses can't bear the smell of dead blood.

There was a long table in the room, more than the length of a
man, and on it there lay the body of Mr. Davis. The eyes were
bound over with a linen band and the arms were tied across the
back, and the feet were bound together with another band. But

the fearful thing was that the breast being quite bare, the bone of it was split through from the top downwards with an axe! Oh, it was a terrible sight; not one there but turned faint and ill with it, and had to go out into the fresh air. Even Mr. White, who was what you might call a hard nature of a man, was quite overcome and said a prayer for strength in the garden.

At last they laid out the other body as best they could in the room, and searched about to see if they could find out how such a frightful thing had come to pass. And in the cupboards they found a quantity of herbs and jars with liquors, and it came out, when people that understood such matters had looked into it, that some of these liquors were drinks to put a person asleep. And they had little doubt that that wicked young man had put some of this into Mr. Davis's drink, and then used him as he did, and, after that, the sense of his sin had come upon him and he had cast himself away.

Well now, you couldn't understand all the law business that had to be done by the coroner and the magistrates; but there was a great coming and going of people over it for the next day or two, and then the people of the parish got together and agreed that they couldn't bear the thought of those two being buried in the churchyard alongside of Christian people; for I must tell you there were papers and writings found in the drawers and cupboards that Mr. White and some other clergymen looked into; and they put their names to a paper that said these men were guilty, by their own allowing, of the dreadful sin of idolatry; and they feared there were some in the neighbouring places that were not free from that wickedness, and called upon them to repent, lest the same fearful thing that was come to these men should befall them also; and then they burnt those writings. So then, Mr. White was of the same mind as the parishioners, and late one evening twelve men that were chosen went with him to that evil house, and with them they took two biers made very roughly for the purpose and two pieces of black cloth, and down at the cross-road, where you take the turn for Bascombe and Wilcombe,[5] there were other men waiting with torches, and a pit dug, and a great crowd of people gathered together from all round about. And the men that went to the cottage went in with their hats on their heads, and four of them took the two bodies and laid them on the biers and covered them over with the black cloths, and no one said a word, but they bore them down the lane, and they were cast into the pit and covered over with stones and earth, and then Mr. White spoke to the people that were gathered together. My father was there, for he had come back when he heard the news, and he said he never should forget the strangeness of the sight, with the torches burning and those two black things huddled together in the pit, and not a sound from any of the people, except it might be a child or a woman whimpering with the fright. And so, when Mr. White had finished speaking, they all turned away and left them lying there.

They say horses don't like the spot even now, and I've heard there was something of a mist or a light hung about for a long time after, but I don't know the truth of that. But this I do know, that next day my father's business took him past the opening of the lane, and he saw three or four little knots of people standing at different places along it, seemingly in a state of mind about something; and he rode up to them, and asked what was the matter. And they ran up to him and said, "Oh, Squire, it's the blood! Look at the blood!" and kept on like that. So he got off his horse and they showed him, and there, in four places, I think it was, he saw great patches in the road, of blood: but he could hardly see it was blood, for almost every spot of it was covered with great black flies, that never changed their place or moved. And that blood was what had fallen out of Mr. Davis's body as they bore it down the lane. Well, my father couldn't bear to do more than just take in the nasty sight so as to be sure of it, and then he said to one of those men that was there, "Do you make haste and fetch a basket or a barrow full of clean earth out of the churchyard and spread it over these places, and I'll wait here till you come back." And very soon he came back, and the old man that was sexton with him, with a shovel and the earth in a hand-barrow: and they set it down at the first of the places and made ready to cast the earth upon it; and as soon as ever they did that, what do you think? the flies that were on it rose up in the air in a kind of a solid cloud and moved off up the lane towards the house, and the sexton (he was parish clerk as well) stopped and looked at them and said to my father, "Lord of flies, sir,"[6] and no more would he say. And just the same it was at the other places, every one of them.

Charles: But what did he mean, granny?

Grandmother: Well, dear, you remember to ask Mr. Lucas when you go to him for your lesson to-morrow. I can't stop now to talk about it: it's long past bed-time for you already. The next thing was, my father made up his mind no one was going to live in that cottage again, or yet use any of the things that were in it: so, though it was one of the best in the place, he sent round word to the people that it was to be done away with, and anyone that wished could bring a faggot to the burning of it; and that's what was done. They built a pile of wood in the living-room and loosened the thatch so as the fire could take good hold, and then set it alight; and as there was no brick, only the chimney-stack and the oven, it wasn't long before it was all gone. I seem to remember seeing the chimney when I was a little girl, but that fell down of itself at last.

Now this that I've got to is the last bit of all. You may be sure that for a long time the people said Mr. Davis and that young man were seen about, the one of them in the wood and both of them where the house had been, or passing together down the lane, particularly in the spring of the year and at autumn-time. I can't speak to that, though if we were sure there are such things as ghosts, it would seem likely that people like that wouldn't rest quiet. But I can tell you this, that one evening in the month of March, just before your grandfather and I were married, we'd been taking a long walk in the woods together and picking flowers and talking as young people will that are courting; and so much taken up with each other that we never took any particular notice where we were going. And on a sudden I cried out, and your grandfather asked what was the matter. The matter was that I'd felt a sharp prick on the back of my hand, and I snatched it to me and saw a black thing on it, and struck it with the other hand and killed it. And I showed it him, and he was a man who took notice of all such things, and he said, "Well, I've never seen ought like that fly before," and though to my own eye it didn't seem very much out of the common, I've no doubt he was right.

And then we looked about us, and lo and behold if we weren't in the very lane, just in front of the place where that house had stood, and, as they told me after, just where the men set down the biers a minute when they bore them out of the garden gate. You may be sure we made haste away from there; at least, I made your grandfather come away quick, for I was wholly upset at finding myself there; but he would have lingered about out of curiosity if I'd have let him. Whether there was anything about there more than we could see I shall never be sure: perhaps it was partly the venom of that horrid fly's bite that was working in me that made me feel so strange; for, dear me, how that poor arm and hand of mine did swell up, to be sure! I'm afraid to tell you how large it was round! and the pain of it, too! Nothing my mother could put on it had any power over it at all, and it wasn't till she was persuaded by our old nurse to get the wise man over at Bascombe to come and look at it, that I got any peace at all. But he seemed to know all about it, and said I wasn't the first that had been taken that way. "When the sun's gathering his strength," he said, "and when he's in the height of it, and when he's beginning to lose his hold, and when he's in his weakness, them that haunts about that lane had best to take heed to themselves." But what it was he bound on my arm and what he said over it, he wouldn't tell us. After that I soon got well again, but since then I've heard often enough of people suffering much the same as I did; only of late years it doesn't seem to happen but very seldom: and maybe things like that do die out in the course of time.

But that's the reason, Charles, why I say to you that I won't have you gathering me blackberries, no, nor eating them either, in that lane; and now you know all about it, I don't fancy you'll want to yourself. There! Off to bed you go this minute. What's that, Fanny? A light in your room? The idea of such a thing! You get yourself undressed at once and say your prayers, and perhaps if your father doesn't want me when he wakes up, I'll come and say good night to you. And you, Charles, if I hear anything of you frightening your little sister on the way up to your bed, I shall tell your father that very moment, and you know what happened to you the last time.

The door closes, and granny, after listening intently for a minute or two, resumes her knitting. The Squire still slumbers.

THERE WAS A MAN DWELT BY A CHURCHYARD

This, you know, is the beginning of the story about sprites and goblins which Mamilius, the best child in Shakespeare, was telling to his mother the queen, and the court ladies, when the king came in with his guards and hurried her off to prison. There is no more of the story; Mamilius died soon after without having a chance of finishing it. Now what was it going to have been? Shakespeare knew, no doubt, and I will be bold to say that I do. It was not going to be a new story: it was to be one which you have most likely heard, and even told. Everybody may set it in what frame he likes best. This is mine:

There was a man dwelt by a churchyard. His house had a lower story of stone and an upper one of timber. The front windows looked out on the street and the back ones on the churchyard. It had once belonged to the parish priest, but (this was in Queen Elizabeth's days) the priest was a married man and wanted more room; besides, his wife disliked seeing the churchyard at night out of her bedroom window. She said she saw—but never mind what she said; anyhow, she gave her husband no peace till he agreed to move into a larger house in the village street, and the old one was taken by John Poole, who was a widower, and lived there alone. He was an elderly man who kept very much to himself, and people said he was something of a miser.

It was very likely true: he was morbid in other ways, certainly. In those days it was common to bury people at night and by torchlight: and it was noticed that whenever a funeral was toward, John Poole was always at his window, either on the ground floor or upstairs, according as he could get the better view from one or the other.

THERE WAS A MAN DWELT BY A CHURCHYARD

There came a night when an old woman was to be buried. She was fairly well to do, but she was not liked in the place. The usual thing was said of her, that she was no Christian, and that on such nights as Midsummer Eve and All Hallows,[1] she was not to be found in her house. She was red-eyed and dreadful to look at, and no beggar ever knocked at her door. Yet when she died she left a purse of money to the Church.

There was no storm on the night of her burial; it was fair and calm. But there was some difficulty about getting bearers, and men to carry the torches, in spite of the fact that she had left larger fees than common for such as did that work. She was buried in woollen, without a coffin. No one was there but those who were actually needed—and John Poole, watching from his window. Just before the grave was filled in, the parson stooped down and cast something upon the body—something that clinked—and in a low voice he said words that sounded like "Thy money perish with thee." Then he walked quickly away, and so did the other men, leaving only one torch-bearer to light the sexton and his boy while they shovelled the earth in. They made no very neat job of it, and next day, which was a Sunday, the churchgoers were rather sharp with the sexton, saying it was the untidiest grave in the yard. And indeed, when he came to look at it himself, he thought it was worse than he had left it.

Meanwhile John Poole went about with a curious air, half exulting, as it were, and half nervous. More than once he spent an evening at the inn, which was clean contrary to his usual habit, and to those who fell into talk with him there he hinted that he had come into a little bit of money and was looking out for a somewhat better house. "Well, I don't wonder," said the smith one night, "I shouldn't care for that place of yours. I should be fancying things all night." The landlord asked him what sort of things.

"Well, maybe somebody climbing up to the chamber window, or the like of that," said the smith. "I don't know—old mother Wilkins that was buried a week ago to-day, eh?"

"Come, I think you might consider of a person's feelings," said the landlord. "It ain't so pleasant for Master Poole, is it now?"

"Master Poole don't mind," said the smith. "He's been there long enough to know. I only says it wouldn't be my choice. What with the passing bell, and the torches when there's a burial, and all them graves laying so quiet when there's no one about: only they say there's lights—don't you never see no lights, Master Poole?"

"No, I don't never see no lights," said Master Poole sulkily, and called for another drink, and went home late.

That night, as he lay in his bed upstairs, a moaning wind began to play about the house, and he could not go to sleep. He got up and crossed the room to a little cupboard in the wall: he took out of it something that clinked, and put it in the breast of his bedgown. Then he went to the window and looked out into the churchyard.

Have you ever seen an old brass in a church with a figure of a person in a shroud? It is bunched together at the top of the head in a curious way. Something like that was sticking up out of the earth in a spot of the churchyard which John Poole knew very well. He darted into his bed and lay there very still indeed.

Presently something made a very faint rattling at the casement. With a dreadful reluctance John Poole turned his eyes that way. Alas! Between him and the moonlight was the black outline of the curious bunched head. . . . Then there was a figure in the room. Dry earth rattled on the floor. A low cracked voice said "Where is it?" and steps went hither and thither, faltering steps as of one walking with difficulty. It could be seen now and again, peering into corners, stooping to look under chairs; finally it could be heard fumbling at the doors of the cupboard in the wall, throwing them open. There was a scratching of long nails on the empty shelves. The figure whipped round, stood for an instant at the side of the bed, raised its arms, and with a hoarse scream of "YOU'VE GOT IT!"—

At this point H.R.H. Prince Mamilius (who would, I think, have made the story a good deal shorter than this) flung himself with a loud yell upon the youngest of the court ladies present, who responded with an equally piercing cry. He was instantly seized upon by H.M. Queen Hermione, who, repressing an inclination to laugh, shook and slapped him very severely. Much flushed, and rather inclined to cry, he was about to be sent to bed: but, on the intercession of his victim, who had now recovered from the shock, he was eventually permitted to remain until his usual hour for retiring; by which time he too had so far recovered as to assert, in bidding good night to the company, that he knew another story quite three times as dreadful as that one, and would tell it on the first opportunity that offered.

RATS

*"And if you was to walk through the bedrooms now, you'd see
the ragged, mouldy bedclothes a-heaving and a-heaving like seas."
"And a-heaving and a-heaving with what?" he says. "Why, with
the rats under 'em."*[1]

But was it with the rats? I ask, because in another case it was
not. I cannot put a date to the story, but I was young when I
heard it, and the teller was old. It is an ill-proportioned tale, but
that is my fault, not his.

It happened in Suffolk, near the coast. In a place where the
road makes a sudden dip and then a sudden rise; as you go
northward, at the top of that rise, stands a house on the left of
the road. It is a tall red-brick house, narrow for its height; perhaps it was built about 1770. The top of the front has a low tri-
angular pediment with a round window in the centre. Behind it
are stables and offices, and such garden as it has is behind them.
Scraggy Scotch firs are near it: an expanse of gorse-covered land
stretches away from it. It commands a view of the distant sea
from the upper windows of the front. A sign on a post stands
before the door; or did so stand, for though it was an inn of repute once, I believe it is so no longer.

To this inn came my acquaintance, Mr. Thomson, when he
was a young man, on a fine spring day, coming from the University of Cambridge, and desirous of solitude in tolerable
quarters and time for reading. These he found, for the landlord
and his wife had been in service and could make a visitor comfortable, and there was no one else staying in the inn. He had a
large room on the first floor commanding the road and the

view, and if it faced east, why, that could not be helped; the house was well built and warm.

He spent very tranquil and uneventful days: work all the morning, an afternoon perambulation of the country round, a little conversation with country company or the people of the inn in the evening over the then fashionable drink of brandy and water, a little more reading and writing, and bed; and he would have been content that this should continue for the full month he had at disposal, so well was his work progressing, and so fine was the April of that year—which I have reason to believe was that which Orlando Whistlecraft chronicles in his weather record as the "Charming Year."[2]

One of his walks took him along the northern road, which stands high and traverses a wide common, called a heath. On the bright afternoon when he first chose this direction his eye caught a white object some hundreds of yards to the left of the road, and he felt it necessary to make sure what this might be. It was not long before he was standing by it, and found himself looking at a square block of white stone fashioned somewhat like the base of a pillar, with a square hole in the upper surface. Just such another you may see at this day on Thetford Heath.[3] After taking stock of it he contemplated for a few minutes the view, which offered a church tower or two, some red roofs of cottages and windows winking in the sun, and the expanse of sea— also with an occasional wink and gleam upon it—and so pursued his way.

In the desultory evening talk in the bar, he asked why the white stone was there on the common.

"A old-fashioned thing, that is," said the landlord (Mr. Betts), "we was none of us alive when that was put there." "That's right," said another. "It stands pretty high," said Mr. Thomson, "I dare say a sea-mark was on it some time back." "Ah! yes," Mr. Betts agreed, "I 'ave 'eard they could see it from the boats; but whatever there was, it's fell to bits this long time." "Good job too," said a third, " 'twarn't a lucky mark, by what the old men used to say; not lucky for the fishin', I mean to say." "Why ever not?" said Thomson. "Well, I never see it myself," was the answer, "but they 'ad some funny ideas, what I mean, peculiar, them old chaps, and I shouldn't wonder but what they made away with it theirselves."

It was impossible to get anything clearer than this: the company, never very voluble, fell silent, and when next someone spoke it was of village affairs and crops. Mr. Betts was the speaker.

Not every day did Thomson consult his health by taking a country walk. One very fine afternoon found him busily writing at three o'clock. Then he stretched himself and rose, and walked out of his room into the passage. Facing him was another room, then the stair-head, then two more rooms, one looking out to the back, the other to the south. At the south end of the passage was a window, to which he went, considering with himself that it was rather a shame to waste such a fine afternoon. However, work was paramount just at the moment; he thought he would just take five minutes off and go back to it, and those five minutes he would employ—the Bettses could not possibly object—to looking at the other rooms in the passage, which he had never seen. Nobody at all, it seemed, was indoors; probably, as it was market day, they were all gone to the town, except perhaps a maid in the bar. Very still the house was, and the sun shone really hot; early flies buzzed in the window-panes. So he explored. The room facing his own was undistinguished except for an old print of Bury St. Edmunds; the two next him on his side of the passage were gay and clean, with one window apiece, whereas his had two. Remained the southwest room, opposite to the last which he had entered. This was locked; but Thomson was in a mood of quite indefensible curiosity, and feeling confident that there could be no damaging secrets in a place so easily got at, he proceeded to fetch the key of his own room, and when that did not answer, to collect the keys of the other three. One of them fitted, and he opened the door. The room had two windows looking south and west, so it was as bright and the sun as hot upon it as could be. Here there was no carpet, but bare boards; no pictures, no washing-stand, only a bed, in the farther corner: an iron bed, with mattress and bolster, covered with a bluish check counterpane. As featureless a room as you can well imagine, and yet there was something that made Thomson close the door very quickly and yet quietly behind him and lean against the window-sill in the passage, actually quivering all over. It was this, that under the counterpane someone lay, and not only lay, but stirred. That it was some *one* and not some *thing* was certain, because the shape of a head was unmistakable on the bolster; and yet it was all covered, and no one lies with covered head but a dead person; and this was not dead, not truly dead, for it heaved and shivered. If he had seen these things in dusk or by the light of a flickering candle, Thomson could have comforted himself and talked of fancy. On this bright day that was impossible. What was to be done? First, lock the door at all costs. Very gingerly he approached it and bending down listened, holding his breath; perhaps there might be a sound of heavy breathing, and a prosaic explanation. There was absolute silence. But as, with a rather tremulous hand, he put the key into its hole and turned it, it rattled, and on the instant a stumbling padding tread was heard coming towards the door. Thomson fled like a rabbit to his room and locked himself in: futile enough, he knew it was; would doors and locks be any obstacle to what he suspected? but it was all he could think of at the moment, and in fact nothing happened; only there was a time of acute suspense—followed by a misery of doubt as to what to do. The impulse, of course, was to slip away as soon as possible from a house which contained such an inmate. But only the day before he had said he should be staying for at least a week more, and how if he changed plans could he avoid the suspicion of having pried into places where he certainly had no business? Moreover, either the Bettses knew all about the inmate, and yet did not leave the house, or knew nothing, which equally meant that there was nothing to be afraid of, or knew just enough to make them shut up the room, but not enough to weigh on the spirits: in any of these cases it seemed that not much was to be feared, and certainly so far he had had no sort of ugly experience. On the whole the line of least resistance was to stay.

Well, he stayed out his week. Nothing took him past that door, and, often as he would pause in a quiet hour of day or night in the passage and listen, and listen, no sound whatever issued from that direction. You might have thought that Thomson would have made some attempt at ferreting out stories connected with the inn—hardly perhaps from Betts, but from the parson of the parish, or old people in the village; but no, the reticence which commonly falls on people who have had strange experiences, and believe in them, was upon him. Nevertheless, as the end of his stay drew near, his yearning after some kind of explanation grew more and more acute. On his solitary walks he persisted in planning out some way, the least obtrusive, of getting another daylight glimpse into that room, and eventually arrived at this scheme. He would leave by an afternoon train—about four o'clock. When his fly was waiting, and his luggage on it, he would make one last expedition upstairs to look round his own room and see if anything was left unpacked, and then, with that key, which he had contrived to oil (as if that made any difference!), the door should once more be opened, for a moment, and shut.

So it worked out. The bill was paid, the consequent small talk gone through while the fly was loaded: "pleasant part of the country—been very comfortable, thanks to you and Mrs. Betts—hope to come back some time," on one side: on the other, "very glad you've found satisfaction, sir, done our best—always glad to 'ave your good word—very much favoured we've been with the weather, to be sure." Then, "I'll just take a look upstairs in case I've left a book or something out—no, don't trouble, I'll be back in a minute." And as noiselessly as possible he stole to the door and opened it. The shattering of the illusion! He almost laughed aloud. Propped, or you might say sitting, on the edge of the bed was—nothing in the round world but a scarecrow! A scarecrow out of the garden, of course, dumped into the deserted room. . . . Yes; but here amusement ceased. Have scarecrows bare bony feet? Do their heads loll on to their shoulders? Have they iron collars and links of chain about their necks? Can they get up and move, if never so stiffly, across a floor, with wagging head and arms close at their sides? and shiver?

The slam of the door, the dash to the stair-head, the leap downstairs, were followed by a faint. Awaking, Thomson saw

Betts standing over him with the brandy bottle and a very re-
proachful face. "You shouldn't a done so, sir, really you
shouldn't. It ain't a kind way to act by persons as done the best
they could for you." Thomson heard words of this kind, but
what he said in reply he did not know. Mr. Betts, and perhaps
even more Mrs. Betts, found it hard to accept his apologies and
his assurances that he would say no word that could damage
the good name of the house. However, they *were* accepted.
Since the train could not now be caught, it was arranged that
Thomson should be driven to the town to sleep there. Before he
went the Bettses told him what little they knew. "They says he
was landlord 'ere a long time back, and was in with the 'igh-
waymen that 'ad their beat about the 'eath. That's how he come
by his end: 'ung in chains, they say, up where you see that stone
what the gallus stood in. Yes, the fishermen made away with
that, I believe, because they see it out at sea and it kep' the fish
off, according to their idea. Yes, we 'ad the account from the
people that 'ad the 'ouse before we come. 'You keep that room
shut up,' they says, 'but don't move the bed out, and you'll find
there won't be no trouble.' And no more there 'as been; not
once he haven't come out into the 'ouse, though what he may do
now there ain't no sayin'. Anyway, you're the first I know on
that's seen him since we've been 'ere: I never set eyes on him
myself, nor don't want. And ever since we've made the servants'
rooms in the stablin', we ain't 'ad no difficulty that way. Only I
do 'ope, sir, as you'll keep a close tongue, considerin' 'ow an
'ouse do get talked about": with more to this effect.

The promise of silence was kept for many years. The occasion of my hearing the story at last was this: that when Mr.
Thomson came to stay with my father it fell to me to show him
to his room, and instead of letting me open the door for him, he
stepped forward and threw it open himself, and then for some
moments stood in the doorway holding up his candle and looking narrowly into the interior. Then he seemed to recollect himself and said: "I beg your pardon. Very absurd, but I can't help
doing that, for a particular reason." What that reason was I
heard some days afterwards, and you have heard now.

AFTER DARK IN THE PLAYING FIELDS

The hour was late and the night was fair. I had halted not far from Sheeps' Bridge[1] and was thinking about the stillness, only broken by the sound of the weir,[2] when a loud tremulous hoot just above me made me jump. It is always annoying to be startled, but I have a kindness for owls. This one was evidently very near: I looked about for it. There it was, sitting plumply on a branch about twelve feet up. I pointed my stick at it and said, "Was that you?" "Drop it," said the owl. "I know it ain't only a stick, but I don't like it. Yes, of course it was me: who do you suppose it would be if it warn't?"

We will take as read the sentences about my surprise. I lowered the stick. "Well," said the owl, "what about it? If you will come out here of a Midsummer evening like what this is, what do you expect?" "I beg your pardon," I said, "I should have remembered. May I say that I think myself very lucky to have met you to-night? I hope you have time for a little talk?" "Well," said the owl ungraciously, "I don't know as it matters so particular to-night. I've had me supper as it happens, and if you ain't too long over it—ah-h-h!" Suddenly it broke into a loud scream, flapped its wings furiously, bent forward and clutched its perch tightly, continuing to scream. Plainly something was pulling hard at it from behind. The strain relaxed abruptly, the owl nearly fell over, and then whipped round, ruffling up all over, and made a vicious dab at something unseen by me. "Oh, I *am* sorry," said a small clear voice in a solicitous tone. "I made sure it was loose. I do hope I didn't hurt you." "Didn't 'urt me?" said the owl bitterly. "Of course you 'urt me, and well you know it, you young infidel. That feather was no more loose than—oh, if I could git at you! Now I shouldn't wonder but what you've throwed me all out of balance. Why can't you let a person set quiet for two minutes at a time without you must come creepin' up and—well, you've done it this time, anyway. I shall go straight to 'eadquarters and"—(finding it was now addressing the empty air)—"why, where have you got to now? Oh, it is too bad, that it is!"

"Dear me!" I said, "I'm afraid this isn't the first time you've been annoyed in this way. May I ask exactly what happened?"

"Yes, you may ask," said the owl, still looking narrowly about as it spoke, "but it 'ud take me till the latter end of next week to tell you. Fancy coming and pulling out anyone's tail feather! 'Urt me something crool, it did. And what for, I should like to know? Answer me that! Where's the *reason* of it?"

All that occurred to me was to murmur, "The clamorous owl that nightly hoots and wonders at our quaint spirits."[3] I hardly thought the point would be taken, but the owl said sharply: "What's that? Yes, you needn't to repeat it. I 'eard. And I'll tell you what's at the bottom of it, and you mark my words." It bent towards me and whispered, with many nods of its round head: "Pride! stand-offishness! that's what it is! *Come not near our fairy queen*"[4] (this in a tone of bitter contempt). "Oh, dear no! we ain't good enough for the likes of them. Us that's been noted time out of mind for the best singers in the Fields: now, ain't that so?"

"Well," I said, doubtfully enough, "*I* like to hear you very much: but, you know, some people think a lot of the thrushes and nightingales and so on; you must have heard of that, haven't you? And then, perhaps—of course I don't know—perhaps your style of singing isn't exactly what they think suitable to accompany their dancing, eh?"

"I should kindly 'ope not," said the owl, drawing itself up. "Our family's never give in to dancing, nor never won't neither. Why, what ever are you thinkin' of!" it went on with rising temper. "A pretty thing it would be for me to set there hiccuppin' at them"—it stopped and looked cautiously all round it and up and down and then continued in a louder voice—"them little ladies and gentlemen. If it ain't sootable for them, I'm very sure it ain't sootable for me. And" (temper rising again) "if they expect me never to say a word just because they're dancin' and carryin' on with their foolishness, they're very much mistook, and so I tell 'em."

From what had passed before I was afraid this was an imprudent line to take, and I was right. Hardly had the owl given its last emphatic nod when four small slim forms dropped from a bough above, and in a twinkling some sort of grass rope was thrown round the body of the unhappy bird, and it was borne off through the air, loudly protesting, in the direction of Fellows' Pond.[5] Splashes and gurgles and shrieks of unfeeling laughter were heard as I hurried up. Something darted away over my head, and as I stood peering over the bank of the pond, which was all in commotion, a very angry and dishevelled owl scrambled heavily up the bank, and stopping near my feet shook itself and flapped and hissed for several minutes without saying anything I should care to repeat.

Glaring at me, it eventually said—and the grim suppressed rage in its voice was such that I hastily drew back a step or two—" 'Ear that? Said they was very sorry, but they'd mistook me for a duck. Oh, if it ain't enough to make anyone go reg'lar distracted in their mind and tear everythink to flinders for miles round." So carried away was it by passion, that it began the process at once by rooting up a large beakful of grass, which alas! got into its throat; and the choking that resulted made me really afraid that it would break a vessel. But the paroxysm was mastered, and the owl sat up, winking and breathless but intact.

Some expression of sympathy seemed to be required; yet I was chary of offering it, for in its present state of mind I felt that the bird might interpret the best-meant phrase as a fresh insult. So we stood looking at each other without speech for a very awkward minute, and then came a diversion. First the thin voice of the pavilion clock, then the deeper sound from the Castle quadrangle, then Lupton's Tower, drowning the Curfew Tower by its nearness.[6]

"What's that?" said the owl, suddenly and hoarsely. "Midnight, I should think," said I, and had recourse to my watch. "Midnight?" cried the owl, evidently much startled, "and me too wet to fly a yard! Here, you pick me up and put me in the tree; don't, I'll climb up your leg, and you won't ask me to do that twice. Quick now!" I obeyed. "Which tree do you want?" "Why, my tree, to be sure! Over there!" It nodded towards the Wall. "All right. Bad-calx tree[7] do you mean?" I said, beginning to run in that direction. " 'Ow should I know what silly names you call it? The one what 'as like a door in it. Go faster! They'll be coming in another minute." "Who? What's the matter?" I asked as I ran, clutching the wet creature, and much afraid of stumbling and coming over with it in the long grass. "*You'll* see fast enough," said this selfish bird. "You just let me git on the tree, *I* shall be all right."

And I suppose it was, for it scrabbled very quickly up the trunk with its wings spread and disappeared in a hollow without a word of thanks. I looked round, not very comfortably. The Curfew Tower was still playing St. David's tune[8] and the little chime that follows, for the third and last time, but the other bells had finished what they had to say, and now there was silence, and again the "restless changing weir"[9] was the only thing that broke—no, that emphasized it.

Why had the owl been so anxious to get into hiding? That of course was what now exercised me. Whatever and whoever was coming, I was sure that this was no time for me to cross the open field: I should do best to dissemble my presence by staying on the darker side of the tree. And that is what I did.

All this took place some years ago, before summertime came in. I do sometimes go into the Playing Fields at night still, but I come in before true midnight. And I find I do not like a crowd after dark—for example at the Fourth of June fireworks.[10] You see—no, you do not, but I see—such curious faces: and the people to whom they belong flit about so oddly, often at your elbow when you least expect it, and looking close into your face, as if they were searching for someone—who may be thankful, I think, if they do not find him. "Where do they come from?"

Why, some, I think, out of the water, and some out of the ground. They look like that. But I am sure it is best to take no notice of them, and not to touch them.

Yes, I certainly prefer the daylight population of the Playing Fields to that which comes there after dark.

WAILING WELL

In the year 19— there were two members of the Troop of Scouts[1] attached to a famous school, named respectively Arthur Wilcox and Stanley Judkins. They were the same age, boarded in the same house, were in the same division, and naturally were members of the same patrol. They were so much alike in appearance as to cause anxiety and trouble, and even irritation, to the masters who came in contact with them. But oh how different were they in their inward man, or boy!

It was to Arthur Wilcox that the Head Master said, looking up with a smile as the boy entered chambers, "Why, Wilcox, there will be a deficit in the prize fund if you stay here much longer! Here, take this handsomely bound copy of the *Life and Works of Bishop Ken,*[2] and with it my hearty congratulations to yourself and your excellent parents." It was Wilcox again, whom the Provost noticed as he passed through the playing fields, and, pausing for a moment, observed to the Vice-Provost, "That lad has a remarkable brow!" "Indeed, yes," said the Vice-Provost.[3] "It denotes either genius or water on the brain."

As a Scout, Wilcox secured every badge and distinction for which he competed. The Cookery Badge, the Map-making Badge, the Life-saving Badge, the Badge for picking up bits of newspaper, the Badge for not slamming the door when leaving pupil-room, and many others. Of the Life-saving Badge I may have a word to say when we come to treat of Stanley Judkins.

You cannot be surprised to hear that Mr. Hope Jones[4] added a special verse to each of his songs, in commendation of Arthur

Wilcox, or that the Lower Master burst into tears when handing him the Good Conduct Medal in its handsome claret-
coloured case: the medal which had been unanimously voted to
him by the whole of Third Form. Unanimously, did I say? I am
wrong. There was one dissentient, Judkins *mi.*,[5] who said that
he had excellent reasons for acting as he did. He shared, it
seems, a room with his major. You cannot, again, wonder that
in after years Arthur Wilcox was the first, and so far the only
boy, to become Captain of both the School and of the Oppidans,[6] or that the strain of carrying out the duties of both positions, coupled with the ordinary work of the school, was so
severe that a complete rest for six months, followed by a voyage round the world, was pronounced an absolute necessity by
the family doctor.

It would be a pleasant task to trace the steps by which he attained the giddy eminence he now occupies; but for the moment enough of Arthur Wilcox. Time presses, and we must
turn to a very different matter: the career of Stanley Judkins—
Judkins *ma*.

Stanley Judkins, like Arthur Wilcox, attracted the attention
of the authorities; but in quite another fashion. It was to him
that the Lower Master said, with no cheerful smile, "What,
again, Judkins? A very little persistence in this course of conduct, my boy, and you will have cause to regret that you ever
entered this academy. There, take that, and that, and think
yourself very lucky you don't get that and that!" It was Judkins,
again, whom the Provost had cause to notice as he passed
through the playing fields, when a cricket ball struck him with
considerable force on the ankle, and a voice from a short way
off cried, "Thank you, cut-over!" "I think," said the Provost,
pausing for a moment to rub his ankle, "that that boy had better fetch his cricket ball for himself!" "Indeed, yes," said the
Vice-Provost, "and if he comes within reach, I will do my best
to fetch him something else."

As a Scout, Stanley Judkins secured no badge save those
which he was able to abstract from members of other patrols.
In the cookery competition he was detected trying to introduce
squibs into the Dutch oven of the next-door competitors. In the

tailoring competition he succeeded in sewing two boys together very firmly, with disastrous effect when they tried to get up. For the Tidiness Badge he was disqualified, because, in the Midsummer schooltime, which chanced to be hot, he could not be dissuaded from sitting with his fingers in the ink: as he said, for coolness' sake. For one piece of paper which he picked up, he must have dropped at least six banana skins or orange peels. Aged women seeing him approaching would beg him with tears in their eyes not to carry their pails of water across the road. They knew too well what the result would inevitably be. But it was in the life-saving competition that Stanley Judkins's conduct was most blameable and had the most far-reaching effects. The practice, as you know, was to throw a selected lower boy, of suitable dimensions, fully dressed, with his hands and feet tied together, into the deepest part of Cuckoo Weir,[7] and to time the Scout whose turn it was to rescue him. On every occasion when he was entered for this competition Stanley Judkins was seized, at the critical moment, with a severe fit of cramp, which caused him to roll on the ground and utter alarming cries. This naturally distracted the attention of those present from the boy in the water, and had it not been for the presence of Arthur Wilcox the death-roll would have been a heavy one. As it was, the Lower Master found it necessary to take a firm line and say that the competition must be discontinued. It was in vain that Mr. Beasley Robinson[8] represented to him that in five competitions only four lower boys had actually succumbed. The Lower Master said that he would be the last to interfere in any way with the work of the Scouts; but that three of these boys had been valued members of his choir, and both he and Dr. Ley[9] felt that the inconvenience caused by the losses outweighed the advantages of the competitions. Besides, the correspondence with the parents of these boys had become annoying, and even distressing: they were no longer satisfied with the printed form which he was in the habit of sending out, and more than one of them had actually visited Eton and taken up much of his valuable time with complaints. So the life-saving competition is now a thing of the past.

In short, Stanley Judkins was no credit to the Scouts, and

there was talk on more than one occasion of informing him that
his services were no longer required. This course was strongly
advocated by Mr. Lambart: but in the end milder counsels prevailed, and it was decided to give him another chance.

So it is that we find him at the beginning of the Midsummer
Holidays of 19— at the Scouts' camp in the beautiful district of
W (or X) in the county of D (or Y).

It was a lovely morning, and Stanley Judkins and one or two
of his friends—for he still had friends—lay basking on the top
of the down. Stanley was lying on his stomach with his chin
propped on his hands, staring into the distance.

"I wonder what that place is," he said.

"Which place?" said one of the others.

"That sort of clump in the middle of the field down there."

"Oh, ah! How should I know what it is?"

"What do you want to know for?" said another.

"I don't know: I like the look of it. What's it called? Nobody
got a map?" said Stanley. "Call yourselves Scouts!"

"Here's a map all right," said Wilfred Pipsqueak,[10] ever re-
sourceful, "and there's the place marked on it. But it's inside the
red ring. We can't go there."

"Who cares about a red ring?" said Stanley. "But it's got no
name on your silly map."

"Well, you can ask this old chap what it's called if you're so
keen to find out." "This old chap" was an old shepherd who
had come up and was standing behind them.

"Good morning, young gents," he said, "you've got a fine
day for your doin's, ain't you?"

"Yes, thank you," said Algernon de Montmorency, with native politeness. "Can you tell us what that clump over there's
called? And what's that thing inside it?"

"Course I can tell you," said the shepherd. "That's Wailin'
Well, that is. But you ain't got no call to worry about that."

"Is it a well in there?" said Algernon. "Who uses it?"

The shepherd laughed. "Bless you," he said, "there ain't from
a man to a sheep in these parts uses Wailin' Well, nor haven't
done all the years I've lived here."

"Well, there'll be a record broken to-day, then," said Stanley Judkins, "because I shall go and get some water out of it for tea!"

"Sakes alive, young gentleman!" said the shepherd in a startled voice, "don't you get to talkin' that way! Why, ain't your masters give you notice not to go by there? They'd ought to have done."

"Yes, they have," said Wilfred Pipsqueak.

"Shut up, you ass!" said Stanley Judkins. "What's the matter with it? Isn't the water good? Anyhow, if it was boiled, it would be all right."

"I don't know as there's anything much wrong with the water," said the shepherd. "All I know is, my old dog wouldn't go through that field, let alone me or anyone else that's got a morsel of brains in their heads."

"More fool them," said Stanley Judkins, at once rudely and ungrammatically. "Who ever took any harm going there?" he added.

"Three women and a man," said the shepherd gravely. "Now just you listen to me. I know these 'ere parts and you don't, and I can tell you this much: for these ten years last past there ain't been a sheep fed in that field, nor a crop raised off of it—and it's good land, too. You can pretty well see from here what a state it's got into with brambles and suckers and trash of all kinds. *You've* got a glass, young gentleman," he said to Wilfred Pipsqueak, "you can tell with that anyway."

"Yes," said Wilfred, "but I see there's tracks in it. Someone must go through it sometimes."

"Tracks!" said the shepherd. "I believe you! Four tracks: three women and a man."

"What d'you mean, three women and a man?" said Stanley, turning over for the first time and looking at the shepherd (he had been talking with his back to him till this moment: he was an ill-mannered boy).

"Mean? Why, what I says: three women and a man."

"Who are they?" asked Algernon. "Why do they go there?"

"There's some p'r'aps could tell you who they *was*," said the shepherd, "but it was afore my time they come by their end. And why they goes there still is more than the children of men can tell: except I've heard they was all bad 'uns when they was alive."

"By George, what a rum thing!" Algernon and Wilfred muttered: but Stanley was scornful and bitter.

"Why, you don't mean they're deaders? What rot! You must be a lot of fools to believe that. Who's ever seen them, I'd like to know?"

"*I've* seen 'em, young gentleman!" said the shepherd, "seen 'em from near by on that bit of down: and my old dog, if he could speak, he'd tell you he've seen 'em, same time. About four o'clock of the day it was, much such a day as this. I see 'em, each one of 'em, come peerin' out of the bushes and stand up, and work their way slow by them tracks towards the trees in the middle where the well is."

"And what were they like? Do tell us!" said Algernon and Wilfred eagerly.

"Rags and bones, young gentlemen: all four of 'em: flutterin' rags and whity bones. It seemed to me as if I could hear 'em clackin' as they got along. Very slow they went, and lookin' from side to side."

"What were their faces like? Could you see?"

"They hadn't much to call faces," said the shepherd, "but I could seem to see as they had teeth."

"Lor'!" said Wilfred, "and what did they do when they got to the trees?"

"I can't tell you that, sir," said the shepherd. "I wasn't for stayin' in that place, and if I had been, I was bound to look to my old dog: he'd gone! Such a thing he never done before as leave me; but gone he had, and when I came up with him in the end, he was in that state he didn't know me, and was fit to fly at my throat. But I kep' talkin' to him, and after a bit he remembered my voice and came creepin' up like a child askin' pardon. I never want to see him like that again, nor yet no other dog."

The dog, who had come up and was making friends all round, looked up at his master, and expressed agreement with what he was saying very fully.

The boys pondered for some moments on what they had heard: after which Wilfred said: "And why's it called Wailing Well?"

"If you was round here at dusk of a winter's evening, you wouldn't want to ask why," was all the shepherd said.

"Well, I don't believe a word of it," said Stanley Judkins, "and I'll go there next chance I get: blowed if I don't!"

"Then you won't be ruled by me?" said the shepherd. "Nor yet by your masters as warned you off? Come now, young gentleman, you don't want for sense, I should say. What should I want tellin' you a pack of lies? It ain't sixpence to me anyone goin' in that field: but I wouldn't like to see a young chap snuffed out like in his prime."

"I expect it's a lot more than sixpence to you," said Stanley. "I expect you've got a whisky still or something in there, and want to keep other people away. Rot I call it. Come on back, you boys."

So they turned away. The two others said, "Good evening" and "Thank you" to the shepherd, but Stanley said nothing. The shepherd shrugged his shoulders and stood where he was, looking after them rather sadly.

On the way back to the camp there was great argument about it all, and Stanley was told as plainly as he could be told all the sorts of fools he would be if he went to the Wailing Well.

That evening, among other notices, Mr. Beasley Robinson asked if all maps had got the red ring marked on them. "Be particular," he said, "not to trespass inside it."

Several voices—among them the sulky one of Stanley Judkins—said, "Why not, sir?"

"Because not," said Mr. Beasley Robinson, "and if that isn't enough for you, I can't help it." He turned and spoke to Mr. Lambart in a low voice, and then said, "I'll tell you this much: we've been asked to warn Scouts off that field. It's very good of the people to let us camp here at all, and the least we can do is to oblige them—I'm sure you'll agree to that."

Everybody said, "Yes, sir!" except Stanley Judkins, who was heard to mutter, "Oblige them be blowed!"

Early in the afternoon of the next day, the following dialogue was heard. "Wilcox, is all your tent there?"

"No, sir, Judkins isn't!"

"That boy is *the* most infernal nuisance ever invented! Where do you suppose he is?"

"I haven't an idea, sir."

"Does anybody else know?"

"Sir, I shouldn't wonder if he'd gone to the Wailing Well."

"Who's that? Pipsqueak? What's the Wailing Well?"

"Sir, it's that place in the field by—well, sir, it's in a clump of trees in a rough field."

"D'you mean inside the red ring? Good heavens! What makes you think he's gone there?"

"Why, he was terribly keen to know about it yesterday, and we were talking to a shepherd man, and he told us a lot about it and advised us not to go there: but Judkins didn't believe him, and said he meant to go."

"Young ass!" said Mr. Hope Jones, "did he take anything with him?"

"Yes, I think he took some rope and a can. We did tell him he'd be a fool to go."

"Little brute! What the deuce does he mean by pinching stores like that! Well, come along, you three, we must see after him. Why can't people keep the simplest orders? What was it the man told you? No, don't wait, let's have it as we go along."

And off they started—Algernon and Wilfred talking rapidly and the other two listening with growing concern. At last they reached that spur of down overlooking the field of which the shepherd had spoken the day before. It commanded the place completely; the well inside the clump of bent and gnarled Scotch firs was plainly visible, and so were the four tracks winding about among the thorns and rough growth.

It was a wonderful day of shimmering heat. The sea looked like a floor of metal. There was no breath of wind. They were all exhausted when they got to the top, and flung themselves down on the hot grass.

"Nothing to be seen of him yet," said Mr. Hope Jones, "but we must stop here a bit. You're done up—not to speak of me. Keep a sharp look-out," he went on after a moment, "I thought I saw the bushes stir."

"Yes," said Wilcox, "so did I. Look . . . no, that can't be him. It's somebody though, putting their head up, isn't it?"

"I thought it was, but I'm not sure."

Silence for a moment. Then:

"That's him, sure enough," said Wilcox, "getting over the hedge on the far side. Don't you see? With a shiny thing. That's the can you said he had."

"Yes, it's him, and he's making straight for the trees," said Wilfred.

At this moment Algernon, who had been staring with all his might, broke into a scream.

"What's that on the track? On all fours—O, it's the woman. O, don't let me look at her! Don't let it happen!" And he rolled over, clutching at the grass and trying to bury his head in it.

"Stop that!" said Mr. Hope Jones loudly—but it was no use. "Look here," he said, "I must go down there. You stop here, Wilfred, and look after that boy. Wilcox, you run as hard as you can to the camp and get some help."

They ran off, both of them. Wilfred was left alone with Algernon, and did his best to calm him, but indeed he was not much happier himself. From time to time he glanced down the hill and into the field. He saw Mr. Hope Jones drawing nearer at a swift pace, and then, to his great surprise, he saw him stop, look up and round about him, and turn quickly off at an angle! What could be the reason? He looked at the field, and there he saw a terrible figure—something in ragged black—with whitish patches breaking out of it: the head, perched on a long thin neck, half hidden by a shapeless sort of blackened sun-bonnet. The creature was waving thin arms in the direction of the rescuer who was approaching, as if to ward him off: and between the two figures the air seemed to shake and shimmer as he had never seen it: and as he looked, he began himself to feel something of a waviness and confusion in his brain, which made him guess what might be the effect on someone within closer range of the influence. He looked away hastily, to see Stanley Judkins making his way pretty quickly towards the clump, and in proper Scout fashion; evidently picking his steps with care to avoid treading on snapping sticks or being caught by arms of brambles. Evidently, though he saw nothing, he suspected some sort of ambush, and was trying to go noiselessly. Wilfred saw all that, and he saw more, too. With a sudden and dreadful sinking at the heart, he caught sight of someone among the trees, waiting: and again of someone—another of the hideous black figures—working slowly along the track from another side of the field, looking from side to side, as the shepherd had described it. Worst of all, he saw a fourth—unmistakably a man this time—rising out of the bushes a few yards behind the wretched Stanley, and painfully, as it seemed, crawling into the track. On all sides the miserable victim was cut off.

Wilfred was at his wits' end. He rushed at Algernon and shook him. "Get up," he said. "Yell! Yell as loud as you can. Oh, if we'd got a whistle!"

Algernon pulled himself together. "There's one," he said, "Wilcox's: he must have dropped it."

So one whistled, the other screamed. In the still air the sound carried. Stanley heard: he stopped: he turned round: and then indeed a cry was heard more piercing and dreadful than any that the boys on the hill could raise. It was too late. The crouched figure behind Stanley sprang at him and caught him about the waist. The dreadful one that was standing waving her arms waved them again, but in exultation. The one that was lurking among the trees shuffled forward, and she too stretched out her arms as if to clutch at something coming her way; and the other, farthest off, quickened her pace and came on, nodding gleefully. The boys took it all in in an instant of terrible silence, and hardly could they breathe as they watched the horrid struggle between the man and his victim. Stanley struck with his can, the only weapon he had. The rim of a broken black hat fell off the creature's head and showed a white skull with stains that might be wisps of hair. By this time one of the women had reached the pair, and was pulling at the rope that was coiled about Stanley's neck. Between them they overpowered him in a moment: the awful screaming ceased, and then the three passed within the circle of the dump of firs.

Yet for a moment it seemed as if rescue might come. Mr. Hope Jones, striding quickly along, suddenly stopped, turned, seemed to rub his eyes, and then started running *towards* the field. More: the boys glanced behind them, and saw not only a troop of figures from the camp coming over the top of the next down, but the shepherd running up the slope of their own hill. They beckoned, they shouted, they ran a few yards towards him and then back again. He mended his pace.

Once more the boys looked towards the field. There was nothing. Or, was there something among the trees? Why was there a mist about the trees? Mr. Hope Jones had scrambled over the hedge, and was plunging through the bushes.

The shepherd stood beside them, panting. They ran to him and clung to his arms. "They've got him! In the trees!" was as much as they could say, over and over again.

"What? Do you tell me he've gone in there after all I said to him yesterday? Poor young thing! Poor young thing!" He would have said more, but other voices broke in. The rescuers from the camp had arrived. A few hasty words, and all were dashing down the hill.

They had just entered the field when they met Mr. Hope Jones. Over his shoulder hung the corpse of Stanley Judkins. He had cut it from the branch to which he found it hanging, waving to and fro. There was not a drop of blood in the body.

On the following day Mr. Hope Jones sallied forth with an axe and with the expressed intention of cutting down every tree in the clump, and of burning every bush in the field. He returned with a nasty cut in his leg and a broken axe-helve.[11] Not a spark of fire could he light, and on no single tree could he make the least impression.

I have heard that the present population of the Wailing Well field consists of three women, a man, and a boy.

The shock experienced by Algernon de Montmorency and Wilfred Pipsqueak was severe. Both of them left the camp at once; and the occurrence undoubtedly cast a gloom—if but a passing one—on those who remained. One of the first to recover his spirits was Judkins *mi*.

Such, gentlemen, is the story of the career of Stanley Judkins, and of a portion of the career of Arthur Wilcox. It has, I believe, never been told before. If it has a moral, that moral is, I trust, obvious: if it has none, I do not well know how to help it.

THE EXPERIMENT

A NEW YEAR'S EVE GHOST STORY
(Full directions will be found at the end)

The Reverend Dr. Hall was in his study making up the entries for the year in the parish register: it being his custom to note baptisms, weddings, and burials in a paper book as they occurred, and in the last days of December to write them out fairly in the vellum book that was kept in the parish chest.

To him entered his housekeeper, in evident agitation. "Oh, sir," said she, "whatever do you think? The poor Squire's gone!"

"The Squire? Squire Bowles? What are you talking about, woman? Why, only yesterday—"

"Yes, I know, sir, but it's the truth. Wickem, the clerk, just left word on his way down to toll the bell—you'll hear it yourself in a minute. There now, just listen."

Sure enough the sound broke on the still night—not loud, for the Rectory did not immediately adjoin the churchyard. Dr Hall rose hastily.

"Terrible, terrible," he said. "I must see them at the Hall at once. He seemed so greatly better yesterday." He paused. "Did you hear any word of the sickness having come this way at all? There was nothing said in Norwich. It seems so sudden."

"No, indeed, sir, no such thing. Just caught away with a choking in his throat, Wickem says. It do make one feel—well, I'm sure I had to set down as much as a minute or more, I come over that queer when I heard the words—and by what I could understand they'll be asking for the burial very quick. There's some can't bear the thought of the cold corpse laying in the house, and——"

"Yes: well, I must find out from Madam Bowles herself or Mr. Joseph. Get me my cloak, will you? Ah, and could you let Wickem know that I desire to see him when the tolling is over?" He hurried off.

In an hour's time he was back and found Wickem waiting for him. "There is work for you, Wickem," he said, as he threw off his cloak, "and not overmuch time to do it in."

"Yes, sir," said Wickem, "the vault to be opened to be sure—"

"No, no, that's not the message I have. The poor Squire, they tell me, charged them before now not to lay him in the chancel. It was to be an earth grave in the yard, on the north side." He stopped at an inarticulate exclamation from the clerk. "Well?" he said.

"I ask pardon, sir," said Wickem in a shocked voice, "but did I understand you right? No vault, you say, and on the north side? Tt-tt! Why the poor gentleman must a been wandering."

"Yes, it does seem strange to me, too," said Dr. Hall, "but no, Mr. Joseph tells me it was his father's—I should say stepfather's—clear wish, expressed more than once, and when he was in good health. Clean earth and open air. You know, of course, the poor Squire had his fancies, though he never spoke of this one to me. And there's another thing, Wickem. No coffin."

"Oh dear, dear, sir," said Wickem, yet more shocked. "Oh, but that'll make sad talk, that will, and what a disappointment for Wright, too! I know he'd looked out some beautiful wood for the Squire, and had it by him years past."

"Well, well, perhaps the family will make it up to Wright in some way," said the Rector, rather impatiently, "but what you have to do is to get the grave dug and all things in a readiness—torches from Wright you must not forget—by ten o'clock to-morrow night. I don't doubt but there will be somewhat coming to you for your pains and hurry."

"Very well, sir, if those be the orders, I must do my best to carry them out. And should I call in on my way down and send the women up to the Hall to lay out the body, sir?"

"No: that, I think—I am sure—was not spoken of. Mr. Joseph will send, no doubt, if they are needed. No, you have enough without that. Good night, Wickem. I was making up the registers when this doleful news came. Little had I thought to add such an entry to them as I must now."

All things had been done in decent order. The torchlighted cortège had passed from the Hall through the park, up the lime avenue to the top of the knoll on which the church stood. All the village had been there, and such neighbours as could be warned in the few hours available. There was no great surprise at the hurry.

Formalities of law there were none then, and no one blamed the stricken widow for hastening to lay her dead to rest. Nor did anyone look to see her following in the funeral train. Her son Joseph—only issue of her first marriage with a Calvert of Yorkshire—was the chief mourner.

There were, indeed, no kinsfolk on Squire Bowles's side who could have been bidden. The will, executed at the time of the Squire's second marriage, left everything to the widow.

And what was "everything"? Land, house, furniture, pictures, plate were all obvious. But there should have been accumulations in coin, and beyond a few hundreds in the hands of agents—honest men and no embezzlers—cash there was none. Yet Francis Bowles had for years received good rents and paid little out. Nor was he a reputed miser; he kept a good table, and money was always forthcoming for the moderate spendings of his wife and stepson. Joseph Calvert had been maintained ungrudgingly at school and college.

What, then, had he done with it all? No ransacking of the house brought any secret hoard to light; no servant, old or young, had any tale to tell of meeting the Squire in unexpected places at strange hours. No, Madam Bowles and her son were fairly non-plussed. As they sat one evening in the parlour discussing the problem for the twentieth time:

"You have been at his books and papers, Joseph, again today, haven't you?"

"Yes, mother, and no forwarder."

"What was it he would be writing at, and why was he always sending letters to Mr. Fowler at Gloucester?"

"Why, you know he had a maggot[1] about the Middle State of the Soul. 'Twas over that he and that other were always busy. The last thing he wrote would be a letter that he never finished. I'll fetch it. . . . Yes, the same song over again.

"Honoured friend,—I make some slow advance in our studies, but I know not well how far to trust our authors. Here is one lately come my way who will have it that for a time after death the soul is under control of certain spirits, as Raphael, and another whom I doubtfully read as Nares,[2] but still so near to this state of life that on prayer to them be may be free to come and disclose matters to the living. Come, indeed, he must, if he be rightly called, the manner of which is set forth in an experiment. But having come, and once opened his mouth, it may chance that his summoner shall see and hear more than of the hid treasure which it is likely he bargained for; since the experiment puts this in the forefront of things to be enquired. But the eftest[3] way is to send you the whole, which herewith I do; copied from a book of recipes which I had of good Bishop Moore."[4]

Here Joseph stopped, and made no comment, gazing on the paper. For more than a minute nothing was said, then Madam Bowles, drawing her needle through her work and looking at it, coughed and said, "There was no more written?"

"No, nothing, mother."

"No? Well, it is strange stuff. Did ever you meet this Mr. Fowler?"

"Yes, it might be once or twice, in Oxford, a civil gentleman enough."

"Now I think of it," said she, "it would be but right to acquaint him with—with what has happened: they were close friends. Yes, Joseph, you should do that: you will know what should be said. And the letter is his, after all."

"You are in the right, mother, and I'll not delay it." And forthwith he sat down to write.

From Norfolk to Gloucester was no quick transit. But a letter went, and a larger packet came in answer; and there were more evening talks in the panelled parlour at the Hall. At the close of one, these words were said: "Tonight, then, if you are certain of yourself, go round by the field path. Ay, and here is a cloth will serve."

"What cloth is that, mother? A napkin?"

"Yes, of a kind: what matter?" So he went out by the way of the garden, and she stood in the door, musing, with her hand on her mouth. Then the hand dropped and she said half aloud: "If only I had not been so hurried! But it *was* the face cloth, sure enough."

It was a very dark night, and the spring wind blew loud over the black fields: loud enough to drown all sounds of shouting or calling. If calling there was, there was no voice, nor any that answered, nor any that regarded—yet.

Next morning, Joseph's mother was early in his chamber. "Give me the cloth," she said, "the maids must not find it. And tell me, tell me, quick!"

Joseph, seated on the other side of the bed with his head in his hands, looked up at her with bloodshot eyes. "We have opened his mouth," he said. "Why in God's name did you leave his face bare?"

"How could I help it? You know how I was hurried that day! But do you mean you saw it?"

Joseph only groaned and sunk his head in his hands again. Then, in a low voice, "He said you should see it, too."

With a dreadful gasp she clutched at the bedpost and clung to it. "Oh, but he's angry," Joseph went on. "He was only biding his time, I'm sure. The words were scarce out of my mouth when I heard like the snarl of a dog in under there." He got up and paced the room. "And what can we do? He's free! And I daren't meet him! I daren't take the drink and go where he is! I daren't lie here another night. Oh, why did you do it? We could have waited."

"Hush," said his mother: her lips were dry. " 'Twas you, you know it, as much as I. Besides, what use in talking? Listen to me: 'tis but six o'clock. There's money to cross the water: such as they can't follow. Yarmouth's not so far, and most night boats sail for Holland, I've heard. See you to the horses. I can be ready."

Joseph stared at her. "What will they say here?"

"What? Why, cannot you tell the parson we have wind of property lying in Amsterdam which we must claim or lose? Go, go; or if you are not man enough for that, lie here again to-night." He shivered and went.

That evening after dark a boatman lumbered into an inn on Yarmouth Quay, where a man and a woman sat, with saddle-bags on the floor by them.

"Ready, are you, mistress and gentleman?" he said. "She sails before the hour, and my other passenger he's waitin' on the quay. Be there all your baggage?" and he picked up the bags.

"Yes, we travel light," said Joseph. "And you have more company bound for Holland?"

"Just the one," said the boatman, "and he seem to travel lighter yet."

"Do you know him?" said Madam Bowles: she laid her hand on Joseph's arm, and they both paused in the doorway.

"Why no, but for all he's hooded I'd know him again fast enough, he have such a cur'ous way of speakin', and I doubt you'll find he know you, by what he said. 'Goo you and fetch 'em out,' he say, 'and I'll wait on 'em here,' he say, and sure enough he's a-comin' this way now."

Poisoning of a husband was petty treason then, and women guilty of it were strangled at the stake and burnt. The Assize records of Norwich tell of a woman so dealt with and of her son hanged thereafter, convict on their own confession, made before the Rector of their parish, the name of which I withhold, for there is still hid treasure to be found there.

Bishop Moore's book of recipes is now in the University Library at Cambridge, marked Dd 11, 45, and on the leaf numbered 144 this is written:

An experiment most ofte proved true, to find out tresure hidden in the ground, theft, manslaughter, or anie other thynge. Go to the grave of a ded man, and three tymes call hym by his nam at the hed of the grave, and say. Thou, N., N., N., I coniure the, I re-quire the, and I charge the, by thi Christendome that thou takest

leave of the Lord Raffael and Nares and then askest leave this
night to come and tell me trewlie of the tresure that lyith hid in
such a place. Then take of the earth of the grave at the dead
bodyes hed and knitt it in a lynnen clothe and put itt under thi
right eare and sleape theruppon: and wheresoever thou lyest or
slepest, that night he will come and tell thee trewlie in waking or
sleping.

THE MALICE OF INANIMATE OBJECTS

The Malice of Inanimate Objects is a subject upon which an old friend of mine was fond of dilating, and not without justification. In the lives of all us, short or long, there have been days, dreadful days, on which we have had to acknowledge with gloomy resignation that our world has turned against us. I do not mean the human world of our relations and friends: to enlarge on that is the province of nearly every modern novelist. In their books it is called "Life" and an odd enough hash it is as they portray it. No, it is the world of things that do not speak or work or hold congresses and conferences. It includes such beings as the collar stud, the inkstand, the fire, the razor, and, as age increases, the extra step on the staircase which leads you either to expect or not to expect it. By these and such as these (for I have named but the merest fraction of them) the word is passed round, and the day of misery arranged. Is the tale still remembered of how the Cock and Hen went to pay a visit to Squire Korbes? How on the journey they met with and picked up a number of associates, encouraging each with the announcement:

> To Squire Korbes we are going
> For a visit is owing.

Thus they secured the company of the Needle, the Egg, the Duck, the Cat, possibly—for memory is a little treacherous here—and finally the Millstone: and when it was discovered that Squire Korbes was for the moment out, they took up positions in his mansion and awaited his return. He did return, wearied no doubt by a day's work among his extensive properties. His nerves were first jarred by the raucous cry of the Cock. He threw himself into his armchair and was lacerated by the Needle. He went to the sink for a refreshing wash and was splashed all over by the Duck. Attempting to dry himself with the towel he broke the Egg upon his face. He suffered other indignities from the Hen and her accomplices, which I cannot now recollect, and finally, maddened with pain and fear, rushed out by the back door and had his brains dashed out by the Millstone that had perched itself in the appropriate place. "Truly," in the concluding words of the story, "this Squire Korbes must have been either a very wicked or a very unfortunate man."[1] It is the latter alternative which I incline to accept. There is nothing in the preliminaries to show that any slur rested on his name, or that his visitors had any injury to avenge. And will not this narrative serve as a striking example of that Malice of which I have taken upon me to treat? It is, I know, the fact that Squire Korbes's visitors were not all of them, strictly speaking, inanimate. But are we sure that the perpetrators of this Malice are really inanimate either? There are tales which seem to justify a doubt.

Two men of mature years were seated in a pleasant garden after breakfast. One was reading the day's paper, the other sat with folded arms, plunged in thought, and on his face were a piece of sticking plaster and lines of care. His companion lowered his paper. "What," said he, "is the matter with you? The morning is bright, the birds are singing. I can hear no aeroplanes or motor bikes."

"No," replied Mr. Burton, "it is nice enough, I agree, but I have a bad day before me. I cut myself shaving and spilt my tooth powder."

"Ah," said Mr. Manners, "some people have all the luck," and with this expression of sympathy he reverted to his paper. "Hullo," he exclaimed, after a moment, "here's George Wilkins dead! You won't have any more bother with him, anyhow."

"George Wilkins?" said Mr. Burton, more than a little excitedly. "Why, I didn't even know he was ill."

"No more he was, poor chap. Seems to have thrown up the

sponge[2] and put an end to himself. Yes," he went on, "it's some days back: this is the inquest. Seemed very much worried and depressed, they say. What about, I wonder? Could it have been that will you and he were having a row about?"

"Row?" said Mr. Burton angrily. "There was no row: he hadn't a leg to stand on: he couldn't bring a scrap of evidence. No, it may have been half-a-dozen things: but Lord! I never imagined he'd take anything so hard as that."

"I don't know," said Mr. Manners, "he was a man, I thought, who did take things hard: they rankled. Well, I'm sorry, though I never saw much of him. He must have gone through a lot to make him cut his throat. Not the way I should choose, by a long sight. Ugh! Lucky he hadn't a family, anyhow. Look here, what about a walk round before lunch? I've an errand in the village."

Mr. Burton assented rather heavily. He was perhaps reluctant to give the inanimate objects of the district a chance of getting at him. If so, he was right. He just escaped a nasty purl[3] over the scraper at the top of the steps: a thorny branch swept off his hat and scratched his fingers, and as they climbed a grassy slope he fairly leapt into the air with a cry and came down flat on his face. "What in the world?" said his friend coming up. "A great string, of all things! What business—Oh, I see—belongs to that kite" (which lay on the grass a little farther up). "Now if I can find out what little beast has left that kicking about, I'll let him have it—or rather I won't, for he shan't see his kite again. It's rather a good one, too." As they approached, a puff of wind raised the kite and it seemed to sit up on its end and look at them with two large round eyes painted red, and, below them, three large printed red letters. I.C.U. Mr. Manners was amused and scanned the device with care. "Ingenious," he said, "it's a bit off a poster, of course: I see! Full Particulars, the word was." Mr. Burton on the other hand was not amused, but thrust his stick through the kite. Mr. Manners was inclined to regret this. "I dare say it serves him right," he said, "but he'd taken a lot of trouble to make it."

"Who had?" said Mr. Burton sharply. "Oh, I see, you mean the boy."

"Yes, to be sure, who else? But come on down now: I want to leave a message before lunch." As they turned a comer into the main street, a rather muffled and choky voice was heard to say "Look out! I'm coming." They both stopped as if they had been shot.

"Who *was* that?" said Manners. "Blest if I didn't think I knew"—then, with almost a yell of laughter he pointed with his stick. A cage with a grey parrot in it was hanging in an open window across the way. "I *was* startled, by George: it gave you a bit of a turn, too, didn't it?" Burton was inaudible. "Well, I shan't be a minute: you can go and make friends with the bird." But when he rejoined Burton, that unfortunate was not, it seemed, in trim for talking with either birds or men; he was some way ahead and going rather quickly. Manners paused for an instant at the parrot window and then hurried on laughing more than ever. "Have a good talk with Polly?" said he, as he came up.

"No, of course not," said Burton, testily. "I didn't bother about the beastly thing."

"Well, you wouldn't have got much out of her if you'd tried," said Manners. "I remembered after a bit; they've had her in the window for years: she's stuffed." Burton seemed about to make a remark, but suppressed it.

Decidedly this was not Burton's day out. He choked at lunch, he broke a pipe, he tripped in the carpet, he dropped his book in the pond in the garden. Later on he had or professed to have a telephone call summoning him back to town next day and cutting short what should have been a week's visit. And so glum was he all the evening that Manners' disappointment in losing an ordinarily cheerful companion was not very sharp.

At breakfast Mr. Burton said little about his night: but he did intimate that he thought of looking in on his doctor. "My hand's so shaky," he said, "I really daren't shave this morning."

"Oh, I'm sorry," said Mr. Manners, "my man could have managed that for you: but they'll put you right in no time."

Farewells were said. By some means and for some reason Mr. Burton contrived to reserve a compartment to himself. (The train was not of the corridor type.) But these precautions avail little against the angry dead.

I will not put dots or stars, for I dislike them, but I will say that apparently someone tried to shave Mr. Burton in the train, and did not succeed overly well. He was however satisfied with what he had done, if we may judge from the fact that on a once white napkin spread on Mr. Burton's chest was an inscription in red letters: GEO. W. FECI.[4]

Do not these facts—if facts they are—bear out my suggestion that there is something not inanimate behind the Malice of Inanimate Objects? Do they not further suggest that when this malice begins to show itself we should be very particular to examine and if possible rectify any obliquities in our recent conduct? And do they not, finally, almost force upon us the conclusion that, like Squire Korbes, Mr. Burton must have been either a very wicked or a singularly unfortunate man?

A VIGNETTE

You are asked to think of the spacious garden of a country rectory,[1] adjacent to a park of many acres, and separated therefrom by a belt of trees of some age which we knew as the Plantation. It is but about thirty or forty yards broad. A close gate of split oak leads to it from the path encircling the garden, and when you enter it from that side you put your hand through a square hole cut in it and lift the hook to pass along to the iron gate which admits to the park from the Plantation. It has further to be added that from some windows of the rectory, which stands on a somewhat lower level than the Plantation, parts of the path leading thereto, and the oak gate itself can be seen. Some of the trees, Scotch firs and others, which form a backing and a surrounding, are of considerable size, but there is nothing that diffuses a mysterious gloom or imparts a sinister flavour— nothing of melancholy or funereal associations. The place is well clad, and there are secret nooks and retreats among the bushes, but there is neither offensive bleakness nor oppressive darkness. It is, indeed, a matter for some surprise when one thinks it over, that any cause for misgivings of a nervous sort have attached itself to so normal and cheerful a spot, the more so, since neither our childish mind when we lived there nor the more inquisitive years that came later ever nosed out any legend or reminiscence of old or recent unhappy things.

Yet to me they came, even to me, leading an exceptionally happy wholesome existence, and guarded—not strictly but as carefully as was any way necessary—from uncanny fancies and fear. Not that such guarding avails to close up all gates. I should be puzzled to fix the date at which any sort of misgiving about the Plantation gate first visited me. Possibly it was in the years just before I went to school, possibly on one later summer afternoon of which I have a faint memory, when I was coming back after solitary roaming in the park, or, as I bethink me, from tea at the Hall: anyhow, alone, and fell in with one of the villagers also homeward bound just as I was about to turn off the road on to the track leading to the Plantation. We broke off our talk with "good nights," and when I looked back at him after a minute or so I was just a little surprised to see him standing still and looking after me. But no remark passed, and on I went. By the time I was within the iron gate and outside the park, dusk had undoubtedly come on; but there was no lack yet of light, and I could not account to myself for the questionings which certainly did rise as to the presence of anyone else among the trees, questionings to which I could not very certainly say "No," nor, I was glad to feel, "Yes," because if there were anyone they could not well have any business there. To be sure, it is difficult, in anything like a grove, to be quite certain that nobody is making a screen out of a tree trunk and keeping it between you and him as he moves round it and you walk on. All I can say is that if such an one was there he was no neighbour or acquaintance of mine, and there was some indication about him of being cloaked or hooded. But I think I may have moved at a rather quicker pace than before, and have been particular about shutting the gate. I think, too, that after that evening something of what Hamlet calls a "gain-giving"[2] may have been present in my mind when I thought of the Plantation. I do seem to remember looking out of a window which gave in that direction, and questioning whether there was or was not any appearance of a moving form among the trees. If I did, and perhaps I did, hint a suspicion to the nurse the only answer to it will have been "the hidea of such a thing!" and an injunction to make haste and get into my bed.

Whether it was on that night or a later one that I seem to see myself again in the small hours gazing out of the window across moonlit grass and hoping I was mistaken in fancying any movement in that half-hidden corner of the garden, I cannot now be sure. But it was certainly within a short while that I began to be

visited by dreams which I would much rather not have had—
which, in fact, I came to dread acutely; and the point round
which they centred was the Plantation gate.

As years go on it but seldom happens that a dream is disturb-
ing. Awkward it may be, as when, while I am drying myself
after a bath, I open the bedroom door and step out on to a pop-
ulous railway platform and have to invent rapid and flimsy excuses for the deplorable *déshabillé*. But such a vision is not
alarming, though it may make one despair of ever holding up
one's head again. But in the times of which I am thinking, it did
happen, not often, but oftener than I liked, that the moment a
dream set in I knew that it was going to turn out ill, and that
there was nothing I could do to keep it on cheerful lines.

Ellis the gardener might be wholesomely employed with rake
and spade as I watched at the window; other familiar figures
might pass and repass on harmless errands; but I was not deceived. I could see that the time was coming when the gardener
and the rest would be gathering up their properties and setting
off on paths that led homeward or into some safe outer world,
and the garden would be left—to itself, shall we say, or to
denizens who did not desire quite ordinary company and were
only waiting for the word "all clear" to slip into their posts of
vantage.

Now, too, was the moment near when the surroundings began to take on a threatening look; that the sunlight lost power
and a quality of light replaced it which, though I did not know
it at the time, my memory years after told me was the life-
less pallor of an eclipse. The effect of all this was to intensify
the foreboding that had begun to possess me, and to make me
look anxiously about, dreading that in some quarter my fear
would take a visible shape. I had not much doubt which way
to look. Surely behind those bushes, among those trees, there
was motion, yes, and surely—and more quickly than seemed
possible—there was motion, not now among the trees, but on
the very path towards the house. I was still at the window, and
before I could adjust myself to the new fear there came the impression of a tread on the stairs and a hand on the door. That
was as far as the dream got, at first; and for me it was far

enough. I had no notion what would have been the next development, more than that it was bound to be horrifying.

That is enough in all conscience about the beginning of my dreams. A beginning it was only, for something like it came again and again; how often I can't tell, but often enough to give me an acute distaste for being left alone in that region of the garden. I came to fancy that I could see in the behaviour of the village people whose work took them that way an anxiety to be past a certain point, and moreover a welcoming of company as they approached that corner of the park. But on this it will not do to lay overmuch stress, for, as I have said, I could never glean any kind of story bound up with the place.

However, the strong probability that there had been one once I cannot deny.

I must not by the way give the impression that the whole of the Plantation was haunted ground. There were trees there most admirably devised for climbing and reading in; there was a wall, along the top of which you could walk for many hundred yards and reach a frequented road, passing farmyard and familiar houses; and once in the park, which had its own delights of wood and water, you were well out of range of anything suspicious—or, if that is too much to say, of anything that suggested the Plantation gate.

But I am reminded, as I look on these pages, that so far we have had only preamble, and that there is very little in the way of actual incident to come, and that the criticism attributed to the devil when he sheared the sow is like to be justified. What, after all, was the outcome of the dreams to which without saying a word about them I was liable during a good space of time? Well, it presents itself to me thus. One afternoon—the day being neither overcast nor threatening—I was at my window in the upper floor of the house. All the family were out. From some obscure shelf in a disused room I had worried out a book, not very recondite: it was, in fact, a bound volume of a magazine in which were contained parts of a novel. I know now what novel it was, but I did not then, and a sentence struck and arrested me. Someone was walking at dusk up a solitary lane by an old mansion in Ireland, and being a man of imagination he was suddenly forcibly impressed by what he calls "the aerial image of the old house, with its peculiar malign, sacred, and skulking aspect" peering out of the shade of its neglected old trees.[3] The words were quite enough to set my own fancy on a bleak track. Inevitably I looked, and looked with apprehension, to the Plantation gate. As was but right it was shut, and nobody was upon the path that led to it or from it. But as I said a while ago, there was in it a square hole giving access to the fastening; and through that hole, I could see—and it struck like a blow on the diaphragm—something white or partly white. Now this I could not bear, and with an access of something like courage— only it was more like desperation, like determining that I must know the worst—I did steal down and, quite uselessly, of course, taking cover behind bushes as I went, I made progress until I was within range of the gate and the hole. Things were, alas! worse than I had feared; through that hole a face was looking my way. It was not monstrous, not pale, fleshless, spectral. Malevolent I thought and think it was; at any rate the eyes were large and open and fixed. It was pink and, I thought, hot, and just above the eyes the border of a white linen drapery hung down from the brows.

There is something horrifying in the sight of a face looking at one out of a frame as this did; more particularly if its gaze is unmistakably fixed upon you. Nor does it make the matter any better if the expression gives no clue to what is to come next. I said just now that I took this face to be malevolent, and so I did, but not in regard of any positive dislike or fierceness which it expressed. It was, indeed, quite without emotion: I was only conscious that I could see the whites of the eyes all round the pupil, and that, we know, has a glamour of madness about it. The immovable face was enough for me. I fled, but at what I thought must be a safe distance inside my own precincts I could not but halt and look back. There was no white thing framed in the hole of the gate, but there was a draped form shambling away among the trees.

Do not press me with questions as to how I bore myself when it became necessary to face my family again. That I was upset by something I had seen must have been pretty clear, but I am very sure that I fought off all attempts to describe it. Why I make a lame effort to do it now I cannot very well explain: it undoubtedly has had some formidable power of clinging through many years to my imagination. I feel that even now I should be circumspect in passing that Plantation gate; and every now and again the query haunts me: Are there here and there sequestered places which some curious creatures still frequent, whom once on a time anybody could see and speak to as they went about on their daily occasions, whereas now only at rare intervals in a series of years does one cross their paths and become aware of them; and perhaps that is just as well for the peace of mind of simple people.

THE FENSTANTON WITCH

Nicholas Hardman and Stephen Ashe were two Fellows of the King's College in Cambridge: they had come like all their contemporaries from the sister College at Eton where they had spent their lives from about the age of six to that of sixteen, and at the time we encounter them they were both men of about thirty years old. Hardman was the son of a Lincolnshire parson, living at Thorganby-on-the-Wolds, while Ashe's father was a yeoman-farmer of Ospringe in Kent.[1]

Hardman was black, dour and saturnine with a rasping voice and a strong Lincolnshire accent which cannot be reproduced here. Ashe had the sturdy and somewhat slow intelligence of his Kentish ancestors: "a good friend and a bad enemy" represents the opinion which the men of his year held of him. Both were in priests' orders, and each, we might suppose, looked forward in the fullness of time to occupying College livings,[2] marrying and bringing up a son or two: one most likely to reproduce his father's career; another, perhaps, to go on the land and become a reputable farmer in a small way.

I say we might suppose their aspirations to have been of this nature: for such was the programme of a majority of Fellows of Colleges at that time. But there is an entry in the book called Harwood's *Alumni*[3] which shows that they entertained ideas of a very different sort; and it has occurred to me that it may be worthwhile to tell the story of what they adventured and what came of it.

I have alluded more than once to "their times" but I have not yet told when they lived. Anne was on the throne of England, Scotland, Ireland and France, and Dr. James Roderick was Pro-

vost of the College,[4] having been elected by the Fellows in pref-
erence to Sir Isaac Newton, whom the Prince of Orange, King
William the Third of blessed memory, would have intruded
into that pasture. The Fellows of King's had indicated their
right of election and the Lower Master of Eton occupied the
Lodge—he was known as one of the "four Smoking Heads"—
while Sir Isaac lived in the Observatory over Trinity Great Gate,
and, according to popular legends, gently remonstrated with his
dog Diamond, or cut holes in his door to admit his cat and kit-
ten.[5] The University was a happy, sleepy place in those days,
one is apt to think; but after all, what with the Church in danger and the excitement of depriving Dr. Richard Bentley, then
Master of Trinity, of his degrees,[6] there was probably no lack
of sport to be had within the precincts. And certainly just outside them there was more than there is now. Snipe were shot on
Parker's Piece, and the dreary expanse of undrained fen was the
haunt of many a strange fowl, not to speak of other inhabitants
of whom I may one day find an occasion to tell.

But it is time to leave generalities. The two sheep to whom
we must return—and I am afraid they were black ones—were
very close friends; but few men in the University, or indeed in
the King's College itself, could boast of more than a speaking
acquaintance with either. They occupied one room in the Old
School of King's, north of the Chapel, which room was always
locked when they were out. And these were not days when Fellows, nor less still Scholars, were in the habit of dropping into
each other's abodes to partake of casual hospitality in the way
of tobacco or whiskey and water. The common life, such as it
was, was confined to Chapel, Hall and the Fellows' Parlour.

All that was known of Hardman and Ashe's way of employ-
ing "their leisure" was that they went for long walks together
and smoked apparently very bad tobacco when they came back.

It was a fine afternoon in October when these events began, or
to speak more truly, came to a head, which seemed to show
what manner of men were Nicholas Hardman and Stephen
Ashe. Chapel service, we may be sure, was at three, and both of
our friends were there, staring at each other from opposite stalls.
The reedy and pedalless organ helped the rather infirm and

jaded choir through a new verse anthem by Dr. Blow[7] during
which the snoring of Provost Roderick was not doubtfully
heard. At near four, Dr. Tudway,[8] the organist, played out the
scant congregation with a march of his own composition. The
choirmen hurried off to go through a similar performance at
Trinity. The boys rushed off to whatever haunts in the town they
had emerged from. The Provost strolled to his Lodge, then at the
eastern end of the Chapel, and the Fellows and Scholars made
their way across the strip of ground on the north side, holding
on their caps—for a strong west wind was blowing the yellow
leaves about—and so into the Old Court, and to dine in Hall. A
coarse meal, I expect it was, and a silent one. The Vice Provost
and three or four Seniors occupied one table on the dais; the
Masters of Arts—among whom were Hardman and Ashe—
filled a second along with the Fellow-Commoners, and the Bach-
elors and Undergraduate Fellows and Scholars, two more. There
may have been about fifty people in the room. Not much passed
at dinner, which lasted about forty minutes; but afterwards the
Fellows returned to the parlour and the Scholars to their rooms.
With these last we are not concerned, but we may as well follow
the Seniors. They are sitting at a large table, clothless, with some
decanters of wine (I don't know whether port or claret: much
depends upon the date of Lord Methuen's treaty with Portugal),[9]
and something like a conversation has broken out.

"Where did ye ride today, Mr. Bates?" said Mr. Glynne.

"Only so far as Fenstanton."[10]

"Fenstanton. Ah, is that where the witch was ducked last
week? Lord Blandford was riding by at the time" (this was the
Duke of Marlboro's son and heir who died shortly afterwards
and was now a Fellow-Commoner),[11] "and his Lordship made
some hot-headed show at rescuing the old creature. Has there
been any stir made? Dodgson of Magdalene[12] has this living,
but I doubt, if he hath not moved, no one will. 'Tis a lost place,
Fenstanton, for all it be on the Huntingdon road." This from
Mr. Glynne, who had rather a knack for monopolising conversation.

"Well, to tell the truth," says Bates, "I had not heard of the
matter, but the bell was tolling for a burying as I rode through,

and I happened to meet Dodgson coming from his beer and pipe, as I judge, to the churchyard. He did let fall something which could fit with what you say. Pray, did you hear the name, Glynne, Galpin or Gibson; some word with a 'G' in it?"

"Gibson? Mother Gibson! That was the name for a guinea! So that ducking has finished the poor creature," said good-natured Glynne. "These fen-rustics are little but hate. I know the coroner should have sat, and there should have been a dozen strung up at the Assizes, and in any but Dodgson's parish there would have been. But Lord! the man thinks of nothing but his tithes and his beer."

"Matthews[13] had the parsonage before Dodgson," said Bates, "and in his time there were four attempts at ducking that old woman. Not a boy nor man in the parish, he told me, but was ready to swear she had signed herself away.[14] But Matthews threatened to call in the sheriff, and he would have done it too, and so they kept mum in his time."

"For all that," said Glynne, "I remember his saying in this parlour that when he looked at her he was half in a mind to believe the tale. He pointed her out to me one day, and it is sure that she might have sat for a portrait of the Enemy as far as her eyes were concerned: they were as red as blood and the pupils like a goat's." With which Mr. Glynne was silent and shuddered slightly.

"Did they bury her in the churchyard, Bates?" said Dr. Morell, the Vice Provost.[15]

"Yes, Mr. Vice Provost. I noticed a grave dug on the north side, which I take it was for her."

"All this talk about burying witches puts me in mind of William of Malmesbury's tale that Dr. Gale printed not so long back."[16] This was from a new contributor to the conversation, Mr. Newborough, afterwards Head Master of Eton,[17] who was more bookishly inclined than many of his compeers. "Do you know it, Mr. Glynne? You should look at Malmesbury": and he proceeded to tell the story which Southey had put into rhyme under the name of the "Old Woman of Berkeley."[18] After that came a short discussion of the Witch of Endor;[19] then the conversation drifted to Dr. Hody's book on the Versions of the

Bible,[20] then by a not uncommon fate to Dr. Bentley's last enormities, and thence back to the old question of College livings and probable vacancies.

In the midst of this, Hardman and Ashe made their bow to the Vice Provost and went out. They had neither of them made any remark since dinner but Dr. Morrell, an observant man, noticed that they had taken a very considerable interest in the early part of the conversation.

"Two dull dogs gone," said Mr. Glynne, when the door closed behind them: "I pity their wives if ever they marry and their parishes if ever they take 'em."

"Quiet enough if they are dull," said Newborough.

"I don't know that, Newborough," said Morrell. "The man that has chambers under theirs doesn't always sleep best. What can keep those two men treading about the whole night, as I am told they do, and what have they on their minds that makes them sigh and moan like two sick owls, as Burton says?[21] You know everyone in College, Glynne; tell me, pray, were you ever in Hardman's and Ashe's chambers?"

"Not I," said Glynne. "I knocked at their door one day, I recollect, last year. Such a clatter as they made before they opened it, I vow I never heard, but all I can tell of the matter is that Hardman was as pale as a ghost when he opened to me, and that the place smelled as sweet as a bonfire of old rags and bones. Hardman made swift to ask my business, and then shut the door in my face!"

"Well," said the Vice Provost, "he might have spared himself the question, Glynne. I never knew you have any business in this life yet. Never matter! 'Tis time to turn unto the coffeehouse, gentlemen. I have told Dr. Cotes that we should be there before eight, and the clocks are giving the quarter now."

The company adjourned therefore to a coffeehouse on the Market Place, and smoked clay pipes till ten with Dr. Roger Cotes[22] and some other gentlemen from Trinity, Queens' and Bene't Colleges.[23]

The curfew bell was ringing and it was a fine night when Hardman and Ashe, each with a packet and a stick, emerged

from the gates of King's College and told the porter—a fud-
dling old ruffian, as were most College servants of that day—
that they were not like to be returning that night. Neither said
any word until they were clear of the town and on the Huntingdon road. Then said Nicholas Hardman, "If all goes as it
should tonight, Ashe, we shall know a matter worth knowing."

"Yes, Nick, and there will be a matter worth having in one of
these bundles," said Ashe: "I dare swear though that there will
be some disappointment. Newborough's tale of the old witch
set me a-thinking. You have the book upon you, Nick?"

"Book, what book? Dr. Gale's print of Malmesbury, I suppose? A fat folio of a stone weight. Is it likely?"

"No, not Malmesbury. *Our* book, *the* book, I mean."

"Call me fool if you like, Stephen, but don't ask such another question: have I come forth without my head? That is as
likely as it would be for me to leave the book in my chambers.
But why, pray, does that ass Newborough's old story set you
thinking?"

"Why, only, that if the same gentry that came for their friend
in that story were thinking of waiting upon *our* friend at Fenstanton tonight, it is like we may see trouble."

Hardman gave a snort. "And if they did, do you think a circle
is broken so easily? Have I nothing here that avails to make them
give back? Still, you are right in a way, Stephen, as you have been
before. If we are later in the field than they, there may be trouble,
even danger. But what we would have is not what they want. If
we get the three locks of hair and the winding sheet, we are masters of the Elementals. The *others* want the soul."

It was a thought that seemed to back both of them for a moment, and they were silent. So the clouds flew across the moon,
and the wind blew over the bare fields, and the bells of Cambridge came more faintly to the ear, as they walked quietly on
towards the sleeping village of Fenstanton.

Those who remember the road between Cambridge and Fenstanton will bear me out when I say that it is eleven miles long,
and presents few features of interest. There is an occasional
wayside inn, a few farms lie a little off the road, and on a clear

day we may see the lantern and western tower of Ely, and a
good many nearer church towers. The church that lies nearest
to the road is that of Lolworth,²⁴ on the left hand, some five or
six miles out. There was something doing at Lolworth when
Hardman and Ashe passed it. The bell was going, and the windows lighted. Nocturnal funerals were almost the rule in Queen
Anne's time for any one who claimed to be a magnate, so that
it did not surprise the lookers-on when they saw two lines of
torches working their way slowly through the trees near the
church, and when they saw a figure in white flit out of the south
porch to meet the *cortège*, they knew that it must be the parson.
Yet a few moments, and the procession was in the church: then
they walked on again, for they had paused a moment.

The turning out of the main road towards Lolworth church
lay some little distance ahead, and down the lane were coming a
group of figures at a great pace. They reached the road and
turned down it towards the travellers: who were a little daunted
thereby, because they did not wish to be recognised as Cambridge parsons at that hour of the night. There appeared to be
seven people clustering round one in the midst, and their action
and gait was like that of watchmen who had taken a prisoner.
The party came on, and it seemed as if this conjecture might fit
the situation, for the person in the midst was plainly reluctant,
and as plainly was being hurried on by the rest. Hardman and
Ashe drew toward the hedge to let these men pass, and their
eyes were riveted upon the face of the captured man. It was not
lightly to be forgotten, for it is not often that any one beholds
the face of a man who has lost all hope, and yet has room in his
brain for an unspeakable fear. This is the sight which those two
ill-starred priests were now looking upon: and they saw moreover that, in spite of his terror and desperation, the captive
could look nowhere save straight in front of him, for anything
seemed tolerable rather than to see the faces of the seven who
were about him. When they pictured the scene themselves
thereafter, they realised that his was the only face of which they
had caught a sight at all; nay, it even seemed to them that there
was no other face for their eyes to catch.

The thing was passed; it passed quite silently, and for many

moments these two men stayed breathless to within an ace of
sudden flight or swooning. They knew that they had seen that
which no mourner at that funeral had seen, and it was in their
minds that it is not always well for those whose eyes are
opened. It may happen to some to see the mountain full of
bones and chariots of fire,[25] but to others are also shown very
different sights from that. Yet the natures of both were so ob-
stinate and dogged that neither would broach to the other the
thought of returning, and giving up the dismal project they had
in their minds. They went on.

Soon they sighted Fenstanton spire, and half a mile further
they left the road and made their way across the fields to the
side where the churchyard was accessible away from the street.
It was not a difficult wall to climb, yet they were unnerved and
took several minutes to get over it. Then they proceeded to go
through the sinister rites and ceremonies which were to safe-
guard them against those powers with which they supposed
themselves to be leagued, for they are treacherous allies, as
those tell who claim to know the heart of the matter. On the
north side of the dark church, even in its shadow, and not more
than ten yards from a new-made grave—the only one on that
side of the building—they picked out a space where the grass
was shortest, and drew two large circles, one within the other.
And in the space between the circles they marked out with some
pains the symbols of the planets and a few Hebrew letters
which were meant to indicate names of angels and of the Great
Power, whose aid, by one of the strange contradictions of art
magic, they promised themselves they would gain for the work
they were at. When their defence was completed they stopped,
and Ashe looked at his time-piece. The time was something
short of a quarter to twelve, so they must wait till the middle of
night was reached.

And now—what was it that these two educated clergymen
proposed to themselves? And how came it that they were on an
enterprise which one associates, not always correctly, with the
darkest mediaevalism and the most defective civilisation?

You have guessed that they were earnest and credulous students of art magic: how came such men to be in Cambridge in

the reign of Queen Anne? I can only answer that in that day there were many such men in Germany, and the instinct which prompts men to seek intercourse with the unseen peoples of the air is one that may come to the surface in any civilisation and in any century. Many have a sneaking idea that the intercourse has been sometimes gained, but that is little to the point.

That which Hardman and Ashe were determined upon was the obtaining of an ingredient for future spells, which should end in making them able to command the forces of nature to a degree which they believed many to have obtained before them. They meant on this night—and they were confident of accomplishing it—to go through certain forms of words which would have power to make the corpse of the old woman buried that day rise out of the grave and come to them, and give them—it is horrid to think of—the portion of the grave-clothes and the locks of hair of which Hardman spoke when they were on the road. Then should the body return to the earth as it was, and the soil be replaced over it. They were to go back to their College the next day; and in seven days' time, who so rich and powerful as Nicholas Hardman and Stephen Ashe, Esquires?

It was with a strange kind of exaltation that, as midnight came near, Hardman drew from his bosom a paper book, about a hundred years old, ill-written and full of diagrams like that which had just been drawn upon the ground, and within whose compass both of them were standing. He began to read, or intone, a Latin form of conjuration, a sinister kind of Church service, in which the most sacred of names were freely employed; and to this Ashe made the set appointed refrains. The night had been disturbed throughout and windy, but no rain had fallen and the thin clouds kept covering the moon, which was by this time low and near the horizon. The wind rattled in the louvres of the tower, and every now and then swung the tongue of a bell so that it sounded in a dim and far off fashion. Nicholas Hardman read on, and read faster and louder, and Ashe responded at short intervals. They had now entered upon the 91st Psalm: "*Qui Habitat,*" "Whoso dwelleth," and they were just promising themselves deliverance from the terror that walks in darkness[26] when a blacker cloud than usual left the moon's face and Stephen Ashe fell like an ox at the feet of Hardman. For it seems that it had been determined that these fools should be answered according to their folly.

I have said that the miserable and criminous old woman whom the fen-men had killed was buried a bare ten yards away from the two conjurors: and their eyes were fixed upon her grave as the point to which their spells were directed. Looking over at the grave, Hardman beheld crouched upon it a shape which there was small likelihood of his ever forgetting. It was the figure, one would say, at first sight, of an enormous bat, with folded wings and hints of head approaching the human form. In a short moment, Hardman caught sight of the folds of wrinkled skin or hide that hung down from the cheeks, of the wide ears which shone transparent in the moonlight, and of the two lines of dusky red fire which marked the two almost closed eyes. And further, he declared afterwards, he saw the earth heap upon which this being was crouched stir and wave beneath it. Not long was he allowed to remain a spectator, for this terrific appearance rose to its height and for a minute seemed to look about as if for a victim whom it knew to be near. Hardman, almost at the pitch of despair, yet trusted dimly in his charmed circle. But the creature on a sudden turned full in his direction and stepped swift and straight towards him, but flinching for an instant at angelic names or planetary symbols. In another moment, its talons were raised toward his face, and he knew no more.

It was Ashe who helped him back to Cambridge in the morning of the next day: and it was Ashe also who, for the twenty years that he survived, sheltered him in the parsonage of Willoughton[27] and ministered to him, himself a stricken man. But Hardman never saw light again.

The College at large never learned the rights of the story. Two days after the catastrophe, Mr. Glynne says to Mr. Morrell, being Vice Provost, "What did you do at the Fellows' Meeting this morning, Mr. Vice?"

"Sealed the presentation to Weedon Lois,[28] and received a declaration, Glynne."

"A royal declaration or what?"

"No, Glynne; Mr. Provost will tell you about it maybe, if you ask him."

So off goes Mr. Glynne to the Lodge. But Provost Roderick is pale, which is not natural to him, and not smoking, which is decidedly unnatural, and disturbed and uncommunicative. Mr. Glynne can only learn that it is a matter which the Seniors have decided to keep private. During the next week, a barrowload of matters from one set of chambers in the King's College is wheeled off in the direction of Barton[29] and does not come back: and most of the Seniors are very regular in their attendance in the Chapel for some months.

I cannot help connecting these events I have set down with that entry in the Protocollum book, which states that two gentlemen, being Fellows of the College, were permitted to register a solemn abjuration of all unlawful acts in the practicing of which they had grievously transgressed, and that it was agreed that the Provost and Seniors shall exercise their utmost discretion to the end that this matter be kept strictly private to the Seniority.

TWELVE MEDIEVAL
GHOST-STORIES

These stories were I believe first noticed in the recent *Catalogue of the Royal Manuscripts,* where a brief analysis of them is given which may well have excited the curiosity of others besides myself. All that Casley has to say of them in the old catalogue is "Exemplaria apparitionum spirituum (saec.) xv."[1]

I took an early opportunity of transcribing them, and I did not find them disappointing: I hope others will agree that they deserved to be published.

The source is the Royal MS. 15. A. xx in the British Museum. It is a fine volume of the twelfth and early thirteenth centuries containing some tracts of Cicero and the *Elucidarium.* It belonged to Byland Abbey (Yorkshire) and later to John Theyer.

On blank pages in the body of the book (ff. 140–3) and at the end (fo. 163 *b*) a monk of Byland has written down a series of ghost-stories of which the scenes are laid in his own neighbourhood. They are strong in local colour, and though occasionally confused, incoherent, and unduly compressed, evidently represent the words of the narrators with some approach to fidelity.

To me they are redolent of Denmark. Any one who is lucky enough to possess E. T. Kristensen's delightful collections of *Sagn fra Jyllana*[2] will be reminded again and again of traits which occur there. Little as I can claim the quality of "folklorist" I am fairly confident that the Scandinavian element is really prominent in these tales.

The date of the writing cannot be long after 1400 (*c.* 1400 is the estimate in the catalogue). Richard II's reign is referred to as past. A study of local records, impossible to me, might not improbably throw light upon the persons mentioned in the stories.

The hand is not a very easy one, and the last page of all is really difficult: some words have baffled me. The Latin is very refreshing.

M. R. JAMES

British Museum MS. Royal 15 A. xx.

I. De quodam spiritu cuiusdam mercenarii de Ryeuall' qui adiuuit hominem ad portandum fabas.

Quidam homo equitauit super equum suum portantem super se vnum modium fabarum. Qui equus cepsitauit [sc. cesp-] in via et fregit tibiam. Quo percepto vir tulit fabas super dorsum suum proprium: et dum iret per viam vidit quasi equum stantem super pedes posteriores, pedibus anterioribus sursum erectis. Qui perterritus prohibuit equum in nomine ihesu christi ne noceret ei. Quo facto ibat cum eo quasi equus, et post paululum apparuit in figura acerui de feno rotantis,[3] et lumen erat in medio. Cui dixit viuus Absit quod inferas mihi malum. Quo dicto apparuit in figura hominis, et ille coniurauit eum. Tunc spiritus dixit ei nomen suum et causam et remedium,[4] et addidit Permitte me portare fabas et adiuuare te. Et fecit sic usque ad torrentem sed noluit transire vlterius, et viuus nesciuit qualiter saccus fabaram iterum ponebatur super dorsum suum. Et postea fecit spiritum absolui et missas cantari pro eo et adiutus est.

[I. Concerning the ghost of a certain laborer of Ryedale who helped a man carry beans.

A certain man was riding on horseback with a sack of beans slung over the horse's back. His horse happened to stumble in the road and broke its leg. Upon realizing what had happened, the man hoisted the beans over his own back and, as he trudged down the road, he saw what appeared to be a horse standing on its hind legs, holding its front legs high up in front of itself. Thoroughly terrified at this, the man beseeched the horse in the name of Jesus Christ not to hurt him. After he did so, the apparent horse walked along beside him and, in a short time, it appeared in the shape of a rolling bale of hay, with a light glowing from its center. At this the living man said to it, "Begone, lest you do me harm!" After these words, the apparition appeared in the guise of a human being, and the man swore it to reveal its story.[5] Then the ghost told him its name and the reason it was abroad, and how it might be helped. And it added, "Allow me to help you by carrying your sack of beans." And it did so all the way to the river's edge, but it did not want to go any farther than that. And the man did not know how it happened that his sack of beans was placed again on his own back. And later on he saw to it that the spirit was absolved and he had masses sung on its behalf, and thus it was helped.]

II. De mirabili certacione inter spiritum et viuentem in tempore regis Ricardi secundi.

Dicitur quod quidam scissor cognomine [*blank*] Snawball equitando remeauit ad domum suam in ampilforth quadam nocte de Gillyng, et in via audiuit quasi sonitum anates [s]e lauantes [*corr. from* anas se lauans] in torrente et paulopost aspexit quasi coruum circa faciem suam volantem et descendentem vsque ad terram, alis suis concucientibus solum quasi deberet mori. Qui scissor de equo suo descendit ut caperet coruum et interim vidit sintillas ignis spargentes de lateribus eiusdem corui. Tunc signauit se et prohibuit eum ex parte dei ne inferret illi dampnum aliquod illa vice. Qui euolauit cum eiulatu magno quasi spacium lapidis †encardi†[6] Tunc iterum ascendit equum suum et paulopost predictus coruus obuiauit illi in volando et percussit eum in latere et prostrauit in terra scissorem equitantem de equo suo. Qui taliter solotenus prostratus iacuit quasi in extasi et exanimis, valde timens. Tandem resurgens et constans in fide pugnauit cum eo cum gladio suo quousque fuerat lassus, et videbatur sibi quasi percuteret t[er]ricidiu[m] more[7] et prohibuit eum et defendit ex parte dei, dicens Absit quod habeas potestatem nocendi mihi in hac vice, sed recedas. Qui rursus euolauit cum eiulatu horribili quasi per spacium sagitte volantis. Tercia vero vice apparuit eidem scissori ferenti crucem gladii sui super pectus suum pre timore et obuiauit ei in figura canis anulati.[8] Quo viso scissor cogitauit secum animatus in fide. Quid de me fiet? coniurabo eum in nomine trinitatis et per virtutem sanguinis Ihesu Christi de quinque plagis quod loqueretur cum eo et ipsum nullatenus lederet sed staret immobilis et responderet ad interrogata et diceret ei nomen suum et causam pene sue cum remedio competenti. Et fecit ita. Qui

coniuratus exalans terribiliter et ingemiscens. Sic et sic feci[9]
et excommunicatus sum pro tali facto. Vadas igitur ad talem
sacerdotem petens absolucionem pro me. Et oportet me implere
nouies viginti missas pro me celebrandas. et ex duobus vnum
eligas. Aut redeas ad me tali nocte solus, referens responsum de
hiis que dixi tibi et docebo te quomodo sanaberis, et ne timeas
visum ignis materialis[10] in medio tempore. Aut caro tua putres-
cet et cutis tua marcescet et dilabetur a te penitus infra breue.
Scias igitur quia hodie non audiuisti missam neque ewangelium
Iohannis scilicet "In principio" neque vidisti consecracionem
corporis et sanguinis domini obuiaui tibi ad presens, alioquin
non haberem plenarie potestatem tibi apparendi. Et cum loqueretur cum eo fuit quasi igneus et conspexit per os eius sua in-
teriora et formauit verba sua in intestinis et non loquebatur
lingua. Idem quidem scissor petebat licenciam a predicto spiritu
quod poterit habere alium socium secum in redeundo, qui respondit. Non. sed habeas super te quatuor euangelia euangelist'
et titulum trihumphalem videlicet Ihesus Nazarenus propter
duos alios spiritus hic commorantes, quorum vnus nequit loqui
coniuratus et est in specie ignis vel dumi et alter est in figura venatoris, et sunt in obuia valde periculosi. Facias vlterius fidem
huic lapidi quia non diffamabis ossa mea nisi sacerdotibus cele-
brantibus pro me, et aliis ad quos mitteris ex parte mea qui pos-
sunt mihi prodesse Qui fidem fecit lapidi de hoc secreto non
reuelando prout superius est expressum. Demum cordurauit eu-
mdem spiritum quod iret vsque ad hoggebek[11] vsque ad redi-
tum eius. Qui respondit Non. non. non. eiulando. Cui scissor
dixit. Tune vadas ad bilandbanke, et letus efficitur. Dictus vero
vir infirmabatur per aliquot dies, et statim conualuit et iuit Eboraco ad predictum presbiterum, qui dudum excommunicauit
eum, petens absolucionem. Qui renuit absoluere eum, vocans
sibi alium capellanum ipsum consulendo. At ille vocauit adhuc
alium, et alius tercium de absolucione huius musitantes.[12] Cui
primo dixit scissor. Domine scitis intersigna que suggessi in auribus vestris. Qui respondit. Vere, fili. Tandem post varios trac-
tatus inter partes isdem scissor satisfecit et soluit quinque
solidos et recepit absolucionem inscriptam in quadam cedula,

adiuratus quod non diffamaret mortuum sed infoderet illam in sepulcro suo penes caput eius secrete. Qua accepta ibat ad quendam fratrem Ric. de Pikeri[n]g nobilem confessorem sciscitans si dicta absolucio esset sufficiens et legitima. Qui respondit quod sic. Tunc idem scissor transiuit ad omnes ordines fratrum Eboraci et fecit fere omnes predictas missas celebrari per duos aut tres dies. et rediens domum fodit predictam absolucionem prout sibi fuerat imperatum in sepulcro. Hiis vero omnibus rite completis venit domum, et quidam presumptuosus vicinus eius audiens quod oportet ipsum referre eidem spiritui que gesserat in Eboraco in tali nocte, adiurauit cum dicens. Absit quod eas ad predictum spiritum nisi premunias me de regressu tuo et de die et hora. Qui taliter constrictus ne displiceret deo premuniit ipsum excitans a sompno et dixit Iam vado. Si volueris mecum venire, eamus, et dabo tibi partem de scriptis meis que porto super me propter timores nocturnos. Cui alter respondit. Vis tu quod eam tecum? qui respondit. Tu videris. ego nolo precipere tibi. Tunc alter finaliter dixit. Vadas ergo in nomine domini et deus expediat te in omnibus.[13] Quibus dictis venit ad locum constitutum et fecit magnum circulum crucis,[14] et habuit super se quatuor ewangelia et alia sacra verba, et stetit in medio circuli ponens quatuor monilia[15] in modum crucis in fimbriis eiusdem circuli, in quibus monilibus inscripta erant verba salutifera scilicet Ihesus Nazarenus etc. et expectauit aduentum spiritus eiusdem. Qui demum venit in figura capre et ter circa iuit circulum prefatum dicendo a. a. a. qua coniurata cecidit prona in terra et resurrexit in figura hominis magne stature et horribilis et macilenti ad instar vnius regis mortui depicti.[16] Et sciscitatus si labor eius aliqualiter proficeret ei respondit Laudetur deus quod sic. et steti ad dorsum hora nona quando infodisti absolucionem meam in sepulcro et timuisti. nec mirum, quia tres diaboli fuerunt ibidem presentes, qui omnimodis tormentis puniebant me postquam coniurasti me prima vice vsque ad absolucionem meam, suspicantes se permodicum tempus me in sua custodia habituros ad puniendum. Scias igitur quod die lune proxime futura ego cum aliis triginta spiritibus ibimus in gaudium sempiternum. Tu ergo vadas ad torrentem

talem et inuenies lapidem latum quem eleues et sub illo lapide
capias petram arenaciam. laues eciam totum corpus cum aqua
et frica cum petra et sanaberis infra paucos dies.[17] Qui interro-
gatus de nominibus duorum spirituum respondit. Non possum
dicere tibi illorum nomina. Iterum inquisitus de statu eorundem
asseruit quod unus illorum erat secularis et bellicosus et non
fuit de ista patria, et occidit mulierem pregnantem et non
habebit remedium ante diem iudicii, et videbis eum in figura
bouiculi sine ore et oculis et auribus, et nullatenus quamuis coniuretur poterit loqui. Et alius erat religiosus in figura venatoris
cum cornu cornantis, et habebit remedium et coniurabitur per
quendam puerulum nondum pubescentem domino disponente.
Postea inquisuit eundem spiritum de suo proprio statu. qui respondit ei. Tu detines iniuste capucium et togam quondam am-
ici et socii tui in guerra vltra mare. Satisfacies ergo ei vel grauiter
lues. Qui respondit Nescio vbi est. Cui alter respondit In tali
villa habitat prope castellum de Alnewyke. Vlterius inquisitus
Quod est culpa mea maxima? respondit. Maxima culpa tua est
causa mei. Cui viuus Quo modo et qualiter hoc? Dixit Quia
populus peccat de te menciens et alios mortuos scandalizans et
dicens Aut est ille mortuus qui coniurabatur aut ille vel ille. Et
inquisiuit eundem spiritum Quid igitur fiet? Reuelabo ergo
nomen tuum. Qui respondit Non. Sed si manseris in tali loco
eris diues et in tali loco eris pauper, et habes aliquos inimicos.[18]
Tandem spiritus respondit Non possum longius stare et loqui
tibi. Quibus discedentibus ab inuicem predictus surdus et mu-
tus et cecus bouiculus ibat cum viuente vsque ad villam de ampilford, quem coniurauit omnibus modis quibus sciuit, sed nullo
modo potuit respondere. Spiritus autem alius per ipsum adiutus
consuluit cum quod poneret optima sua scripta in suo capite dum
dormiret et non dicas amplius vel minus quam que precipio
tibi, et respicias ad terram et ne respicias ignem materialem ista
nocte ad minus. Qui rediens domum per dies aliquot grauiter
egrotabat.

[II. Concerning a fantastic interchange between a ghost and a
man during the reign of King Richard II.

It is said that a tailor named Snawball, while riding his horse
home one night from Gilling back to Ampleforth, heard a

sound in the road like ducks splashing in a river. And soon after this he saw what appeared to be a crow flying around his face, and it landed on the ground and was flapping its wings so violently it seemed about to die. So the tailor got down off his horse in order to pick up the crow and, as he was doing so, he saw scattered sparks of fire coming from the sides of the bird. He then made the sign of the cross and ordered with the help of God that the bird do him no harm at this meeting. Then the bird flew up with a great caw to the distance of a stone's throw. After that the tailor got back up on his horse, but soon that same crow flew to meet him and slammed right into his side, knocking the tailor off his horse and onto the ground. He lay there helpless with the wind knocked out of him, nearly unconscious, in great fear. Finally getting up with resolve, the tailor fought the bird with his sword until he became tired, and it seemed as if he were fighting against a bale of peat moss; still he held him back and defended himself with the help of God, saying: "May the power you have to do me harm in this place be gone! Get thee hence!" And again the crow flew off with a dreadful cawing, as far as an arrow flying through the air. And for a third time the ghost appeared to this same tailor, who held his sword like a crucifix in front of his chest out of fear, and this time it confronted him in the guise of a dog wearing a collar. When he saw this the tailor reflected to himself in earnest and thought: "What could happen to me? I will command it, in the name of the Trinity and by the strength of the blood of Jesus Christ of the five wounds, to speak to me and in no way to harm me, but to stand still and answer the questions asked of it and so to tell its name and the reason for its plight and an appropriate remedy." And he did so. And the spirit, having been addressed, sighed most horribly and groaned, "I did this and that, and I was excommunicated for a terrible misdeed. Would you go, therefore, to a priest, seeking absolution for me? For what I need to do is to ask the priest to celebrate 180 masses on my behalf. And at that point you will have a choice: either you can come back to me alone some night, bringing the answer to these instructions I gave you, at which time I will show you how you can be healed, and in the meantime you needn't fear the sight of burning matter; or your flesh will rot and your skin wither and drop off of you completely in an instant. You ought to know, in any case, that because today you have not heard mass nor evidently the gospel of John 'In the beginning . . .' nor have you seen the consecration of the body and blood of our Lord poured out for you, I was able to appear to you now; otherwise I would not have had the power to do so."

And while the ghost was speaking with the tailor, it appeared that he was on fire and the tailor could see through his mouth down to his innards and saw that he didn't speak with his tongue but formed his words from his stomach. Then the tailor asked this same spirit for permission to have a companion with him on the return trip, but the spirit answered, "No. But you may have the four evangelists above you and the victorious name of Jesus Christ because near here two other souls are also lingering. One of them is under a spell unable to speak, and he appears in the guise of fire or a bush; and the other is in the guise of a hunter, and they are extremely dangerous when encountered. Finally you are to swear on this stone that you will not disclose my bones to anyone except to the priests celebrating mass for me and to others to whom you will be sent who might come forward to help me." And the tailor swore his oath by the stone that he would not reveal the secret, as explained above. Finally, he entreated this same ghost to go away as far as Hoggebek until his return, but the spirit replied, "No, no, no," with a wail. To him the tailor said, "Then go to Bilandbank." And the ghost was persuaded.

The same man took ill for several days, but as soon as he improved, he went to York seeking absolution from the priest mentioned above who had previously excommunicated the ghost. The priest refused to absolve him and called another chaplain to consult with him about the case. But he called in yet another clergyman, and that one called in yet a third, to contemplate the absolution of the ghost. The tailor said to the chief priest, "Father, you understand the significance of the things that I whispered in your ears." And he answered, "Yes, my son." Finally, after a going-over of the differing opinions, the tailor had his way. He paid a total of five coins and received the absolution, inscribed on a tablet, having vowed that he would not defame the dead man but would secretly bury the tablet in his grave near his head. So once he had the absolution, he went to consult a certain Friar Richard of Pikering, the well-known confessor, in order to ascertain whether the aforementioned document was sufficient and legitimate. The friar replied that it was. Then the tailor went to all the orders of monks around York and saw to it that all the masses mentioned earlier were celebrated in the course of two or three days. And on his way home, he buried the document mentioned above in the grave exactly as he had been instructed. Once he had completed these tasks, the tailor went home. But a nosy neighbor of his, hearing that he needed to report that very night to the same ghost the things he had accomplished in York, accosted him, saying: "Don't you dare go to this ghost of yours unless you warn me in advance of the day and time you are going!" And the tailor, constrained in this fashion and not wanting to displease God, did forewarn his neighbor, waking him while he slept and saying, "I am going now. If you want to come with me, let's go, and I will gve you some of the incantations that I carry with me to keep away fears of the night." And the neighbor said to him, "Do you want me to come with you?" He answered, "It appears that you want to. But I don't mean to suppose that you do." Then his neighbor said with conviction, "You go, then, in the name of the Lord, and may God grant you quick resolve in everything you do."

So once these words had been uttered, the tailor went to the appointed place and drew a great circle on the ground with a cross, and he held above him the four gospels and other holy texts. Then he stood in the middle of the circle and placed four crosses adorned with saints' relics around the edges of his circle; on these reliquaries were inscribed healing words such as "Jesus of Nazareth" and so forth, and he awaited the arrival of the ghost. The ghost appeared at length in the form of a goat, and walked three times around the circle bleating "Baa, baa, baa!" After it had been sworn to confession, it fell flat on the ground and got up in the form of a man of huge stature both horrible and emaciated, like the image on one of those paintings

of dead kings. And when the tailor inquired whether his effort
had been at all useful for it, the ghost replied, "Yes, it has, and
God be praised for it! I stood at your back during the ninth
hour while you buried my absolution in the grave and you were
frightened. And no wonder, because three devils were there in
that very place, who had been punishing me with all sorts of
torments after you swore me to confession on our first meeting
until my absolution, hoping that they would have me in their
power in order to punish me a little longer. You may know
therefore that next Monday I will go with thirty other spirits
into eternal joy. You therefore are to go to a certain river where
you will find a wide stone that you are to lift up. And you are to
pick up some sandy gravel from under that stone. Then you are
to wash your entire body with water and rub yourself with the
gravel, and you will be completely healthy in just a few days."

And when the tailor had asked him for the names of two of
the spirits, he answered, "I cannot tell you the names of the
others." And having been asked again about the situation of the
others, the ghost revealed that one of them had been a layman
and was belligerent, and wasn't of this country, and he had
killed a pregnant woman and would not get his chance for
penance before the day of judgment. "And you will see him in
the shape of a bullock without mouth, eyes, or ears, and no
matter how often he is sworn to confession, he will not be able
to speak. Another one, who had been of a religious order, is in
the guise of a hunter blowing his horn, and he will have a
chance for penance, for he will be sworn to confession by a
young lad, not yet of age, according to God's plan."

Afterwards the tailor asked the ghost about his own particular
situation, and he told him, "You are unjustly keeping back the
cape and tunic of your former friend and companion in the war
beyond the sea. Make restitution to him therefore, or you will
atone for it severely." And the tailor replied, "I don't know
where he is!" And the other answered him, "He is dwelling in a
certain village near the castle Alnwick." When further asked,
"What is my biggest problem?" the spirit said, "Your biggest
problem is because of me." To him the mortal man asked,
"How and why?" The spirit said, "Because people are sinning

against you by lying and defaming other dead men, saying, 'It is either that dead man who was being sworn to confession, or that one, or that one.'" And the tailor asked the ghost, "Then what is to be done? Shall I reveal your name?" But the ghost answered, "No. But if you will have stayed in one place you will be rich, and in another place you will be poor, and you have powerful enemies." At length the ghost said, "I cannot stay here any longer talking to you." And while they were departing from their meeting, the aforementioned deaf, mute, and blind bullock walked along with the living man to the village of Ampleford. And the tailor implored this spirit, in all the ways he could think of, to reveal his situation, but the spirit was not able to respond in any way. However, the other ghost, who had been helped by him, advised him to put his most important documents under his pillow while he slept and said, "Do not reveal more or less than the things I am directing you, look at the ground and don't gaze at anything that is burning for tonight at least." The tailor, upon returning home, became seriously ill for several days.]

III. De spiritu Roberti filii Roberti de Boltebi de Killeburne comprehenso in cimiterio.

Memorandum quod predictus Robertus iunior moriebatur et sepeliebatur in cymiterio sed solebat egredi de sepulcro in noctibus et inquietare villanos et deterrere ac canes ville sequebantur cum et latrabant magnaliter. Tandem iuuenes ville mutuo loquebantur proponentes comprehendere eum si aliquo modo potuissent et conuenientes ad cimiterium. Sed illo viso fugerunt omnes exceptis duobus quorum vnus nomine Robertus Foxton comprehendit eum in egressu de cimiterio et posuit eum super le kirkestile, altero acclamante viriliter Teneas firmiter quousque veniam ad te. Cui alter respondit Vadas cicius ad parochianum ut coniuretur, quia deo concedente quod habeo firmiter tenebo vsque ad aduentum sacerdotis. Qui quidem parochialis presbiter festinauit velociter et coniurauit eum in nomine sancte trinitatis et in virtute Ihesu Christi quatinus responderet ei ad interrogata. quo coniurato loquebatur in interioribus visceribus et non cum lingua sed quasi in vacuo dolio,[19] et confitebatur delicta sua diuersa. Quibus cognitis presbiter

absoluit eum sed onerauit predictos comprehensores ne reue-
lare[n]t aliqualiter confessionem eius, et de cetero requieuit in
pace, deo disponente.

Dicitur autem quod ante assolucionem volebat stare²⁰ ad
hostia domus et fenestras et sub parietibus et muris quasi aus-
cultans. fforsitan exspectans si quis vellet egredi et coniurare
cum suis necessitatibus succurrendo. Referunt aliqui quod erat
adiuuans et consenciens neci cuiusdam viri. et fecit alia mala de
quibus non est dicendum per singula ad presens.²¹

[III. Concerning the spirit of Robert, son of Robert de
Bolteby of Killeburne, who was caught in the graveyard.

It is worth remembering that Robert Jr., mentioned above,
had died and was entombed in the graveyard, but that he used
to come out of his tomb at night and waken and frighten the villagers, and the dogs of the village would follow him, barking
wildly. Finally, the young men of the village joined together and
said that they were determined to catch him by any means they
could, and they went together to the graveyard. But upon spot-
ting him, all but two of them fled. One named Robert Foxton
caught hold of him as he was exiting the graveyard and pushed
him up against the litchgate, while the other boy shouted
bravely, "Hold him tight until I can get to you!" To him his
friend replied, "Go quickly and get the rector to swear him to
confession, because what God is empowering me to hold tight,
I can continue to hold until a priest comes!" Indeed then the local priest hurried as quickly as he could and commanded the
ghost in the name of the Holy Trinity and by the power of Jesus
Christ to answer questions put to him. Having been thus commanded, he spoke then from deep within his abdomen like an
empty barrel, not using his tongue, and he confessed to various
sins he had committed. And once these things had come to
light, the priest absolved him, but he admonished the ghost-
snatchers mentioned above that they were on no account to reveal the confession and thus the spirit would rest in peace for
the future, according to God's plan.

For it is said that, before his absolution, the spirit used to
lurk around under the windows of houses and alongside the
walls, as if listening. Possibly realizing that it needed to be

absolved, it was waiting in the hope that someone might come out and swear it to confession. Some people assert that he had been an accessory and had knowledge of the murder of a certain man, and that he had committed other crimes which must not be mentioned here.]

IV. Iterum tradunt veteres quod quidam nomine Iacobus Tankerlay quondam Rector de Kereby sepeliebatur coram capitulo Bellelande et solebat egredi in noctibus vsque kereby et quadam nocte exsufflauit oculum concubine sue ibidem et dicitur quod abbas et conuentus fecerunt corpus eius effodi de tumulo cum cista sua et coegerunt Rogerum Wayneman cariare illum vsque ad Gormyr[e] et dum iactaret predictam cistam in aquam fer[e] pre timore boues demergerentur. Absit quod ego taliter scribens sim in aliquo periculo, quia sicut audiui a senioribus ita scripsi. Misereatur ei omnipotens, si tamen fuerit de numero saluandorum.[22]

[IV. Again the old folk recount that a certain man, Jacob Tankerlay by name, formerly rector of Kereby, after having been clearly buried in the presence of his dear little Bellalande, used to wander abroad at night over to the village of Kereby; and on a certain night he gouged out the eye of his own mistress. And after this it is said that the abbot and a group of locals had his body dug up from his tomb, in his very coffin, and they persuaded Roger Wayneman to convey it as far as Gormyre; and that as Roger was heaving the aforementioned coffin into the water, his oxen were nearly drowned from fright. May no harm come to me in writing this, for I have written it exactly as I heard from the elders. May the Almighty take pity on Jacob Tankerlay, if indeed he be among the number of those who are meant to be saved.]

V. Item est mirabile dictu quod scribo. Dicitur quod quedam mulier cepit quendam spiritum et portauit in domum quandam super dorsum suum in presencia hominum quorum vnus retulit quod vidit manus mulieris demergentes in came Spiritus profunde, quasi caro eiusdem Spiritus esset putrida et non solida sed fantastica.[23]

[V. What I am writing is indeed astonishing to relate: The story goes that a certain woman caught a kind of ghost and carried it on her back into her very house in the presence of a group of people, one of whom recounted that he saw the woman's hands plunged deep into the flesh of the thing, as if its flesh were rotten and not solid, but like a phantasm.]

VI. De quodam canonico de Newburg post mortem capto quem [*blank*] comprehendit.

Contigit quod ipse cum magistro aratorum pariter loquebatur et in agro gradiebatur. Et subito predictus magister fugit valde perterritus [fugit] et alter luctabatur cum quodam spiritu qui dilacerauit turpiter vestes suas. Sed tandem optinuit victoriam et coniurauit eum. Qui coniuratus confitebatur se fuisse talem canonicum de Newburg et excommunicatum pro quibusdam cocliaribus argenti que in quodam loco abscondit. Supplicauit ergo viuenti quod adiret ad locum predictum et acciperet illa, reportando Priori suo et peteret absolucionem. Qui fecit ita et inuenit dicta choclearia argenti in loco memorato Qui absoltitus in pace deinceps requieuit. Prefatus tamen vir egrotauit et elanguit per multos dies. et affirmauit quod apparuit sibi in habitu canonicorum.²⁴

[VI. How a certain clergyman from Newbury was apprehended after his death.

It happened that a man was walking side by side in a field with the local farm overseer, when suddenly that same overseer became wildly terrified and fled, and the other man grappled with a kind of phantom that viciously tore apart his clothes. But eventually the man achieved victory over the phantom and swore it to reveal its story. And the phantom, having been sworn to confess, did confess that, in fact, it had been a clergyman from Newbury and that he had been excommunicated for the sake of some silver spoons that he had taken and hidden in a certain place. He pleaded therefore with the living man to go to the place after he told him where it was and to remove those spoons, and in taking them back to his priory on his behalf, to ask that the clergyman be absolved. So the man did just that, and he found the silver spoons just as described in the place mentioned. And the phantom, having duly been absolved, rested in peace from that time on. And yet the man in this story became sick and was laid up for many days, and he claimed that the phantom appeared to him dressed as a clergyman.]

VII. De quodam spiritu alibi coniurato qui fatebatur se grauiter puniri eo quod erat mercenarius cuiusdam patris familias et furabatur garbas illius quas dabat bobus suis vt apparerent corpulenti; et aliud quod plus se grauat, quod non profunde sed superficietenus arabat terram suam, volens quod boues eius forent pingues, et affirmauit quod erant quindecim Spiritus in loco vno grauiter puniti pro delictis suis que faciebant. Supplicauit igitur quod suggereret domino suo pro indulgencia et absolucione quatinus posset optinere remedium oportunum.

[VII. This story is about a certain soul who had been sworn to confession elsewhere, and who said he had been punished severely for the reason that, when he had been the hired hand of a certain landowner, he used to steal the scraps that the landowner was accustomed to give his cows in order to fatten them up. And he related another thing that weighed heavily upon him, namely that he used to plow the man's land only superficially, not deep, hoping all the while that his cows would grow fat all the same. Moreover, he insisted that there were fifteen spirits all in a single place, who had been severely punished for the sins they used to commit. He prayed therefore that he might convince his lord to grant leniency and forgiveness, to the extent that he could devise a fitting remedy.]

VIII. Item de alio spiritu sequente Willelmum de Bradeforth et vociferante how how how. ter. per tres vices. Contigit quod quarta nocte circa mediam noctem remeauit ad nouum locum de villa de Ampilford, et dum rediret per viam audiuit vocem terribilem clamantem longe post se quasi in monte, et paulo post iterum clamauit similiter sed proprius. et tercia vice vociferabatur per viam compendii vltra se.[25] et demum vidit pallidum equum, et canis eius latrauit paululum, sed valde timens abscondit se inter tibias eiusdem Willelmi. Quo facto Willelmus prohibuit eundem spiritum in nomine domini et in virtute

sanguinis Ihesu Christi quod discederet et non impediret viam
eius. quo audito recessit ad instar cuiusdam canvas²⁶ reuoluentis
quatuor angulis et volutabat. Ex quo colligitur quod fuit spiritus desiderans magnaliter coniurari et efficaciter adiuuari.²⁷

[VIII. Likewise here is a story about another ghost who followed William of Bradeforth on three successive occasions,
yowling "Ow! Ow! Ow!" each time. And it happened that on
the fourth night, around about midnight, William went over to
a new place in the village of Ampleforth and, while he was returning along the road, he heard a terrible voice shrieking in the
distance behind him, as if coming from the hills. Shortly after
that the voice cried out again in a similar fashion but much
closer. Then for the third time it made its cry at the crossroads
up ahead of him. And at that moment he caught sight of a pale
horse. His dog gave a few feeble barks but, being thoroughly
terrified, tried to hide itself between William's legs. At this
William commanded the apparition to stay back, in the name
of the Lord and by the power of the blood of Jesus Christ, and
to get out of the way and not block his path. Upon hearing this,
the apparition faded into a shape something like a wine-vat,
whirling at four angles, and started rolling away. It was inferred
from this that it was a soul seeking fervently to be sworn to
confession and thus to be helped in the most crucial way.]

IX. *Item de spiritu hominis de Aton²⁸ in Clyueland.* Refertur
quod sequebatur virum per quater viginti milliaria qui deberet
coniurare et succurrere ei. Qui coniuratus confitebatur se fuisse
excommunicatum pro re quadam / sex denariorum / sed post
absolucionem et satisfaccionem factam requieuit in pace. In his
omnibus ostendit se deus cum nil malum est impunitum remu-
neratorem iustum et cum nil bonum a conuerso irremuneratum.

Dicitur quod idem spiritus priusquam esset coniuratus iactauit
viuentem vltra sepem et suscepit eum ex altera parte in descensu.
Qui coniuratus respondit Si fecisses sic imprimis non tibi nocuissem † . . . ter†²⁹ in talibus locis fuisti perterritus et ego feci hoc.

[IX. Here is another ghost story, this one about a person from
Aton, in Clyveland. The story goes that a ghost followed for
twenty-four miles a man who might be someone to swear it to

confession and thus help it in its need. And once it had been sworn to confession, it admitted that it had been excommunicated over the matter of six coins, but that after it had received absolution, and performed penance, it rested in peace. In all these things God reveals himself, because the one who atones suffers no harm and is not punished yet, on the other hand the one who does not atone does suffer and no good comes to him.

It is said that this same spirit, before it was sworn to confession, had thrown a person over a hedge, catching him on the other side as he fell. And after it had made its confession, it explained to the man: "If you had sworn me to confession in the first place, I would not have treated you roughly, but instead you were paralyzed with fear, so I did it."]

Verso blank

The stories are continued on the last three pages of the volume (ff. 163 b, 164). I omit one extract "de triplici genere confessionis"³⁰ and a story taken from a book, of which the catalogue gives this synopsis. A servant guilty of adultery with his mistress, and suspected by his master, is taken to a "vates qui habet spiritum phitonis,"³¹ but on the way he repents and lashes himself, whereby the spirit loses his memory. Caesarius of Heisterbach has many such tales.

X. Quomodo latro penitens post confessionem euanuit ab oculis demonis.

Contigit olim in Exon. quod quidam fossor magnus laborator et comestor mansit in quadam cellula spaciose domus que habebat plures cellulas cum muris intermixtis et ubi [ui: *perhaps* non nisi?] vnum domicilium. hic autem fossor esuriens solebat sepius ascendere per quandam scalam in domicilium et amputare carnes ibidem suspensas et coquere et inde comedere eciam in quadragesima. Dominus vero domus videns carnes suas sic amputatas inquisiuit a domesticis suis de hoc facto. Negantibus autem omnibus et se purgantibus per iuramenta. minabatur ille quod vellet ire ad maleficum quendam nigromanticum et sciscitari per ipsum hoc factum mirandum. Quo audito fossor ille valde timuit et ibat ad fratres et confitebatur delictum suum in

secreto et sacramentaliter absoluebatur. Prefatus quidem dominus domus vt minabatur ibat ad nigromanticum, et ille vnxit
vnguem cuiusdam pueruli et per incantaciones suas inquisiuit ab
eo quid videret. Qui respondit Garcionem video coma tonsum.
Cui dixit Coniures igitur eum quod appareat tibi in pulcherima
forma qua poterit. Et fecit sic. Et affirmauit puerulus Ecce aspi-
cio valde pulcrum equum. Et postea vidit quendam hominem in
tali figura quasi fossorem predictum ascendentem per scalam et
carnes amputantem cum equo pariter consequente. Et clericus inquisiuit Quid faciunt iam homo et equus? et respondit infans
Ecce coquit et comedit carnes illas. Et vlterius inquisitus Et quid
nunc facit? Et ait puerulus Vadunt pariter ad ecclesiam fratrum.
sed equus exspectat pre foribus et homo intrat et flexis genibus
loquitur cum quodam fratre qui ponit manum suam super caput
eius. Iterum clericus inquisiuit a puerulo Quid faciunt nunc? Cui
respondit Ambo simul euanuerunt ab oculis meis et amplius non
video eos, et nescio sine dubio vbi sunt.[32]

[X. How a penitent thief, after he made his confession, disappeared before the eyes of a demon.

It happened once in Exon that a certain digger, a great worker
and eater, stayed in a spacious room in a house that had many
storerooms arranged within its walls, all in the one building.
This digger, however, being hungry, used to climb up often, using a ladder that was in the building, and cut down the meat that
was hanging there and cook and eat it; and it lasted him forty
days. And the master of the house, seeing that his meat had been
cut down like that, questioned his servants about the deed. But
they all denied it and swore under oath that they told the truth.
And the master threatened that he was of a mind to seek out a
well-known evil sorcerer and to find out from him about this unusual occurrence. And after hearing this, the digger was in great
fear, and he went to some monks and confessed his sin in private, and he was absolved by the sacrament. But the aforementioned master of the house went out, as he had threatened, to the
sorcerer. The sorcerer anointed the fingernail of a certain young
lad and questioned him through his incantations as to what he
saw. And the boy said, "I see Garcio with a haircut." Then the
sorcerer said to him, "You are to command him to appear to you

in the most beautiful form that he can." And the boy did so. And the lad announced, "Behold! I am looking at a most beautiful horse." And after that he saw a certain man, who looked just like the digger, climbing a ladder and cutting down meat, with the horse following. And a cleric asked, "What are the man and the horse doing now?" And the young one answered, "Behold, he is cooking and eating those meats." And he was questioned further, "And what is he doing now?" And the lad said, "They are going together to the monks' church. But the horse is waiting in front of the doors while the man in going in and kneeling down and speaking to a monk who is placing his hand on the man's head." Again the cleric asked the boy, "What are they doing now?" And he answered, "Both disappeared together before my eyes and I am not seeing them anymore, and, without a doubt, I don't know where they are."]

XI. De opere dei mirando qui vocat ea que non sunt. tanquam ea que sunt. et qui potest facere quando et quicquid vult. et de quodam miro.

Est memorie comendatum quod quidam homo de Clyueland cognomine Ricardus Rountre relinquens vxorem suam grauidam ibat ad tumbam sancti Iacobi cum aliis quam pluribus qui quadam nocte pernoctabant in quadam silua prope viam regiam. hinc est quod quilibet illorum vigilabat per quoddam spacium noctis propter timorem nocturnum, et ceteri securius dormiebant. Contigit quod in illa parte noctis qua prefatus homo fuit custos et vigil noctis audiebat magnum sonitum transiencium per viam regalem. et aliqui sedebant et equitabant super equos oues et boues et quidam super alia animalia, et vniuersa pecora que fuerunt sua mortuaria quando moriebantur. Tandem vidit quasi paruulum volutantem in quadam caliga super terram. Et coniurauit ipsum Quis esset et quare sic volutasset? Respondit Non oportet te me coniurare Tu enim eras pater meus et ego filius tuus abortiuus sine baptismo et absque nomine sepelitus. Quo audito isdem peregrinus exuit se suam camisiam et induit puerulum suum imponens ei nomen in nomine sancte Trinitatis. et tulit secum illam veterem caligam in testimonium huius rei. Qui quidem infans taliter nominatus

vehementer exultabat et de cetero iuit pedibus suis erectus qui
super terram antea volutabat. Completa vero peregrinacione
fecit conuiuium vicinis suis et peciit ab vxore sua caligas suas.
Que ostendit vnam et alteram non inuenit caligam. Tunc mari-
tus suus ostendit illi caligam in quo puer inuoluebatur, et hoc
mirabatur. Obstetricibus autem confitentibus veritatem de morte
et sepultura pueri in predicta caliga fiebat diuorcium inter maritum et vxorem eius quod fuit compater filii sui taliter abortiui.
Sed credo quod hoc diuorcium displicuit valde deo.[33]

[XI. Concerning a marvelous work of God who calls forth
things that do not exist, just as he calls forth things that do exist, and who is able to do whatever he wants whenever he wants,
and concering one miracle in particular.

It should be remembered that a certain man from Clyveland
named Richard Rountree, leaving his pregnant wife, went to
the tomb of St. Jacob, with a large group of others. And one
night they spent the night in a certain forest near the royal
road. And here various of them kept watch through a portion
of the night because of nocturnal fears, while the others slept
safely. And it happened that, in the part of the night during
which the aforementioned man was watchman and awake in
the night, he heard a great commotion of travelers on the royal
road. And some were sitting or riding on horses, sheep, and
cows, and others on other animals. And all this livestock were
those that had borne them to their graves when they had died.
Finally he saw what seemed to be a very young one rolling
across the ground in a sort of boot. And he demanded of this
one, "Who are you, and why are you rolling?" And it answered, "You are not allowed to accost me. For you were my
father and I am your son. I died by abortion, without benefit of
baptism, and thus buried without even a name." And when he
had heard this, the same pilgrim removed his own shirt and put
it on his son, bestowing upon him a name in the name of the
Holy Trinity, and took the old boot with him as a testimony to
this occurrence. And indeed the infant rejoiced greatly, having
been officially named in this way, and for the future he who
previously had rolled over the ground walked erect on his own
legs. And having completed his pilgrimage, the man held a

party with his neighbours and asked his wife for his boots. She produced one of them, but couldn't find the other boot. Then her husband showed her the boot in which the boy had been rolling, and she was amazed at this. Yet after the obstetricians had confessed the truth about the death and burial of the boy in the boot mentioned earlier, a divorce was had between the husband and his wife, because she had suffered along with her son in such an abortion. But I believe that this divorce greatly displeased God.]

[This page is difficult to read, blurred, and the writing in places is gone.]

XII. De sorore veteris Ade de Lond comprehensa post mortem secundum relacionem antiquorum.

Memorandum quod predicta mulier in cimiterio de Ampilford sepeliebatur et infra breue post mortem comprehendebatur per Willelmum Trower seniorem et coniurata confitebatur se ipsam peragrare viam suam in nocte propter quasdam cartas quas tradidit iniuste Ade fratri suo. Hinc est quod olim quadam discordia otta inter maritum suum et ipsam, in preiudicium predicti viri sui et propriorum filiorum optulit fratri suo predictas cartas. ita quod post mortem suam frater suns expulsit maritum suum de domo sua, videlicet vno toft et crofte cum pertinenciis in Ampilford, et in Heslarton de vna bouata terre cum pertinenciis, per violenciam. Supplicabat igitur predicto Willelmo quod suggereret eidem fratri quod vellet redonare marito suo et filiis easdem cartas, et restituere illis terram suam. alioquin nullo modo posset in pace requiescere ante diem iudicii. Qui quidem Willelmus secundum iussionem suam suggessit predicto Ade. sed ille renuit cartas restituere, dicens non credo [. . .] hiis dictis. Cui ille. Verus est in omnibus sermo meus, vnde deo concedente audietis sororem vestram vobis colloquentem de hac materia infra breue. Et altera nocte rursus comprehendit illam ac attulit ad cameram prefati Ade, et loquebatur cum eo. Cui respondit induratus frater suus secundum quosdam. Si ambulaueris imperpetuum nolo predictas cartas redonare. Cui respondit illa ingemiscens. Iudicet deus inter me

et te ob quam causam. Scias ergo quia vsque ad mortem tuam
minime requiescam. vnde post mortem tuam tu peragrabis loco
mei. Dicitur vlterius quod dextera manus illius pendebat iusum
et erat valde nigra. Et interrogabatur qua de causa, respondebat
quia sepius pugnando [?] extendit illam, iurando falsum. Tandem coniurata fuit ad alterum locum propter timorem nocturnum et terrorem gentis ville. Peto tamen veniam si forte offendi
in scribendo contra veritatem. Dicitur tamen quod Adam [de
lond *above line*] iunior vero heredi partim satisfecit post
mortem Ade senioris.

[XII. Concerning the sister of old Adam de Lond, apprehended after her death, according to the report of venerable
persons.

It should be remembered that the above-mentioned woman
had been entombed in the graveyard of Ampleforth. A short
time after her death, she was apprehended by William Trower
Senior. After he had sworn her to confess her situation, she confessed that she herself wandered along her street at night because of certain documents that she had handed over unjustly to
her brother Adam. The fact is that once, after a quarrel had
arisen between her husband and herself, in an act prejudicial
against her above-mentioned husband and against her own sons,
she delivered the documents in question to her brother. Thus after her death her brother drove her husband violently from his
own property, it being a homestead and stables with acreage extending to Ampleforth, and some grazing land with acreage in
Heslarton. Therefore she begged this William to suggest to her
brother that he give the documents back to her husband and
sons and restore their land to them, otherwise she would not at
all be able to rest in peace prior to the day of judgment. Thus
William made the suggestion to Adam, following her bidding.
But he refused to return the documents, saying, "I don't believe
[. . .] what you have told me." And William said to him, "My
story is true at every point, and, God willing, you will hear your
sister talking to you about this matter quite soon."

And on another night he apprehended her again and took her
to Adam's room, and she spoke with him. But according to
certain persons, her hardened brother said, "Even if you were

to wander for eternity, I won't return the documents." And groaning she said to him, "Let God decide this matter between you and me. You should know, however, that because of this I will not rest well until your death, and that after your death you will wander in my place." It is said further that his right hand dangled and was dark black. And when he was asked the reason for this, he said that it was because he often strained it while fighting [?], but he was lying. Finally the woman who had revealed all this went to a different locale, because of the nocturnal fears and terrors of the village people. Nevertheless I ask forgiveness if by chance I have erred in writing against the truth. And yet it is said that Adam de Lond Junior did partly satisfy the heirs after Adam's Senior's death.]

—*translated by Leslie Boba Joshi*

APPENDIX

INTRODUCTION TO *GHOSTS*
AND MARVELS

At the outset of this preface I must make it quite clear that the choice of the stories which it introduces is not mine. I am glad that it is not, for I have been saved much trouble, and I am also free to comment (if I desire it) adversely on anything that does not please me. But the stage of comment has not yet been reached; general remarks are expected first, and these are to me an obstacle, not lightly got over.

Often have I been asked to formulate my views about ghost stories and tales of the marvellous, the mysterious, the supernatural. Never have I been able to find out whether I had any views that could be formulated. The truth is, I suspect, that the *genre* is too small and special to bear the imposition of far-reaching principles. Widen the question, and ask what governs the construction of short stories in general, and a great deal might be said, and has been said. There are, of course, instances of whole novels in which the supernatural governs the plot; but among them are few successes. The ghost story is, at its best, only a particular sort of short story, and is subject to the same broad rules as the whole mass of them. Those rules, I imagine, no writer ever follows. In fact, it is absurd to talk of them as rules; they are qualities which have been observed to accompany success.

Some such qualities I have noted, and while I cannot undertake to write about broad principles, something more concrete is capable of being recorded. Well, then: two ingredients most valuable in the concocting of a ghost story are, to me, the atmosphere and the nicely managed crescendo. I assume, of course, that the writer will have got his central idea before he undertakes the story at all. Let us be introduced to the actors in a placid way; let us see them going about their ordinary business, undisturbed by forebodings, pleased with their surroundings; and into this calm environment let the ominous thing put out its head, unobtrusively at first, and then more insistently, until it holds the stage. It is not amiss sometimes to leave a loophole for a natural explanation; but, I would say, let the loophole be so narrow as not to be quite practicable. Then, for the setting. The detective story cannot be too much up-to-date: the motor, the telephone, the aeroplane, the newest slang, are all in place there. For the ghost story a slight haze of distance is desirable. "Thirty years ago," "Not long before the war," are very proper openings. If a really remote date be chosen, there is more than one way of bringing the reader in contact with it. The finding of documents about it can be made plausible; or you may begin with your apparition and go back over the years to tell the cause of it; or (as in "Schalken the Painter")[1] you may set the scene directly in the desired epoch, which I think is hardest to do with success. On the whole (though not a few instances might be quoted against me) I think that a setting so modern that the ordinary reader can judge of its naturalness for himself is preferable to anything antique. For some degree of actuality is the charm of the best ghost stories; not a very insistent actuality, but one strong enough to allow the reader to identify himself with the patient; while it is almost inevitable that the reader of an antique story should fall into the position of the mere spectator.

These are personal impressions. Many other views are current, and have been justified in practice. This collection shows how various are the methods which have made their appeal to the public, for there is none of these tales that has not had its vogue. A few pedantic comments upon some of them may be allowed. The dates, which, in particular, look pedantic, are really not without their use and meaning.

Defoe's "Mrs. Veal" (1706), we are told by Sir Walter Scott, was a successful device for selling off an edition of *Drelincourt on Death* which threatened to be a drug in the market.[2] There is no question but that Defoe was perfectly capable of writing such a narrative as this without anything to base it on. But in this case doubts have been expressed, not of the truth but of the untruth of his particular tale, and, though I cannot point to any investigation of it, I remember that Mr. Andrew Lang refers to "Mrs. Veal" as being no imposture, but an attempt to record an occurrence believed to be real.[3] Whether imagined or reported, it is an admirable piece of narrative.

"Wandering Willie's Tale" (1824),[4] that acknowledged masterpiece, has its roots, as may have been suspected by many readers, in old folk-lore. Scottish parallels I cannot cite, but a Danish one is to be found in the story of Claus the coachman of Fru Ingeborg Skeel of Voergaard.

"Fru Ingeborg was Skeel's widow, and of Skeel it is told that some years before his death he got by wrongful means some fields from the village of Agersted. They are still called Agersted fields, and still belong to Voergaard. Now Skeel had been hard enough on the peasants, but his widow was far worse. One day she was driving to church—it was the anniversary of her husband's death—and she said to the coachman 'I wish to know how it is with my husband that's gone.' The coachman—Claus was his name, and he was a free-spoken man—made answer: 'Well, my lady, it's not so easy to find out, but I'm sure he's not suffering from cold.' She was very angry, and threatened the man that unless by the third Sunday from then he brought her news from her husband of how he fared, he should lose his life.

"Claus knew she was a woman of her word, and first went to ask advice of a priest who was said to be as learned as any bishop, but he could only tell him that he had a brother, a priest in Norway, that knew more than he; Claus had best go to him. He did so, and this priest, after some thought, said: 'Well, I can bring about a meeting between you, but it will be a risky thing for you if you are afraid of him: you will have to give the message yourself.' It was settled that at night they should go out

into a great wood and call up the lord. When they got there the
priest set to work to read—till the hair stood upright on Claus's
head. In a little time they heard a terrible noise, and a fiery red
carriage with horses that threw out sparks of fire all about them
came driving through the wood, and pulled up beside them.
Claus recognized his master. 'Who is it would speak with me?'
roared he from the carriage. Claus took off his hat and said,
'My lady's regards to my lord, and she would know how he has
fared since he died.' 'Tell her,' said the lord, 'that I am in hell,
and there's a chair in making for her. It's finished, all but one
leg, and when that is done, she will be fetched, unless she gives
back Agersted. And to prove that you have talked with me, I
give you this ring of my betrothal, which you may give her.'

"The coachman held out his hat, and into it there fell a ring;
but the carriage and horses had vanished. On the third Sunday
Claus took his stand outside the church when Lady Ingeborg
came driving up. When she saw him she asked at once what
message he had brought, and Claus told her what he had seen
and heard, and gave her the ring, which she recognized.

" 'Good,' said she, 'you have saved your life, and I shall join
my husband when I am dead—that will no doubt be so—but I
will never give up Agersted.' "

In other versions the land is given back, and somewhere
among E. T. Kristensen's multitudinous collections[5] there is, I
am confident, a version in which a receipt for rent actually
plays a part.

Three stories, "Ligeia," "The Werewolf,"[6] "Schalken the
Painter," all date from 1838–9. The first represents the dream-
like, rhapsodic, quasi-allegorical *genre*. The editor of Poe's tales
in "Everyman's Library"[7] calls it "so moulded and perfect, that
it offers no crevice for the critical knife," and doubtless it would
be possible to collect other equally enthusiastic descriptions.
Evidently in many people's judgements it ranks as a classic.
"The Werewolf" is undeniably old-fashioned ("Prepare therefore to listen to a strange story") and, as undeniably, well told.
But "Schalken" conforms more strictly to my own ideals. It is
indeed one of the best of Le Fanu's good things. We have (if I
may be bibliographical for a moment) two texts of Schalken.

The one given here is the original, which appeared in the *Dublin University Magazine* in 1839, as one of the "Purcell Papers," and was reprinted in 1883 under that title. The other appeared in a rare anonymous volume issued at Dublin in 1851, and called *Ghost Stories and Tales of Mystery*. Here each story in the book is headed by a motto—felicitously chosen—from the Bible. That of "Schalken" is from Job. "For he is not a man as I am, that we should come together; neither is there any that might lay his hand upon us both. Let him, therefore, take his rod away from me, and let not his fear terrify me."

The story then begins, "There exists at this moment in perfect preservation a remarkable work of Schalken," and the little dialogue between Father Purcell and Captain Vandael is all transferred to the third person; the whole preamble is shortened, and there are many variants throughout the text, which ends with the words—"Rose Velderkaust, whose mysterious fate must always remain matter of speculation,"—the second, and rather unnecessary, description of the picture being omitted. Where, by the way, is that picture? That it was a real one is fairly plain, but I have never seen it, and know no print of it. Most likely Le Fanu saw it in a private house. If so, there is every probability that it has not survived the more generous outbursts of the friends of freedom.

The two stories by Bulwer Lytton and George Eliot both date from 1859.[8] The first is deservedly famous. Does it owe some of its details to the "veridical" history of the haunted mill at Willington, inhabited by the Proctor family?[9] I have thought so. Of this story also there are two forms, in the later of which the encounter with the Comte-de-St-Germain-Cagliostro gentleman does not appear. In parenthesis, I wonder whether many readers share my annoyance at the old trick of writing "Mr. J—— of G—— street."

Probably it will be agreed that "The Open Door" (1885) is the most *beautiful* story in the volume. I class it with the equally beautiful book *A Beleaguered City*,[10] and put these two very much in the forefront of Mrs. Oliphant's excursions into the other world. In this case again I have wondered whether a very old story did not furnish the motif of this. I mean the history of

Mr. Ruddle of Launceston. He tells it himself as a veritable experience he went through in the year 1665. Here, too, there was a young boy who was troubled by the appearance of the ghost of a woman, whom he knew to have been dead about eight years, which met him in a field every day on his way to school. The story is interestingly told: I do not know if it has ever been critically treated. The only text I can now lay hands on is in *News from the Invisible World,* by T. Charley.[11] Mr. Ruddle keeps counsel as to what the ghost (whom he eventually interviewed and exorcized) said to him: the end was that "it quietly vanished, and neither doth appear since, or ever will more, to any man's disturbance."

So many of the best stories of this class are variants on old themes—indeed, so inevitable is it that they should be based to a greater or less extent on tradition, that I count it no depreciation of an author to show that some old tale may have been at the back of his mind when he was devising his new one.

But I do not think that "The Monkey's Paw" (1902), nor any other of Mr. Jacobs's supernatural stories, can thus be provided with an ancestry.[12] They seem absolutely original. They are always terrible, and they are wonderful examples of the art, which I commended at the outset, of leaving a loophole for a rationalistic explanation, which is, after all, not quite practicable. You are sure that the ghost did intervene, but sometimes you will find it quite difficult to put your finger on the moment when it did so.

On the other stories of this collection, all of which I hope may be enjoyed, I have little to offer in the way of comment. Mr. Wells's "Crystal Egg" (1900)[13] is a delightful instance of his unequalled power of pressing natural science into the service of fiction. Mr. Blackwood seems to have laid the scene of "Ancient Sorceries" (1908) at Laon—though, happily, the cathedral there is not a ruin.[14] Mere commendation of such stories as "The Body-Snatcher" (1884) and "The Moon Slave" (1901) is alike impertinent and useless.[15]

I hope it will be generally allowed that this is indeed a representative collection of the ghost stories of two hundred years. Of course every reader of it who is at all versed in this branch of literature will have his own addition or substitution to suggest—just as I have myself. But I am prepared to say that on one ground or another every one of the stories has a claim to its place here.

Let me end a desultory preface with the passage which justifies all ghost stories, and puts them in their proper place:

> *Hermione.* Pray you, sit by us
> And tell's a tale.
>   *Mamilius.* Merry or sad shall't be?
>   *Her.* As merry as you will.
>   *Mam.* A sad tale's best for winter; I have one
> Of sprites and goblins.
>   *Her.*   Let's have that, good sir.
> Come on, sit down: come on, and do your best
> To fright me with your sprites; you're powerful at it.
>   *Mam.* There was a man—
>   *Her.*   Nay, come, sit down; then on.
>   *Mam.* —Dwelt by a churchyard: I will tell it softly;
> Yond crickets shall not hear it.
>   *Her.*   Come on, then,
> And give't me in mine ear.[16]

SOME REMARKS ON GHOST STORIES

Very nearly all the ghost stories of old times claim to be true narratives of remarkable occurrences. At the outset I must make it clear that with these—be they ancient, medieval or post-medieval—I have nothing to do, any more than I have with those chronicled in our own days. I am concerned with a branch of fiction; not a large branch, if you look at the rest of the tree, but one which has been astonishingly fertile in the last thirty years. The avowedly fictitious ghost story is my subject, and that being understood I can proceed.

In the year 1854 George Borrow narrated to an audience of Welshmen "in the tavern of Gutter Vawr, in the county of Glamorgan," what he asserted to be "decidedly the best ghost story in the world." You may read this story either in English, in Knapp's notes to *Wild Wales,* or in Spanish, in a recent edition with excellent pictures (*Las Aventuras de Pánfilo*). The source is Lope de Vega's *El Peregrino en su patria,* published in 1604.[17] You will find it a remarkably interesting specimen of a tale of terror written in Shakespeare's lifetime, but I shall be surprised if you agree with Borrow's estimate of it. It is nothing but an account of a series of nightmares experienced by a wanderer who lodges for a night in a "hospital," which had been deserted because of hauntings. The ghosts come in crowds and play tricks with the victim's bed. They quarrel over cards, they squirt water at the man, they throw torches about the room. Finally they steal his clothes and disappear; but next morning the clothes are where he put them when he went to bed. In fact they are rather goblins than ghosts.

Still, here you have a story written with the sole object of inspiring a pleasing terror in the reader; and as I think, that is the true aim of the ghost story.

As far as I know, nearly two hundred years pass before you find the literary ghost story attempted again. Ghosts of course figure on the stage, but we must leave them out of consideration. Ghosts are the subject of quasi-scientific research in this country at the hands of Glanville, Beaumont,[18] and others; but these collectors are out to prove theories of the future life and the spiritual world. Improving treatises, with illustrative instances, are written on the Continent, as by Lavater.[19] All these, if they do afford what our ancestors called amusement (Dr. Johnson decreed that *Coriolanus* was "amusing"),[20] do so by a side-wind. *The Castle of Otranto* is perhaps the progenitor of the ghost story as a literary genre,[21] and I fear that it is merely amusing in the modern sense. Then we come to Mrs. Radcliffe, whose ghosts are far better of their kind, but with exasperating timidity are all explained away; and to Monk Lewis, who in the book which gives him his nickname is odious and horrible without being impressive.[22] But Monk Lewis was responsible for better things than he could produce himself. It was under his auspices that Scott's verse first saw the light: among the *Tales of Terror and Wonder*[23] are not only some of his translations, but

"Glenfinlas" and the "Eve of St. John," which must always rank as fine ghost stories. The form into which he cast them was that of ballads which he loved and collected, and we must not forget that the ballad is the direct line of ancestry of the ghost story. Think of "Clerk Saunders," "Young Benjie," the "Wife of Usher's Well." I am tempted to enlarge on the *Tales of Terror,* for the most part supremely absurd, where Lewis holds the pen, and jigs along with such stanzas as:

> All present then uttered a terrified shout;
>   All turned with disgust from the scene.
> The worms they crept in, and the worms they crept out,
> And sported his eyes and his temples about,
>   While the spectre addressed Imogene.

But proportion must be observed.

If I were writing generally of horrific books which include supernatural appearances, I should be obliged to include Maturin's *Melmoth,*[24] and doubtless imitations of it which I know nothing of. But *Melmoth* is a long—a cruelly long—book, and we must keep our eye on the short prose ghost story in the first place. If Scott is not the creator of this, it is to him that we owe two classical specimens—"Wandering Willie's Tale" and the "Tapestried Chamber."[25] The former we know is an episode in a novel; anyone who searches the novels of succeeding years will certainly find (as we, alas, find in *Pickwick* and *Nicholas Nickleby!*) stories of this type foisted in; and possibly some of them may be good enough to deserve reprinting. But the real happy hunting ground, the proper habitat of our game is the magazine, the annual, the periodical publication destined to amuse the family circle. They came up thick and fast, the magazines, in the thirties and forties, and many died young. I do not, having myself sampled the task,[26] envy the devoted one who sets out to examine the files, but it is not rash to promise him a measure of success. He will find ghost stories; but of what sort? Charles Dickens will tell us. In a paper from *Household Words,* which will be found among *Christmas Stories* under the name of "A Christmas Tree"[27] (I reckon it among the

best of Dickens's occasional writings), that great man takes occasion to run through the plots of the typical ghost stories of his
time. As he remarks, they are "reducible to a very few general
types and classes; for, ghosts have little originality, and 'walk'
in a beaten track." He gives us at some length the experience of
the nobleman and the ghost of the beautiful young housekeeper
who drowned herself in the park two hundred years before;
and, more cursorily, the indelible bloodstain, the door that will
not shut, the clock that strikes thirteen, the phantom coach, the
compact to appear after death, the girl who meets her double,
the cousin who is seen at the moment of his death far away in
India, the maiden lady who "really did see the Orphan Boy."
With such things as these we are still familiar. But we have
rather forgotten—and I for my part have seldom met—those
with which he ends his survey: "Legion is the name of the German castles where we sit up alone to meet the spectre—where
we are shown into a room made comparatively cheerful for our
reception" (more detail, excellent of its kind, follows), "and
where, about the small hours of the night, we come into the
knowledge of divers supernatural mysteries. Legion is the name
of the haunted German students, in whose society we draw yet
nearer to the fire, while the schoolboy in the corner opens his
eyes wide and round, and flies off the footstool he has chosen
for his seat, when the door accidentally blows open."

As I have said, this German stratum of ghost stories is one of
which I know little; but I am confident that the searcher of
magazines will penetrate to it. Examples of the other types will
accrue, especially when he reaches the era of Christmas Numbers, inaugurated by Dickens himself. His Christmas Numbers
are not to be confused with his *Christmas Books,* though the
latter led on to the former. Ghosts are not absent from these,
but I do not call the *Christmas Carol* a ghost story proper;
while I do assign that name to the stories of the Signalman and
the Juryman (in "Mugby Junction" and "Dr. Marigold").[28]

These were written in 1865 and 1866, and nobody can deny
that they conform to the modern idea of the ghost story. The
setting and the personages are those of the writer's own day;
they have nothing antique about them. Now this mode is not

absolutely essential to success, but it is characteristic of the majority of successful stories: the belted knight who meets the spectre in the vaulted chamber and has to say "By my haildom," or words to that effect, has little actuality about him. Anything, we feel, might have happened in the fifteenth century. No; the seer of ghosts must talk something like me, and be dressed, if not in my fashion, yet not too much like a man in a pageant, if he is to enlist my sympathy. Wardour Street has no business here.

If Dickens's ghost stories are good and of the right complexion, they are not the best that were written in his day. The palm must I think be assigned to J. S. Le Fanu, whose stories of "The Watcher" (or "The Familiar"), "Mr. Justice Harbottle," "Carmilla," are unsurpassed, while "Schalken the Painter," "Squire Toby's Will," the haunted house in *The House by the Churchyard*, "Dickon the Devil," "Madam Crowl's Ghost,"[29] run them very close. Is it the blend of French and Irish in Le Fanu's descent and surroundings that gives him the knack of infusing ominousness into his atmosphere? He is anyhow an artist in words; who else could have hit on the epithets in this sentence: "The aerial image of the old house for a moment stood before her, with its peculiar malign, sacred and skulking aspect."[30] Other famous stories of Le Fanu there are which are not quite ghost stories—"Green Tea" and "The Room in the Dragon Volant"; and yet another, "The Haunted Baronet,"[31] not famous, not even known but to a few, contains some admirable touches, but somehow lacks proportion. Upon mature consideration, I do not think that there are better ghost stories anywhere than the best of Le Fanu's; and among these I should give the first place to "The Familiar" (alias "The Watcher").

Other famous novelists of those days tried their hand— Bulwer Lytton for one. Nobody is permitted to write about ghost stories without mentioning "The Haunters and the Haunted." To my mind it is spoilt by the conclusion; the Cagliostro element (forgive an inaccuracy) is alien. It comes in with far better effect (though in a burlesque guise) in Thackeray's one attempt in this direction—"The Notch in the Axe," in the *Roundabout Papers*.[32] This to be sure begins by being a skit partly on Dumas, partly on Lytton; but as Thackeray warmed to his work he got interested in the story and, as he says, was quite sorry to part with Pinto in the end. We have to reckon too with Wilkie Collins. *The Haunted Hotel,* a short novel, is by no means ineffective; grisly enough, almost, for the modern American taste.[33]

Rhoda Broughton, Mrs. Riddell, Mrs. Henry Wood, Mrs. Oliphant—all these have some sufficiently absorbing stories to their credit. I own to reading not infrequently "Featherston's Story" in the fifth series of *Johnny Ludlow,* to delighting in its domestic flavour and finding its ghost very convincing. (*Johnny Ludlow,* some young persons may not know, is by Mrs. Henry Wood.)[34] The religious ghost story, as it may be called, was never done better than by Mrs. Oliphant in "The Open Door" and "A Beleagured City"; though there is a competitor, and a strong one, in Le Fanu's "Mysterious Lodger."[35]

Here I am conscious of a gap; my readers will have been conscious of many previous gaps. My memory does in fact slip on from Mrs. Oliphant to Marion Crawford and his horrid story of "The Upper Berth," which (with "The Screaming Skull" some distance behind) is the best in his collection of *Uncanny Tales,* and stands high among ghost stories in general.[36]

That was I believe written in the late eighties. In the early nineties comes the deluge, the deluge of the illustrated monthly magazines, and it is no longer possible to keep pace with the output either of single stories or of volumes of collected ones. Never was the flow more copious than it is today, and it is only by chance that one comes across any given example. So nothing beyond scattering and general remarks can be offered. Some whole novels there have been which depend for all or part of their interest on ghostly matter. There is *Dracula,*[37] which suffers by excess. (I fancy, by the way, that it must be based on a story in the fourth volume of Chambers's *Repository,* issued in the fifties.)[38] There is *Alice-for-Short,*[39] in which I never cease to admire the skill with which the ghost is woven into the web of the tale. But that is a very rare feat.

Among the collections of short stories, E. F. Benson's three volumes rank high,[40] though to my mind he sins occasionally by stepping over the line of legitimate horridness. He is however blameless in this aspect as compared with some Americans, who compile volumes called *Not at Night* and the like.[41] These are merely nauseating, and it is very easy to be nauseating. I, *moi qui vous parle,* could undertake to make a reader physically sick, if I chose to think and write in terms of the Grand Guignol. The authors of the stories I have in mind tread, as they believe, in the steps of Edgar Allan Poe and Ambrose Bierce (himself sometimes unpardonable), but they do not possess the force of either.

Reticence may be an elderly doctrine to preach, yet from the artistic point of view I am sure it is a sound one. Reticence conduces to effect, blatancy ruins it, and there is much blatancy in a lot of recent stories. They drag in sex too, which is a fatal mistake; sex is tiresome enough in the novels; in a ghost story, or as the backbone of a ghost story, I have no patience with it.

At the same time don't let us be mild and drab. Malevolence and terror, the glare of evil faces, "the stony grin of unearthly malice," pursuing forms in darkness, and "long-drawn, distant screams," are all in place, and so is a modicum of blood, shed with deliberation and carefully husbanded; the weltering and wallowing that I too often encounter merely recalls the methods of M. G. Lewis.

Clearly it is out of the question for me to begin upon a series of "short notices" of recent collections; but an illustrative instance or two will be to the point. A. M. Burrage in *Some Ghost Stories*,[42] keeps on the right side of the line, and if about half of his ghosts are amiable, the rest have their terrors, and no mean ones. H. R. Wakefield, in *They Return at Evening* (a good title),[43] gives us a mixed bag, from which I should remove one or two that leave a nasty taste. Among the residue are some admirable pieces, very inventive. Going back a few years I light on Mrs. Everett's *The Death Mask*,[44] of a rather quieter tone on the whole, but with some excellently conceived stories. Hugh Benson's *Light Invisible* and *Mirror of Shalott* are too ecclesiastical.[45] K. and Hesketh Prichard's "Flaxman Low" is most ingenious and successful, but rather over-technically "occult."[46] It seems impertinent to apply the same criticism to Algernon

Blackwood, but "John Silence" is surely open to it.[47] Mr Elliott
O'Donnell's multitudinous volumes I do not know whether to
class as narratives of fact or exercises in fiction. I hope they may
be of the latter sort, for life in a world managed by his gods and
infested by his demons seems a risky business.

So I might go on through a long list of authors; but the remarks one can make in an article of this compass can hardly be
illuminating. The reading of many ghost stories has shown me
that the greatest successes have been scored by the authors who
can make us envisage a definite time and place, and give us
plenty of clear-cut and matter-of-fact detail, but who, when the
climax is reached, allow us to be just a little in the dark as to
the working of their machinery. We do not want to see the
bones of their theory about the supernatural.

All this while I have confined myself almost entirely to the
English ghost story. The fact is that either there are not many
good stories by foreign writers, or (more probably) my ignorance has veiled them from me. But I should feel myself un-
grateful if I did not pay a tribute to the supernatural tales of
Erckmann-Chatrian. The blend of French with German in
them, comparable to the French-Irish blend in Le Fanu, has
produced some quite first-class romance of this kind. Among
longer stories, "La Maison Forestière" (and, if you will, "Hughes
le Loup"); among shorter ones "Le Blanc et le Noir," "Le Rêve
du Cousin Elof" and "L'Oeil Invisible" have for years delighted
and alarmed me. It is high time that they were made more accessible than they are.[48]

There need not be any peroration to a series of rather dis-
jointed reflections. I will only ask the reader to believe that,
though I have not hitherto mentioned it, I have read *The Turn
of the Screw*.[49]

GHOSTS—TREAT THEM GENTLY!

What first interested me in ghosts? This I can tell you quite definitely. In my childhood I chanced to see a toy Punch and Judy set,
with figures cut out in cardboard. One of these was The Ghost. It

was a tall figure habited in white with an unnaturally long and narrow head, also surrounded with white, and a dismal visage.

Upon this my conceptions of a ghost were based, and for years it permeated my dreams.

Other questions—why I like ghost stories, or what are the best, or why they are the best, or a recipe for writing such things—I have never found it easy to be so positive about. Clearly, however, the public likes them. The recrudescence of ghost stories in recent years is notable: it corresponds, of course, with the vogue of the detective tale.

The ghost story can be supremely excellent in its kind, or it may be deplorable. Like other things, it may err by excess or defect. Bram Stoker's *Dracula* is a book with very good ideas in it, but—to be vulgar—the butter is spread far too thick. Excess is the fault here: to give an example of erring by defect is difficult, because the stories that err in that way leave no impression on the memory.

I am speaking of the literary ghost story here. The story that claims to be "veridical" (in the language of the Society of Psychical Research)[50] is a very different affair. It will probably be quite brief, and will conform to some one of several familiar types. This is but reasonable, for, if there be ghosts—as I am quite prepared to believe—the true ghost story need do no more than illustrate their normal habits (if normal is the right word), and may be as mild as milk.

The literary ghost, on the other hand, has to justify his existence by some startling demonstration, or, short of that, must be furnished with a background that will throw him into full relief and make him the central feature.

Since the things which the ghost can effectively do are very limited in number, ranging about death and madness and the discovery of secrets, the setting seems to me all-important, since in it there is the greatest opportunity for variety.

It is upon this and upon the first glimmer of the appearance of the supernatural that pains must be lavished. But we need not, we should not, use all the colours in the box. In the infancy of the art we needed the haunted castle on a beetling rock to put us in the right frame: the tendency is not yet extinct, for I have but just read a story with a mysterious mansion on a desolate height in Cornwall and a gentleman practising the worst sort of magic.[51] How often, too, have ruinous old houses been described or shown to me as fit scenes for stories!

"Can't you imagine some old monk or friar wandering about this long gallery?" No, I can't.

I know Harrison Ainsworth could: *The Lancashire Witches* teems with Cistercians and what he calls votaresses in mouldering vestments, who glide about passages to very little purpose. But these fail to impress. Not that I have not a soft corner in my heart for *The Lancashire Witches,* which—ridiculous as much of it is—has distinct merits as a story.[52]

It cannot be said too often that the more remote in time the ghost is the harder it is to make him effective, always supposing him to be the ghost of a dead person. Elementals and such-like do not come under this rule.

Roughly speaking, the ghost should be a contemporary of the seer. Such was the elder Hamlet and such Jacob Marley. The latter I cite with confidence and in despite of critics, for, whatever may be urged against some parts of *The Christmas Carol,* it is, I hold, undeniable that the introduction, the advent, of Jacob Marley is tremendously effective.

And be it observed that the setting in both these classic examples is contemporary and even ordinary. The ramparts of the Kronborg and the chambers of Ebenezer Scrooge were, to those who frequented them, features of every-day life.

But there are exceptions to every rule. An ancient haunting can be made terrible and can be invested with actuality, but it will tax your best endeavours to forge the links between past and present in a satisfying way. And in any case there must be ordinary level-headed modern persons—Horatios—on the scene, such as the detective needs his Watson or his Hastings[53] to play the part of the lay observer.

Setting or environment, then, is to me a principal point, and the more readily appreciable the setting is to the ordinary reader the better. The other essential is that our ghost should make himself felt by gradual stirrings diffusing an atmosphere of uneasiness before the final flash or stab of horror.

Must there be horror? you ask. I think so. There are but two really good ghost stories I know in the language wherein the elements of beauty and pity dominate terror. They are Lanoe Falconer's "Cecilia de Noel"[54] and Mrs. Oliphant's "The Open Door." In both there are moments of horror; but in both we end by saying with Hamlet: "Alas, poor ghost!"[55] Perhaps my limit of two stories is overstrict; but that these two are by very much the best of their kind I do not doubt.

On the whole, then, I say you must have horror and also malevolence. Not less necessary, however, is reticence. There is a series of books I have read, I think American in origin, called *Not at Night* (and with other like titles), which sin glaringly against this law. They have no other aim than that of Mr. Wardle's Fat Boy.[56]

Of course, all writers of ghost stories do desire to make their readers' flesh creep; but these are shameless in their attempts. They are unbelievably crude and sudden, and they wallow in corruption. And if there is a theme that ought to be kept out of the ghost story, it is that of the charnel house. That and sex, wherein I do not say that these *Not at Night* books deal, but certainly other recent writers do, and in so doing spoil the whole business.

To return from the faults of ghost stories to their excellence. Who, do I think, has best realised their possibilities? I have no hesitation in saying that it is Joseph Sheridan Le Fanu. In the volume called *In a Glass Darkly* are four stories of paramount excellence, "Green Tea," "The Familiar," "Mr. Justice Harbottle," and "Carmilla." All of these conform to my requirements: the settings are quite different, but all seen by the writer; the approaches of the supernatural nicely graduated; the climax adequate. Le Fanu was a scholar and a poet, and these tales show him as such. It is true that he died as long ago as 1873, but there is wonderfully little that is obsolete in his manner.

Of living writers I have some hesitation in speaking, but on any list that I was forced to compile names of E. F. Benson, Blackwood, Burrage, de la Mare[57] and Wakefield would find a place.

But, although the subject has its fascinations, I see no use in being pontifical about it. These stories are meant to please and amuse us. If they do so, well; but, if not, let us relegate them to the top shelf and say no more about it.

PREFACE TO *COLLECTED GHOST STORIES*

IN accordance with a fashion which has recently become common, I am issuing my four volumes of ghost stories under one cover, and appending to them some matter of the same kind.

I am told they have given pleasure of a certain sort to my readers: if so, my whole object in writing them has been attained, and there does not seem to be much reason for prefacing them by a disquisition upon how I came to write them. Still, a preface is demanded by my publishers, and it may as well be devoted to answering questions which I have been asked.

First, whether the stories are based on my own experience? To this the answer is No: except in one case, specified in the text, where a dream furnished a suggestion.[58] Or again, whether they are versions of other people's experiences? No. Or suggested by books? This is more difficult to answer concisely. Other people have written of dreadful spiders—for instance, Erckmann-Chatrian in an admirable story called *L'Araignée Crabe*[59]—and of pictures which came alive: the State Trials give the language of Judge Jeffreys and the courts at the end of the seventeenth century: and so on. Places have been more prolific in suggestion: if anyone is curious about my local settings, let it be recorded that S. Bertrand de Comminges and Viborg are real places:[60] that in *Oh, Whistle, and I'll come to you,* I had Felixstowe in mind; in *A School Story,* Temple Grove, East Sheen; in *The Tractate Middoth,* Cambridge University Library; in *Martin's Close,* Sampford Courtenay in Devon: that the cathedrals of Barchester and Southminster[61] were blends of Canterbury, Salisbury, and Hereford: that Herefordshire was the imagined scene of *A View from a Hill,* and Seaburgh in *A Warning to the Curious* is Aldeburgh in Suffolk.

I am not conscious of other obligations to literature or local legend, written or oral, except in so far as I have tried to make my ghosts act in ways not inconsistent with the rules of folklore. As for the fragments of ostensible erudition which are scattered about my pages, hardly anything in them is not pure invention; there never was, naturally, any such book as that which I quote in the *Treasure of Abbot Thomas.*

Other questioners ask if I have any theories as to the writing of ghost stories. None that are worthy of the name or need to be repeated here: some thoughts on the subject are in a preface to *Ghosts and Marvels.* [*The World's Classics,* Oxford, 1924.] There is no receipt for success in this form of fiction more than in any other. The public, as Dr. Johnson said, are the ultimate judges: if they are pleased, it is well; if not, it is no use to tell them why they ought to have been pleased.[62]

Supplementary questions are: Do I believe in ghosts? To which I answer that I am prepared to consider evidence and accept it if it satisfies me. And lastly, Am I going to write any more ghost stories? To which I fear I must answer, Probably not.

Since we are nothing if not bibliographical nowadays, I add a paragraph or two setting forth the facts about the several collections and their contents.

"Ghost Stories of an Antiquary" was published (like the rest) by Messrs. Arnold in 1904. The first issue had four illustrations by the late James McBryde. In this volume *Canon Alberic's Scrap-book* was written in 1894[63] and printed soon after in the *National Review. Lost Hearts* appeared in the *Pall Mall Magazine.* Of the next five stories, most of which were read to friends at Christmas-time at King's College, Cambridge, I only recollect that I wrote *Number 13* in 1899,[64] while *The Treasure of Abbot Thomas* was composed in summer 1904.

The second volume, "More Ghost Stories," appeared in 1911. The first six of the seven tales it contains were Christmas productions, the very first (*A School Story*) having been made up for the benefit of the King's College Choir School. *The Stalls of Barchester Cathedral* was printed in the *Contemporary*

Review: Mr. Humphreys and His Inheritance was written to fill up the volume.

"A Thin Ghost and Others" was the third collection, containing five stories and published in 1919. In it, An Episode of Cathedral History and The Story of a Disappearance and an Appearance were contributed to the Cambridge Review.

Of six stories in "A Warning to the Curious," published in 1925, the first, The Haunted Dolls' House, was written for the library of Her Majesty the Queen's Dolls' House, and subsequently appeared in the Empire Review. The Uncommon Prayer-book saw the light in the Atlantic Monthly, the title-story in the London Mercury, and another, I think A Neighbour's Landmark, in an ephemeral called The Eton Chronic. Similar ephemerals were responsible for all but one of the appended pieces (not all of them strictly stories), whereof one, Rats, composed for At Random, was included by Lady Cynthia Asquith in a collection entitled Shudders. The exception, Wailing Well, was written for the Eton College troop of Boy Scouts, and read at their camp-fire at Worbarrow Bay in August, 1927. It was then printed by itself in a limited edition by Robert Gathome Hardy and Kyrle Leng at the Mill House Press, Stanford Dingley.

Four or five of the stories have appeared in collections of such things in recent years, and a Norse version of four from my first volume, by Ragnhild Undset, was issued in 1919 under the title of Aander og Trolddom.

STORIES I HAVE TRIED TO WRITE

I have neither much experience nor much perseverance in the writing of stories—I am thinking exclusively of ghost stories, for I never cared to try any other kind—and it has amused me sometimes to think of the stories which have crossed my mind from time to time and never materialized properly. Never properly: for some of them I have actually written down, and they repose in a drawer somewhere. To borrow Sir Walter Scott's most frequent quotation, "Look on (them) again I dare not."[65]

They were not good enough. Yet some of them had ideas in them which refused to blossom in the surroundings I had devised for them, but perhaps came up in other forms in stories that did get as far as print. Let me recall them for the benefit (so to style it) of somebody else.

There was the story of a man travelling in a train in France.[66] Facing him sat a typical Frenchwoman of mature years, with the usual moustache and a very confirmed countenance. He had nothing to read but an antiquated novel he had bought for its binding—*Madame de Lichtenstein* it was called.[67] Tired of looking out of the window and studying his *vis-à-vis,* he began drowsily turning the pages, and paused at a conversation between two of the characters. They were discussing an acquaintance, a woman who lived in a largish house at Marcilly-le-Hayer.[68] The house was described, and—here we were coming to a point—the mysterious disappearance of the woman's husband. Her name was mentioned, and my reader couldn't help thinking he knew it in some other connexion. Just then the train stopped at a country station, the traveller, with a start, woke up from a doze—the book open in his hand—the woman opposite him got out, and on the label of her bag he read the name that had seemed to be in his novel. Well, he went on to Troyes, and from there he made excursions, and one of these took him—at lunch-time—to—yes, to Marcilly-le-Hayer. The hotel in the Grande Place faced a three-gabled house of some pretensions. Out of it came a well-dressed woman *whom he had seen before.* Conversation with the waiter. Yes, the lady was a widow, or so it was believed. At any rate nobody knew what had become of her husband. Here I think we broke down. Of course, there was no such conversation in the novel as the traveller thought he had read.

Then there was quite a long one about two undergraduates spending Christmas in a country house that belonged to one of them. An uncle, next heir to the estate, lived near. Plausible and learned Roman priest, living with the uncle, makes himself agreeable to the young men. Dark walks home at night after dining with the uncle. Curious disturbances as they pass through the shrubberies. Strange, shapeless tracks in the snow round the house, observed in the morning. Efforts to lure away

268

M. R. JAMES

the companion and isolate the proprietor and get him to come out after dark. Ultimate defeat and death of the priest, upon whom the Familiar, baulked of another victim, turns.

Also the story of two students of King's College, Cambridge, in the sixteenth century (who were, in fact, expelled thence for magical practices), and their nocturnal expedition to a witch at Fenstanton, and of how, at the turning to Lolworth, on the Huntingdon road, they met a company leading an unwilling figure whom they seemed to know. And of how, on arriving at Fenstanton, they learned of the witch's death, and of what they saw seated upon her newly-dug grave.[69]

These were some of the tales which got as far as the stage of being written down, at least in part. There were others that flitted across the mind from time to time, but never really took shape. The man, for instance (naturally a man with *something* on his mind), who, sitting in his study one evening, was startled by a slight sound, turned hastily, and saw a certain dead face looking out from between the window curtains: a dead face, but with living eyes. He made a dash at the curtains and tore them apart. A pasteboard mask fell to the floor. But there was no one there, and the eyes of the mask were but eyeholes. What was to be done about that?

There is the touch on the shoulder that comes when you are walking quickly homewards in the dark hours, full of anticipation of the warm room and bright fire, and when you pull up, startled, what face or no-face do you see?

Similarly, when Mr. Badman[70] had decided to settle the hash of Mr. Goodman and had picked out just the right thicket by the roadside from which to fire at him, how came it exactly that when Mr. Goodman and his unexpected friend actually did pass, they found Mr. Badman weltering in the road? He was able to tell them something of what he had found waiting for him—even beckoning to him—in the thicket: enough to prevent them from looking into it themselves. There are possibilities here, but the labour of constructing the proper setting has been beyond me.

There may be possibilities, too, in the Christmas cracker, if the right people pull it, and if the motto which they find inside has the right message on it. They will probably leave the party early, pleading indisposition; but very likely a *previous engagement of long standing* would be the more truthful excuse.

In parenthesis, many common objects may be made the vehicles of retribution, and where retribution is not called for, of malice. Be careful how you handle the packet you pick up in the carriage-drive, particularly if it contains nail-parings and hair. Do not, in any case, bring it into the house. It may not be alone . . . [71] (Dots are believed by many writers of our day to be a good substitute for effective writing. They are certainly an easy one. Let us have a few more . . . . . .)

Late on Monday night a toad came into my study: and, though nothing has so far seemed to link itself with this appearance, I feel that it may not be quite prudent to brood over topics which may open the interior eye to the presence of more formidable visitants.[72] Enough said.

Explanatory Notes

Abbreviations used in the notes are as follows:

CGS	*The Collected Ghost Stories of M. R. James* (1931)
CM	*Count Magnus and Other Ghost Stories*, edited by S. T. Joshi (Penguin, 2005)
Cox1	Michael Cox, *M. R. James: An Informal Portrait* (1983)
Cox2	*Casting the Runes*, edited by Michael Cox (1987)
GSA	*Ghost-Stories of an Antiquary* (1904)
KJV	Bible (King James Version)
MGSA	*More Ghost Stories of an Antiquary* (1911)
MRJ	M. R. James
OED	*Oxford English Dictionary*
PT	*A Pleasing Terror* (2001)
TG	*A Thin Ghost and Others* (1919)
WC	*A Warning to the Curious* (1925)

INTRODUCTION

1. Cox2, 143.
2. See CM 255–56
3. See "An M. R. James Letter," edited by Jack Adrian, PT 638–43.

THE RESIDENCE AT WHITMINSTER

First published in *TG* and reprinted in *CGS*, "The Residence at Whitminster" richly evokes an eighteenth-century setting in its account of a magical talisman used for sorcery by a young boy. As with several other of MRJ's tales, it brings into play his almost pathological fear of spiders.

MRJ derived the title of *TG* from a phrase in the story, "a withered heart makes an ugly thin ghost" (p. 122).

1. Whitminster is a village in Gloucestershire in southwest England, five miles northwest of Stroud. There appears to be no church to which MRJ's story could apply, and his use of the name may be coincidental. "Dissolution" refers to Henry VIII's dissolution of the English monasteries between 1536 and 1540 following his break with the Papacy and the establishment of the Church of England in 1534.
2. A fictitious peerage.
3. A *rath* is an Irish term referring to "an enclosure (usually of a circular form) made by a strong earthen wall, and serving as a fort and place of residence for the chief of a tribe; a hill-fort" (*OED*).
4. Aesculapius was the Graeco-Roman god of the medical art.
5. Rhadamistus was a prince of Armenia in the first century C.E. (see Tacitus, *Annals* 12.44–51). He is also the subject of Handel's opera *Radamisto* (1720), based on a libretto by Nicholas Haym, itself based on Domenico Lalli's *Amor tirannico*. But neither in Tacitus nor in Handel is there a scene corresponding to the one described here.
6. Cleodora (Kleodora) was a physician mentioned by Apollodorus (*Library* 2.19). Antigenes is the name of at least three different Greek physicians mentioned by Galen and other writers.
7. The reference is to *The Count of Monte Cristo* (1844) by Alexandre Dumas père (1802–1870). The hero, Edmond Dantès, the Count of Monte Cristo, secures a large house in Auteuil (a suburb of Paris) upon his escape from imprisonment.
8. *The Talisman* (1825), a novel by Sir Walter Scott (1771–1832). It focuses on a talisman (a jewel) that appears to have magical curative powers.
9. A *sawfly* is "an insect of the family *Tenthredinidae,* distinguished by the sawlike constructor of the oripositor" (*OED*). It is highly destructive to vegetation.
10. *Daddy-long-legs* was originally a slang term for the crane fly ("A two-winged fly of the genus *Tipula* or family *Tipulidae,* characterized by very long legs" [*OED*]), but later came to be applied to spiders of a similar shape, chiefly of the genus *Phalangium*.
11. Anna Seward (1747–1809), called the Swan of Lichfield, was a British poet and letter-writer who settled in Lichfield, in Staffordshire, when she inherited a large sum of money from her father. She was acquainted with Lichfield's most famous scion, Samuel

Johnson. Her *Letters,* published in six volumes (1811), are as sac-charine as her poetry.

12. Apparently a misquotation of Shakespeare's "If ever been where bells have knoll'd to church" (*As You Like It* 2.7.114).

13. *Mickle* is an archaic adjective meaning "great."

14. A *black draught* is "A purgative medicine consisting of an infu-sion of senna with sulphate of magnesia and extract of liquorice" (*OED*).

15. *Quietus* is Latin for "a state of repose"; adopted into English, it came to mean "death." For its most celebrated usage see Shake-speare, *Hamlet* 3.1.75–76: "When he himself would his quietus make/With a bare bodkin."

16. Miss Bates is the loquacious and tiresome aunt of Jane Fairfax in Jane Austen's *Emma* (1816).

17. *S. T. P.* = *Sacrosanctae Theologiae Professor* (professor of sacred theology). *S. T. B.* = *Sacrosanctae Theologiae Bachelor* (bachelor of sacred theology). *Praeb. senr.* = *Praebenda senior* (senior prebendary). *Praeb. junr.* = *Praebenda junior* (junior prebendary). A prebendary is the holder of a prebend (i.e., a stipend granted to him from church revenues), or a canon of a cathedral or collegiate church who holds a prebend.

18. John Debrett (1752–1822), *Debrett's Peerage of England, Scot-land, and Ireland* (1803; annually updated to the present day), a comprehensive listing of the British nobility.

19. In the Bible, it was not Saul but the Witch of Endor, at Saul's in-sistence, who raised the spirit of Samuel (1 Samuel 28:7–20).

THE DIARY OF MR. POYNTER

This tale was first published in *TG* and reprinted in *CGS*. It demon-strates MRJ's ability to invest the commonest objects of household use—in this case, a set of curtains—with supernatural menace. Some features of the story (see, e.g., n. 8) remain unexplained, and perhaps we are meant to leave the story with the Shakespearean sentiment expressed at its conclusion.

Further Reading

Rosemary Pardoe, "Hercules and the Pointed Cloth," *Ghosts & Schol-ars* no. 31 (2000): 49–50.

1. F.S.A. = Fellow of the Society of Antiquaries. MRJ was a member. Trinity Hall (not to be confused with Trinity College) is one of the colleges of Cambridge University, founded in 1350. Rendcomb Manor appears to be fictitious, but there is a Rendcomb in Gloucestershire.

2. A *dower-house* is a house comprising a portion of a deceased husband's estate which the law allows a widow to occupy for her life.

3. Acrington is fictitious.

4. Thomas Hearne (1678–1735), British antiquary and librarian at the Bodleian Library at Oxford, performed landmark work in organizing and cataloguing the library and in preparing editions of early British historical sources. He was involved in numerous religious and scholarly controversies. His reputation now rests largely upon his diaries, published as *Remarks and Collections of Thomas Hearne* (1885–1921; eleven volumes).

5. There were numerous British and American organizations in the later nineteenth century opposed to vivisection (medical experimentation on live animals). MRJ probably refers to the London and Provincial Anti-Vivisection Society, founded in 1877.

6. Bermondsey is a district in southeast London.

7. "[A] snapper-up of unconsidered trifles." Shakespeare, *The Winter's Tale* 4.3.26.

8. Cox2 (327) believes this to be a misquotation of "As ragged as Lazarus in the painted cloth" (Shakespeare, 1 *Henry IV* 4.2.26). However, Rosemary Pardoe (see Further Reading) believes the reference to be to *Love's Labor's Lost* 5.2, where a number of characters are performing in a pageant; one of the characters states, "You will be scraped out of the painted cloth for this" (5.2.570–71), and Hercules enters shortly thereafter. The "painted cloth" refers to a wall painting depicting the Nine Worthies who are being represented in the pageant. MRJ's reference remains cryptic, and appears to be an allusion to the controversy surrounding the authorship of the Shakespeare plays.

9. The Feast of Simon and Jude occurs on 28 October, commemorating St. Simon and St. Jude, two of the twelve apostles.

10. A *Commoner* in this context is "One who pays for his commons, *i.e.* a student or undergraduate not on the foundation" (*OED*). University College is one of the colleges at Oxford, founded in 1249.

11. Absalom is depicted in the bible as a handsome youth and the third son of David. When his half-brother Ammon seduced their sister, Tamar, Absalom brought about Ammon's death (2 Samuel

13:1–39). After some years in exile, he returned to David's court but sought to overthrow his father, leading to his ignominious death (2 Samuel 18:9–17).

12. A *cavalier* was a supporter of King Charles I against the Parliamentary party (the Roundheads) in the English Civil War.

13. Robert Plot (1640–1696), *The Natural History of Staffordshire* (1686).

14. "There are more things in heaven and earth, Horatio, / Than are dreamt of in your philosophy." Shakespeare, *Hamlet* 1.5.166–67.

AN EPISODE OF CATHEDRAL HISTORY

"An Episode of Cathedral History" was first published in the *Cambridge Review* (10 June 1914) and reprinted in *TC* and *CGS*. It must have been written no later than May 1913, for on 18 May 1913 A. C. Benson writes in his diary: "Monty read us a very good ghost story, with an admirable verger very humorously portrayed—the ghost part weak" (quoted in Cox2, 328). One of the most substantial of MRJ's later ghost stories, it emphasizes his distaste at the bungling "restoration" of English churches in the mode of the Gothic revival: in this case, such a restoration elicits a supernatural response from the baleful tenant of a centuried altar tomb. Bill Read (see Further Reading) suggests that there are actually two monsters in the story, one in the tomb and one wandering the countryside seeking to free its mate from its imprisonment.

Further Reading

Rosemary Pardoe, "The Demon in the Cathedral," *All Hallows* no. 1 (1989): 25–26.

Bill Read, "The Mystery of the Second Satyr," *Ghosts & Scholars* no. 31 (2000): 46–47.

1. Southminster is a village in Essex, two miles north of Burnham-on-Crouch. There is a church there, with portions dating to Norman times, but no cathedral. In the preface to *CGS* (see p. 262), MRJ remarks that this fictitious church and that in "The Stalls of Barchester Cathedral" were "blends of Canterbury, Salisbury, and Hereford." See further n. 7.

2. In Charles Dickens's unfinished final novel, *The Mystery of Edwin Drood* (1870), Dick Datchery is the name adopted by a mysterious character whose real name is never revealed. MRJ, a

great devotee of Dickens, wrote an article on the novel, "The Edwin Drood Syndicate" (*Cambridge Review,* November and December 1905). See further n. 4.

3. A *Chapter* is "The body of canons of a collegiate or cathedral church, presided over by the dean" (*OED*).

4. In *The Mystery of Edwin Drood,* Jack Jaspers is Drood's uncle and a leading suspect as his murderer. Durdles is a stonemason at the cathedral where Jaspers is choirmaster.

5. The *Perpendicular period* refers to a style of English architecture prevalent in the fifteenth century, characterized by the vertical lines of its tracery. The church in the real Southminster is of this style.

6. MRJ refers to Bell's Cathedral Series, a series of books on British cathedrals published by George Bell & Sons (London) from 1896 to 1932.

7. The Cathedral of St. Ethelbert in Hereford, Herefordshire, features a mix of styles from Norman to Perpendicular. In 1786, the western tower fell, causing considerable damage; the reconstruction was clumsily made by James Wyatt, with later revisions by Lewis Cottingham (1841) and Sir Gilbert Scott (1863), and further reconstruction of the west front completed in 1905. MRJ was strongly opposed to restorations of this sort.

8. In this sense, *affection* means "An abnormal state of body; malady, disease" (*OED*).

9. See "The Diary of Mr. Poynter," n. 1.

10. A *diaper-ornament* refers to a pattern or design resembling a diaper (a "fabric . . . consisting of lines crossing diamond-wise, with spaces variously filled up by parallel lines, a central leaf or dot, etc." [*OED*]) used to decorate a flat surface, as a panel or wall.

11. Apparently an allusion to John Stevens Henslow (1796–1861), botanist and Church of England clergyman, and Alfred Lyall (1796–1865), philosopher and traveler. Both were Cambridge men (Henslow at St. John's College, Lyall at Trinity). Henslow, a friend of Charles Darwin, was presiding at the celebrated meeting of the British Association in Oxford in October 1860 when Thomas Henry Huxley vigorously disputed with Bishop Samuel Wilberforce over the theory of evolution. Lyall's chief work was in logic, but he contributed an essay on "The History of the Mediaeval Church" to the *Encyclopaedia Metropolitana* (1829–43). He was also rector of Hambledown, Kent.

12. A reference to Charles Simeon (1759–1836), British leader of the Evangelical Revival, which laid special stress on conversion and

salvation by faith in the atoning death of Jesus Christ. MRJ's father was an Evangelical and was disappointed that his son did not pursue a career in the church.

13. A *set-out* is a slang term meaning "A commotion, disturbance, 'to-do' " (*OED*).

14. The *Venite* is Psalm 95 (*"Venite, exultemus Domino"* = "O come let us sing unto the Lord") used as a canticle at matins or morning prayer in the Anglican service. It is, however, not sung on Easter or on the nineteenth day of the month, when the canticle is sung in the ordinary course of the Psalms.

15. *Decani* refers to the members of a choir on the decanal (south) side of the choir in antiphonal singing.

16. i.e., a crowbar.

17. A reference to Jesus's celebrated utterance, "Judge not, that ye may not be judged" (Matthew 5:25).

18. From Isaiah 34:14 (Vulgate): "There hath the lamia lain down and found rest for itself" (KJV). A *lamia* is a monster out of Roman popular mythology, often thought to devour children. The use of the imperfect tense is significant here, suggesting that the lamia is no longer in the tomb.

THE STORY OF A DISAPPEARANCE
AND AN APPEARANCE

This tale first appeared in the *Cambridge Review* (4 June 1913) and was reprinted in *TG* and *CGS*. It makes much use of the characters and general atmosphere of Punch and Judy shows. Punch (short for Punchinello) and Judy shows were shows involving puppets or marionettes and a series of recurring characters. The shows were of Italian origin (as MRJ alludes to in the story; see p. 66) and were probably introduced to England in the later seventeenth century. Aside from Punch and his wife, Judy, the characters mentioned by MRJ are a dog named Toby (sometimes played by an actual dog); the Baby; Jack Ketch, the hangman; Beadle, an officer of the law; and the Foreigner (usually a black man), who can only say the word *"Shallabala!"* (MRJ mentions a character named Turncock, but his role in Punch and Judy shows cannot be verified.) In most of the shows, Punch usually bludgeons many of the characters to death before himself being castigated or killed. MRJ later acknowledged that an early exposure to the figure of the Ghost in Punch and Judy shows helped to trigger his interest in the supernatural (see "Ghosts— Treat Them Gently!" [p. 258]).

Further Reading

Roger Craik, "Nightmares of Punch and Judy in Ruskin and M. R. James," *Fantasy Commentator* no. 49 (Fall 1996): 12–14.

1. Presumably an archaic name for Chrishall, a village in Essex, six miles east of Royston.
2. Woodley is a city in Berkshire, three miles east of Reading. It is about fifty-five miles southwest of Chrishall.
3. The reference is to the Bow Street runners, a group of constables associated with the Bow Street Police Office in central London, serving as detectives and thief-takers. Their role, however, had largely been superseded by the establishment of Scotland Yard in 1829.
4. *Qui vive* is French for "(long) live who?" The expression "On the *qui vive*" means to be on the alert or lookout.
5. Boniface is the genial innkeeper in George Farquhar's play *The Beaux' Stratagem* (1707).
6. Boz was the pseudonym of Charles Dickens in his first three books, *Sketches by Boz* (1836), *The Pickwick Papers* (1836–37), and *Oliver Twist* (1837–38).
7. "And he [Jacob] answered her [Rebecca]: Thou knowest that Esau my brother is a hairy man, and I am a smooth" (Genesis 27:11).
8. A *bagman* is "A commercial traveller, whose business it is to show samples and solicit orders on behalf of manufacturers, etc." (*OED*). Cf. Dickens's ghost story "The Story of the Bagman's Uncle," in *The Pickwick Papers*.
9. Pan-pipes were common accompaniments to Punch and Judy shows.
10. Henry Fuseli (Heinrich Füssli, 1741–1825), Swiss painter who worked chiefly in England. There is no painting by Füseli entitled "The Vampire"; MRJ probably refers to the widely reproduced painting *The Nightmare* (1781), depicting a monster (probably an incubus) resting upon a sleeper's chest.
11. An allusion to the conventional view that British poet George Gordon, Lord Byron, (1788–1824) was a misanthrope.
12. A *vail* in this context means "A gratuity given to a servant or attendant; a tip" (*OED*).
13. *To wolve,* as pertains to the organ, means "To give forth a hollow wailing sound like the howl of a wolf, from a deficient wind-supply" (*OED*). *OED* cites this passage (also one from J. S. Le Fanu's *Uncle Silas,* 1864) in its definition.

14. *The Pickwick Papers* was initially issued in a series of monthly installments from April 1836 to November 1837.

TWO DOCTORS

This story (first published in *TG* and reprinted in *CGS*) is a supernatural puzzle in which the reader is challenged to piece together the solution. As Lance Arney (see Further Reading) suggests, MRJ is careful to provide sufficient clues for a reasonably complete reconstruction of events. (Those readers who have not read the story, or who wish to attempt a reconstruction for themselves, are advised not to read the following paragraph until after they have finished the story.)

The protagonists' names, Dr. Quinn and Dr. Abell, are significant in suggesting the Cain and Abel story in Genesis 4:2–15; but unlike the biblical account, in this tale it is Dr. Abell who kills Dr. Quinn—and by supernatural means. Abell's supernatural powers (apparently secured by a deal with the Devil) are suggested by the otherwise unexplained "matter of the bedstaff" (by which we are probably meant to assume that Abell had learned to manipulate inanimate objects by sorcery) as well as by Dr. Quinn's discomfort with his bedclothes (suggesting that Abell had cast a spell on them). Quinn, therefore, seeks new bedclothes. Abell had stolen the burial sheets of a deceased nobleman (hence the reference to "a coronet and a bird," the mark of nobility), sold them to an unscrupulous dealer, and (perhaps the one unexplained detail in the story) contrived to have the dealer sell these garments to Quinn for the purpose of making new bedsheets out of them. The bedsheets then suffocate Quinn, killing him.

Further Reading

Lance Arney, "An Elucidation (?) of the Plot of M. R. James's 'Two Doctors,'" *Studies in Weird Fiction* no. 8 (Fall 1990): 26–35.

1. Gray's Inn, a collection of buildings in central London, has been the home of London's most prestigious law offices since the fourteenth century.
2. Islington, a district now in the north of London, was settled in the early fourteenth century. In the early eighteenth century it was still relatively sparsely populated, with a number of broad parks and mansions with substantial gardens. It was a popular resort for tea gardens and other amusements.

3. Battle Bridge was formerly a village north of London, now occupied by the district of King's Cross.

4. *Distinguo* (Latin for "I draw a distinction") was a term used by medieval scholastic philosophers in a variety of ways to segregate qualities or relations.

5. St. Jerome (345?–420), biblical scholar who translated the Bible from the original languages into Latin (the Vulgate). MRJ alludes to Jerome's *Vita Pauli Primi Eremitae* [The Life of St. Paul, the First Hermit] (ch. 8), in which the hermit St. Antony of Egypt (251?–356) encounters a satyr: "So then Antony . . . continued on his way. Nor was it long till in a rocky valley he saw a dwarfish figure of no great size, its nostrils joined together, and its forehead bristling with horns: the lower part of its body ended in goat's feet. Unshaken by the sight, Antony, like a good soldier, caught up the shield of faith and the buckler of hope. The creature thus described, however, made to offer him dates as tokens of peace: and perceiving this, Antony hastened his step, and asking him who he might be, had this reply: 'Mortal am I, and one of the dwellers in the desert, whom the heathen worship, astray in diverse error, calling us Fauns, and Satyrs, and Incubi.'" See *The Desert Fathers,* translated by Helen Waddell (New York: Henry Holt, 1936), 45.

6. Milton, *Paradise Lost* 4.677–78.

7. The Royal Society, founded in 1660, is the oldest scientific body in the world.

8. A *bolus* is "A medicine of round shape adapted for swallowing, larger than an ordinary pill" (*OED*).

9. *Tickleminded* is a compound form of the now rare or dialectic adjective *tickle,* "Easily moved to feeling or action; easily affected in any way; not firm or steadfast" (*OED*).

THE HAUNTED DOLLS' HOUSE

"The Haunted Dolls' House" was first published in the *Empire Review* (February 1923) and reprinted in *WC* and *CGS*. The story was written, as MRJ states in the preface to *CGS* (see p. 264), for the library of Queen Mary's Dolls' House. Queen Mary (wife of King George V) conceived the idea of the dolls' house in 1920. Situated at Windsor Castle (near Eton) and under the guidance of the architect Sir Edwin Lutyens, it became the most elaborate dolls' house in the world, taking more than three years to design and furnish. MRJ, who as Provost of Eton dined once every summer with King George and Queen Mary, was one of numerous authors asked to contribute to the dolls' house library (in which books no larger than a postage stamp would be housed), among them Max Beerbohm, Hilaire Belloc, Sir Arthur Conan Doyle (who contributed an extremely rare Sherlock Holmes squib, "How Watson Learned the Trick"), Thomas Hardy, and many others; some of this work (but not MRJ's story) was included in *The Book of the Queen's Dolls' House,* edited by A. C. Benson, Lawrence Weaver, and E. V. Lucas (1924; two volumes). See Mary Stewart-Wilson and David Crippes, *Queen Mary's Dolls' House* (1988). MRJ states at the end of the story that the basic plot is a variant of "The Mezzotint" (*GSA* and *CGS*), but in fact the only resemblance between the tales is the core notion of works of art (a dolls' house and a mezzotint, respectively), normally inanimate, coming to life and depicting activity supernaturally. MRJ is correct in believing that there is sufficient "variation" between the two stories to allow them to stand as independent entities.

1. Strawberry Hill Gothic refers to a house built by Horace Walpole (1717–1797), author of the first Gothic novel, *The Castle of Otranto* (1764). Shortly after he received a substantial inheritance from his father in 1745, Walpole purchased a house in Twickenham (now a suburb of London) and transformed it into what he called "a little Gothic castle" named Strawberry Hill. The house ultimately helped to give birth to the Gothic revival of the nineteenth century, just as Walpole's novel ushered in the era of the Gothic novel.

2. An *ogival hood* is a rooflike projection over a window in the shape of an ogive, or the diagonal groin or rib of a vault. A *crocket* is "One of the small ornaments placed on the inclined sides of pinnacles, pediments, canopies, etc., in Gothic architecture" (*OED*).

3. French for "A platform, to which one ascends by steps, in front of a church, mansion, or other large building, and upon which the door or doors open" (*OED*).

4. A *posset* is "A drink composed of hot milk curdled with ale, wine, or other liquor, often with sugar, spices, or other ingredients; formerly much used as a delicacy, and as a remedy for colds or other affections" (*OED*).

5. A *truckle-bed* is "A low bed running on tracks or castors, usually pushed beneath a high or 'standing' bed when not in use" (*OED*). In American usage, a trundle-bed.

6. As noted in *PT* (297n11), the Vagrancy Acts of 1713 and 1744

stipulated that two justices of the peace were required to commit persons to an insane asylum if they were deemed to present a danger to the community.

7. MRJ apparently uses the verb *to physic(k)* in the sense of "to puzzle," a meaning not attested in *OED*.

8. The Canterbury and York Society was established in 1904 for the purpose of printing bishop's registers and other ecclesiastical records.

9. St. Stephen's Church and Coxham are fictitious.

10. M. Vitruvius Pollio (first century B.C.E.) was a Roman architect and engineer and author of *De Architectura* (On Architecture), a treatise that, when it was rediscovered in the fifteenth century, was instrumental in launching the classical revival in architecture.

THE UNCOMMON PRAYER-BOOK

First published in the *Atlantic Monthly* (June 1921) and reprinted in *WC* and *CGS*, "The Uncommon Prayer-book" is a relatively elementary tale of supernatural vengeance, in which a book dealer who steals some unusual seventeenth-century prayer books meets his fitting comeuppance. The Jewish name of this dealer—alternately Homberger and Poschwitz—and his unsavory character suggest a hint of anti-Semitism. The title of the story is an obvious play on the Book of Common Prayer, the official service book of the Church of England (see further n. 13 below).

1. Gaulsford and Leventhorp House are fictitious.

2. Longbridge is a village in Warwickshire, two miles south of Warwick; but MRJ was probably intending to coin a fictitious locale.

3. All the sites—the river Tent, the towns Stanford St. Thomas, Stanford Magdalene, and Kingsbourne Junction—are fictitious. Cox2 (331) believes the locale to be based upon the valley of the Teme in Hereford and Worcester, with the two Stanfords referring to the actual towns of Stanford on Teme and Stanford Bridge.

4. Brockstone is fictitious.

5. i.e., Gregorian chant (or plainsong), the traditional music for the Latin rite, named after Pope Gregory the Great (540?–604; Pope 590–604), although the surviving music has little to do with him. Plainsong is entirely monophonic and is sung in unmeasured time values. It was revived in the nineteenth century in the Anglican rite as an outgrowth of the Oxford Movement.

6. The London plague occurred in 1665–66, killing an estimated 56,000 people. See Daniel Defoe's historical novel, *A Journal of the Plague Year* (1722).

7. The artist is depicting the defeat of Oliver Cromwell (1599–1658; Lord Protector of Great Britain, 1649–58) and some of the leading members of the parliamentary party—Henry Ireton (1611–1651), commander of the cavalry; John Bradshaw (1602–1659), president of the High Court of Justice that tried and condemned King Charles I to death; and Hugh Peter or Peters (1598–1660), a Puritan divine who was falsely accused of being the king's executioner—by forces supporting King Charles II, who was restored to the throne in 1660.

8. Lady Anne Sadleir (1585–1671/2), a royalist and literary patron who donated many manuscripts to Trinity College, Cambridge. MRJ catalogued the manuscripts at Trinity College in 1900–04. One of her donations was the Trinity Apocalypse, which MRJ edited for the Roxburghe Club in 1909.

9. A fictitious magazine, based upon the actual magazine *Country Life*.

10. Abbey Dore is an abbey of the Cistercian order in Herefordshire, founded in 1147. MRJ writes of it in *Abbeys* (London: Great Western Railway Co., 1925): "The site and buildings were granted to John Scudamore; a descendant, John, Viscount Scudamore, is the memorable name for us in connection with Dore. He was an enthusiastic churchman of the Laudian type. Laud induced him to give up the tithes which he held of the Abbey's property, and he himself in 1633 restored the transepts and choir of the Abbey church, beautified it, and gave it for the use of the parish. Whether he built the tower in the angle of the south transept, or whether that is in part pre-Dissolution work, is not agreed. Most attribute it to Scudamore. In any case, what he did here has deserved our respect and gratitude. His restored church was reconsecrated on Palm Sunday (March 30), 1634" (p. 116).

11. Thomas Dallam (1575–1630?) and his sons, Robert (1602?–1665), Ralph (d. 1673), and George (d. 1684), were celebrated organ builders in the later Elizabeth, Jacobean, and Restoration eras.

12. Psalm 109 reads in part: "The Lord at thy right hand hath broken kings in the day of his wrath. He shall judge among nations, he shall fill ruins: he shall crush the heads in the land of many" (5–6).

13. The Book of Common Prayer (BCP) was first printed in 1549, in

the reign of Edward VI, and revised in 1552. It was suppressed by the Catholic Queen Mary (r. 1553–58) but restored in 1559 by Queen Elizabeth I. Puritan objections to the BCP led to its replacement in 1645 by the Directory of Public Worship, compiled by the Westminster Assembly, and penalties were put in place for using the BCP. After the Restoration, the BCP was returned to use, with a further revision in 1662.

14. Arlingworth is fictitious.
15. There are two Norwoods in England, one in Derbyshire and the other in the London area, near Croydon. The latter site is presumably meant here.
16. This celebrated image was first devised in "'Oh, Whistle, and I'll Come to You, My Lad'" (GSA and CGS): "what he chiefly remembers about it is a horrible, an intensely horrible, face *of crumpled linen*" (CM 99).

A NEIGHBOUR'S LANDMARK

"A Neighbour's Landmark" was first published in the *Eton Chronic* (17 March 1924) and reprinted in WC and CGS (with the addition of the concluding note regarding Sir John Fox's *The Lady Ivie's Trial*). The title derives from the Book of Common Prayer, in the section "A Commination, or denouncing of God's anger and judgement against sinners": "Cursed is he that removeth his neighbour's landmark" (cf. Deuteronomy 19:14: "Thou shalt not take nor remove thy neighbour's landmark"). The story is based (as MRJ suggests at the end) on the trial of Theodosia Bryan, Lady Ivy (or Ivie), in the late seventeenth century.

Further Reading

Jacqueline Simpson, "Landmarks and Shrieking Ghosts," *Ghosts & Scholars* no. 25 (1997): 42–44.

1. In Christian doctrine, there are two different types of mercy, Works of Corporal Mercy (feeding the hungry, burying the dead, etc.) and Works of Spiritual Mercy (correcting sinners, bearing wrongs patiently, etc.).
2. A fictitious citation from the *Times Literary Supplement*. MRJ had considerable sympathy for the Victorian era and did not appreciate early twentieth-century criticisms of its social and religious conventions, as embodied in the work of Lytton Strachey and others.

3. *The Conduct of the Allies* (1711) is a celebrated tract by Jonathan Swift condemning the Whig government for becoming involved in the War of the Spanish Succession (1702–13) against England's true interests. The titles of the other two pamphlets are either fictitious or too imprecise to be clearly identified.

4. Most of these titles appear to be fictitious. *A Letter to a Convocation-Man* (1701) is an anonymous pamphlet by a clergyman commenting upon the canons for the Church of England. The Right Rev. Jonathan Trelawny was Lord Bishop of Winchester (or Winton) from 1706 to his death in 1721.

5. Many of Swift's hundreds of tracts were published pseudonymously, or anonymously, and some bibliographers believe that they have even now not been fully identified.

6. The Society for Promoting Christian Knowledge was founded in 1698. The Dean of Canterbury in 1711 was George Stanhope (1660–1728; dean 1704–28), criticized for being a political time-server.

7. It was this couplet that MRJ's Cambridge colleague A. E. Housman referred to as "good poetry" (cited in Cox1, 145).

8. Myles Birket Foster (1825–1899), British painter and book illustrator best known for *Pictures of English Landscapes* (1862).

9. Alfred Lord Tennyson, *In Memoriam: A. H. H.* (1850), stanza 54, line 20.

10. Sir Walter Scott, "Glenfinlas; or, Lord Ronald's Coronach" (1801), 1.184. For MRJ's comment on this weird poem, see "Some Remarks on Ghost Stories" (p. 253).

11. MRJ was a diligent reader of the State Trials, as he indicates in the preface to Sir John Fox's *The Lady Ivie's Trial* (Oxford: Clarendon Press, 1929), which he cites at the end of the story as the source of his information on Theodosia Bryan: "It is not until 1648 that we begin to get really lively reports. From that date till the end of the century the volumes contain the cream of the collection . . . those of the Popish Plot, the reign of James II, and the years immediately following the Revolution are undoubtedly the richest; and, I should say, among them, the trials in which the figure of Jeffreys appears. Things are never dull when he is at the bar or on the bench" (cited in Cox1, 145).

12. Shadwell is a district in Stepney in eastern London.

13. George Jeffreys, first baron Jeffreys of Wem (1648–1689), a notorious figure in Stuart England. As recorder of London (1678–80) he exercised severity in the "Popish Plot," in which

Jesuits were falsely accused of trying to assassinate King Charles II. As lord chief justice (1683–85) he held the "bloody assize" after the suppression of Monmouth's rebellion. He was later lord chancellor (1685–88), but fell into disgrace and died in the Tower of London. He is a central figure in MRJ's "Martin's Close" (*MGSA* and *CGS*).

A VIEW FROM A HILL

"A View from a Hill" first appeared in the *London Mercury* (May 1925) and was was reprinted in *WC* and *CGS*. All the locales cited in the story—Fulnaker Abbey, Oldbourne Church, Lambsfield, Wanstone, Ackford, and Thorfield—are fictitious, but in the preface to *CGS* (see p. 262) MRJ states that "Herefordshire was the imagined scene" of the story. The tale relies upon the common superstition that corpses, especially those of hanged criminals, possess supernatural powers. In this case, a pair of binoculars that had incorporated the substance of a hanged man's eyes allows one of the characters (whose blood, resulting from a cut, triggers the supernatural effect) to see through the binoculars with the dead man's eyes.

Further Reading

Martin Byrom, "A Wander Round Withybush," *Ghosts & Scholars* no. 19 (1995): 32–33.

1. As noted in *PT* (325n2), the character of Squire Richards appears to be based upon MRJ's friend, the antiquarian Dr. Henry Owen of Poyston, near Haverfordwest in Pembrokeshire. Owen (discussed in MRJ's *Eton and King's,* 1925) and MRJ first met in 1912–13 when the former was on the Royal Commission on Public Records.
2. MRJ alludes to the conventional belief that Rodrigo Borgia (1431–1503), who became Pope Alexander VI in 1492 and was the father of Cesare and Lucrezia Borgia, possessed a ring containing poison. The ring is cited in "The Ash-Tree" (*CM* 42).
3. "She lived unknown, and few could know / When Lucy ceased to be." William Wordsworth, "She Dwelt among the Untrodden Ways" (1800), ll. 9–10.

A WARNING TO THE CURIOUS

"A Warning to the Curious" was first published in the *London Mercury* (August 1925) and reprinted in *WC* and *CGS*. As MRJ notes in his preface to *CGS* (see p. 262), the fictitious town of Seaburgh, where the tale is set, is based on the Suffolk town of Aldeburgh, where MRJ's maternal grandmother lived; he visited her frequently until her death in 1870. Many of the locales described in the story, including the beach and the Martello Tower, remain today very much as MRJ described them (see Darroll Pardoe in Further Reading). The story makes clever use of the old British legend that certain magical coins buried on the coast in Anglo-Saxon times are designed to prevent the landing of enemy ships. Mike Pincombe suggests provocatively that the story "is at some level an expression of James's own perhaps slightly suppressed sense of guilt at occupying himself with what he regarded as the relatively trivial business of scholarship whilst others were dying for their country" in World War I.

The notes in *PT* (341–55) have interesting information on variant readings found in the manuscript of the story (now at the Pierpont Morgan Library, New York).

Further Reading

Darroll Pardoe, "A Visit to Seaburgh," *Ghosts & Scholars* no. 15 (1993): 35–36.

Rosemary Pardoe, "The Manuscript of 'A Warning to the Curious,'" *Ghosts & Scholars* no. 32 (2001): 47–49.

Mike Pincombe, "'No Thoroughfare': The Problem of Paxton in 'A Warning to the Curious,'" *Ghosts & Scholars* no. 32 (2001): 42–46.

1. In Dickens's *Great Expectations* (1860–61), the opening chapters deal with Little Pip's wandering the marsh country in Kent, where he lives, and coming upon an escaped prisoner hiding there.
2. A *shingle* in this sense means "A beach or other tract covered with loose roundish pebbles" (*OED*).
3. A *martello tower* is "a small circular fort with massive walls, containing vaulted rooms for the garrison, and having on top a platform for one or two guns; usually erected on a coast to prevent the landing of enemies" (*OED*). *Martello* is usually capitalized, reflecting its derivation as a corruption of Cape Mortella in Corsica.
4. Froston is fictitious.
5. The kingdom of East Anglia was established by Anglo-Saxon

migrants in the late fifth and early sixth centuries in what is now Norfolk and Suffolk. Some years after its last king, St. Edmund, was martyred in 870, it was incorporated into a united England by Edward the Elder (r. 899–924).

6. Rædwald, the earliest king of the East Angles whose career can be reconstructed, was king for part of the period between 616 and 633; he probably died in 624. Rendlesham is a town in Suffolk, four miles northeast of Woodbridge and about twenty miles from the coast. As noted in Cox2 (334), a silver crown purporting to be Rædwald's was indeed dug up at this time, but, as MRJ remarks in *Suffolk and Norfolk* (London: J. M. Dent, 1930), it "was melted down almost at once, so that we know nothing of its quality" (p. 11).

7. An Anglo-Saxon royal palace is properly defined as a place visited by a king and queen and their family, with a retinue of people and horses. A total of 193 royal palaces are known from Anglo-Saxon times, of which 155 are identified as to locale and name and 38 by name only. So far as is known, there is no royal palace under the sea off the East Anglian coast.

8. The "war of 1870" was the Franco-Prussian War (actually 1870–71); England was not involved in the conflict. The "South African War" was the Boer War (1899–1902).

9. The reference is to the Crown Jewels, a set of jewels dating from the twelfth to the seventeenth century, housed in the Tower of London and used when a new monarch is crowned.

10. In this sense, *boots* (a singular noun) refers to "The name for the servant in hotels who cleans the boots; formerly called *boot-catcher* or *-catch*" (*OED*).

11. i.e., the moon at Easter.

12. A reference to John Bunyan's *The Pilgrim's Progress* (1678–84), in which Christian has to pass successively through the Valley of Humiliation (where he fights the devil Apollyon) and the Valley of the Shadow of Death, during which he has to pass by one of the gates to Hell. MRJ alludes to Apollyon in " 'Oh, Whistle, and I'll Come to You, My Lad' " (*CM* 87).

AN EVENING'S ENTERTAINMENT

First published in *WC* and reprinted in *CGS*, "An Evening's Entertainment" is one of the relatively few tales by MRJ that do not involve an actual ghost and that make extensive use of pagan (as opposed to satanic or anti-Christian) magic. There is some suggestion that it was written merely to flesh out *WC* to proper book length, as was the case with "Mr. Humphreys and His Inheritance" (in *MGA*): MRJ writes to Gwendolen McBryde on 3 October 1925: "The ghost story book is finished. I had to write another one instead of the one I was at, which would not come out" (*Letters to a Friend* [London: Edward Arnold, 1956], p. 135). But the tale, in spite of its almost flippant opening, carries powerful implications of horror under its seemingly bland surface.

1. The *OED* dates the expression *Rawhead and Bloody-Bones* to the treatise *Wyll of Deuyll* (c. 1550), attributed to George Gascoigne. *OED* defines the term as "The name of a nursery bugbear." The work in question is properly *The Wyll of the Deuyll, and Last Testament* (1548), an anti-Catholic tract. Gascoigne's authorship cannot be confirmed.

2. MRJ refers to three widely reprinted textbooks for young adults. The first appears to be Jane Marcet (1769–1858), *Conversations in Chemistry* (1806), although Marcet wrote several other books of similar title, e.g., *Conversations on Political Economy* (1816), *Conversations on Natural Philosophy* (1819), *Conversations for Children* (1838), etc. The second is Jeremiah Joyce (1763–1816), *Dialogues in Chemistry* (1809). The third is John Ayrton Paris (1785–1856), *Philosophy in Sport Made Science in Earnest* (1827), a treatise with illustrations by George Cruikshank.

3. *Woundy* is an archaic adverb meaning "Very; extremely; excessively" (*OED*). *OED* cites a usage from Le Fanu's *Uncle Silas* (1864), whence MRJ probably derived it.

4. Cf. MRJ's discussion of the abbey of Cerne in Dorset: "That the sanctuary is really old I have little doubt; I have always supposed that it was set up here as a counterblast to the worship of the wicked old giant who is portrayed on the side of Trendle Hill just beyond the Abbey. He is surely of very great antiquity, and is perhaps the most striking monument of the early paganism of the country. Whether he is British or Saxon, who shall say? Some have thought that he represents what Caesar describes—a wicker figure in which troops of victims were enclosed and then burnt to death. On this hypothesis the figure would have been marked out by a palisade of wattles on the ground, and the victims, bound, crowded into the enclosure. In any case, here must have been an important heathen sanctuary, and a fit place consequently for champions of the new religion to set up their standard" (*Abbeys*, p. 149).

5. Bascombe and Wilcombe are fictitious.
6. In the Old and New Testaments, the etymology of the name Beelzebub (properly Beelzebul), usually considered a synonym for Satan, is "lord of flies."

THERE WAS A MAN DWELT BY A CHURCHYARD

This story or sketch was first published in *Snapdragon* (an Eton magazine) for 6 December 1924 and reprinted in *CGS*. It is the first of four tales that MRJ wrote after completing *WC*, his last separately published ghost story collection. For the source of the title and for the character of Mamilius, see MRJ's introduction to *Ghosts and Marvels* (p. 251).

1. Midsummer Eve (June 23) and All Hallows Eve (October 31) were considered two of the dates of the Witches' Sabbath, although May Eve (April 30), or *Walpurgisnacht,* was considered an even more potent occasion.

RATS

"Rats" was first published in *At Random* (an Eton magazine) on 23 March 1929 and reprinted in Lady Cynthia Asquith's anthology *Shudders* (London: Hutchinson, 1929) and in *CGS*. The title is deliberately misleading, for it is very unlikely that actual rats, either real or supernatural, are involved. The tale might well have been inspired by the passage in Dickens that is quoted as an epigraph.

1. From Charles Dickens, "Tom Tiddler's Ground" (*All the Year Round,* Christmas 1861). See Dickens's *Christmas Stories* (The New Oxford Illustrated Dickens, Volume 11) (London: Oxford University Press, 1956), p. 294.
2. Apparently a reference to Orlando Whistlecraft's *The Weather Record of 1856* (London: Thwaite, 1857). Whistlecraft wrote several similar works, including *The Climate of England* (1840) and *The Magnificent and Notably Hot Summer of 1846* (1846).
3. i.e., the heath outside of Thetford, a city in Norfolk, twelve miles north of Bury St. Edmunds. Cf. MRJ's *Suffolk and Norfolk:* "Thetford I will not treat of now, only pausing to note that not far from the Bury road, on the west side, you may catch sight of a

block of stone on the heath which I have always taken to be the base of a gibbet: certainly the locality would have suited highwaymen" (p. 66).

AFTER DARK IN THE PLAYING FIELDS

This story, first published in *College Days* (an Eton magazine) for 28 June 1924, was collected in *CGS*. The first of MRJ's tales set explicitly at Eton (the other is "Wailing Well"), it is remarkably similar in tone and atmosphere to MRJ's juvenile fantasy *The Five Jars* (1922), which also features a talking owl. The title alludes to the Playing Fields northeast of the college, the southwest part of which borders upon the Provost's garden.

1. Sheeps' Bridge is a small bridge leading across the Jordan (a stream that empties into the Thames) from the Playing Fields to the Shooting Fields.
2. The reference is to Romney Weir, upstream from Sheep's Bridge. A *weir* in this context is a body of water resulting from a dam placed across a river or canal.
3. Shakespeare, *A Midsummer-Night's Dream* 2.2.6–7.
4. The italicized phrase is from *A Midsummer-Night's Dream* 2.2.12.
5. Fellows' Pond is a pond on the northeast edge of the Playing Fields, just west of Sheep's Bridge.
6. Lupton's Tower, named after Robert Lupton (Provost, 1504–35), who commissioned it, is a splendid tower forming the eastern side of the School Yard. The Castle quadrangle and Curfew Tower are sites associated with nearby Windsor Castle.
7. The reference is to the Wall Game, a type of ball game invented at Eton. "Calx" denotes the two areas at the end of the Wall (on the northwest end of the Playing Fields) where it is possible to score a goal. Bad Calx is at the Slough end, or the end facing Slough Road.
8. St. David's tune is a musical setting of Psalm 1.
9. The quotation (if it is a quotation) is unidentified. For *weir* see n. 2.
10. June 4 is School Speech Day at Eton, commemorating the birthday of King George III, who took a special interest in Eton and its pupils. (He was actually born on May 24, 1738.) Among the festivities are a procession of boats from Fellows' Eyot to Surly Hall and a display of fireworks opposite the Playing Fields.

WAILING WELL

This story—published as a separate booklet (Mill House Press, 1928) and collected in *CGS*—is set near Worbarrow Bay in Dorset, referred to in the story as "the beautiful district of W (or X) in the county of D (or Y)," where the Boy Scouts had camped in 1927 when MRJ read them the story on 27 July. The *Eton College Chronicle* obituary of MRJ (18 June 1936) states that after MRJ's recital "several boys had a somewhat disturbed night as the scene of the story was quite close to Camp" (quoted in Cox1, 208). A far more substantial story than "After Dark in the Playing Fields," it is perhaps the most effective of the tales not included in MRJ's four ghost story collections, containing rich characterization of the schoolboy protagonists and a dark humor that underscores the grim horror of the scenario.

1. The Boy Scouts were established at Eton in 1919 for the purpose of developing resourcefulness and ingenuity. Common activities included bridge-building without materials, cooking without pots and pans, and the like.
2. There is no work of exactly this title. MRJ refers either to *The Works of . . . Thomas Ken* (1721; four volumes) or two early biographies, W. L. Bowles's *The Life of Thomas Ken* (1830) or John Lavicount Anderdon's *Life of Thomas Ken* (1851). Ken (1637–1711) was bishop of Bath and Wells (1685–91) but was deprived of his post for being a nonjuror (i.e., one who refused to swear allegiance to the new king and queen, William III and Mary, in 1689).
3. The vice-provost at the time of the writing of this story was Hugh V. Macnaghten (1862–1929), author of *Fifty Years of Eton* (1924). He and MRJ were not notably cordial to each other.
4. William Hope-Jones, an instructor of mathematics and a leader of the Boy Scouts.
5. i.e., Judkins *minor* ("the younger"), the younger brother (otherwise not named) of Stanley Judkins, referred to later as Judkins *ma.* (i.e., *major* = "the elder").
6. Oppidans (from the Latin *oppidum*, town) are fee-paying students who board in town, as opposed to the King's Scholars (Collegers), who receive scholarships and are housed in dormitories on the Eton grounds. There has frequently been considerable tension between Oppidans and Collegers. MRJ was a Colleger during his Eton years (1876–82).

7. Cuckoo Weir is a bathing place for nonswimmers, just below Ward's Mead.

8. A. C. Beasley Robinson and Julian Lambart (mentioned later in the text) were two Masters who were leading forces behind the Boy Scouts.

9. H. G. Ley, the Precentor (i.e., the Master responsible for the teaching of music).

10. As noted in *PT* (390n13), Pip, Squeak, and Wilfred were three characters (a penguin, a dog, and a rabbit, respectively) that appeared in a popular comic strip in the *Daily Mirror* (1919–46).

11. An *axe-helve* is the handle of an axe.

THE EXPERIMENT

First published in the *Morning Post* (London), 31 December 1930, "The Experiment" is one of two tales (the other being "The Malice of Inanimate Objects") that appeared in MRJ's lifetime subsequent to the submission of *CGS* to the publisher. It is a tale whose denouement is unclear because of the difficulty of interpreting the nature of the creature (Nares) MRJ has invented for the tale.

Further Reading

Steve Duffy, "Nares," *Ghosts & Scholars* no. 31 (2000): 50.

Rosemary Pardoe, "'The Experiment': Story Notes," *Ghosts & Scholars M. R. James Newsletter* no. 3 (January 2003): 22–24.

1. In this sense (now archaic), *maggot* means "A whimsical or perverse fancy; a crochet" (*OED*).

2. In the apocryphal books of Tobit and 1 Enoch, Raphael is one of the seven archangels who stand in the presence of God. Nares (Latin for "nostrils") is evidently a creature of MRJ's invention.

3. i.e., most convenient. *OED's* only citation of this superlative of *eft* is Shakespeare, *Much Ado about Nothing* 4.2.38: "Yea, marry, that's the eftest way."

4. John Moore (1646–1714), bishop of Norwich (1691–1707) and then of Ely (1707–14). Upon his death, his immense library of 29,000 books and 1800 manuscripts were sold to King George I, who then donated them to Cambridge.

THE MALICE OF INANIMATE OBJECTS

This story appeared in *Masquerade* (Eton College), June 1933. As with "Rats," the tale's title is deliberately misleading, for it does not suggest that inanimate objects are endowed with "malice," but rather that they are agents in the working out of supernatural vengeance.

1. This is a quite accurate paraphrase of the fairy-tale "Herr Korbes" in the Brothers Grimms' *Fairy Tales*. The couplet is MRJ's rendering of the Grimms' "Als hinaus / Nach den Herrn Korbes seinem Haus." The Grimms' version merely states that Herr Korbes was a "wicked" (*böser*) man. For the Grimm text, see Jakob and W. K. Grimm, *Kinderund Hausmärchen* (Düsseldorf: Verlag L. Schwann, 1949), pp. 190–91.
2. *To throw up the sponge* is British slang for to give in or give up (in this context, to abandon any hope for living).
3. A *purl* is British slang for "An act of whirling, hurling, or pitching head-over-heels or head-foremost" (*OED*).
4. "I, George W[ilkins] made (or did) [this]," a standard Latin inscription on *objets d'art* to identify the artist who fashioned the object in question.

A VIGNETTE

The first of MRJ's fugitive tales to be published posthumously, "A Vignette" appeared in the *London Mercury* for November 1936. An editor's note prefacing the story states:

"A Vignette" is undoubtedly the last ghost story written by the late Dr. M. R. James, provost of Eton, and probably his last piece of continuous writing intended for the Press. It came into being in this way. Mr. Owen Hugh Smith was good enough to ask Dr. James to try to recapture the mood in which he wrote *Ghost Stories of an Antiquary,* and to let me have something in similar vein for the Christmas number of *The London Mercury* (1935). The answer was that he would do his best. On December 12th of that year he sent off to me the manuscript, written in pencil, from The Lodge, Eton College, with the following letter:

I am ill satisfied with what I enclose. It comes late and is short and ill written. There have been a good many events conspiring to keep it back, besides a growing inability. So pray don't use it unless it has some quality I do not see in it.

I send it because I was enjoined to do something by Mr. Owen Smith.

It was then too late for our Christmas number, or, indeed, for the January number; so it was agreed that it should be held over till one of the closing months of this year.

At the moment of going to press, I see it announced that the original manuscripts of his *Ghost Stories* are to appear at Sotheby's sale on November 9th (written on foolscap paper). The original of "A Vignette," of course, is not among them. Like the others, it is written on lined foolscap.

Its chief virtue lies in its apparently straightforward autobiographical significance, especially in its recounting of youthful dreams MRJ had that may have led him to the composition of ghostly tales.

1. i.e., Livermore rectory near Bury St. Edmunds, where MRJ grew up.
2. "It is but foolery, but it is such a kind of gain-giving, as would perhaps trouble a woman." Shakespeare, *Hamlet* 5.2.215–16. "Gain-giving" here means misgiving.
3. The quotation is from J. Sheridan Le Fanu's novel *The House by the Churchyard,* serialized in the *Dublin University Magazine* (October 1861–February 1863) and published in book form in 1863. The quotation is from Chapter 11; the exact quotation is as follows: "As the aërial aspect of the old house for a moment stood before her [Old Sally], with its peculiar, malign, sacred, and skulking aspect, as if it had drawn back in shame and guilt under the melancholy old elms among the tall hemlock and nettles." The magazine version prints "sacred" as "scared," and some MRJ scholars believe this to be the correct reading; but sacred (in the sense of awe inspiring), the reading of the first edition, must be correct, and is the reading both in the magazine version of "A Vignette" and in the citation in MRJ's essay "Some Remarks on Ghost Stories" (p. 255).

THE FENSTANTON WITCH

Unpublished in MRJ's lifetime, "The Fenstanton Witch" was first published in *Ghosts & Scholars* no. 12 (1990) and reprinted in *PT*. The manuscript of the tale is in the Cambridge University Library. Rosemary Pardoe has recently reexamined the manuscript and produced a much more accurate transcription than previous editions; this transcription appears on her website (www.users.globalnet.co.uk/~pardos/Archive Fenstanton.html) and is reproduced here by her gracious permission.

"The Fenstanton Witch" is the only one of the "Stories I Have Tried to Write" (see p. 266) that MRJ actually completed. It is a substantial work that richly evokes the early eighteenth-century ambience of Cambridge; however, its historical details are contradictory, and would probably have been corrected if MRJ had polished the story. It is stated at the outset that the story takes place in the reign of Queen Anne (1702–14), but other details (see, e.g., n. 17) suggest an earlier date. Nevertheless, its effective use of witchcraft and sorcery outweighs any of its historical errors.

Further Reading

Rosemary Pardoe, " 'The Fenstanton Witch': Story Notes," *Ghosts & Scholars M. R. James Newsletter* no. 2 (September 1902): 14–18.

1. The first site mentioned is now simply Thorganby, a village in Lincolnshire eight miles southwest of Grimsby. Ospringe is a village in Kent, one mile southwest of Faversham.
2. In this sense, a *living* means a benefice or ecclesiastical employment in a parish church.
3. Thomas Harwood (1767–1842), *Alumni Etonenses* (1797), a descriptive list of Eton alumni from 1443 to 1797.
4. Apparently an error for Charles Roderick, who was successively head master of Eton (1680–89) and provost (1689f.) and vice-chancellor of King's College.
5. Sir Isaac Newton (1642–1727) had been a fellow of King's College since 1667, remaining there until 1695. He was reputed to have had a dog named Diamond who on one occasion knocked over a candle and set fire to some of his manuscripts, whereupon Newton is supposed to have said, "Oh Diamond! Diamond! thou little knowest the mischief done." But this story, reported half a century after Newton's death, is almost certainly apocryphal, and he probably owned no pets.
6. Richard Bentley (1662–1742), the greatest classical scholar of his age, became master of Trinity College in 1699. In 1714 he was put on trial for the questionable dismissal of Edmund Miller (a barrister holding the physic fellowship) and for the use of college funds for expensive repairs. After years of litigation, during which the

university voted to deprive Bentley of his degrees and of the regius professorship of divinity (which he had contrived to bestow upon himself in 1717), King George I restored Bentley's degrees in 1722.

7. John Blow (1649–1708), a well-known British composer and organist.

8. Thomas Tudway (1650?–1726), organist at King's College from 1670 until his death, although his duties were severely curtailed after 1706 as a result of his having spoken slightingly of Queen Anne. He was also a composer and collected a large quantity of English church music in manuscript from the Reformation to the death of Queen Anne.

9. The diplomats John Methuen (1650–1706) and his son, Sir Paul Methuen (1672?–1757), as successive ministers to Portugal, managed to negotiate diplomatic and commercial treaties with Portugal in 1703 that resulted in Great Britain's securing a monopoly on Portugal's trade for the rest of the eighteenth century, including the importation of port wine, usually shipped from the city of Oporto in Portugal.

10. Fenstanton is a town in Cambridgeshire, two miles south of St. Ives and ten miles northwest of Cambridge.

11. MRJ refers to John Churchill, first duke of Marlborough (1650–1722), celebrated British army officer, and his eldest son, John (Jack), first marquis of Blandford (1686–1703). Blandford died of smallpox on 20 February 1703.

12. Dodgson is fictitious.

13. Matthews is fictitious.

14. i.e., she had sold her soul to the devil.

15. Morell is fictitious.

16. William of Malmesbury (1090?–1142?), British historian and Benedictine monk, wrote numerous historical and ecclesiastical works, notably the *Gesta Regum Anglorum* [Deeds of the English Kings]. The story of the witch of Berkeley is found in Book 2, chapter 13 of that work. In the story, a woman of Berkeley, "addicted to witchcraft," is told by a jackdaw that her son and other members of her family have been killed as punishment for her sins. On her deathbed, the woman summons the surviving members of her family, along with a monk and a nun, and beseeches them to ward off evil spirits by the following method: "sew up my corpse in the skin of a stag; lay it on its back in a stone coffin; fasten down the lid with lead and iron; on this lay a stone, bound round with three iron chains of enormous weight; let there be psalms sung for fifty nights, and masses said for an equal number

of days." But the precautions are useless: on the first two nights, demons come and break into the church, causing havoc; on the third night, an especially powerful demon snatches up the woman's body, places her on a black horse, and suddenly vanishes—"her pitiable cries, however, for assistance, were heard for nearly the space of four miles." See William of Malmesbury, *Chronicle of the Kings of England,* translated by J. A. Giles (1847; reprinted London: George Bell & Sons, 1895), 230–32.

By "Dr. Gale" MRJ refers to Thomas Gale (1635–1702), a King's Scholar at Trinity College (1655–62), and successively fellow (1659f.) and tutor (1663–72) before becoming dean of York. In collaboration with William Fulman (1632–1688), Gale compiled *Rerum Anglicarum Scriptores Veteres* (1684–91; three volumes), a collection of writings on Great Britain by early English writers; volume 1 contains several works by William of Malmesbury, but the *Gesta Regum Anglorum* is not one of them.

17. John Newborough, head master of Eton (1690–1711). If this tale is set in the reign of Queen Anne, Newborough would already be head master and no longer at Cambridge.

18. Robert Southey's "The Old Woman of Berkeley" was first published in his *Poems* (1799).

19. See "The Residence at Whitminster," n. 19.

20. Humphrey Hody (1659–1707), a scholar at Wadham College, Oxford, and author of *De Bibliorum Textibus Originalibus, Versionibus Graecis, et Latina Vulgata* [On the Original Texts of the Bible, the Greek Versions, and the Latin Vulgate] (1705).

21. Evidently a reference to *The Anatomy of Melancholy* (1621) by Robert Burton (1577–1640), although no phrase of exactly this sort can be found in the work.

22. Roger Cotes (1682–1716), fellow of Trinity, professor of mathematics and experimental science, and friend of Sir Isaac Newton.

23. i.e., Corpus Christi College. It was situated near St. Benedict's (Bene't's) Church.

24. Lolworth is a village six miles northwest of Cambridge.

25. Cf. 2 Kings 2:11: "And it came to pass, as they still went on, and talked, that, behold, there appeared a chariot of fire, and horses of fire, and parted them both asunder; and Elijah went up by a whirlwind into heaven."

26. Cf. Psalm 91.5–6: "Thou shalt not be afraid . . . for the pestilence that walketh in darkness."

27. Willoughton is a village in Lincolnshire, seven miles northeast of Gainsborough and about 100 miles northwest of Cambridge.

28. Weedon Lois is a village in Northamptonshire, six miles north of Brackley. As Pardoe remarks, the living there has been in the gift of King's College since the Reformation.
29. Barton is a village about three miles southwest of Cambridge.

TWELVE MEDIEVAL GHOST-STORIES

This document first appeared in the *English Historical Review* 37 (July 1922): 413–22. It was first reprinted (with a translation of the Latin text by M. Benzinski) in Hugh Lamb's anthology *The Man-Wolf and Other Horrors* (1978); another version (with a translation by Pamela Chamberlaine) appears in Peter Haining's edition of *M. R. James: The Book of the Supernatural* (1979; U.S. edition published as *M. R. James: The Book of Ghost Stories*), and yet another version (with an anonymous translation) appears in *PT*. The translation presented here, by Leslie Boba Joshi, adheres more closely to the Latin text than previous versions. This is the first time that the Latin text, as well as all of MRJ's footnotes (identified below with his initials), have been reprinted. The translation is presented in brackets following each story.

Further Reading

Rosemary Pardoe, "Scrying the Horse-Demon," *Ghosts & Scholars* no. 31 (2000): 43–45.

Jacqueline Simpson, "Ghosts in Medieval Yorkshire," *Ghosts & Scholars* no. 27 (1998): 40–44 (reprinted in *PT* 631–37).

Jacqueline Simpson, "Repentant Soul or Walking Corpse? Debatable Apparitions in Medieval England," *Folklore* 114 (March 2003): 389–402.

1. "Examples of spiritual apparitions, fifteenth century." MRJ is referring to David Casley, compiler of *A Catalogue of the Manuscripts of the King's Library* (1734), revised as *A Catalogue of the Harleian Collection of Manuscripts* (1759–63), now in the British Library.
2. Evald Tang Kristensen (1843–1929), Danish compiler of *Sagn fra Jylland* (1880), *Danske sagn, som de har lydt i folkemunde* (1928–39; seven vols.), and other volumes of Danish folk and fairy-tales.
3. So in II a ghost is said to appear "in specie dumi" (as I read it), i.e. of a thorn-bush. In several of these stories the ghosts are liable to many changes of form. [MRJ]

4. The reason of his "walking" and how he could he helped. [MRJ]
5. The verb *coniurare,* used frequently in these stories, literally means "to swear to confession," but can also mean "to beseech" or "to command." In this translation, the verb is variously translated depending on the context.
6. The word is a mystery to me. It seems to begin with *e* and ends with *di.* There is a mark of contraction. [MRJ]
7. *more* I take to be the genitive of *mora,* a moor or marsh. The other word I do not know nor find, but guess it to mean a turf or peat-stack. [MRJ]
8. A dog with a chain on its neck. [MRJ]
9. Great pains are taken throughout to conceal the name of the ghost. He must have been a man of quality, whose relatives might have objected to stories being told about him. [MRJ]
10. At the end of the story we have "ne respicias ignem materialem ista nocte ad minus." In the Danish tales something like this is to be found. Kristensen, *Sagn og overtro,* 1866, no. 585: After seeing a phantom funeral the man "was wise enough to go to the stove and look at the fire before he saw (candle- or lamp-)light. For when people see anything of the kind they are sick if they cannot get at fire before light." *Ibid.* no. 371: "he was very sick when he caught sight of the light." The same in no. 369. In part ii of the same (1888), no. 690: "When you see anything supernatural, you should peep over the door before going into the house. You must see the light before the light sees you." Collection of 1883, no. 193: "When he came home, he called to his wife to put out the light before he came in, but she did not, and he was so sick they thought he would have died." These examples are enough to show that there was risk attached to seeing light after a ghostly encounter. Does *ignis materialis* mean simply a fire of wood here? [MRJ]
11. I suppose, in order that the ghost might not haunt the road in the interval before the tailor's return. [MRJ]
12. The reluctance of the priest at York to absolve, and the number of advisers called in, testify to the importance of the case. [MRJ]
13. The conduct of the officious neighbour who insists upon being informed of the tailor's assignation with the ghost and then backs out of accompanying him, is amusing. [MRJ]
14. Whether a circle enclosing a cross or a circle drawn with a cross I do not know. [MRJ]
15. Small "reliquaries" such as could be worn on the person. [MRJ]
16. I think the allusion is to the pictures of the Three Living and

Three Dead so often found painted on church-walls. The Dead and Living are often represented as kings. [MRJ]

17. The need of a prescription for healing the tailor was due to the blow in the side which the crow (raven?) had given him. [MRJ]

18. This does not seem to follow logically upon the prohibition to tell the ghost's name. I take it as advice to the tailor to change his abode. "If you take up your abode—reside—in such a place you will prosper; if in such a place you will be poor; and you have some enemies (where you now are)." [MRJ]

19. "quasi in vacuo dolio" is a picturesque touch. These ghosts do not twitter and squeak like those of Homer. [MRJ] On several occasions Homer refers to ghosts—or, more properly, the souls of the dead—as making sounds of this kind. See, e.g., *Odyssey* 24.6–9: "And as when bats in the depths of an awful cave flitter and gibber, when one of them has fallen out of his place in the chain that the bats have formed by holding one on another; so, gibbering, they [the souls of the suitors] went their way together" (translated by Richmond Lattimore).

20. "volebat stare," "he would stand." [MRJ]

21. There is the same caution here about mentioning the crimes of the dead man. [MRJ]

22. When Wayneman was throwing the coffin into Gormyre the oxen which drew his cart almost sank in the marsh for fear. This, I suppose, is the sense of the rather obscure sentence. [MRJ]

23. This is most curious. Why did the woman catch the ghost and bring it indoors? [MRJ]

24. A daylight ghost, as it seems. The seer and the head ploughman are walking together in the field. Suddenly the ploughman has a panic and runs off, and the other finds himself struggling with a ghost. Probably the prior had excommunicated the stealer of the spoons "whoever he might be" without knowing who he was, as in the case of the Jackdaw of Rheims. [MRJ]

25. "per viam compendii vltra se," at the cross-road ahead of him. [MRJ]

26. Du Cange gives the forms "canava," "canavis," and "canvoys." [MRJ]

27. For three nights William of Bradford had heard the cries. On the fourth night he met the ghost. And I suspect he must have been imprudent enough to answer the cries, for there are many tales, Danish and other, of persons who answer the shrieking ghost with impertinent words, and the next moment they hear it close to their car. Note the touch of the frightened dog. [MRJ]

28. "Aton," the catalogue suggests, may be Ayton. The ghost throws him over the hedge and catches him as he falls on the other side. So the Troll, whose (supposed) daughter married the blacksmith, when he heard that all the villagers shunned her, came to the church on Sunday before service when all the people were in the churchyard and drove them into a compact group. Then he said to his daughter, "Will you throw or catch?" "I will catch," said she, in kindness to the people. "Very well, go round to the other side of the church." And he took them one by one and threw them over the church, and she caught them and put them down unhurt. "Next time I come," said the Troll, "she shall throw, and I will catch—if you don't treat her better." Not very relevant, but less known than it should be. [MRJ]

29. The word after "nocuissem" I cannot read: it ends -ter. [MRJ]

30. "Concerning the threefold sort of confession."

31. "Priest who had the spirit of a python [i.e., sorcerer]."

32. The wizard "anoints" the nail of the child, not the palm of the hand. He, I suppose, and not the master of the house, is the *clericus* who asks the questions. [MRJ]

33. There are multitudinous examples of the nightly processions of the dead, but I do not know another case in which they ride on their own "mortuaries" (the beasts offered to their church, or claimed by it, at their decease): it is a curious reminiscence of the pagan fashion of providing means of transport for the dead by burying beasts with them. Evidently the wife was not accessory to the indecent burial of the child, and the sympathy of the writer is with her. The divorce does seem superfluous, since, though sponsors were not allowed to marry, here was but one sponsor: but I know not the canon law. [MRJ]

APPENDIX

In the course of the 1920s and 1930s, MRJ had frequent occasion to comment on the nature, history, and theory of the ghost story. In this appendix, several significant documents are printed. Aside from these articles, MRJ also wrote several essays on his favorite Victorian weird writer, J. Sheridan Le Fanu (see *PT* 491–509), but as these have less direct relevance to MRJ's own thoughts on the ghost story, they are not included here.

MRJ's "Introduction" to V. H. Collins's anthology *Ghosts and Marvels* (London: Oxford University Press, 1924) is his first discussion of the practice of ghost story writing since his brief preface to *MGA* (see *CM* 255–56). Not much is known about Vere Henry Collins aside from the fact that he edited numerous thematic compilations of English literature, including *Ghosts and Marvels* (1924), *More Ghosts and Marvels* (1929), and *Poems of Action* (1913). MRJ's comments suggest that he would have compiled the volume somewhat differently.

"Some Remarks on Ghost Stories," first published in the London *Bookman* for December 1929 (an immense issue devoted exclusively to the weird tale and featuring contributions by Algernon Blackwood, Arthur Machen, and other noted writers), is MRJ's most exhaustive discussion of the ghost story—both a theoretical account of how ghost stories ought to be written and a potted history of the weird tale. MRJ's bias toward reticence and indirection is evident in his censure of what he perceives to be contemporary writers' excessive use of gore and sexual imagery.

"Ghosts—Treat Them Gently!" first appeared in the London *Evening News* (17 April 1931). A more personal article than his other discussions of the ghost story, it again emphasizes those principles—chiefly the avoidance of occultist jargon, the need for relative contemporaneity of setting, and the focus on the "horror and malevolence" of the supernatural phenomenon—that MRJ utilized in his own work.

MRJ's preface to *CGS* provides fascinating clues as to the real sources (topographical and otherwise) of his tales, as well as their dates of writing and publication.

"Stories I Have Tried to Write" was first published in the *Touchstone* (30 November 1929), an Eton magazine, and reprinted in *CGS*. It tells of several plot synopses that MRJ had devised but not developed into fully formed tales; several of them were in fact written up as actual tales or fragments of tales, with some modifications of plot details.

1. A story by J. Sheridan Le Fanu, first published in the *Dublin University Magazine* (May 1839) and reprinted in a revised version in *Ghost Stories and Tales of Mystery* (1851); the original text was reprinted in the posthumous volume, *The Purcell Papers* (1880).

2. Daniel Defoe, *The Apparition of Mrs. Veal* (1706). Sir Walter Scott's belief (expressed in his essay "Daniel Defoe," in *Miscellaneous Prose Works* [1827], vol. 4) that the work was written to promote the sale of Charles Drelincourt's *The Christian's Defence against the Fears of Death* (1675; a translation of *Les Consolations de l'âme fidèle contre les frayeurs de la mort*, 1651) has now been discredited.

3. The citation is from Andrew Lang (1844–1930), *History of English*

Literature (London: Longmans, Green, 1912), pp. 416–17. MRJ had cited Lang, a Scottish folklorist and critic, in "Martin's Close" (see *CM* 213).

4. Sir Walter Scott, "Wandering Willie's Tale," a chapter of the novel *Redgauntlet* (1824).

5. See "Twelve Medieval Ghost-Stories," n. 2.

6. Edgar Allan Poe, "Ligeia" (*American Museum* [Baltimore], September 1838; in *Tales of the Grotesque and Arabesque*, 1840); Captain Frederick Marryat, "The Werewolf" (a chapter of *The Phantom Ship*, 1839).

7. The Irish poet and critic Padraic Colum wrote the introduction to the Everyman's Library edition of Poe's *Tales of Mystery and Imagination* (1908).

8. Edward Bulwer-Lytton, "The Haunted and the Haunters; or, The House and the Brain" (*Blackwood's Edinburgh Magazine*, August 1859); George Eliot, "The Lifted Veil" (*Blackwood's Edinburgh Magazine*, July 1859).

9. See Mrs. Crowe's *Night Side of Nature*, and Stead's *Real Ghost Stories*. [MRJ] [MRJ refers to Catherine Crowe's *The Night Side of Nature* (1848) and W. T. Stead's *Real Ghost Stories* (1897), both of which feature the haunted mill mentioned by MRJ. Others believe that Bulwer-Lytton's story is based upon the haunted house at 50 Berkeley Square, London, to which MRJ himself alludes in "A School Story" (*CM* 121).]

10. Margaret Oliphant, "The Open Door" (*Blackwood's Edinburgh Magazine*, January 1882), *A Beleagured City* (1880).

11. MRJ apparently refers to T. Ottway, *The Spectre; or, News from the Invisible World* (1835), later published as *News from the Invisible World* (1844). "Charley" may be a transcriptional error by V. H. Collins or MRJ's typist.

12. W.W. Jacobs, "The Monkey's Paw" (*Harper's*, September 1902). For other of Jacobs's weird tales, see *The Monkey's Paw and Other Tales of Mystery and the Macabre* (Academy Chicago, 1997).

13. H. G. Wells, "The Crystal Egg" (*New Review*, 1897; in *Tales of Space and Time*, 1900).

14. Algernon Blackwood, "Ancient Sorceries," in *John Silence—Physician Extraordinary* (1908). The tale is set in Laon, a town in southern France.

15. Robert Louis Stevenson, "The Body Snatcher" (*Pall Mall Magazine*, Christmas 1884); Barry Pain, "The Moon-Slave" (*Stories in the Dark*, 1901).

16. From Shakespeare, *A Winter's Tale* 2.1.22–32.

17. MRJ refers to Scottish writer George Borrow (1803–1881), whose *Wild Wales: Its People, Language and Scenery* (1862) was based on his travels through Wales in 1854. In chapter 99 of that work, he alludes to a ghost story told by Spanish writer Lope de Vega (1562–1635); the actual story can be found in William I. Knapp's *Life, Writings, and Correspondence of George Borrow* (London: John Murray, 1899), vol. 2, 120–24. Lope's *Las Aventuras de Pánfilo: Cuentos de espantos* was first published as the fifth part of *El Pelegrino en su patria* (1604). MRJ appears to refer to an illustrated edition published in 1920 (Madrid: Jiménez Fraud).

18. Joseph Glanvill (1636–1680), *Saducismus Triumphatus* (1681), one section of which purports to prove "the real existence of apparitions, spirits and witches." Glanvill is mentioned in "Martin's Close" (*CM* 198). John Beaumont (d. 1731), *An Historical, Physiological and Theological Treatise of Spirits, Apparitions, Witchcrafts, and Other Magical Practices* (1705).

19. Ludwig Lavater (1527–1586), *De Spectris, Lemuribus et Magnis atqve Insolitis Fragoribus* (1570), translated into English as *Of Ghosts and Spirites Walking by Nyght* (1572).

20. Samuel Johnson's comment on *Coriolanus* appears in his edition of Shakespeare (1765). See *Johnson on Shakespeare* (The Yale Edition of the Works of Samuel Johnson, vol. 8) (New Haven: Yale University Press, 1968), p. 823.

21. See "The Haunted Dolls' House," n. 1.

22. Ann Radcliffe, whose best-known work is *The Mysteries of Udolpho* (1794). Matthew Gregory ("Monk") Lewis, author of *The Monk* (1796).

23. *Tales of Wonder* (1801) was an anthology of supernatural balladry edited by Lewis; *Tales of Terror* (1801) was an anonymous parody of that volume.

24. Charles Robert Maturin, *Melmoth the Wanderer* (1824), often believed to be the last and the greatest of the early Gothic novels.

25. "The Tapestried Chamber" (*Keepsake for 1829*, 1828).

26. MRJ refers to his diligent hunting of periodicals in search for previously unrecognized works by J. Sheridan Le Fanu, embodied in his critical and bibliographical notes in *Madam Crowl's Ghost and Other Tales of Mystery* (1923).

27. Dickens, "A Christmas Tree" (*Household Words*, Christmas 1850), in *Christmas Stories* (The New Oxford Illustrated Dickens, Volume 11) (London: Oxford University Press, 1956), 1–18.

28. Dickens, *A Christmas Carol* (1843). "No. 1 Branch Line: The Signal-Man," a segment of *Mugby Junction* (*All the Year Round*, Christmas 1866). By "the Juryman" MRJ refers to "To Be Taken with a Grain of Salt" (later retitled "The Trial for Murder"), a segment of *Doctor Marigold's Prescriptions* (*All the Year Round*, Christmas 1865).

29. Le Fanu, "The Watcher" (*Dublin University Magazine*, November 1847; in *Ghost Stories and Tales of Mystery*, 1851), revised as "The Familiar," in *In a Glass Darkly* (1872). "Mr. Justice Harbottle," in *In a Glass Darkly*. "Carmilla" (*Dark Blue*, December 1871–March 1872; in *In a Glass Darkly*). For "Schalken the Painter," see n. 1 above. "Squire Toby's Will" (*Temple Bar*, January 1868). For *The House by the Churchyard*, see "A Vignette," n. 3. "Dickon the Devil" (*Dark Blue*, Christmas 1872). "Madam Crowl's Ghost" (*All the Year Round*, 31 December 1870). The last two tales are included in *Madam Crowl's Ghost and Other Tales of Mystery* as is "Squire Toby's Will."

30. See "A Vignette," n. 3.

31. "Green Tea" (*All the Year Round*, 23 October–13 November 1869); in *In a Glass Darkly*. "The Room in the Dragon Volant" (*London Society*, February–June 1872); in *In a Glass Darkly*. "The Haunted Baronet" (*Belgravia*, July–November 1870); in *Chronicles of Golden Friars* (1871).

32. William Makepeace Thackeray, "The Notch in the Axe" (*Cornhill Magazine*, April–June 1862), in *Roundabout Papers* (1863).

33. Wilkie Collins, *The Haunted Hotel* (1879), a blood-and-thunder novella full of horrifying dreams and gruesome murders.

34. Ellen (Price) Wood (Mrs. Henry Wood), *Johnny Ludlow: Fifth Series* (1890).

35. Le Fanu, "The Mysterious Lodger" (*Dublin University Magazine*, January–February 1850).

36. F. Marion Crawford, "The Upper Berth" (*The Broken Shaft*, edited by Henry Norman [1886]) and "The Screaming Skull" (*Red Magazine*, December 1908), both included in *Wandering Ghosts* (1911), published in the United Kingdom as *Uncanny Tales* (1911).

37. Bram Stoker, *Dracula* (1897).

38. MRJ refers to *Chambers's Repository of Instructive and Amusing Tracts* (1852–54; twelve volumes). In *M. R. James: The Book of the Supernatural* (1979), Peter Haining claims that he has found the story—an anonymous tale entitled "The Vampire of Kring"— and prints the text of it; but he gives the date of its appearance as

14 January 1856: either this date is erroneous, or Haining found the item in a different periodical altogether.

39. William de Morgan, *Alice-for-Short* (1907).

40. E. F. Benson, *The Room in the Tower* (1912), *Visible and Invisible* (1923), and *Spook Stories* (1928). Benson would write one more volume of ghost stories, *More Spook Stories* (1934), and other weird tales are scattered elsewhere in his work. He was a longtime friend of MRJ's, having heard MRJ recite his first ghost stories to the Chitchat Society in 1893.

41. Actually, the "Not at Night" series—beginning with *Not at Night!* (1925) and concluding with *The Night at Night Omnibus* (1937)—was assembled by a British editor, Christine Campbell Thomson, although much of the contents was selected from the American pulp magazine *Weird Tales*. An American editor, Herbert Asbury, published a volume entitled *Not at Night* (1928), apparently a pirated edition of some of the early "Not at Night" volumes. It was quickly withdrawn from publication and is now very rare.

42. *Some Ghost Stories* (1927), one of several volumes of ghost stories written by A. M. Burrage.

43. *They Return at Evening* (1928), one of seven volumes of ghost stories published by H. Russell Wakefield.

44. Mrs. H. D. Everett, *The Death-Mask and Other Stories* (1920), an extremely scarce volume; reprinted, with additions, by Ghost Story Press (1995).

45. Robert Hugh Benson, *The Light Invisible* (1903) and *A Mirror of Shalott* (1906), two collections of short stories narrated by priests.

46. K[ate] and Hesketh Prichard, a mother-and-son writing team who wrote many stories involving the psychic detective Flaxman Low, published in *Pearson's Magazine* (1898–99). They were collected in the volume *Ghosts* (1899).

47. See n. 13 above.

48. Emile Erckmann and Alexandre Chatrian, who published under the byline Erckmann-Chatrian. MRJ refers to *La Maison forestière* (1866), translated as "The Wild Huntsman"; "Hugues-de-Loup" (*Constitutionel*, May 1859), usually translated as "The Man-Wolf"; "Le Blanc et le noir" (*Contes des bords du Rhin*, 1862), translated as "The White and the Black"; "Le Rêve du cousin Elof" (in *Contes fantastiques*, 1860); "L'Oeil invisible" (*L'Artiste*, 1857), translated as "The Invisible Eye."

49. Henry James, *The Turn of the Screw* (1898).
50. Properly, the Society for Psychical Research, founded in the United Kingdom in 1882; an American branch was founded in 1885.
51. It has not been determined which work MRJ is referring to here. Perhaps it is J. B. Priestley's *Benighted* (1927; published in the United States as *The Old Dark House*), but this novel is set in Wales, not Cornwall.
52. W. Harrison Ainsworth, *The Lancashire Witches* (1849), a non-supernatural historical novel about a celebrated witch trial in the seventeenth century.
53. The reference is to Dr. John Watson, Sherlock Holmes's companion in the stories of Sir Arthur Conan Doyle, and Captain Hastings, the companion of Hercule Poirot in the detective stories of Agatha Christie.
54. Lanoe Falconer (pseudonym of Mary Elizabeth Hawker, 1848–1908), *Cecilia de Noël* (1891); reprinted in *The Virago Book of Victorian Ghost Stories,* edited by Richard Dalby (London: Virago, 1988).
55. Shakespeare, *Hamlet* 1.5.4.
56. Mr. Wardle is a character in *The Pickwick Papers*. The Fat Boy is Joe, his servant, who immediately goes to sleep after a task he has performed is done. MRJ is therefore suggesting that the *Not at Night* books are soporific.
57. Walter de la Mare, British author of *The Riddle and Other Stories* (1922), *The Connoisseur and Other Stories* (1926), and other volumes of weird tales, along with the supernatural novel *The Return* (1910).
58. " 'Oh, Whistle, and I'll Come to You, My Lad.' "
59. Erckmann-Chatrian, "L'Araignée crabe" (in *Contes fantastiques,* 1860); usually translated as "The Crab Spider" or "The Waters of Death."
60. Used in "Canon Alberic's Scrap-book" and "Number 13," respectively.
61. Used in "The Stalls of Barchester Cathedral" and "An Episode of Cathedral History," respectively.
62. James Boswell quotes Samuel Johnson as saying: "A man who writes a book, thinks himself wiser or wittier than the rest of mankind; he supposes that he can instruct or amuse them, and the public to whom he appeals, must, after all, be the judges of his pretensions." Boswell, *Life of Johnson* (1791), under the date 1749.
63. Actually written in 1892 or 1893 (see *CM* 258).

64. Actually, MRJ probably wrote the story in 1900 (see *CM* 267).
65. The quotation ("I am afraid to think what I have done; / Look on't again I dare not") is actually from Shakespeare, *Macbeth* 2.2.50–51.
66. The following is the plot description of an untitled fragmentary tale published as "Marcilly-le-Hayer" (*PT* 426–28).
67. Cited as *Caroline de Lichtenfeld* in the fragment.
68. Marcilly-le-Hayer is a village in the province of Champagne-Ardenne in northern France, about twenty miles west of Troyes.
69. This is a plot description of "The Fenstanton Witch" (p. 212), not published in MRJ's lifetime. MRJ has transferred the story to the early eighteenth century, and the protagonists are not "students" but Fellows of King's College.
70. Mr. Badman is the protagonist of John Bunyan's *The Life and Death of Mr. Badman* (1680), a companion to *The Pilgrim's Progress;* but MRJ is referring here to Mr. Goodman and Mr. Badman generically as characters representing good and evil.
71. This appears to be a description of the unfinished story "John Humphreys" (*PT* 429–39), an early version of "Mr. Humphreys and His Inheritance" (*MGA*).
72. Cf. a letter to Gwendolen McBryde (11 November 1929): "Now here is a thing. This morning they sent me a new edition of *In a Glass Darkly* [by J. Sheridan Le Fanu] . . . and I read Green Tea and other things—I write at night—and just now as I re-entered my room what should I see but a toad hopping across the floor? Fortunately a smallish toad. It has retired behind the curtains near the door. Will it clasp my leg as I go out? and what does it portend?" *Letters to a Friend,* p. 159.

CLICK ON A CLASSIC
www.penguinclassics.com

The world's greatest literature at your fingertips

Constantly updated information on more than a thousand titles,
from Icelandic sagas to ancient Indian epics, Russian drama to
Italian romance, American greats to African masterpieces

•

The latest news on recent additions to the list, updated
editions, and specially commissioned translations

•

Original essays by leading writers

•

A wealth of background material, including biographies
of every classic author from Aristotle to Zamyatin, plot
synopses, readers' and teachers' guides, useful web links

•

Online desk and examination copy assistance for academics

•

Trivia quizzes, competitions, giveaways, news on
forthcoming screen adaptations

...ner of the world, on every subject under the sun, Penguin represents
...nd variety—the very best in publishing today.

..r complete information about books available from Penguin—including
Penguin Classics, Penguin Compass, and Puffins—and how to order them, write
to us at the appropriate address below. Please note that for copyright reasons the
selection of books varies from country to country.

In the United States: Please write to *Penguin Group (USA), P.O. Box 12289
Dept. B, Newark, New Jersey 07101-5289* or call *1-800-788-6262.*

In the United Kingdom: Please write to *Dept. EP, Penguin Books Ltd, Bath
Road, Harmondsworth, West Drayton, Middlesex UB7 0DA.*

In Canada: Please write to *Penguin Books Canada Ltd, 90 Eglinton Avenue East,
Suite 700, Toronto, Ontario M4P 2Y3.*

In Australia: Please write to *Penguin Books Australia Ltd, P.O. Box 257,
Ringwood, Victoria 3134.*

In New Zealand: Please write to *Penguin Books (NZ) Ltd, Private Bag 102902,
North Shore Mail Centre, Auckland 10.*

In India: Please write to *Penguin Books India Pvt Ltd, 11 Panchsheel Shopping
Centre, Panchsheel Park, New Delhi 110 017.*

In the Netherlands: Please write to *Penguin Books Netherlands bv, Postbus 3507,
NL-1001 AH Amsterdam.*

In Germany: Please write to *Penguin Books Deutschland GmbH, Metzlerstrasse
26, 60594 Frankfurt am Main.*

In Spain: Please write to *Penguin Books S. A., Bravo Murillo 19, 1° B, 28015
Madrid.*

In Italy: Please write to *Penguin Italia s.r.l., Via Benedetto Croce 2, 20094 Corsico,
Milano.*

In France: Please write to *Penguin France, Le Carré Wilson, 62 rue Benjamin
Baillaud, 31500 Toulouse.*

In Japan: Please write to *Penguin Books Japan Ltd, Kaneko Building, 2-3-25
Koraku, Bunkyo-Ku, Tokyo 112.*

In South Africa: Please write to *Penguin Books South Africa (Pty) Ltd, Private Bag
X14, Parkview, 2122 Johannesburg.*

P.O. 0005542205 202